AF250189

Scion of Lightning

The Stormcrafter Chronicles

J.T. Moy

Copyright © 2022 by J.T. Moy. All rights reserved.

Published by Centaurus Press, Auckland, New Zealand. See www. jtmoy.com for further publications. 19052022

Cover illustration and design by Jeff Brown Graphics.

No part of this work may be copied, published or sold without the author's permission, except for the use of brief quotations in critical articles or reviews.

All the characters in this book are fictitious. No relationship is intended to anyone living or dead.

ISBN 978-0-473-59740-5 (Kindle)
ISBN 978-0-473-59739-9 (Epub)
ISBN 978-0-473-59738-2 (Hardback)
ISBN 978-0-473-59737-5 (Paperback)

For Fen, Hannah, and Daniel.
Thanks for when you tried to stay out of my way.

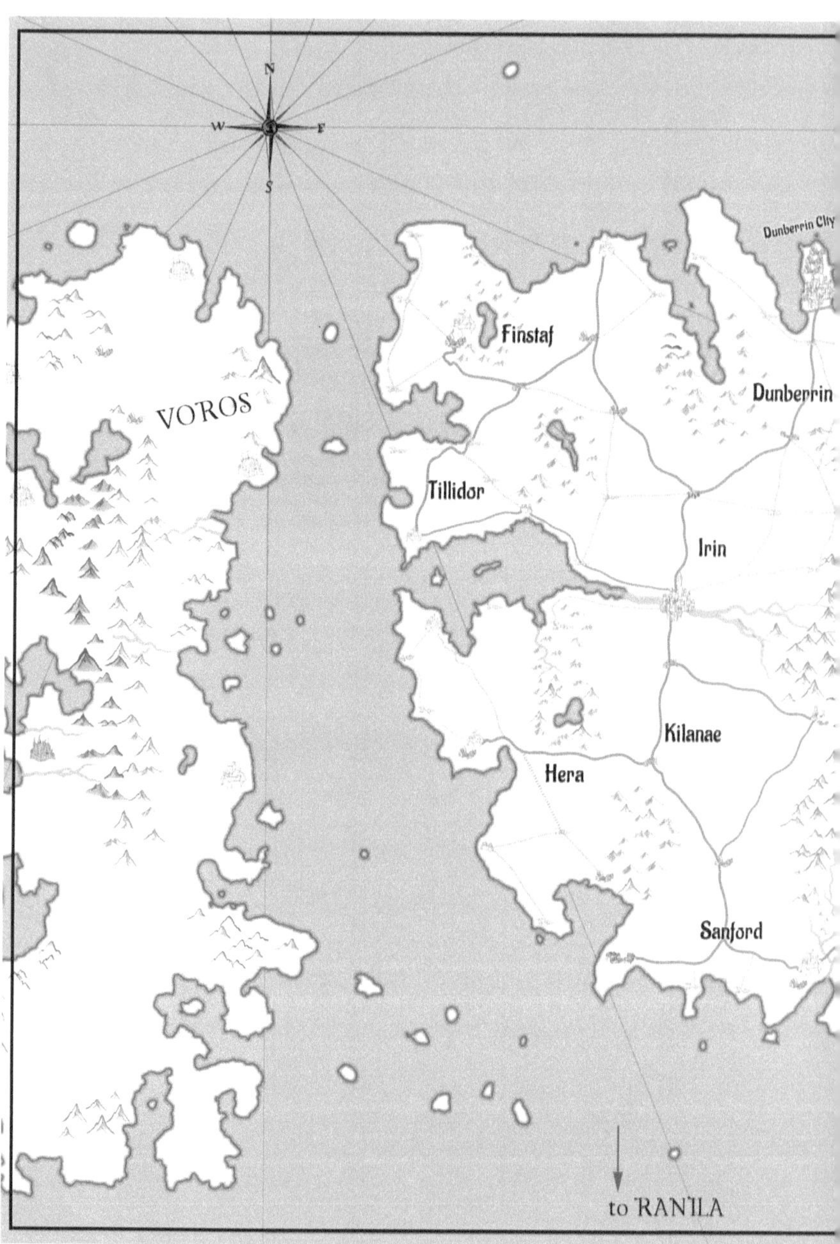

N
W
E
S
VOROS
Finstaf
Tillidor
Dunberrin City
Dunberrin
Irin
Kilanae
Hera
Sanford
to RANILA

FAUCONY
to PIHAAT
STROCK
Jurn
ELLIPTA
to ZURA
ASCORIA
HUSVAN
Cerik
NERABOA

Chapter 1

The Frostbear

A dozen conscripts stalked between massive giantwood trees as a storm exhausted itself over the forest. They hoped for the return of birdsong and insect chirrups, but heard nothing but the squelch of their boots on muddy leaves.

The young men edged forward with arrows nocked to their hunting bows. Swords swayed at their hips, and their gazes turned to every flicker of movement as they sought their prey.

A thirteenth man, a king's ranger, led the way.

He stopped and listened.

Forest sounds returned to their rear, but not ahead.

The ranger fanned out the fingers of his left hand and gestured for the less experienced men to spread out. He resumed the advance.

Jaks Rauhalik was at the back of the group. Tall

with a head of brown hair, he bore the square jaw and aquiline nose of a nobleman's son. On any other day, his eyes would have drifted as he daydreamed of great battles and heroes, but today his gaze focused on the hunt.

Determined to impress Ranger Cromer, on this week of survival exercises at the end of their two-year mandatory conscription, he couldn't make any more errors. All his hopes of joining the army as a career soldier depended on it. For protecting his kingdom, as his older sister did, was the noblest of professions.

But yesterday, unfortunately, he'd taken a fall, just before a squad mate loosed an arrow at a deer. The sound of him skidding down a muddy slope had scared the animal off and earned Jaks an admonishment from the ranger and the inglorious position at the back of the squad.

They had been tracking a frostbear all morning; that is, the *ranger* had been tracking the bear, and the inexperienced conscripts were following like lion cubs learning to hunt.

Without the deadly archer, a frostbear would have been completely out of the conscripts' capabilities.

Twelve-foot tall and two tons in weight, it was a formidable beast that required at least a squad of experienced soldiers to bring down—or a master ranger who could shoot unerringly for the heart. Yet, its size was not its greatest strength. Silence was. Frostbears were arcane predators with an innate ability to magically absorb sound. They were massive, silent killers of the forest whose victims never even heard them coming.

The beast had come from the much wilder northern mountains to this tree-felling region and had already slaughtered seven woodsmen over the past several months. It was the conscripts' training exercise to assist the ranger to kill it. Nothing like a giant bear to challenge one's survival skills.

They had not yet seen the frostbear, relying on Ranger Cromer's tracking skills to follow its lumbering path over the mountains. But it had been three hours now, and the rain had hindered their progress significantly.

Another half hour passed, and the forest grew thicker. The full sounds of the forest had returned, and the conscripts' formation loosened, their postures less anxious and eyes less vigilant. Surely, the master ranger would call a rest break soon.

Jaks was tired and bored. He un-nocked his arrow and returned it to his hip quiver. Far easier to walk without the arrow knocking against underbrush and branches.

His only friend in the squad—and friend since childhood—Minto Piccaton, had also lost interest in the hunt. A foot shorter than Jaks, but of stockier build, he had a square face dotted with freckles and a head topped with a scruff of brown hair. A carefree spirit, he was the jollity that countered Jaks's earnestness. As they tramped behind the rest of the squad, Minto hissed at him and veered closer.

"I've been thinking. Could your father help us get into the King's Rangers? Is it worth asking him?" questioned the freckled youth.

The question froze Jaks in his tracks. "My father would rather spit on me than help," he replied through gritted teeth. "You would not want anything to do with him. I can assure you of that." He felt bad being so blunt with his friend, but thinking about his father sent chills through his body.

"His lordship looked pleasant enough at the Royal Parade last year. Why are you so foul of him?" he said over his shoulder as he clambered over a rotted tree trunk.

"Would a pleasant man do this?" Jaks stopped again and raised his left hand, baring the stub of his little finger for Minto to see. "Forget about him. Our only path forward is if we can get a commendation from the master ranger." He gritted his teeth at the thought of their trainer's disapproving glares.

Jaks's attention drew to the empty woods in front of them, devoid of any sign of their fellow conscripts. "Oh, hell—we've lost them again. We need to find the trail, quick."

"I thought they went that way?" Minto pointed toward a patch of dense forest rising ahead of them. He looked up at the sun through the thick canopy of branches and leaves.

"But aren't those their footprints?" Jaks pointed in the opposite direction, toward a muddy clearing. He cursed and pulled on the buckles of the pack that were always slipping because of his bony shoulders.

They milled around the clearing for a couple of minutes, looking for a clear trail.

It was then that Jaks noticed there were no birds or insects to hear.

The forest had gone quiet.

"Don't move," Jaks whispered to Minto.

His friend froze in his steps. "What—"

"Shhh . . ." Jaks slowly reached for the arrow he'd returned to the quiver, cursing himself for letting down his guard.

A flicker of movement caught his eye. There, forty yards to his left, a huge, brown-furred beast lumbered between the bases of two giantwoods, crushing bushes and undergrowth beneath it, but astonishingly without making a sound.

Crouching, hoping the knee-high undergrowth would camouflage him, Jaks trembled in his attempt to nock the arrow.

The frostbear raised its snout and sniffed the air. Its head was massive, as big as one of the army's warlions, with jaws that could certainly bite his arm off as a snack.

"*Grafuk*," swore Minto in a panicky voice. "We've got to hide."

He was right. The two of them alone couldn't take it out. The ranger's plan had been to surround the frostbear and pepper it with arrows—individuals running away if it came for them—enraging it into rearing up on its hind legs, where the ranger would kill it with a heartshot.

Sniffing the ground, the bear ambled closer and behind another giantwood. It paused, its backside and two rear legs still visible.

"Quick, move." Jaks jogged in a crouch in the opposite direction.

Around enormous trees and through dense underbrush they fled, dodging low branches and leaping fallen trees until they ran out of breath behind a gray boulder.

Silence still embraced them.

"Did it follow us?" asked Minto, puffing and sweating heavily.

Jaks peeked over the boulder.

Thirty yards distant, the frostbear had its nose to the undergrowth, coming their direction. It was tracking them.

A wave of panic flooded over Jaks. Desperately, he looked around—and then upward.

The giantwoods were notoriously difficult to climb. Their wide bases were more like cliff faces than regular trees and their lowest branches thin and weak, if they could even be reached.

A stand of ironwood trees rose nearby. Yes, their

narrower trunks and wider spread of branches were reachable and more likely to take their weight. Although nowhere near the height of their majestic cousins, if he could even get halfway up, Jaks was sure he'd be out of reach of the twelve-foot-tall bear.

He tapped Minto on the shoulder and pointed at the gray-barked ironwoods.

Running to the closest tree, Jaks threw away his pack and bow—they would only slow him down—grabbed the lowest branches, and shoved his foot between two of the sturdiest. Then the next ones, and again and again, he climbed.

Fearing to look down, he pulled and pushed his way up through the branches, not stopping until the branches were too thin to climb any higher. Minto was in the tree next to him, but having chosen a taller specimen, he was up higher by two yards.

Jaks's tree shook violently. Gasping in fright, he stared down.

The bear was pushing against the ironwood, its giant front paws pressed against the waist-thick trunk. Evil-looking claws dug into the bark. Dark eyes stared up at Jaks and the beast opened its mouth, baring rows of triangular teeth.

A deafening roar blasted at Jaks's feet. Its arcane powers allowed the frostbear to stalk in silence, but also, if it chose, to terrify with loudness.

The tree shook again. A branch broke in Jaks's grip. A foot slipped from between a fork of branches. He wrapped his arms around the upper trunk, paralyzed in fear, and unable to do anything but scream in terror and void his bladder.

The beast rose higher on its hind legs, front paws clawing up the ironwood.

Minto yelled at the frostbear from the other tree and threw arrows from his quiver—having also abandoned his bow to free his hands—trying to distract the frostbear.

The tree swayed sharply. Branches snapped and cracked. Jaks's grip slipped. His foot swung wildly.

The bear swung its paw and a claw hooked Jaks's boot and tore it from him.

A warhorn blared from the forest and shouts surrounded the stand of ironwoods. Almost a dozen men encircled Jaks's tree from a range of twenty yards and began loosing arrows at the frostbear. The ranger and the conscripts had come to the rescue.

Arrows thudded into the animal's back and legs. Some, unable to penetrate the thick fur and hide, bounced off and fell to the ground along with Minto's thrown ones. Others bounced off its thick skull or missed completely and thumped into nearby trees. The few that penetrated angered the giant and distracted it from its tree-bound prey.

Bellowing, the bear dropped to all fours and charged toward a hapless conscript with a spent bow in his hands.

The youth screamed and ran.

Hiss. Another flurry of arrows. Only two stuck but were enough distraction that the bear turned again and charged toward another conscript. The unfortunate youth tripped as he turned to flee and fell with an anguished cry.

Twang. A single arrow zipped through the air and into the bear's eye.

Half blinded and fully enraged, the frostbear rose to its full height, searching for the archer to tear apart.

Twang. A second arrow thudded into the beast's chest. As the bear roared and staggered clumsily, a third shaft followed and embedded in the same spot.

Two heartshots—the frostbear collapsed into the undergrowth, moaning.

Two final breaths and the brown-furred chest never rose again.

Cheers broke out and the conscripts filtered out of the woods to examine their conquest. Several nudged it gingerly with their swords. Declaring it dead, they whooped and hollered.

Jaks descended, shivering at the sight of the deep gouges in the trunk as his hands passed over them. His torn-off boot rested at the foot of the tree, a large hole in the sole, a reminder of the bear's deadly claws. As he pushed it back on, he trembled, knowing that with another shake of the tree, he would've fallen and been torn apart.

"You all right?" Minto asked, down from his own

perch. "Almost got you, it did." He gestured at Jaks's boot.

"Nah. Would've kicked it in the nose," replied Jaks with faked confidence.

Nodding, his freckled friend picked up his arrows from around the base of the ironwood. Finding Jaks's bow undamaged, he handed it back to him.

A voice called out from the conscripts around the dead bear.

"Have a nice climb, ladies?" spoke a thick-necked thug named Baden. "You're good bear-bait, I have to admit. He was gonna eat you up." He lunged at them, chomping his teeth, and then laughed. In their conscript squad called the "Thorns"—to demark them from the other dozen or so conscript units active around the kingdom—Baden ranked as the senior conscript.

"Fuck off, Baden." Jaks squared off against the smirking youth. "You would've run too."

Ranger Cromer stood up from behind the bear, where he'd been studying his marksmanship, and strode through the circle, silencing the hecklers. He was a cutting figure in weathered black leather and an arrow-thin beard. Female conscripts swooned after him as though he were a dashing pirate, but his cold demeanor kept all but the most brazen from his attention. But none of that mattered to Jaks as the ranger descended on them with flaring nostrils and blazing eyes.

He stood before Jaks and Minto. "A few minutes later and you idiots would've been dead. You're lucky I realized it'd circled back behind us as soon as I did." He pointed his bow tip at them and scowled. "Stop getting separated from your squad. It is not that hard."

"Sorry, sir," Jaks said with his eyes downcast.

"Sir, the underbrush got really thick and we couldn't see anyone—" Minto started.

"Don't give me excuses." The ranger loomed over them. "You two are the worst conscripts I have ever been cursed with in these forests—that's twice you've gotten lost now. Now, after we get this thing buried, you're going to get your weedy asses over that ridge and lead us south until sundown. Go off course, and you make your own way back to Dunberrin."

The master ranger returned to the main squad and began snapping orders. Shovels were produced, and a grave was dug. Jaks and Minto went to help.

Two hours later, the bear, minus a few body parts taken as tokens, lay beneath a pile of dirt, and it was time to return to base.

Minto led the way, Jaks a few paces behind, and Ranger Cromer tracing their steps. There were a few more jibes and jokes from the other conscripts at their expense, but the scowling ranger shushed them and they walked in silence.

A while later, they came to a rocky stream, wide but shallow, running down from the mountains ahead. The cold water soaked through Jaks's boots— especially quick in his left through the hole at its base. He followed his friend across the stream and then climbed the opposite bank to find him staring into the sky.

Minto pointed upward. "Look at that."

Jaks followed his gesture and saw a bright yellow speck trailed by a long tail falling through the clouds toward the distant mountains.

"Meteor," he said. "Make a wish and get moving."

He pushed Minto's hand away and walked on, not wanting to be chewed out by the ranger again.

"It looks close . . . really close. Like it might land near us," Minto said, adjusting his sword belt and striding to keep up with Jaks.

They made their way back into the forest edge, which was on a slope getting higher and colder toward the mountains.

Jaks and Minto continued to catch glimpses of the bright meteor through the speckled canopy overhead. It seemed to be getting closer to them. The speck turned into a large burning glow.

Then it dimmed—the front glow first, then the tail disappeared. He heard a distant hissing sound from its direction and glimpsed an object disappearing into the shadows of a distant mountain.

Minto waggled a finger. "It's just over there! Probably no more than a day's trek from here, I reckon."

Ranger Cromer caught up. "Stop gawping. Nothing to get excited about. It's just a lump of rock," he said and pushed past them. The trees had thinned into a clearing with a small crag of rocks. "All right. This'll do. Stop and set camp."

The Thorns spread out around the area to set up their shelters and a campfire. Subdued chatter about the meteor went around, but everyone soon lost interest.

That night, Jaks woke to the sound of water splashing against his makeshift tent. Two feet were planted by his shelter and their owner was urinating against the oilskin near his head. Jaks scrambled out, cursing and swearing at the vandal. Baden grinned at him in the moonlight.

"Didn't see you there, bear-bait," the senior conscript said.

"Hell, you didn't," Jaks forcibly whispered back, not wanting to wake anyone. "Don't push me. You'll regret it one day." He kicked the tent and splattered the brute with his own urine.

Baden stepped back in annoyance and hiked up his breeches. "Your watch now, city-boy," he said, as he walked to his own shelter. Then over his shoulder he added, "Better guard your back."

Muttering in disgust, Jaks slapped on his sword belt and went to clamber up the crag of rocks overlooking the campsite. Other cohorts of conscripts were fast friends who played, drank, and stood loyally alongside each other. But Jaks's group was rude and cruel toward outsiders—and Jaks and Minto had been outsiders to them from the beginning.

The only two city-born recruits in the Thorns, they were assumed to be privileged and haughty, despite Jaks's efforts to befriend the rest of the squad. He always had a supportive word or a lending hand if anyone stumbled or needed help with their training exercises or duties. However, the city-country split and Minto's unhelpful reminders to the others of Jaks's father's status as a lord castellan—even though he'd been disowned—kept them excluded. The crux had come when they'd expressed disgust at Baden's vile game where he'd cajoled the other conscripts into kicking a dead cat back and forth like a ball. From there, the senior conscript had taken extra efforts to ostracize the two. Fortunately, Jaks and Minto were strong friends from childhood and continued their shared interests in heraldry and ancient stories of lore, regardless of their status in the group.

As he sat, Jaks's anger soon turned to wonder as he gazed up at the night sky and saw two more glowing white streaks blast across the black. They flared and faded but far more distant than the meteor from earlier that day; however, they were still spectacular to behold.

Over the next two hours, he sat with knees pulled up and wrapped under his fur jacket, listening to the rustle of the trees and snores of his campmates as he stared into the abyss, hoping to see more of the mysterious phenomena. However, none else appeared but the stars and moon.

Eventually, he slid down and prodded the next watcher awake.

Fatigued, he went to his sleeping mat and dragged it away from the urine-stenched canopy. Lying down, images of the frostbear shaking the tree and its shark-like maw gaping at him flashed through his mind. He stared into the dark, worried the beast would come back.

Hours later, he finally succumbed to sleep—and dreamed fitfully of a giant bear who transformed into his father and then chased him through dark woods until he fell down a staircase in the middle of the forest; catching him, it proceeded to devour him. He half-woke, and the dream began again.

The next morning when they had broken camp, Ranger Cromer called the squad together for the day's survival exercise.

Jaks rubbed his eyes, poorly rested from a disturbed night.

"Pair up. From here to the White Cliff is an easy eight hours. Get yourselves to the base cave there." He pointed at a far-off mountain with a sheer white cliff face to the south. "If you're not at the base by tomorrow midday—you had better be dead, because that is the only excuse I will accept."

Baden stood up. "Sir, I'll be there this evening," he said, greasing favor with the ranger.

"But I know who probably won't." Cromer glowered at Jaks and Minto as the group readied to leave.

Jaks stared at the ground, riled up by the ranger's words; the man was expecting them to fail.

He would show Cromer he wasn't a complete failure.

Chapter 2

The Meteor

Jaks and Minto were the second pair to be sent off, ten minutes after Baden and his partner.

Tall trees enveloped them as they left the clearing. A pair of fantails fluttered after them, darting over the forest floor, spearing beetles and worms unveiled by their footsteps. The sky was clouding over and threatening another downpour.

"Let's not get lost today," Jaks said. "We really need a win to get the ranger on our side."

"Don't worry about it." Minto grinned cheerfully. He slapped Jaks on the back as he brushed past. "There's always second chances. If we get to the base on time, he'll forget about yesterday."

"Yeah, we'll be fine." Jaks nodded.

Minto widened his steps and sweat glistened his brow. "And . . . that meteor landed in that valley over there. I have never seen one before. We should have a quick look."

"Not sure that's a good idea," said Jaks, intrigued with the concept but conflicted by the need to do well on their trek that day.

"We've got heaps of time," said Minto. "If we don't get to the cliffs by tonight, I'll take the blame, okay? Okay."

He smiled at his friend's boundless optimism. Jaks had to admit, after seeing the meteors in the sky last night, he would love to see one up close.

Two hours later, the threat of rain clouds had passed, but Minto's curiosity had not.

"This way. I'm sure the valley is over here. Looks like something circling over it," said Minto. He pushed his thumbs into his belt and walked faster.

"Carrion birds?" Jaks hurried to catch up.

By midday, they had climbed steadily to where the trees thinned and were much smaller than their sisters below. Jaks looked back over the lower forest and then searched for the White Cliffs but could only see jagged outlines of mountains. He did not know where they were.

Less than a mile away, the flight of dark wings continued to spiral and swoop.

"We really should go back down. I think we're lost." Jaks grabbed Minto's elbow to slow him.

"It's just over this crest, I think." Minto pulled away

from him and gestured rapidly. "I don't think they're birds."

At the top of the ridgeline, they looked into the next valley and gasped at the sight below.

On the valley floor, a pod the size of a giant boulder rested against a shattered tree stump. Its gray surface was smooth and symmetrical, and a huge orange sail, with thin black tethers, lay tangled over nearby trees.

He saw that the dark wings belonged to a thunder of dragons. A half dozen bronze-colored ones, bodies the size of a dog but wings measuring six times their width. Two other dragons perched on top of the bulbous object; one of them slid to the ground, its claws unable to grip the surface, whilst the other twisted its head around and flicked its forked tongue over the object.

Minto crashed down the slope. He yelled and drew his sword, slapping it against its sheath. The startled dragons jumped into the air and took flight to join their packmates overhead.

Jaks hurried to join his friend beside the mysterious object, pulling out his sword and keeping a wary eye to the sky. Hopefully, the dragons would fly off back to their roost. Although they were smaller than the army's trained war dragons—and not red fire-breathers nor black acid-spitters—all dragons were dangerous, especially if they attacked in unison.

But seeing the dragons spiraling higher, Jaks gingerly prodded the boulder-like object with the tip of his sword. "This is no mere rock. It looks metal." His eyebrows furrowed. "I wonder if it's dangerous?"

Minto walked around from the other direction, caressed it, and then pushed against it. "Do you think it's valuable? We could be rich, Jaks! I bet some merchant or forgemaster would pay a cartload of gold for this." His eyes were wide and darted about.

"What's this?" Jaks lifted part of the sail that still draped the top part of the object and uncovered a dark opening to the inside of it. He swept aside the rest of the orange material and stooped to peer inside.

Minto came up and gave a low whistle.

The midday sun illuminated a small interior. Inside, Jaks could see an empty padded seat with straps and clasps on either side of it. To its left, square and round inlays marked by nonsensical symbols indented the internal surface. And to the other side of the seat, a glass panel clung to a thick metal arm. Some leaves blew into the otherwise empty vessel.

He touched his fingers to the cold exterior. The surface vibrated. Surprised, he quickly withdrew. He could have sworn it responded to his touch. *Is it alive?*

Minto dropped his pack and weapons, and then threw a leg over the edge of the entrance and straddled it.

"What are you doing? You can't climb in there," said

Jaks. "I have a bad feeling about this. We should get back to the forest."

Minto grinned at him as he crammed himself into the tight space and lay in the upward-facing seat. "Bit cramped . . ." He poked some of the inlays, which depressed, clicked, and rose. He moved the panel back and forth. Finally, he reached over his head and thrust an arm into an alcove above the seat. He brought down his hands, pulling out a thin blue tube. He studied the end of it and squeezed—a stream of liquid spouted from the nozzle into his face. Spluttering and wiping his face, he dropped the tube and it stopped flowing. "Water." He laughed.

"Looks like it was made for a person," Jaks remarked. He stood back to cast his eyes around the sparsely wooded mountainside again and briefly up at the circling dragons.

The orange sail stretched from the metal object and up the slope to wrap itself around the bases of three speckled trees. The material bore an emblem repeated several times over the sail, a white circle crisscrossed with lines cradled in a basket of branches. "Is that the symbol of Ranila?" he asked Minto, a self-proclaimed expert of country flags and heraldic symbols.

Minto climbed back out of the vessel and shrugged. "I've never seen that emblem before. I'll get some of it to show Ranger Cromer." He drew his dagger, attacked the thin material, and remarked that it was much tougher than it looked.

Jaks heard several screeches from the dragons overhead and breathed a sigh of relief as they peeled away and winged toward the mountain peaks. The tension eased in his shoulders, and he began to pace the landing site, examining the ground for tracks.

Amongst their own footprints, he found a drag mark heading up to the speckled trees.

"There might be someone here," he hissed to Minto. He hefted his short-sword. The small ashes could easily hide a person beneath the folds of orange fabric covering them.

Minto tucked the cut square under his belt as he kneeled beside Jaks and squinted at the disturbed ground.

They stood and crept forward, their weapons waving unsteadily before them.

In a high-pitched voice, Jaks called out, "Is there someone there?"

He stepped around to the back of the trees and found a woman.

She sat on the ground on a crinkled silver sheet with her back against a tree trunk. The material hanging from the branches cast an orange hue over her. Her dark-blue clothes were tightly fitted and embroidered with emblems and words on her shoulder and chest. An open satchel lay on the ground, and her lower body was blanketed by a second sheet. A bandage circled her forehead and short, raven-black hair framed a face that was unnaturally narrow but bewildering to behold. Wide lips thinned, and huge, brown eyes dilated as she stared at the intruders.

Jaks's face reddened and his heart raced as he drew in a quick breath and drank in her exotic features. Her skin was pale as though not sun-touched for months but flawless, suggesting a similar age to his own. He could not identify her country or race, but he knew that she was beautiful.

She shouted and pointed an object at them, weaving it back and forth between them like targets. Jaks thought it must be a weapon; the way she was pointing it at them was threatening and it looked hard and evil. Although she held it like a crossbow, it was much shorter and had no string or limbs, but despite that, it looked dangerous.

"We won't hurt you," Minto said in a controlled voice, putting his sword back into its scabbard. He nudged Jaks, who sheathed his sword in response and raised his hands.

Still pointing the weapon toward them, she struggled to her feet, favoring her left leg, and slid up against the tree. The silver blanket fell away and Jaks saw that her right lower leg was wrapped in a blood-soaked bandage. She grimaced as she moved.

The three of them stood frozen for several seconds.

Again, she shouted some words at them, but slower this time.

"I do not know what you are saying," said Minto, intoning each word clearly. "Put the weapon down." His right hand lowered and patted the air.

Forehead wrinkling, she squinted at them as though reading their thoughts. After a minute, she sucked in a deep breath and pointed the weapon at the ground. She uttered a few more words and placed a hand on her injured leg.

"I can help you," said Jaks. He moved toward her a few steps, taking confidence when she remained unflinching. Then beside her, he grasped her arm, and she sat with a groan.

Up close, she seemed delicate and small. His gaze lingered on her face.

She glared back at him fiercely.

A hard object prodded him in the ribs. Her weapon against his chest.

Jaks backed away. Ears burning, he retreated and joined Minto outside the shelter.

"Hell's breath. We have to let Ranger Cromer know about this," Minto said and then looked up to position the sun. "Maybe four or five hours of light left. We can get her to the base by night."

"Not with her leg like that. We have to bring back help so we can carry her on a stretcher. Also, he'll want to see this vessel," said Jaks.

After a short debate, they decided Minto would continue to the base cave, as he had better navigation sense, and Jaks would stay with the woman in case the dragons returned to harass her.

It was midafternoon, and rain clouds were rolling in again, when Minto eventually shouldered his pack and weapons and started his trek to find Ranger Cromer and the rest of their conscript unit.

Jaks stared out around the mountainside for several minutes after Minto had left, then shook out his hands, swept back his hair, and went back over to the woman, intent on trying to talk with her.

She was sitting, shivering, with her silver blanket around her shoulders but with her right hand resting atop the material, gripping her unusual weapon. She gazed at him suspiciously, but despite her wariness, her eyes mesmerized him with their size and exoticness.

"How is your injury?" he said slowly.

She stared at his mouth as he spoke but did not respond.

"How is your head?" he tried again, pointing at the dirty bandage. She reached out from under her blanket to touch it and said a few words in lilting, musical tones. The sounds made little sense to him, and his face creased in puzzlement.

She shivered again. Her thin blanket seemed inadequate to keep out the chill, so Jaks removed his fur jacket and held it out to her. The woman looked surprised but pushed aside the crinkly wrap and reached out with her left hand to accept the coat. She rolled up the sleeves, far too long for her arms, and pulled on the garment.

She looked up at him and smiled, then pointed at herself. "Meila," she said.

That must be her name, he realized. Jaks crouched at the shelter entrance, looking at her, and repeated her name carefully, but unable to replicate the lilt associated with it.

She smiled and nodded.

He then said his own name once and mimicked her actions by pointing at himself.

"Jaks," she copied without hesitation.

They repeated the exercise with different objects. The woman led, finding greater ease at pronouncing his words than he at hers. Eventually, she stopped trying to teach him her language at all and simply pointed at objects for Jaks to tell her the names of in Ascorian. Her memory was remarkable and her pronunciation of the words concise but with a slight musical lilt. A pleasant and melodic voice.

At one stage, her forehead creased in concern, and she waved her hand around and said, "Voros." He had not taught her that word and was surprised to hear her say the name of the foreign country far to the west.

"Ascoria," he repeated several times and made a broad sweep with his arms.

She nodded, and her face relaxed.

It became more difficult when they tried to extend beyond naming objects, to explaining things. She was able to extract from him words for "yes," "no," "come," and "go," but after that, they stopped—both exhausted from their awkward efforts.

She yawned and said to him, "Go." Lying down, she pulled the hand weapon into the overlong sleeve and tugged the fur closer around herself like a blanket. She stared blankly over his shoulder and appeared lost in thought.

Jaks left shelter and paced the mountainside, gazing up often for any sign of dragons. Without his coat, he shivered, but navigating the slope soon warmed him. Putting himself to task, he gathered dry branches and steepled them, preparing a campfire for sundown.

Later, he turned to strengthening the makeshift shelter. He rearranged the orange sail, fully covering the three small trees and weighting the edges with large stones but leaving an opening to the front. The material was plentiful and tough, making for a perfect cover.

As the sun faded, he lit the campfire and sat to bask in its warmth.

The woman shuffled to the opposite side, dragging her pack. She lay against it and stared into the flames.

"Ahh," she said, face brightening, minutes later. She rummaged around in her pack, gave a cheerful yelp, and drew out a handful of small bars. She threw one over the fire at Jaks and landed it deftly in front of him. She held up another and pulled at it; a thin wrapper tore away and revealed a brown block. She put it to her mouth and bit. Chewing enthusiastically, she gestured at the bar in front of Jaks.

He picked it up and copied her motions. Sweet flavors flooded his mouth. Sticky, delicious tar clung to his palate.

The woman laughed and smiled when Jaks stuck his finger in his mouth to unstick his teeth.

He chuckled in return and offered her his waterskin.

The rain started an hour after nightfall and drenched the valley. The campfire collapsed and steamed out. Jaks dashed to lend an arm to the woman as she hopped back into the shelter.

Inside, she propped herself against the tree trunk again and said a word he guessed might have been in thanks.

Rain drummed against the sail material and wind blew through the opening. Jaks released a rolled section, weighing the edge down with his backpack, and sealed the entrance against the elements.

The woman pulled the hood of the oversized coat over her head and, with her hand gripping her weapon within the depths of its sleeve, shut her eyes.

Jaks feigned rest as well. When her breathing slowed, he opened his eyes. Although too dark to see, her exquisite features were burned into his mind as though it were daylight. He longed to touch the outline of face, but knew that if he tried, he would learn what that dangerous-looking weapon could do.

Hours later, the rain stopped and Jaks slipped into a fitful sleep, dreaming of dragons and a winged woman soaring over him.

The next morning, the woman recovered a long branch with a Y-shaped end and crooked it under her left arm. As she hopped clumsily around the campsite, the fur coat brushed the ground, further hindering her progress. However, her eyes were full of determination, and she pushed ahead despite the obvious pain from her injured leg.

His conscience told him to help her, but his mouth went dry, and the pit of his stomach fluttered. He was bewildered that she had such an effect on him; he had been around extraordinary women all of his life. In fact, they did not get any tougher than his older sister, Vixhana, a captain in the Order of Nightwraiths, nor more talented than his younger sister, Karisa, who crafted illumancy for spectacular performances before audiences of thousands.

Yet, this foreign woman with a limp disconcerted him completely with her sheer willpower and intensity.

Midmorning, the pack of dragons reappeared. Three patrolled the air while the other three landed to investigate the metal pod again, hopping onto, into, and around the object curiously. Jaks and the woman, resting under their shelter, peered out through the opening and spied on the reptilian beasts.

"I'm sure they know we're here. Hopefully, they're not looking for food." Jaks nocked an arrow to the string of his hunting bow. Wild dragon attacks were rare on the plains, but here in the mountains, they had no fear and preyed on all creatures, including humans. He had never shot at one before. He hoped he would not have to today. Their quickness, scales, and sinuous bodies made them hard targets.

The woman clearly read Jaks's anxiety. She nodded to him and held her weapon in front of her with both hands.

Several minutes later, the three bronzes screeched at one another. One snapped at the others until the other two scraped their chins to the dirt. Then, as though they had made a decision, the dragons turned away from the pod and started toward the improvised shelter.

A beat of wings and one hurled itself through the air, landing several yards from the entrance. The other two followed with a flurry of wings and could be heard landing on either side, but out of sight, hidden by the walls of the shelter. And behind them, a screech and a thump announced a fourth dragon: one of the overhead beasts completing the encirclement.

With wings extended and claws scratching at the ground, the lead dragon snarled and hissed at the two humans.

The woman made a coarse utterance and raised her weapon at the beast.

Jaks whipped about as light filled the shade behind them. A dragon was twisting its neck under the orange sail and had raised the edge. Trembling, he drew his bowstring to his cheek. The end of the arrow wavered over the torso of his target. The dragon's head weaved back and forth like a snake with a gaping mouth of daggers.

Thuck. Jaks released the bowstring. *Zip.* The arrow missed the dragon's head. But piercing the tent, it passed through and struck the body of the beast. With a screech, it recoiled and flailed out of sight.

Hands still shaking, he nocked another arrow and turned toward a tent wall where a set of sharp teeth clamped the orange sail outside and pulled at the material.

Squelch. A queer sound drew Jaks's attention to the shelter entrance.

Blood and gore stained the mountain outside the entrance to the tent. Two disembodied wings and a decapitated dragon's head remained; the rest was a smear of red and gray turned inside-out, as though the beast had been squashed by a giant's foot.

The woman cried out. Her weapon arm swung

toward Jaks. A dragon had collapsed the tent wall and was now rearing up on its haunches, ready to lunge.

The beast exploded.

A second splatter of muscle, scales, and bone pasted the mountainside. No hammer, no missile, no visible effort he could see—yet the beast was obliterated.

Jaks recoiled in horror. The arrow fell off the string of his bow and flipped to the ground, but he did not need it any longer—the screeches and the sound of retreating wings indicated that the remaining dragons had taken flight.

"How . . ." His question faltered as he stared at the weapon in the woman's hand. A chill ran along his spine. He backed away from her. The same weapon had been trained on him less than a day before. She could have killed him and Minto in less than a blink. *What manner of magic is this?*

She replied with some soothing noises as though he were a startled puppy, and she tucked the weapon away into a pocket of the fur coat.

He lowered his bow and forced a twisted smile. If she had wanted to harm him, she could have already at any time that day.

A distant screech carried in the wind, tailing the fleeing dragons. With two of their kind dead and another injured by Jaks's arrow, surely, they would keep their distance for some time. Some species were vengeful for their dead, but Jaks could not remember if dragons were one of them. They would need to stay vigilant.

For the next hour, Jaks dug a shallow hole using a small shovel that conscripts carried, mainly for latrine duty, and buried the remains of the dead.

Later that morning, a loud moan emanated from the now-repaired shelter. Jaks discovered the woman slowly unwinding the bandage around her leg, pain etching her face.

Without a thought, Jaks dropped the bow from his hands and kneeled beside her. He hesitated as he reached for the edge of the bandage.

She nodded, and he began peeling away the rest of the sodden material.

She followed his every movement, wincing and grimacing.

Jaks cringed, empathizing with her pain. He stretched his mind for a way to distract her from staring at the wound.

He started singing.

In his childhood, his mother would sing quietly whenever she tended his, or his sisters', grazes and cuts. Her soothing song calmed and said everything would be all right. Although far less dulcet than his mother, he hoped his singing might help Meila.

It was a children's lullaby about a baby crying and

being rocked to sleep. A song that every child had heard, that had existed forever.

He immediately felt like an idiot and was about to stop.

She lifted her head and stared at Jaks. Her breathing slowed, and her face relaxed. She nodded encouragement and curled a little smile.

When the song finished, Jaks began a repetition— and Meila also began to sing.

She sang exactly a verse behind, but instead of words she sang in las. She had an acute musical ear. They sang in rounds, his baritone voice and her alto dancing and weaving, as though they had sung together for years, perfectly partnered in pitch and tone.

Jaks smiled and laughed in delight as they completed their song.

Meila's gaze was warm and grateful.

They looked at each other, unsure what to say, then murmured and uttered a few words. Eventually, they stopped altogether when she winked at him and laughed.

His hands had paused during their song. Resuming his task, he unraveled the last of the bandage with a couple more turns.

Beneath, the wound was raw. A blood-crusted vertical laceration exposing the bone on her shin.

Meila took charge again, clearing the blood and clot from the wound with a flask of water and then covering it with a square of material with a gelatinous blob in the center. She topped it with a second, thicker pad, and proffered a new bandage to Jaks.

Jaks wrapped the wound pad into place as she held still.

With their task done, Meila sat back and studied him. A minute later, she began singing again and raised her eyebrows at him to join.

This time, she sang in her own language. Another lullaby? Although unfamiliar to Jaks, he too had sharp ears and picked up the melody well enough to repeat it the second and third time she sang it.

She clapped her hands, smiled, and motioned for him to take a turn.

For the next hour, the pair shared simple songs and counterpoints. They laughed at their mistakes and paused to teach other trickier verses and phrases. So entranced, Jaks forgot his worries of the future, and the woman never flinched to her injury.

Eventually, his singing companion blinked with fatigue and sought to lie down. She pulled the blanket to her neck and closed her eyes.

He left her to rest, picked up his bow and walked outside to stand watch over the camp. He hummed to himself, thinking he could not remember the last time he'd known such joy as today.

Later that day, as the sun dipped low, and Jaks was readying another fire, several voices called out from the ridgeline of the valley.

A dozen familiar-looking figures angled down the slope. Jaks smiled as he caught sight of Minto. However, his relief evaporated as he realized that the ranger and other Thorn conscripts came with danger in their eyes and their bows half-drawn with nocked arrows.

Ranger Cromer cast an expert eye over the mountainside. He immediately took control, ignoring Jaks's explanation of recent events.

The woman was declared a foreign spy, disarmed, and ordered to be tied up.

The training exercise was over. The ranger ordered that they would return to the City of Dunberrin the next day and hand over the captive for interrogation.

She did not fight but looked pleadingly at Jaks while two burly conscripts forced her up by the arms and a third approached her with a rope. Her face contorted in pain and then anger. The feeling of betrayal was clear in her eyes.

Jaks protested to the Ranger, arguing her innocence. She was no spy. He didn't know what she was doing here, but had he detected no malice in her.

However, the superior officer refused to hear his arguments.

Though she did not understand his words, Jaks turned to her and said quietly, "I'll help you. I'll make sure they don't treat you like a spy." For the path of a spy was execution.

His promise, though, was of little use when they tied her hands and trussed her up to a tree. The anger in her voice displaced all of its musical tones as she then spat what could only be obscenities or curses.

Baden, grinning maliciously, took it upon himself to stand guard over their new prisoner.

Chapter 3

The Siblings

A week after the conscripts returned to Dunberrin with their captive, Jaks battled a troubled mind as he sat amongst a throng of soldiers within the city's massive cathedral.

"Quit fidgeting. It's almost over," Minto whispered next to him.

He stilled his leg—difficult when the droning voice of the Bishop of Dunberrin gnawed inside his ears. He cursed the poor luck of their unit being "privileged" with attending this week's Faithday cathedral service. Wasted time that could otherwise have been spent tracking down the prisoner he knew as Meila.

He was obsessed with her, unable to stop thinking about their short time together: the most exhilarating experience of his eighteen years. And what was more, he had made an oath to aid her plight.

His dead mother's words harangued him: "A broken oath will plague your soul." Her warning against childhood lies and a warning he used to think ridiculous. But since her death, the phrase, like a curse, honor-bound him to his promises.

But despite his inquiries, he could find no rumor or sign of what had happened to her. After the ranger had handed her to the city guard, she had simply vanished.

After this religious tedium was over, perhaps he could get his eldest sister to help locate her? Jaks began jigging his leg again.

Finally, a gong reverberated through the building and the assemblage groaned to their feet as the bishop gave his final blessing.

The cathedral took prominence in the city's cultural district; the magnificent stone building, along with its expansive gardens and cemeteries, cultivated a sense of importance to the area. Although it was commonly thought that the kingdom's official religion was nothing more than a method to harvest money from the populace, as a piece of architecture, it could not be denied that the cathedral lent great beauty to the city.

Beyond the religious grounds, nearby streets sheltered opera houses, theaters, galleries, and taverns that contrasted starkly to the hallowed structure but were the true center of Dunberrin's cultural wealth. Festooned with banners, streamers, and colored lanterns, the district was a spectacle at night.

"I'm off to the tavern. You coming?" Minto asked Jaks as they followed the throng of soldiers tipping into the streets to celebrate the rest of the day of rest.

"Go without me. I've arranged to meet my sisters."

"Your gorgeous sisters! I could go throw dice later . . . I'll join you."

"No, I don't think they would welcome your hellos and come-ons at the foot of our mother's grave." He laughed.

"Well, at least pass on my greetings to them." Minto waved cheerily as he departed with the crowd. "I'd marry either of them in a second. Tell them that?"

"I won't," said Jaks, shaking his head at his friend's boldness.

Over the few minutes it took to walk around the cathedral, Jaks's mood deepened. He stepped onto the short grass of the east cemetery and paced down a solemn row of gray headstones—one of the many that stretched out to the distant low boundary wall. On the other side, two stall-keepers rolled their carts noisily along a wide, cobbled street.

At the center of the graveyard, his sisters stood by their mother's grave. He called out a greeting, and they turned to his voice.

Karisa, only sixteen, looked like a woman several

years older than she was. Even though as tall as her brother and more shapely than her sister, it was the haunted depths of her eyes that betrayed her lost innocence. She hid herself that day in a dowdy, gray shift with a sash tied at the waist and a cape with a hood over her head. Only her opal-blue eyes and a curl of golden hair could be seen.

She carried a small, shaggy dog under her arm. Lowered to its paws, it wandered off to sniff flowers and potted plants along the row of headstones.

Jaks gathered his younger sister into an embrace. "Karisa, how I've missed you," he said.

Her hood slipped and revealed her face lit up with a smile.

He loved his little sister dearly. As children, they had been inseparable: monkeying backstage at their mother's performances, mimicking the actors, and leaning against one another as they listened to their mother sing. A more caring, gentle sibling he could not have had. For her true gift, he knew, was not her beauty or her illumancy magic, but her compassion. Even as they grew older, they still shared an unbreakable bond.

Vixhana was ten years older than Jaks, tall and masculine, with the hard, stern face of a career soldier. Deep-set eyes with heavy brows offset a long, aquiline nose, and a small scar—one of the few injuries she had taken in numerous battles—etched her square jaw. A fur-lined cape covered a suit of black leather armor. Her left hand rested on a longsword at her hip, and in her other hand, she held a bunch of white flowers. She locked her brother with her steely eyes and thrust out her sword hand.

He stared at it momentarily, then grasped her hand. She pulled him into a full embrace, knocking some petals off the flowers.

"What a proper little soldier you make," she said, looking him up and down. "Still scrawny as a lightning rod; even a uniform can't hide those twig legs." She smiled as she let go of his hand and stepped back; in contrast, her own tight-fitting armor undulated and bulged.

Vixhana gave Karisa the bunch of flowers, and the girl knelt beside the headstone to lay them down.

Her fingers trailed over the delicate white blossoms as she whispered quietly to herself. A tear dropped onto the flowers. "I miss her so," she said eventually. "But I can't even remember her face anymore."

"She was beautiful, Karisa," Jaks said hesitantly, wanting to comfort her. "You look so much like her."

"I don't know. I wish I could see her again."

The tiny dog sensed her distress and placed its front paws on her leg and gave her a querulous look. She stroked its head until it dropped away to sniff at the bunch of flowers.

The cathedral bells tolled noon. The streets around the sacred grounds now throbbed with citizens and soldiers, walking at pace between riders on horseback and the occasional horse-drawn carriage.

"Let's eat," Vixhana said. "I know a soldierly tavern where we won't be disturbed." She led the way to a large establishment with a swinging wooden placard marked "The Beer and the Boar."

On entering the tavern, the barkeeper gestured to an empty booth in the furthest reaches of the hall. Men and women, mostly in military uniforms, sat at tables and booths, eating, drinking, and talking; several stopped to nod at the tall captain of the Nightwraiths as they wound their way through the busy eatery.

At the table, Vixhana shouted an order of ale, bread, and stew to the serving boy. He scurried off with a "Yes, ma'am."

"It's only a month until Summer Solstice," said Vixhana as she turned to her siblings. Her eyes alighted on Jaks. "What are you going to do when you complete your conscription? Regular infantry?" she demanded.

"I don't know. Minto wants me to apply for the Rangers with him, but I don't think any of the army units will want me," he said, fiddling with the sleeve of his tunic. "I hear that the magistrate's office might have work. Maybe a job as a clerk?"

"Sounds dull," Vixhana said. But compared to her job, everything was dull. Following her conscription, she had qualified for, then rapidly advanced through the army's elite Order of Nightwraiths—battlefield assassins that terrorized the enemy in their camps and ambushed army lines.

Jaks spun the conversation toward his dilemma, spluttering a question back at her. "Could you find a prisoner for me?"

"Prisoner?"

He leaned forward and detailed his encounter with the mysterious woman in the mountains. Vixhana's brow rose as he described the otherworldly Meila and then furrowed as he outlined the carnage delivered by her weapon.

"Extraordinary," replied Vixhana, tapping her chin with an empty fork. "If I hadn't heard some rumors of a recently caught spy, I would have thought the fluff between your ears had finally got the better of you."

"You know where she is? Where? Can you get me to see her?"

"Sit down. I only know a little about your prisoner," she replied, and then glared at a curious cavalryman at a neighboring table until he averted his eyes. "But I have to agree with your ranger. She does sound like some sort of spy. What else would she be?"

"She's not," he said. "She's lost—"

"In the middle of Ascoria? I think not." Vixhana shook her head, shutting off his defense. His frustration must have shown on his face, as she paused and then sighed. "I'll see what I can find out, brother. But there will be nothing you or I can do if the king decides she's a spy."

Jaks nodded his thanks, hope renewed with his sister's offer.

The serving boy then thumped mugs of ale on the table and returned with a platter of food.

Vixhana turned her attention to the youngest of the three siblings. "You're quiet . . . How are you, little sister? Ready to start your conscription next month?"

Karisa, her dog at her feet under the bench, sat opposite Vixhana. Silent while Jaks and Vixhana had been speaking, she looked up and pulled down her hood. Tresses of golden hair tumbled about her shoulders. The sunlight adored a face blessed with jewel-like eyes that sparkled blue against a sculpted brow and cheekbones. Heart-shaped lips lent to a delicate chin.

A sigh arose from a nearby table.

She ignored the rising pitch of voices around the tavern and said, "I'm not going to do it. My acting troupe is going on tour to Faucony after the Summer Solstice. Ella and I are going to go with them." Her voice was defiant. "You know I would die in the army. The girls are cruel, they cut off your hair, and they scar you."

Vixhana leaned forward, glancing around. "You can't shirk conscription, Karisa. They'll track you down. You know the Pact Countries all have agreements to send back deserters." She scowled and leaned back. "And, if you fled, I would have a duty to report you."

"The only way out is to petition the king. But I hear he doesn't exempt anyone," Jaks added.

Several pairs of eyes around the hall were focused on Karisa, hungrily fixed on her like spectators at a play.

Vixhana leaned forward and returned the stares with a flinty glare. Their attention withered away from the challenge.

Karisa's hair abruptly changed to a mottled gray and shadows contoured her face to a gaunt and sickly appearance. It was as though a gnarled peasant woman had taken her place.

With the magical ability to control light and dark, she was a gifted illumancer able to augment her already natural beauty with ease. But, targeted by obscene attention from admirers—particularly after her portrayal of a dryad princess in a popular play, *Nereen and the Forest*—she had recently taken to obscuring her features.

Jaks frowned momentarily, taken aback by his sister's transformation. But returning to her outburst, and wanting to reassure her, he continued, "The conscription is not that bad. They make up stories like that to scare new recruits. The male and female conscript units may be kept separate, but I can tell you that the girls I do see still have their hair and bear nothing more than a few scratches."

"The two years go fast. When you finish, you can do what you like and go back to live with your troupe," Vixhana said.

"I promise, no one will hurt you," said Jaks. "I made an oath to Mother to look out for you." He tried not to wince as he said the words. Even to his own ears, they sounded weak.

"I don't need you to protect me. I can look after myself." Karisa flared her nostrils and locked in a haughty look. A look not unlike a noblewoman admonishing a feckless servant.

Jaks sighed. Both of his sisters could be as stubborn as mules. *She'll come to her senses.*

But Karisa continued to glare. Defiant.

"Come on, this food isn't going to eat itself," Vixhana said to break the tension and grabbed a bowl of the stew.

They ate and drank in quiet for several minutes.

When the last of the food was gone, Vixhana thumped the table. "I know something that will do you both some good," she said. "Follow me." She threw some silver coins onto the table and strode off as though certain her younger siblings would follow.

Jaks and Karisa exchanged looks of curiosity and followed their sister into the busy streets.

The City of Dunberrin covered a giant finger of land at the northern tip of Ascoria and, as the largest center of commerce and politics in the realm, the most important. A fortified wall sealed the main city from the mainland to the south, and a busy harbor dominated its east coast. Boats and ships ferried passengers and cargo to the Pact

Countries and other nations. Fishing boats brought in their catches to sell in the city's celebrated markets, and merchant carts delivered a constant supply of everything else. Avenues, streets, and alleys of cobblestone sectioned the metropolis into districts of commerce and residence.

Beyond the fortified wall, the "Grand Avenue" reached out toward the pastures and farmlands of the south. On either side of the thoroughfare, though, just outside the main gates, a worker's town of manufactories, iron smelters, and other industries billowed smoke and steam—and spawned waves of stench and dust.

The Rauhalik family were long established in a noble district within the main city, where two generations had been born and raised. Jaks's grandparents, self-exiled from Voros, had brought wealth with them when they arrived in Ascoria and bought a minor title. Their estate consisted of a three-storied manse, stables, and servant quarters, at the base of the city wall.

But since the death of the siblings' mother, it lay abandoned. Jaks had started his compulsory conscription period; Karisa had been sent to live with a Matron in the market district—but instead ran off to join a local theater group; Vixhana continued in the army barracks, as she had been for the past ten years; and their father departed for a distant province.

It was to that estate that Jaks suspected his elder

sister was taking them. The final clue revealed as their path turned onto "Rose Row" with its characteristic stretch of red and purple blooms.

"Vix, I can't go back there," he said, stopping in his steps and his face turning pale.

She stood to the side of the road. A horse and carriage clattered past. Glaring at Jaks, she said, "Get a hold of yourself. It's been two years now. You'll be fine." She slapped him lightly on the back.

Karisa stepped up beside them. Her face hidden under the hood, she clutched her tiny dog to her chest. "No, Vix. It's horrible. I never want to go back inside that place," she said.

"What if Father is there?" Jaks stammered. "He said that I should never return." After Lady Rauhalik's funeral, Lord Rauhalik had thrown Jaks a coin pouch and torn the family insignia from his tabard. Then, as though to a flea-ridden stray, he instructed him, "Be off with you. You are worthless to me." Had he possessed Karisa's charisma or Vixhana's physical prowess, he might have earned his father's respect. But with neither, he was discarded and disowned.

Vixhana pulled her siblings into an alleyway and spoke sharply. "This needs to be done. You must find closure one way or another. Trust me, you need this. Besides, Father's attentions are in the far south now, not here."

Karisa opened her mouth as though she were going

to say something but pursed her lips and switched Ella the dog from one arm to the other.

Vixhana placed a hand on each of their shoulders and turned them to face her. Her face softened. "You both have to move on. Mother's accident was years ago and you act like it was just yesterday. You'll see that it is just a dusty, decrepit building, and then you will be able to close that part of your life off—and then get on with the rest of it." She was well-meaning, from her gruff take on life.

An iron-spike fence surrounded the Rauhalik's city estate. *Surely, it did not always look like a prison*, Jaks thought as Vixhana creaked open the rusted main gate. In its prime, four horses could ride through those gates side-by-side. But the barricade, like the rest of the grounds, was a decayed remnant of its stately past. Weeds overran the foreyard, and a pair of unruly willow trees smothered the cobbled promenade. The stables along the far boundary were a shuttered and empty shell. And far from the street, the three-storied main building, covered with ropey vines, stared at them through a dozen dark windows.

Although Jaks had last lived here with Karisa and their mother just over two years before, it looked to have aged a century.

Vixhana disappeared behind the stables and

returned with an iron key. She unlocked the main door of the manse and led them inside.

As the last to follow, Jaks closed the door and paused as his eyes adjusted to the dim interior. Sunlight filtered through two opaque windows in the foyer. It was as he remembered: wood-paneled walls covered with artwork and frames, capes and hats on wall hooks, and hallways leading off to a maze of corridors and rooms within.

But as he turned to the foot of the stairs, it hit him.

Images flickered and battered at a wedged door in his mind.

Dark hands and a flash of light.

A metallic taste in his mouth. A scream.

Jaks's mind spun, forcing the memories back. *Stay away. Not now.*

Breathing rapidly, he braced himself against the wall.

That dark night when his mother died. Too gruesome, too terrible to allow into his consciousness. He did not want to remember.

Not now. Not ever.

He stumbled out of the foyer, away from the crime.

"Jaks, what's wrong? You look like the breath of a wraith," Karisa said as he entered the main reception hall. She rushed to him and laid hands on his waist.

"I'm fine . . . just wasn't what I expected." He slowed his breathing and sealed his thoughts, forcing a smile to reassure her. "I shouldn't have come back."

"Nonsense. This was your home for sixteen years. Walk around. Get it out of your system," said Vixhana. She paced the length of the far wall and drew aside a velvet curtain.

A long panel of frosted glass illuminated the hall, revealing the carved whirls and rosettes that decorated the ceiling and the crystal chandelier at its center. Padded wooden chairs surrounded several low stone tables in this reception hall where officers, nobles, and dignitaries once smoked cigars and lounged about with glasses of heady liquor.

Karisa put down her little dog. It yapped twice and scampered off, wagging its tail and sniffing about the hall.

The girl then went over to a table and touched the runestone lamp sitting at its center. It sprang to life with a steady, pure light. She pulled back her hood and dropped the cosmetic enchantment from her face and hair, reverting to her normal appearance.

Picking up the light, she walked over to one of the many paintings on the wall. Tears welled in her eyes and rolled down her face.

The oil painting had hung in the exact same spot since Jaks was six years old. Years of dust had gathered on its wooden frame, but it still imbued the essence of their once idyllic family life. Lady Katerin Rauhalik sat on a carved wooden seat, smiling. Wavy blonde tresses framed an aristocratic face and highlighted eyes as blue as the northern sky. At that time a lauded actor and singer on the theater circuit, she wore an embroidered crimson dress for the portrait. Little Karisa smiled, snuggled in her mother's arms, and small Jaks leaned against their chair. On the other side, Vixhana stood in her formal conscript blues, a scowl marring her face. And behind them, their father stared out of the frame.

Captured in the painting, Lord General Sicaro Rauhalik—dark-haired and bearded below soulless eyes —towered like a bear. The corners of his eyes drooped and curled in toward a mouth that never smiled. One gloved hand capped the top of a six-foot warhammer whilst the other gripped his wife's shoulder, possessively. A fur-lined robe draped his massive shoulders and obscured a black breastplate beneath. But despite the fine brushwork and detail, it did not show that Sicaro Rauhalik was a troubled man.

A career soldier, he thrived in wartime and maddened in peace.

After the Unifying Wars, his glory years stalled as the soldiers of his army retired to farms and mines or were amalgamated to other corps—General Sicaro was a general with no army.

A general who festered while the king then played at populist and builder.

And then, the most insulting of acts. On the death of an elderly custodian in a distant, southern province, Sicaro Rauhalik was installed as his replacement: royal castellan over Castle Sanford and a garrison of a mere two hundred soldiers. No matter what fancy titles the king made up, he was little more than the caretaker for the remotest and poorest of provinces in Ascoria. A poor reward for decades of service.

Jaks stared at the painting across the room. His father stared back, eyes demanding an explanation for his intrusion. Fleeting memories returned. Shouts, blood, and dark hands. Always dark hands.

Knees weak and sweat beading his forehead, Jaks collapsed onto a seat. *Not now.* Quicker this time, more prepared, he hummed the first tune that came to his throat and ground a fist into his leg.

Vixhana placed a hand on his shoulder. "It's okay, brother. You need to let it go."

"I tried to stop him. But I couldn't," said Jaks. "You don't know what he was like in those later years."

Her hand went rigid on his shoulder. He could sense her conflict. She had outright denied Jaks's accusations on previous occasions. Refused to believe that their father had pushed their mother down the stairs, repeating the magistrate's conclusions like a parrot. "It was an accident," she would often say to finalize the subject. Jaks suspected she believed him, but her blind adherence to the kingdom's laws prevented her from denying the summary of a king's official.

Vixhana turned her attention to her sister. "Karisa,

bring down that painting. You can take it back with you."

"I don't want a picture with him in it," the girl replied.

"He doesn't have to be in it."

Karisa and Vixhana lifted the heavy frame and leaned it against the wall. The nightwraith slipped out a boot-knife and sliced the canvas, leaving the bearded monster alone in the frame.

Chapter 4

Reunited

Karisa's little dog had wandered back into the foyer. It started yapping again. Karisa apologized and skipped out to find her excitable pet.

Vixhana ejected a breath. "We should go anyway, we've done what we needed to do here. You go ahead," she said to Jaks and went to close the wall-length curtain.

Jaks joined his younger sister in the foyer. She had a leash in her hand and bent down to scold the animal. "Shhh . . . Ella. Stop being silly. What's wrong with you?"

The door opened, and a gush of wind swept over the siblings.

Three large figures loomed in the door frame.

Karisa gave a startled cry and stood. The leash fell to the floor. The dog leapt in front of her and started yapping and growling at the intruders.

Jaks froze on the spot and gasped as his father strode through the entrance.

Lord Sicaro planted his feet squarely and stared at his two youngest children. He wore a chain hauberk and a steel chestplate emblazoned with the Sanford Crest—a falcon with two heads. Battle-scarred boots, built to stomp skulls and wade through blood, adorned his feet, and a longsword hung at his waist. At fifty years old, he stood the size and stature of a bear and towered over them.

"Look at this one," he said, glowering at Jaks, and laughed. "The little runt. Should have drowned him in the horse trough." He walked up to his son and shoved him aside.

Jaks stumbled and fell onto his backside.

The two other men, dressed in similar armor and livery, laughed as they stepped inside the foyer.

The bearded giant's gaze roamed and settled on Karisa. He smiled broadly. "There you are, my love. I've been looking for you everywhere."

Karisa's face twisted in fear. Her dog suddenly gave up its brave face, whimpered, and ran behind her legs.

Chills ran down Jaks's spine. He retreated into the shadows toward the closest door, scuttling backward. *Dark hands. They mustn't find me. Hide.*

Sicaro reached out to take hold of Karisa's chin and tilted her face to appraise it.

"A merry hunt, you've led. The matron said you ran off to the theater, and that dandy of a theatrician refused to tell me a thing until Bako parted him with an ear," he said, gesturing at a balding man behind him. "But what a joyous reunion."

He ran a hand through her thick blonde hair, placed it behind her neck, and pulled her in intimately. "You've grown even more beautiful. I have ached for you, my darling."

Karisa, terrified, pushed at him ineffectually.

Her father tightened his grip until her face contorted in pain.

"Take your hands off her. You're hurting her," Vixhana shouted as she stormed into the foyer.

A henchman dashed forward and imposed himself before her. Her equal in size, the man smirked at her.

Vixhana stared at him and, in an instant, transformed into her nightwraith form. Her features lost all definition, and her outer appearance went black as though dissolved into a swamp of darkness.

If Karisa was unusual in abilities, Vixhana was exceptional. Both gifted in illumancy, the older sister focused her magic on camouflage and distraction in combat, making her an evasive foe. And, in addition, she was a skilled gravmancer, manipulating the weight of any object around her, enabling her to wield enormous swords, hammers, or axes that no ordinary soldier could.

Where Karisa was beauty and grace, Vixhana was stealth and destruction.

There was an explosion of violence as a dark arm picked up the warrior by the throat and threw him across the room in the way that only a gravmancer could. Rendered as light as a puppet for seconds, he hurtled through the air and recovered his full weight just in time to smash heavily against the wall. Several wall hangings fell around the stunned man.

The room danced with shadows.

The darkness that was Vixhana slammed into the second henchman, magically manipulating him and launching him hard against the other wall, where he slumped to the ground with a grunt.

Vixhana coalesced from the shadows and returned to her normal form, an arm's length away from her father.

Sicaro spun his youngest daughter around and wrapped an arm around her neck. Elsewhere, it might have looked like a father tenderly embracing his child, but here the hold was sinister.

Karisa's eyes darted around frantically. She looked at Jaks imploringly, as though willing him to do something.

"Let her go," Vixhana commanded, her hand resting on the pommel of her sword.

"That was unnecessary," their father replied.

His injured henchmen, groaning and cursing, dragged themselves to their feet.

"What do you want?" Vixhana addressed her father, her eyes flitting between all three of the dangerous men.

Sicaro stroked Karisa's golden hair with his free hand. "I've come to take my darling to her new home."

"No, no, no . . ." Karisa cried out in a feeble voice and struggled against his grip. The rolled painting fell to the ground from where she had tucked it under her sash.

"Leave her be. She is her own person. She doesn't want to go with you." Vixhana walked slowly until her back was to the main door. Sicaro twisted to follow her movement, keeping Karisa in front of him.

A tense minute followed as father and eldest daughter stared each other down. Karisa was pale and rigid in her father's arms.

Jaks was behind his father now. He should draw his weapon. Attack unseen. His hand fell to his dagger but he couldn't draw it. His arm was paralyzed with fear. Instead, he could only stare at his father's massive hands. He was a child again, regressed and quivering in the corner.

"Step aside. She's coming with me," Sicaro said calmly and changed his grip on Karisa to drag her by the arm.

Vixhana slowly held up the palms of her hands to him, as though resigning to his will.

"Good girl," he said.

However, surrender was not her intention—a brilliant light, an illumancer's invocation as bright as the midday sun, beamed from Vixhana's palms directly into Sicaro's eyes.

Instinctively, his hands raised to shield his eyes from the blinding light.

Karisa fell from his grasp and scrambled away toward the gaping door. With outstretched hands, she grasped the frame, hurtled through, and sprinted across the foreyard.

Her little dog, bereft of a hiding place beneath her skirts, panicked, and with blunt claws scrabbling against the wooden floor, it fled deep into the house.

Vixhana lunged forward and rammed Sicaro with both fists. The moment before the strike, her gravmancer powers rendered him as light as a doll, negating his massive build and armor. However, just as her knuckles connected, her father invoked his own gravmancy—reversing the weightlessness to normal.

Instead of the potent, magically-augmented blow she had expected to deliver, Vixhana's attack was mitigated to that of a muscular warrior striking another powerfully built warrior—Sicaro staggered sideways and fell heavily to a knee.

The henchmen had recovered, and snarling, started toward her with bared swords.

"Get out!" Vixhana yelled at Jaks, drawing her sword.

He leapt up, charged the closest man, and shoved him as hard as he could. The man stumbled and careened into the bannister of the staircase.

Jaks then ran and fled out the door, only pausing when he reached the estate gates to look back for his older sister.

Vixhana faced the soldiers as they reformed their

fighting stances. She brandished her sword, hunched low, and mutated her appearance into a hideous demon form: illumancer magic elongated her face, sprouted vicious teeth and horns, glowed her eyes red, and cast flames around her body.

The men backed away. With faces full of fear, their weapons went limp in their hands.

Sicaro lurched back to his feet, his eyes clearing from Vixhana's blinding flash. "It's just an illusion, you fools," he shouted, and his sword rasped from its scabbard.

Confronting Vixhana in her demonic guise, he met her glowing eyes.

Vixhana invoked again and melted into a writhing shadow that sucked at the light in the foyer, then vanished out the doorway.

Sicaro stormed to the door. "You can't keep her from me. I will find her," he boomed at the retreating shadow. "Then I will kill you, bitch!"

Several people on the street nearby stared at the source of the shouting for a moment and then hurried away in fright.

Jaks spun from the gate and ran.

Chapter 5

Fleeing the Manse

Jaks and Karisa wound their way through the streets and stumbled into the market district, hand in hand, neither knowing where to go. Midafternoon, and people were shoulder to shoulder, intent on stocking up on vegetables and fruits, haggling with butchers, or perusing knickknacks from stands of artisan crafters.

Going back to Karisa's theater was not an option, nor was taking Karisa back to Jaks's conscript barracks. Their father might be on their heels, still intent on his youngest daughter.

They both breathed a sigh of relief when Vixhana caught up with them. She materialized out of the shadows without warning, startling a young mother with her baby. The woman squealed and hurried away.

"Come with me, you'll be safe in my quarters. We need to figure out what to do with you," Vixhana said to

Karisa and marched off toward the army district, beckoning them along.

The district sheltering the barracks and half of the military ranks of the kingdom ran along the western bay of the city. A ten-foot wall segregated the military compound from the rest of the city and housed many thousands of professional soldiers, a few hundred conscripts, and a naval base.

Vixhana vouched for Karisa—the only of them without military attire—to the Gate Sergeant and passed into the drill area. Being a rest day, the massive field of compacted dirt was empty but for flagpoles around the circumference flying the yellow and blue of Ascoria.

Although Karisa was new to the district, she commented that it seemed eerily quiet even for a Faithday. Vixhana informed her that four regiments of soldiers had recently vacated and marched west to reinforce the coasts of the Hera and Finstaf provinces against increasing numbers of Vor raids. "That'll be why," she explained.

The nightwraiths' quarters were tunneled deep beneath the barracks of the regular army, hidden and protected by a runestoned maze of magical shadows and darkness. Although their father, as a royal castellan, could enter the army district, he only had control over the garrison troops at Sanford and no longer held power over regimented soldiers as he once did.

In Vixhana's personal chambers within the

underground base, Karisa breathed a sigh of relief as she sat down on her sister's cot, removed her cape, and pulled a blanket around her shoulders. Her older siblings sat at a small table in the center of the room, next to a rack of knives, swords, and a single shield. Several shelves of clothes and wooden boxes lined the walls.

"What was all that about? Why is he looking for you?" Vixhana asked her sister, her face stony and hard.

Karisa stared at the ground, shuffling her loose shoe about on the floor. Eventually, she said, "Father has been asking after me at the theater for the last few days, but . . . I wanted nothing to do with him. I hoped he'd just go away."

"Okay, but what does he want of you?" Vixhana leaned forward.

Jaks shifted uncomfortably in his chair.

Karisa sank lower onto the bed, looking exhausted and spent. She tucked her knees up to her chest and wrapped the blanket tightly around herself.

She spoke in a small voice. "You weren't there when he came back from the war. He was always drunk, and he would accuse Mother of terrible things—you know she wasn't like that, she'd never do anything like what he accused her of. He wouldn't let her leave the house and dismissed everyone except for the guards to keep us in." Tears formed in Karisa's eyes. "That one time you came home for the weekend, he was so nice for a while, but after a few days, he started accusing her again and beat her . . . it was awful." She sniffed and wiped her eyes.

Vixhana rested her arms on the table and wrung her hands.

Karisa suddenly glared at her. "Why didn't you come back? You were away for years. You could have stopped him—you only came back when she was dead!"

"I couldn't. They needed me on the border, my unit needed me . . ." Vixhana started, then more softly, said, "I'm sorry, I didn't know it was like that."

Jaks frowned. A wave of guilt battered at him. He had been there. He had done nothing.

Karisa glared at her sister for several seconds and then slumped to her side, the anger retreating. Lying on the cot, she stared at the opposite wall with glazed eyes.

"All I could do was try and distract him," said Karisa. "Remember when I was little? I did silly dances and made up stories to make him come away and play with me. He loved the disguises I made up. Angels, sylphs, fairies."

She paused and took a deep breath. "Well, in the last few years, it was the only way I could get him away from her. He used to beat her so much, she lost some teeth and couldn't eat properly for weeks. She always had so many cuts and bruises. I had to protect her. I . . . I just had to."

Jaks had some idea of what she was going to say. For some reason, the knowledge had always been there but sequestered and repressed amongst other shuttered doors.

"He liked me most when I pretended to be older—like one of those painted women." Karisa started gently rocking on the bed. "So, I did. I did those things . . . for him. I used the magic to make myself desirable. I would say things I didn't mean . . . promise him things I didn't have. I lowered my clothes to show him what he wanted." She went quiet for a while and collected herself. "He brought me gifts. Flowers, jewelry, and then clothes of frills and lace. He would make me dance."

"Did he touch you?" Vixhana asked.

Karisa was quiet for a long while. Tears spilled down her face. Her silence answered their sister's question.

"From then, it was only me he came home for. I let him do what he wanted to me—so he wouldn't beat Mother anymore. She couldn't take much more." The girl stopped rocking, closed her eyes, and pulled the blanket over her head.

Vixhana and Jaks stared at the stone floor, not making eye contact or talking, but sinking in their own shame as they tried to comprehend the vile abuse that the youngest and most vulnerable of their family had traded for the protection of their mother.

From her woolen refuge, Karisa's voice became thin and high-pitched as she said, "It was the only way I could protect mommy . . ."

"The filthy bastard. I should have killed him." Vixhana's chair scraped back as she stood, clenching her hands. She pounded a fist into the wall.

"I'm so sorry, I should have tried to help," Jaks said, ashamed of his own inaction and naivety, knowing that at all those times he had simply run to his room and hid. And although he suspected evil, he had never talked openly with Karisa about their father's visits—cowardice and shame had dug the deepest of holes to bury secrets.

Vixhana ground the knuckles of her fist into the table, and her face stormed with rage.

A knock at the door broke the tension, and a servant brought in a bowl with ham, cheese, and cobbled bread, and a jug of water. When he spilled some of the water— trembling at the sight of the furious nightwraith— Vixhana simply waved him out and threw a cloth square over it, then poured the remaining water into cups.

She then looked at Karisa, who had sat up after the servant left. "This is the safest place you can be. He can't come here. It's only a month until Summer Solstice, and then he won't be able to bother you once you're a conscript."

Karisa remained silent and sipped from her cup.

Jaks had an idea. "After basic training, maybe you could apply to be a signaler for the regular army instead of doing the full conscription. A recruit from my unit did that after the first six weeks, and his illumancy wasn't anywhere as good as yours."

Vixhana's eyes rose as she thought on this. "Not a

bad idea. Signalers keep back from the heavy combat. In fact, you could have it easy. Once you're in the regular army, you only need to stay in for one year, instead of the two if you stayed a conscript. You would just have to learn to signal, of course." She reached for the bread and tore off a chunk. "And, if you were regular army, he wouldn't dare touch you, as one of the king's professional soldiers."

Karisa brightened at the idea, and after eating some bread and half a pear, agreed to stay within the regimented order and protection of the army.

But whether she was fully accepting of the idea, or simply agreeing to please her older siblings, Jaks was unsure.

"I promise you, Karisa. It'll turn out fine. I'll always be there for you," said Jaks, affirming the oath his mother had implored of him.

Chapter 6

The Creatures of the Forest

Two days later, the conscripts of the Thorns unit returned with Ranger Cromer to the northern mountain range of Ascoria. This time, however, they approached from the east, many leagues distant from their encounter with the foreign woman.

With no further word about Meila, Jaks's last hope was with his eldest sister and her military connections. The only indication she had even existed was a sketch he'd made of her lying in his pocket.

They set up camp as the sun dipped toward the end of the day. Around them, giantwoods, some as wide as castle towers, stretched up to the clouds. A family of squirrels scurried around a nearby trunk and knocked bits of bark to the forest floor in their hunt for nuts and bugs to eat. The leaf-strewn gaps between each of the mighty trees spared plentiful ground for the conscripts to spread out their camping gear.

Jaks noticed Baden and a few of the other men glaring at him as he gathered firewood around the campground. He was glad their conscription period would be over in a few weeks. After two years of shoves and putdowns, he would be rid of these ruffians when the Summer Solstice arrived.

"This is all your fault," a voice interrupted his thoughts. "If you'd just killed that spy, or just left her to die, we wouldn't have to be doing this all again." Baden shoved him in the back. Firewood spilled from Jaks's arms as he stumbled.

Jaks turned to face the senior conscript and raised his fists. "You shouldn't have done that."

"Go on. Take a jab," the brute said, raising his chin and sneering at him.

"You're not worth it. I'd probably kill you and end up court-martialed for it." Jaks said, his voice trembling with false bravado. He lowered his fists.

"You couldn't kill a gnat," said Baden. "Weakling." He spat at the fallen firewood and stalked off.

Minto rushed over. "You can't keep letting him get away with that sort of thing," he said, glowering at Baden and his cronies.

"It's only a few more weeks. I'm used to it," Jaks said.

But Minto was right. Jaks was tired of bullies. Instead of keeping it bottled up; instead of looking away; instead of thinking everyone else was better than him, he needed to stand up for himself.

The next morning, once the conscripts had downed hardtack and dried fruit, Ranger Cromer gathered the Thorns for the day's assignment.

"Leave your packs here. Hunting gear only," the gnarly woodsman said from his perch on a fallen log. He whittled away at a stick with swift slices of his knife as he spoke. "Hunt, fish, or forage—but do not steal. Use your wits and find some food. Prepare me a dinner feast."

They were to go out individually to hone their lone-wolf skills. Baden and a few others headed toward denser forest for deer; the majority, including Minto, toward a river or stream; and Jaks remained in the giantwood forest. He did not want to get lost. He would stay near the camp to forage and hunt.

Dappled sunlight shimmered through the trees as Jaks walked through the forest of red and gray trunks. He was off to a good start when he stumbled across a couple of thorny bushes bursting with small, juicy berries; unfortunately, they were so delicate that they mushed to a pulp within his leather pouch.

He sighed. He needed something more substantial.

Alone in the forest, his spirits calmed, and his head cleared of the hostility of the previous day. He listened to the wind rustling through the leaves, trees creaking and groaning as they swayed, and watched the birds and insects darting about, but found no trace of larger game.

His fantasy was to bring down a deer or boar. The ranger could not help but be impressed if he saw Jaks roasting a haunch over the campfire that evening. But whether lacking in luck or stalking skill (or both), animals always seemed to be aware of him and dashed away before he could bring his bow to aim. Even rabbits and squirrels seldom dallied long enough to give him the chance of loosing an arrow. It was as though he emitted some energy that warned them of his approach.

He circled in wider and wider arcs from the campsite, keeping watch for forest dragons—protective of their tree groves and liable to attack humans who strayed near their nesting sites—and listened out for the furtive shufflings and flaps of lone wyverns, who, more vicious and fearless than their dragon cousins, would stalk down their prey over many hours or even days.

Jaks stumbled upon a small creek burbling with water from molten snow high up in the mountains. He followed it to a point where he found deer tracks beside a natural ford. There were no animals around, but he did find a spot to hide and wait—a giantwood that had grown irregularly into a steepled recess at its base, big enough to back into and stack up branches to create a hunting hide.

As he scanned the forest for signs of a deer or boar, growing bored, his mind drifted to imagining a battle scene that Vixhana had told him of from the Unifying Wars. She and a swarm of nightwraiths, each hidden by their lightvoid invocations, charged across a field fought over for days before their arrival. In his mind, she leapt the wall of pikemen and landed behind the enemy formation—he'd forgotten whose army they had been; it didn't matter—then cleaved through their rear with a giant double-bladed axe. She would materialize to strike, then vanish, only to reappear dozens of yards away to smash her axe through more hapless soldiers. As she, and others, reaped confusion from the rear, even more attacked from the other sides. He was grinning as the images ran through his mind—but then something caught his eyes.

A small brown face across the creek.

The face stared at him.

Alarmed, Jaks blinked and narrowed his eyes to focus. He had been daydreaming again and was caught unaware.

Beady, brown eyes peered at him from a thicket of shrubs.

The bushes quivered, and the face disappeared.

Jaks rubbed his eyes. Were they playing up, or was that a dryad—a guardian and watcher of the forest? He had never seen one before, except for his sister performing as one on stage. However, he doubted they really looked as enchanted and svelte as Karisa's "Princess Nereen." *Something* had been there. If it had been one of the rare forest folk, might it warn game animals away from his hunting hide?

Jaks decided that he still had a chance of game at the

water crossing, and staying in the hideout was safer than wandering about.

A few hours later, the sun reached its peak. Boredom and the gentle babbling of the creek lulled him into a doze. Images of the beautiful foreign woman filled his mind. He dreamt of rescuing her from whatever prison she was in and running off with her to some exotic land.

A tug at his belt snapped him out of his nap.

Startled, he stood up, knocking away most of the branches that he had stacked up in front of his hide.

His hunting bow and an arrow clattered to the ground.

Again, the tugging at his waist. A doll-like creature hung by the handle of his shortsword, both of its tiny hands gripping the sheathed weapon.

"Get away from me!" he yelled as he stumbled out of the giantwood shelter, knocking the miniature thief away from him.

The creature fell on its back with a small cry. Empty-handed, it scrambled out of sight.

Jaks returned to the shelter to grab his hunting bow and quiver, then backed away from the tree. He looked up and down it, but there was no hint of the creature.

Rattled, Jaks jogged away from the creek with his bow in hand and a nocked arrow at the ready, throwing back glances for signs of pursuit.

When he reached a small clearing, he stopped. He listened to the forest as he had been taught: the chirruping of insects returned and the songs of birds sounded brightly. The danger was gone.

But, oddly, amongst the sounds of branches swishing and leaves rustling, a distressed mew carried in from the east. A sound like a wounded cat.

Puzzled and curious, but wary from his encounter with the forest creature, he walked toward the cries, keeping his bow tense and gaze alert.

It was another forest creature, similar to the one that had tried to steal his knife. This one, however, was hanging by the wrist, a noose ensnaring its limb. The rope was taut and tied to the top of a strong sapling that bent slightly with each of the creature's struggles.

Knee height, the creature had wild brown hair, mottled bark-colored skin, and what seemed like a dress of leaves. Its face was rounded and smooth, with brown eyes and a lipless mouth.

It pulled and gnawed at the rope around its wrist with little effect, but stopped at the sudden appearance of the human and whimpered.

Jaks felt sympathy for the trapped creature hanging by its wrist.

Two more of the creatures appeared. Partially obscured by a tree, they all stared wide-eyed at him.

He put down his bow. "I won't hurt you. I can help." One of the creatures stared at the sword on his belt. He unsheathed it and placed it on the ground in front of him.

"You can use it to cut the rope."

The tiny creature slid out barefoot, looked around cautiously, and reached for the blade. The sword fell from its claw-like hands several times. It was too heavy for it to hold.

Jaks took a step forward and slowly reached for the sword. The small creature retreated and sheltered behind the bough of the tree.

Jaks picked up the blade and advanced on the ensnared creature, who trembled and pulled at the noose a few more times, looking pathetic with its tiny arm drawn taut above its head.

He reached up and sliced through the rope. He thought that the animal trap would have been easily noticed by intelligent creatures such as these, and wondered whether it had been accidentally triggered while they had tried to defuse it.

Freed, but with the knotted noose still around its wrist, the creature ran off behind a tree.

"Wait," Jaks called out, "I can cut the rest off."

All three of the creatures disappeared. When he searched the area for them, all he found was a half-eaten red apple lying on the ground next to the trap.

The rest of that afternoon, Jaks returned to roaming the forest armed with his bow. He loosed two arrows off at rabbits but missed both times.

He was desperate. He needed to salvage his

standing with Ranger Cromer. Had to prove he had at least some skills and capability if he was to have a chance of a proper job in the king's pay. Minto had a good chance of getting in, as did Baden and all the other recruits in their unit. It would be shameful if everyone received a commission and he did not.

Even his claim that he might gain employment as a clerk in the magistrate's office was doubtful. His last coppers would not stretch far before he would be forced to beg in the streets or indenture himself as a covenant-slave to a plantation owner in a Pact Country.

By midafternoon, Jaks had only a pouchful of squashed berries and another of tree fungi that he wasn't even sure were safe to eat.

He started walking back to camp, biting his lip and cursing his poor take, when he heard a mewing sound again. This time it came in long bursts and was melodic like a song.

One of the forest creatures stood near a particularly wide redwood, hopping from one foot to the other and gesturing at him to follow. It appeared to be calling him. Maybe another of their kind was trapped?

Jaks shrugged and followed the creature. He was late already, so another minor diversion would not make much difference.

The creature ran from tree to tree on graceful legs, as though it slid on ice. Sometimes it climbed a few yards up a trunk and leapt to the next, pausing episodically to glance at Jaks. They ascended a hill, and the trees and bushes thickened considerably. When Jaks was puffing heavily and questioning the wisdom of following this creature, they reached the top of the incline and walked onto a grassy plateau.

At the center of the level clearing were several apple trees planted in a neat circle. Red fruit dotted the trees, amongst branches lush with green leaves.

There were hundreds of ripe fruits on the trees and lying on the ground. Jaks picked one up and smiled at the pleasing weight and glossed surface.

The forest creature began running back and forth, heaping apples at Jaks's feet, emitting happy mewling sounds as it worked. Laughing, Jaks filled a large sack with fruit and crammed every pocket he had.

Weighted down but grinning, Jaks was indebted to the little forest guardian—he could return with pride from this survival exercise.

"Thank you," said Jaks as he crouched and looked at the creature obscured by a tree trunk.

Its ethereal face curled a smile in return. It scooted up into the leafy recesses of a tree and sat on a large bough, where it dangled its legs.

He had not eaten all day since leaving camp and crunched into an apple, delighting in the sweetness of the white-fleshed fruit.

Jaks hefted the heavy sack, wiping apple juice from his chin, and marched back to camp.

Chapter 7

The Bully

J aks arrived back at the campsite at sunset to discover the other recruits' preparations and cooking were well advanced. Several fires roasted animals on cooking spits—several fish, rabbits, and a small boar—wafting delicious aromas around the area.

Only Minto acknowledged his return by giving him a cheerful wave.

"Have a look at these beauties," said Jaks, walking over to where Minto was tending to one of the cooking fires.

He dropped his sack next to Minto, noting his two roasting fish, and pulled an apple out to offer to his friend.

Minto examined the apple, bit into it with a satisfying crunch, and nodded his approval with a smile on his face.

"Ranger Cromer isn't back yet," said Minto between

munches of apple. He reached out to rotate his spitted catch. "I only got these two pathetic things all day at the river. Apparently, there was a pond further down that had some handsome wigglers." He flicked his head at one lad beaming with his catch of four fish, each the length of his elbow to fingertips.

The other conscripts had brought back at least a fish or rabbit; however, Baden—of course, thought Jaks—had trumped them all with the boar and two rabbits. Bringing back fresh fruit was acceptable, but far less soldierly in their eyes, given the snide comments a few made as they walked past Jaks's collection.

Night fell, and they waited for their instructor to return. But after an hour tiring of their rumbling bellies, Baden started eating, and the others followed. When they'd finished, only the senior conscript, the fishing prodigy, and Jaks had any food left over.

"Here. I'm going to share these around," said Jaks, giving Minto another fist-sized apple.

"Don't waste them on those idiots. If you think you're being nice, think again; they don't care."

Jaks thought of the forest creature in her leafy dress bringing him fruit that afternoon and decided it would be selfish to keep the apples just for himself. The fruit was a gift from the forest itself.

He told Minto about his encounters with the forest folk, the snare, and the apple orchard. But feeling protective of the little people—who they decided could only have been dryads—he asked his friend to keep the proximity of the dryads secret. It wouldn't take much for a malicious soul to take sport and hunt the gentle beings —something that Baden and his cronies were likely to do if they knew about them.

He stored a few leftover apples in his own pack and took the remaining ones to the middle of the campsite, leaving them sitting in the open sack. He called out to two of the less surly conscripts and told them the apples were for everyone.

A few of the other recruits ambled over to the apples and took up his offer. One even held up an apple and nodded thanks to Jaks.

Baden sauntered over to the sack of apples, picked one up, studied it closely, and walked over to Jaks and Minto.

"You've been messing around with my traps." Baden glared at Jaks, holding the apple accusingly in front of him. "I found one half-eaten at my last one. Some dumbass cut the rope."

Ice ran down Jaks's spine and his mouth formed a circle as he realized it was probably Baden's snare that the dryad had been caught in.

"It was you, wasn't it?" the heavyset youth challenged him, his eyes protruding and lips flat.

Fear coursed through Jaks like frost. He couldn't tell Baden about the dryads, but he couldn't deny damaging his snare either.

"I had to cut it. Got my foot caught in it," he said, thinking fast. "I didn't see it until it was too late."

He got to his feet, his shoulders stooped and head held low.

Baden closed the gap between them. His nostrils flared, and he pointed a finger. "You thought you'd have a laugh and wreck my trap, is what I think." He shoved Jaks in the chest with both hands, causing the taller youth to fall onto his backside.

Jaks sat bewildered for a moment, then fear surged as Baden advanced on him again. Baden's gang gathered around to watch the spectacle.

Not this time. He wouldn't let this thug bully him any longer.

Thoughts of the brave forest creatures, the verbal insults, name-calling, and being pushed around pumped fiery indignation through Jaks's veins.

It was time to take down this brute.

Jaks gritted his teeth and rose to his feet. Anger burned down his back.

Staring directly into Baden's eyes, he stood tall and tensed his shoulders, but his confidence was shaky. He knew he would get flattened by one of the thug's huge hammer hands if he didn't strike first. He raised his fists in front of his face.

"Fucking weakling. I'll smash you." Baden snorted and pulled his fist back.

Summoning the resolve to launch an attack, Jaks imagined hitting the brute in the face and willed himself to attack.

Suddenly, a flash of brilliant light blasted from Jaks's knuckles, accompanied by a sharp crack of sound.

An arc of white struck Baden and exploded in a dazzling ball of fury. The huge conscript was slammed off his feet. Flat on the ground, his arms and legs twitched several times before he went limp and lifeless.

Smoke wafted from a black mark on Baden's face and the cloth tunic over his chest, and a metallic odor cut through the air.

There was a sudden clamor of voices as several of the conscripts swore and shouted in astonishment.

Amazed faces flitted glances back and forth between the immobile body and Jaks, who still stood in a boxer's stance. Minto looked to the sky as though wondering whether a passing storm had been the source of the lightning strike.

Two of the senior conscript's closest associates gingerly approached the body.

Jaks stood rooted to the ground, staring at his hands. The lightning imprint on the backs of his eyes had dissolved, but the memory of the sharp forked lines tracing from his clenched fists to Baden's twisted face was etched in his mind. He stared down at his victim's unmoving body, confused by what had happened. Had he invoked an illumancer flash similar to what Vixhana had used against their father? No, it was much greater than that. He had knocked a grown man down without touching him. He had produced the same energy that traveled with storms. Energy that crackled, burnt—and destroyed.

He staggered a few steps as the enormity of his actions fell heavily on his shoulders. He had killed Baden.

He turned and fled into the darkness.

Branches whipped at his arms, and roots and bushes grabbed at his legs as he ran. The shouting voices of the conscripts trailed off, and the forest became an army of accusing giants as he rushed through.

A thick bough flicked out of the night and bashed him in the face. Pain exploded, stars spun, and he was slapped to the ground, knocking him unconscious.

When he came to, his forehead throbbed. No blood, but a definite promise of a days-long headache. His breathing slowed, and he listened for the mood of the forest. It slept, with the rustling of leaves and the creaking of trees his only companions.

His eyes adjusting to the night, he sat up and stared up at giantwoods silhouetted by the dim light of a clear, starry night sky. The camp was far behind him, and the chilly air embraced him.

Was Baden dead? If he had killed him, he would be tried and executed for murder. Perhaps he could flee to another country as a fugitive to start a new life.

He held his hands to his face. Black fingers in the night. There was no doubt to him that arcs of lightning had come from these hands. But *how?* Up until today, he had never generated even the slightest sign of magic.

Karisa had instructed him how to invoke simple illumancer tricks and illusions when they were younger, but his efforts to mimic her conjurations had always failed.

She would have him recall a happy moment—patting a puppy or watching their mother perform on stage—then encourage him to imagine a light forming on his fingertip. "Then *will* it to happen," she would say as though it were the most natural thing. Then the magic was supposed to begin. She would demonstrate by dancing colored lights along her fingertips. But then all he could do with his fingers was make shadow puppets to her scintillating show.

Jaks stood. His head throbbed harder, feeling like it was going to burst. Hands fumbling along a fallen tree in the dark, he sat.

He had visualized . . . striking Baden. And he had certainly wanted it to happen very strongly, so maybe that counted as willpower. But it was fear that had filled his being, not joy or happiness, and it was forks of lightning, not a simple light, that had channeled through his fists.

Jaks sat in the dark woods for another hour and came to a decision.

"There you are! Ranger Cromer is back," said Minto, after Jaks returned to the camp. He had crept in quietly, evading the sleepy recruit on watch, and had shaken Minto awake under his shelter. "You'd better go see him."

He found the Ranger by a firepit, staring into the embers. He had a cloak wrapped around his shoulders and was poking a stick at the dying fire. As Jaks approached him, he looked up, his eyes pinpoint despite the dark but otherwise unreadable in a face like granite.

Jaks stood at attention and stammered out a few words, but they spilled out in a jumble.

"Shut up. Start again," Cromer directed him, his voice gravelly.

Jaks took a deep breath and told the Ranger about the altercation between Baden and himself, describing the initial shove from Baden through to the lightning strike when the senior conscript was about to attack him a second time.

"Where did it come from . . . this lightning?"

"I don't know. He was about to hit me. It just came out when I was trying to defend myself." Jaks trembled in anticipation of his fate. "Am I under arrest, sir?"

Cromer looked at him hard and threw the stick onto the glowing firepit.

"He isn't dead, boy. Whatever you did knocked him out but didn't kill him." The grim man rose to his feet and kicked dirt over the campfire.

He then pierced Jaks with his intense eyes in the darkness of their sockets. "You're no soldier, boy. You cause too many problems to be a part of my army." The ranger leaned in close to Jaks, his breath sour in Jaks's face. "In a few weeks, you'll be on your backside on the street. Get out of here."

With a dismissive flick of his hand, he sent Jaks slouching back to his shelter.

The rest of the week, Jaks kept to himself, staying at the back of the Thorns when they marched or performed their duties, and keeping his distance during their off time.

Baden, the morning after their clash, was marred by an angry burn on his right cheek and shot Jaks a baleful glare. Whether fearful of Jaks or planning a delayed revenge, neither Baden nor his gang bothered Jaks or Minto for the rest of the week.

When Minto questioned him about the lightning, Jaks would say he could not remember and did not want to talk about it. Thinking on it too hard sent him breaking out in a sweat and grinding his teeth. There was something more to it than just the brief fight with Baden. Something buried deep in his memory, threatening to claw its way up with dark hands. Yes, it was best to forget it and push the incident to the back of his mind, he told himself.

But despite his reprieve from the bullies and time alone, Jaks was miserable. For after the Summer Solstice, he would be homeless, an outcast.

Chapter 8

Conscription Ends

Five days until the end of conscription and Jaks would leave the army. The problem was that he had nowhere to go.

That morning, the Thorns unit was posted to sentry duty on the city wall of Dunberrin. Staggered out along a length of the twenty-foot-wide fortification between two catapult towers, the conscripts sagged under the weight of their armor and weapons as the day rose to its promise of clear skies and damning heat.

Over the battlements, the wall dropped fifty feet to the green waters of the outer canal, and on the other side, a mosaic of buildings, streets, and alleys stretched out for a mile and thinned away to countryside. A dozen pillars of smoke blew across Jaks's view, spewed from manufactories that produced half of the realm's iron goods, leather, cloth, and other basic goods.

Perhaps there, he could find work.

Jaks placed his wooden shield on an embrasure gap in the wall and pulled at the neck opening of his steel breastplate. The leather doublet underneath was rubbing his skin raw, and the sun didn't help his discomfort, either. In his other hand, he held a spear with a polished iron point. Beside him, Minto had laid down his own spear and shield and was crouched over, tightening a bootstrap.

"I hear that the Den of Warlions are looking for apprentices," Minto suggested as he straightened and picked up his gear. Minto had been refused by the Royal Rangers, but he had scored his second choice—apprentice to the Heraldic Corps. A profession that started him out as a simple errand boy for the royal palace, but that could advance to royal representative around the country and, ultimately, a chance to become a diplomat to one of the Pact Countries.

"Absolutely not! I'd rather stir a tanning vat than end up as a lion's breakfast." Jaks's flippant reply hid the fact that he had already applied to the Den and been rejected because of his "inappropriate temperament during conscription." In fact, the leather works were looking to be his best chances for a job, for even the desperate could find work breaking their backs over stinking vats of hides and urine—they just never lasted long at the miserable job.

"How about that clerk's job at the magistrate's office then?" asked Minto, twirling his spear by its blunt end on the stone underfoot.

"Maybe. I haven't heard back from them yet. I think my scribing exam was satisfactory, but they haven't decided how many clerks they're going to take this year," Jaks said. "I really hope I get in. If I were a magistrate one day—"

"You'd be filthy rich and get to execute whoever you like," Minto said with a grin on his face.

Jaks's face turned solemn, his forehead creased, and he stared into the distance.

"No. I'd petition the king to change the justice system." He turned to look at Minto and held his gaze. "I'd make it so that anybody can have a fair say during a trial, so everyone can get justice—not just lords and ladies." He was thinking of the inquest into his mother's death, where only their father had needed to give his recollection of events. He and Karisa had not even been allowed to be present in the magistrate's proceedings.

Minto was quiet for a while, gazing at the far-off mountains that lay beyond the workers' city and farms and pastures below.

"How about that magnificent sister of yours, do you think she'll be impressed when I'm a master herald?" Minto asked, puffing out his chest, trying to turn from the somber direction the conversation had taken.

Jaks grinned and said, "Honestly, I don't think Vix would care whether you were a herald, a governor, or the Emperor of Zura. I don't think she's interested in men in that way." He laughed as Minto's face crumpled with disappointment, and his thoughts turned to Karisa. "You *are* talking about Vixhana, aren't you?"

"Hell yes, even I know that your other sister is beyond my fair charms."

"And barely sixteen," Jaks added. He hadn't seen either of his sisters for three weeks, since he had gone on the second survival exercise. In a few days, he could visit Vixhana and Karisa. He hoped Karisa was coping with the underground bunkers of the nightwraiths and had not changed her mind about her conscription: she had threatened to run away with her acting troupe; he prayed she had not.

And perhaps Vixhana had news on the whereabouts of Meila. He had not forgotten his promise to her, too.

Although he lacked any genuine power or authority, maybe he could help the foreigner argue against her charges of spying. She would need someone who spoke Ascorian. He brightened with hope. If he got that clerk's job at the magistrate's office, he might discover an even better way to help free her.

"Oi, you two get back to your posts, proper like!" a man-at-arms sergeant yelled at them from further down the battlements. Jaks and Minto hurried back to their assigned positions with their spears. Standing eight merlons apart, they stood at attention and stared at the countryside.

At midafternoon came the Changing of the Watch. A new shift of conscripts led by another man-at-arms replaced Jaks and Minto's section of guards. Wearily, the two youths and the rest of the Thorns trudged down a tower stairwell and marched through the army district to their barracks.

The army district felt even emptier than when Karissa had commented on it weeks before. The deployment of four thousand troops to the west coast of the realm, followed by another four thousand a couple of weeks later, had reduced the city's garrison to a ghost town. The chatter and gossip amongst conscripts said that coastal raiders were so frequent and well organized that King Silas was preparing a defense against a Vor invasion.

However, as they neared the central drill area—a huge field that took up almost a quarter of the entire army district and could stand ten thousand men and women at attention—they were greeted by the shouted commands and war cries of ranks of infantry drilling for battle. Three battalions of Royal Pikes practiced defensive maneuvers against fast-moving sections of close-melee soldiers armed with swords and shields. The Pikes maneuvered to counter flanking efforts and bristled their formations with unwavering polearms.

Jaks was impressed with the discipline and coordination of these professional soldiers and felt disappointed at failing to meet the required standards to join them.

The conscripts followed the cobblestone boundaries of the grounds and kept on marching.

Their barracks were in an ancient keep at the end of the army district and had once been the Royal Castle over six hundred years ago. Built without the benefit of magic in its building or maintenance, the keep was now run-down, dark, and damp—nothing like the gravmancer-crafted and purpose-built barracks of the professional soldiers.

Jaks sighed with relief back in their twenty-bed dormitory, having relieved himself of his armor and spear at the foot of his bed, and happily anticipated the thirty-minute break until his section was due in the kitchens for dinner prep.

On his pillow, an envelope awaited him.

His excitement grew, seeing both his addressed name and the wax seal of the Royal Magistrate's Office on the rectangle of paper.

Flicking it open, he unfolded a letter. As his eyes darted from sentence to sentence, his shoulders drooped and his head sank.

He had been rejected.

Minto, seeing him with the letter, asked him the result and gave his commiserations.

Across the room, Baden smirked as he overheard Jaks's rejection. He rubbed at his scarred cheek. Menace lurked in the thug's eyes, but with his imminent transfer to the Royal Lancers—a legendary division of heavy cavalry—following conscription, his opportunities to return the injury were running out.

——————

That night, retribution was delivered in the form of a pillow and fists.

Jaks woke to a smothering pressure over his face. Blinded and unable to breathe, his reflex was to pull the obstruction away; however, his arms and legs were pinned. Iron hands gripped his wrists and ankles.

Pain exploded in his belly. An onslaught of heavy jabs struck his unprotected abdomen. Unable to breathe, he struggled his best, but numerous attackers held him to the cot.

Muffled voices arose near his covered head, but he could not make them out.

The attack renewed and continued for what seemed forever. The face covering stifled his breathing as fists and elbows struck him over and over.

His mind retreated, as it did from time to time. Aware of the physical blows but detached from pain or response.

A shout roused him an unknown time later. The pillow fell from his face and Minto was standing at the side of Jaks's cot with a bared sword. "Get away, you fucking bastards," his friend shouted around the dark dormitory. He waved the blade with one hand and shone a runestone flashlight at a group of retreating shadows with the other.

Jaks rolled to his side and gulped in air. The act of breathing stirred a wave of nausea, and he dry-retched.

The soft front of his body was in pain. From his chest down to his groin, it felt like he had been stomped by a horse. He curled into a ball and moaned.

"Damn whoresons . . ." said Minto. He placed the sword on the ground and gently examined Jaks's injuries. Finding numerous bruises but no blood, he laid a calming hand on the youth's arm and returned to glaring around the room.

Baden's voice rose from beyond the reach of the torch. "Oops, didn't see him there," he said, and laughed.

***

The next morning, Jaks remained in his cot, nauseated and aching from the beating. Minto covered for him when the man-at-arms queried his absence from sentry duty, blaming food poisoning for his infirmity.

Later that day, as the Thorns returned from their duty, an errand boy employed by the Captain of Conscripts trotted up to his bedside and handed him a summons to present himself to the captain in his tower. *Oh, God, more trouble?* Had Baden contrived further devilry, using the commanding officer to exact further revenge?

Midriff aching, Jaks struggled into his uniform and lurched after the waiting messenger.

Jaks had only spoken with Captain Buik once over the past two years. In the initiation week, the short, well-dressed officer had given Jaks his condolences, saying that he had heard that his mother had fallen to her death. "A fine actress. Saw every play she was in. She was so splendid. Such a tragedy," he had said in a clipped and precise manner, and then added, "And your older sister—yes, she was an excellent swordfighter. A nightwraith now, I hear." Fortunately, he had not mentioned his father, for Jaks would have had no reply. Since then, he had only seen the captain from afar: on the drill grounds, on march, or on parade.

The boy led Jaks through the keep to an anteroom and knocked. A voice sounded in reply.

Pushing open the timber door, the boy announced Jaks and stepped back. Unsure of proper protocol, or the reception which he would get, he marched in and stood at attention in front of the captain's huge wooden desk.

Captain Buik sat in a tall carved chair, dressed in an officer's formal uniform decorated with gold tassels over the shoulders and bronze clasps down the front. Partially bald, he had carefully plastered a few strands of hair across his head.

Curiously, another man sat in one of the over-padded armchairs to the side of the room. Attired in a nobleman's clothes—well-cut and tailored with sharp straight lines in the latest fashion—he rested a clipboard and stylus on his knees.

"Conscript Rauhalik, this is Master Cranbrook from the Academy." The captain nodded to the other man. "He is here to evaluate your . . . power."

"Power? I have no powers, sir," Jaks stammered.

The mage stood and walked over to Jaks with an inquisitive look on his gaunt face. He had deep-set eyes as though he neared death, and a scar that ravaged his neck from ear to ear but was partially obscured by a rounded collar. "You look ill, young man," he said.

"Just a sour stomach . . . my lord," replied Jaks, unsure of how to address a member of the Academy. The Academy of the Arcane harbored the elite of mages. Renowned as the center for inventing new implementations of magic and creating powerful artifacts, only the most brilliant and powerful of gravmancers, pyromancers, and suchlike dwelt there. Whilst the army trained battlemages in offensive magic, the Academy trained magesmiths and mancers in everything else.

"Reports are that you invoked lightning." The master sat on the captain's desk, placed his clipboard and stylus down, and folded his arms. "If that is true. You would be the first electromancer since Grandmaster Vinton—the first in over eighty years."

Jaks's stomach churned and his face went pale. *Electromancer?*

"I'm going to need you to do exactly what I say. If I

find you're just a common illusionist or trickster, I'm not interested in you," said the wraith-like mage. "But, if what the Ranger reported to Captain Buik is true—then it would be a waste not to explore your powers somewhat more."

The errand boy took Jaks and Master Cranbrook up to the captain's solar, a sun-soaked room filled with potted plants spilling out sweet scents and cascades of color.

They sat on two wicker chairs at the center of the round tower room. The mage pulled at his collar, leaned forward, and looked intently at the young man. Jaks stared at the man's nose, avoiding the temptation to glance at the scar, wondering how close to death the mage had come.

"Feel. Visualize. And then, will," said the master, flicking each word through the air with his writing stylus. "This is how you harness magical power. Summon the emotion, create a picture in your mind of what you want to do, and then push your willpower into making it happen." He sat back in his chair and looked expectantly at Jaks.

"Wait." The master waved his stylus toward the other end of the room. "Go over there, by that watering can. I don't want to be in the way if something happens."

Jaks faced a metal watering can and tried to recreate the sequence of events from his encounter with Baden. For a few minutes, he ran the scenario over and over, stretching his hands in front of him at the watering can, but nothing happened. He recalled and followed Master Cranbrook's instructions, and nothing happened.

"No, no, no," said the mage. He sighed, tapping his chin with the stylus, and then walked over to Jaks.

"You need to incite and hold your fear." He stopped a few steps from Jaks, placed his hands on his shoulders, and turned him back to face the metal bucket. "Electromancy draws on the feeling that your life, your very existence, is under threat. It comes when you are being chased or attacked by a great evil. Electromancers in the past manifested their greatest invocations when in battle and wounded."

Jaks had never heard of a mage drawing power from fear. It sounded wonderful, but impossible. Fear was the opposite of power. It was what he felt under the heel of someone else's power—like last night in the barracks.

Master Cranbrook continued, "This is not happy, joyous illumancy or anger-driven pyromancy. It is fear, dread, terror. It rips at your deepest being. Tears at your soul." He spoke so passionately, spittle flew from his mouth. "Think of times you have been attacked or felt you might die. Falling from a tower . . . the dread of a bear staring at you . . . the terror of—" He paused, searching for an example.

But Jaks had his own: the terror of his raging father hammering down a heavy gloved fist, sweeping past his head, and smashing a kitchen table to splinters. The terrifying mask of anger stretched over his father's face.

The horror of seeing the dark fist descending toward his mother's head.

Jaks breathed rapidly. Couldn't get enough air into his chest fast enough. He felt as though he was suffocating, as though a pillow smothered his face again. His heart raced and his mind spiraled—and then the room abruptly closed around him and he collapsed to the floor.

For the second time that day, Jaks revived from blacking out. This time, he found himself lying on the ground in the captain's solar. A half-empty bag of dried sheep manure cushioned his head. The side of his head ached and was tender to touch. He had been injured so many times in the past week, he was losing count. He sat up groggy and nauseated.

"You took a bit of a knock as you fell," said Master Cranbrook, examining a hanging plant with conical yellow flowers.

"Sorry, sir. I don't know what happened."

He turned from his botanical study and looked at Jaks. "A panic attack. Something threw your mind into a whirlwind, by the looks of it. Common with battle veterans or torture victims, but sometimes a dire memory can trigger emotions that consume and engulf a mind completely, propelling you back to re-experience your trauma again." He pulled his round collar up higher around the pale scar curving around his neck.

The mage signaled for Jaks to return and sit with him in the wicker chairs. "It may take a while to elucidate whether you have any magic power. Today, your anxiety and . . . indigestion, appear to have won the day."

"Sorry, my lord. The—"

The mage held up a finger to interrupt. "Learning to harness your emotions will give you the best chance of unveiling the presence of magic. If you have the power of electromancy, it will be in the Academy's best interests to help you develop and explore its potential. Grandmaster Vinton documented the use of his lightning power on the battlefield. Indeed, Ascoria would not be here today if it had not been for him. But we know little of the nature of electricity and whether it has other practical uses as well."

Master Cranbrook reclined in his chair, lost in thought for a while, and then finally slid his stylus into a holder on his clipboard.

"Grandmaster Mulgrave needs a clerk at the Academy. He will continue from where we have got to today. And, in turn, you will assist him in his research and administration. It will be up to him to further evaluate your power. Who knows? One day you might apprentice at the Academy."

Master Cranbrook looked at Jaks and arched his eyebrows questioningly.

Tingles of excitement radiated through Jaks's neck and shoulders once he realized he was being offered a second chance at making a difference of some sort.

He nodded.

Despite two dismal years of conscription and two rough weeks at the end, his future had flipped from bleak to bright. He wouldn't have to sleep on the streets and scrape coppers from the gutters, or sell himself in servitude; instead, he had a job and income—and had been given hope to possess the rarest of magical powers.

Chapter 9

The Archway of Perpetual Night

The Summer Solstice festival, heralding the start of the new year, had begun in the City of Dunberrin. The week-long festival summoned provincial nobles to deliver their tithes to the King, brought household retinues and guards, traveling troupes of performers and minstrels, crafters of jewelry and trinkets, and rich and plain country folk wanting to join in on the most exciting event of the year.

Several festivals, markets, and outdoor performances were taking place centered around the market and cultural districts of the main city. However, the usual festivities seemed more subdued than other years, and rumors of war with Voros led to smaller audiences and crowds coming to attend.

Summer Solstice was also when every youth in Ascoria who had reached sixteen years was brought, voluntarily or not, to be sworn into the Royal Conscripts during the Ceremony of Age. Tearful families waved off their sons and daughters to join the army.

However, those new conscripts would not arrive until tomorrow, for today was "The Outgoing," for those who had finished their two years of service. Jaks, along with the rest of the outgoers, would be branded with a completion mark on his arm, given a small stipend, and handed his identity papers.

His last morning in the barracks, Jaks threw his last few possessions into a sack and relished the comfort of being back in comfortable civilian clothes: woolen leggings, a cotton tunic, and an armless leather jerkin.

"Watch out for all those princesses," he said, coming up to Minto, who was closing the trunk at the foot of his cot.

"I wish," replied his mop-haired friend, who then laughed and slid his coin purse into a pocket inside his jerkin.

"Hells, this hurts." Minto rubbed the skin around the Shield and Crossed-Pikes emblem that had been burnt onto his upper arm earlier that morning. "Well, this is it then," he said, and threw Jaks a tense smile. "You'll keep in touch?"

"I'll write you," Jaks replied.

"Write? Hell no, send me a messenger to tell me when your master lets you off duties and we'll meet at the tavern! I might even be able to visit you when I'm on messenger duties."

"I might get Faithdays off?" Jaks said, not even sure

how to get to the Academy, how much he would be paid, or where he would sleep. At the end of his meeting with Master Cranbrook last week, he had simply been told to report to Grandmaster Mulgrave at the Academy on this day, then sent away.

They walked to the district gates amongst the hundreds of other outgoers. A few parents waited for their now-adult children on the avenue outside the army district barbican and sentry post, but most of the conscripts simply walked out and made their own way to their various destinations with excited goodbyes to one another.

"Farewell, old friend. See you again soon," said Minto, and then jogged over to meet with another novice who had also joined the Heralds.

A pang of loss struck Jaks as his friend was swallowed into the crowds.

He sighed and prayed that his next two tasks for the morning would be more satisfactory—for, once he reported to his new job at the Academy, there was no telling when he would have more free time like this.

Jaks heaved his carrysack and headed to the military prison in another attempt to locate the foreign prisoner Meila. He pestered the guards there and then at the three city prisons for word of her. They had none. Again, he had exhausted his limited avenue of inquiry and slumped away.

He wondered whether a palmed coin was needed to

loosen their tongues and gain their cooperation; he knew little of these things.

Vixhana would know. She might have even uncovered the foreigner's whereabouts already.

He swore to himself, shaking his head as he walked toward the nightwraiths' barracks. On reflection, he should have visited his sisters *first* that morning.

The nightwraiths' arch was an enigmatic landmark in the army district near the city wall. A gigantic curve of granite connected two large buildings. At the apex of this archway stood a statue of a warrior raising a greatsword as if to plunge the blade onto anyone who dared to pass below. But most remarkable was the arc below called the Archway of Perpetual Night, a wall of impenetrable darkness where light could not pass or escape. Rumors told that the mysterious complex was filled with this same magical dark and that the elite soldiers crept about with magical night vision and performed bizarre rituals and sacrifices. Nonsense and mystery, Jaks knew from his sister, created to keep curious regular soldiers away.

It was this arch that Vixhana had brought them through after their encounter with their father over a month ago.

At midday, he stepped into the blackness under the

arch and felt his way along the wall of the left building. Several steps, then he followed a gap leading down five steps. Light returned as he entered an enclosed alcove lit with a runestone globe above an ironwood door and barred window. He gave it a sharp rap with his knuckles.

A small slot slid open behind the bars and beady eyes peeked out.

"What do you want?" asked a raspy voice. But before Jaks could answer, the voice continued, "Oh, it's you. What are you doing using this entrance? Shouldn't you be in the kitchen?"

What a curious greeting, thought Jaks.

There was a heavy clank, and the door opened, revealing a gray-haired sentry armored in chain mail and bearing a sheathed shortsword. "Well, get in, lad," the sentry said.

Jaks entered a square guardroom and saw several unmarked doors and passageways.

A second wrinkled guard, with an eyepatch over his left eye, sat at a small table in the middle of the room and was staring at a hand of cards.

"Why don't you use the servants' entrance?" The rough-looking guard frowned at him. "You got lost in the Dark?"

"Oh, I'm not a servant. I just came to visit my sister."

Both of the guards stared at Jaks, the seated one placing down his cards to squint at him.

"Your sister? Who is that, then? You're just that serving boy, you're having us on," the first guard said.

"No, I'm not, not," Jaks stuttered and felt his heart quicken. "She's Captain Vixhana Rauhalik. My other sister is here too, staying with her a short time."

The sentries gaped at Jaks for several seconds, then looked at each other and roared in laughter.

"You said your 'other sister,' you dolt. You meant your *brother*, of course, you two look so alike. Twins, are you? Never mind." The eye-patched guard sat back down, wiping his eyes and still chortling. "You've missed Captain Vixhana. She was deployed several days ago. Sent to the provinces on one of their covert missions," he said, tapping the side of his bulbous nose. "But your brother should be here, of course."

Baffled, Jaks couldn't think of anything to say and simply stood with a puzzled look stuck on his face.

The first guard ducked his head into one of the many doors, and a girl with a cheerful smile came running out after him.

"Take this lad to his brother," the guard instructed the girl and sat down to pick up his hand of cards.

"What brother, sir?" The girl then looked Jaks up and down and a flash of recognition appeared over her face—although Jaks had never met her before. "Oh, I see. He'll be in the kitchen."

"Of course, you dolt. Off you go. I have some coins to win back."

The girl led Jaks through a maze of doors, stairs, and

magically darkened passageways he knew would be impossible for him to remember in finding his way back. How did this child navigate the tunnel complex so easily? He would have to ask his sisters whether illumancers could actually see in the dark.

Finally, they entered a large dining hall filled with long tables and benches, but only a quarter of the seats, at the far end near the servery and kitchen, were occupied by black-armored men and women eating what seemed to be bread, beef, and corn. A few other nightwraiths returned tin trays and dishes to the kitchen and headed into the hallways.

Jaks followed the girl into the kitchen, where two men tidied the servery benches, and several workers out the back were washing dishes and utensils in tubs of soapy water and then stacking the items in piles.

"Oi, your brother is here," the youngster yelled toward the dishwashers.

The workers stared up from their tasks to Jaks.

One tall youth stood up, brushed his hands on his apron, and walked over to him.

The young man's face looked oddly familiar. A moment later, he backstepped and gaped in surprise. The man was his mirror image.

"What?" Jaks blinked several times.

"Jaks, it's me, of course." Karisa dropped part of her illusion for a second and revealed her normal face. "It's just easier like this," she said, and re-invoked her illumancy to complete the mimicry.

A coarse matronly voice called over from the washing area, "Boy, get back to work. Talk to your brother after breakfast." Jaks looked over to see an old woman stacking dishes and glaring at Karisa. He was dumbfounded as his sister scuttled back to her chore.

Jaks waited, rubbing his arm below his newly branded mark of a conscript, and stood awkwardly outside the kitchen. A quarter hour later, Karisa came out drying her hands on her leggings.

Back in Vixhana's quarters, Karisa fell onto a chair and kicked off her shoes. She dropped the mirroring illusion and restored the appearance of her face and hair. But even without magic, the siblings looked similar: noble, refined features and generous lips and eyes. Only Karisa's blonde hair, blue eyes, and the swell of her chest—inherited from their mother—significantly marked her different from him.

"Sorry, Jaks, you must have caught a fright," she said. "After I got here, Vix didn't want any soldiers to bother me, so we decided I should cut my hair, strap my chest, and use an illusion. It's tiring keeping it up, but it's better than fighting off stupid men. I hope you don't mind?"

He laughed and shook his head, then went to sit in another of the chairs beside the round table at the center of the room. He looked about.

Vixhana's bed was tidily made, and they had set another bed up against the opposite wall since the last time he had been here. As he had expected based on the guard's information, his older sister was absent, as were the weapons and shield from her equipment rack.

"You must be excited for tomorrow," he said. "Don't take too much of your own gear. The quartermaster'll supply you a uniform and boots when you get to the conscript's barracks."

He then frowned as a small brown mouse climbed up the table leg and ran over the top to Karisa. It rose on its hind legs, waggled its front paws, and sniffed at her. The teenager took out a small nub of carrot and offered it to the mouse. The rodent scrambled onto her palm and nibbled the vegetable. Cradling the tiny animal, she smiled.

Jaks loved to see his sister happy and didn't press her for a response.

A minute later, however, she lifted her eyes to him and replied, "I've changed my mind. I'm going to run away in the morning." She shot him an anxious look. "You won't tell Vix, will you?"

"What? What do you mean?"

Karisa stroked the mouse a few times, then placed it on the ground. It skittered away beneath Vixhana's cot.

"I found some money that she left in a jar. I'm going to borrow it and buy a berth to Faucony and wait for my troupe." She smiled and looked at him with a sly look on her face. "I'm going to disguise myself as you. You just said you didn't mind."

"That's not what I meant," Jaks said, his voice almost a shout in the small room. "You can't run away. I thought we had a plan. You were going to report for conscription tomorrow."

Karisa continued as though she had not heard. "Father would never leave Ascoria to find me. If I leave the country, he will give up searching for me," said Karisa. "You could come with me. We would be twin brothers on a voyage!" Her face brightened with a smile.

"No. It's not just Father you should worry about. The army would trial you as a deserter and hang you, Karisa." Jaks rose from his seat and stared at her. "You know what Vixhana said about the Pact Countries— they would only need one look at your identity papers and they would send you straight back. If you don't turn up for conscription, you will be marked a wanted criminal. You can't hide forever." He threw his hands up in the air, exasperated.

"I could," Karisa said in a petulant tone of voice. "They would never hang me," she added with less certainty and put a hand to her throat.

"Father can't force you to do anything anymore—it's not your fault he did those things to you, so don't let him make you a criminal and steal your freedom. Do the right thing." Jaks reached out and grasped her arm gently. "When you're in the army, he can't get to you. He only commands his garrison. He is not a general anymore. So, if he tried to take you or hurt you, he would have to answer to King Silas himself." Jaks released her arm and sat down.

She persisted with her stubborn look, a child not

getting what she wanted. "I thought you would want me to be happy after all we went through."

"I do, but you will never be happy, running and hiding for the rest of your life." Jaks's eyes dropped to stare at the table. It was difficult for him to look at her with what he was about to say. "Karisa, I am sorry I was such a coward when we were children. I was so scared of him. I should have done more for you and Mother."

"It wouldn't have made any difference. He would have just beat you even more," she replied. He needed no reminder of the beatings he'd received.

"I promised Mother that I would look out for you if she died. She seemed to know she wouldn't live to an old age."

Karisa's eyes misted and her face softened at the mention of their mother.

The siblings sat in silence for several minutes.

Finally, Karisa found Jaks's hand atop the table and gazed at him. "You are right. It is not our fault how things turned out. It was his fault. He is the criminal, not me. I won't hide. I need to get through this. Running away seems the easiest thing, but you are right, it would be the *worst* thing—I could not live as an outlaw."

Jaks smiled and patted her on the hand. "You are far too pretty to be an outlaw."

"You're so nice, Jaks. You and Mother are the only people who say things like that and don't want something back from me in return."

"That's the way it's supposed to be in families. Here, I brought you these." He reached into his carrysack and extracted a folded document and a small book. "It's a signalers' application form and a signalers' code book. I asked Captain Buik for them before I left. You just need to give him your application before you finish basic training, and he will process them. He will know you; in fact, he said he saw you in a play last year and thought well of your performance."

Karisa drew the objects toward her and looked at them curiously.

"You will be fine tomorrow—you are tougher than me—and if I survived conscription, you certainly will," Jaks said, feeling pleased with himself for averting this disaster. Then, putting on a deep voice, he added, "If anything happens to you, I'll come and set things right. Your big brother will take care of you."

They both laughed.

But even as he made light of his oath, an unusual heaviness fell upon him. A premonition that some mystic cyclone had been triggered and his words would drag him into its perilous path.

Perhaps she was right. Perhaps she would be better off absconding offshore? Their father was seldom denied, and the army was no place to be if a war broke out . . . No. He gritted his teeth. The honorable path was the best path. Vixhana had also wanted this for their sister. *Karisa will be fine.*

Jaks looked over his shoulder to see if anyone had entered the room, but on finding no one, he shivered as though the night itself had laid her fingers upon him.

Chapter 10

The Academy

The midafternoon sun sweltered over Jaks's head as he farewelled Karisa outside the Archway of Perpetual Night. He welcomed the warmth, a stark contrast to the cold subterranean tunnels of the nightwraith barracks.

As he walked away, he cursed his luck that his other sister was away on deployment. Not that he doubted Karisa would follow through with their agreement, but for another reason: Vixhana was his last chance to find Meila.

Already, he was wondering whether the entire escapade in the mountains had been a dream. It was almost as though she had never existed, it was so hard to find any information about her.

But unable to do anything more about Karisa or the foreign woman, he bit his lip and steeled himself for his last destination that day: the Academy.

Make a good impression with his new master, and he could prove he could do something right.

He wiped the sweat from his neck and headed into the foundry district. The narrow streets were lined with workshops of crafters and fine artisans of materials and magic. A horse-drawn carriage, attended by a steely-eyed guard, waited outside one goldsmith's shop. Outside another, a nobleman and his mistress gazed through the barred windows of a jeweler. The beautiful woman pointed a finger at a gem-encrusted bauble and the shop guard unlocked the door to allow them in.

Jaks squeezed past a cart laden with coal bound for one of the many smithies and almost fell over a beggar sitting in the shade of a runestone-hewer's shop awning. The one-legged man rattled a wooden cup at him. Jaks frowned. *There go I but for the grace of God*, he thought.

Jaks dropped a brass coin into the cup, then as an afterthought, he asked the beggar for directions to the Academy.

The man pointed a crooked finger at one of the many chimneys to the south. Taller and wider than any of the others in the district, it spewed a thick column of smoke from its tapered top.

Guided by the landmark at the tip of the peninsula, Jaks came to the harbor's edge.

A prison-like building squatted on a small island connected to the mainland by a land bridge. Windows dotted the bleak stone exterior, and battlements and parapets lined the roof. However, the only sentries that Jaks saw guarded the main gates at the end of the bridge.

Several blue dragons with bodies the size of hawks—less aggressive and smaller than the bronzes that he had fought in the mountains—soared and screeched above the square building. A few others perched on its walls, preening and sinuating their necks to gaze over the area with possessive arrogance. One dived off the rooftop and swooped toward a pair of seagulls beating over the wharves. The birds cried out and winged away. The blue then looped back over the harbor and dove into the sea; a minute later, it dragged up a struggling fish in two of its claws and flew back to the roof of the Academy.

Jaks returned to examining the famed building. This was the closest he'd been to it, despite living in Dunberrin all of his life. Unlike the children's picture-book drawings, or how his mother had described it after taking six-year-old Karisa there to be assessed, it did not look like a majestic castle overlooking the ocean; instead, it appeared dark and grim.

But it was here that the Grandmasters researched and discovered new methods of using the magic energies, and here, in the runic forge, that the most powerful artifacts in the realm were crafted.

Two huge archways greeted his approach. Wooden signs marked one "in" and the other "out." Three guards stood with bored expressions on their faces. When asked the whereabouts of Grandmaster Mulgrave, the middle guard shrugged and pointed at a map panel fixed to the wall behind him, detailing the three floors of the institution: enormous squares with a wide courtyard. He tapped a ground floor area of the map marked, "Metals Laboratory."

As Jaks took his leave from the guards, a man in coal-blackened rags trundled two horses and an empty coal cart out from the exit arch. A clattering of hooves from the other direction saw another carter approaching, his cart full of the black nuggets.

Jaks walked through the archway, along a double-laned tunnel, and out to a dirt courtyard. He had expected the area to open to the sky; instead, a bronze dome roofed the enormous space. The great chimney that had led him here rose from the middle of the courtyard and pierced the dome at its center as though it were the rounded handguard to its blade.

The bottom of the chimney was encircled by workshops stationed by leather-aproned smiths, striking a rhythm with their hammers against anvils. Each station fed on a roaring flume of blue and white fire within a single enormous furnace.

Despite a breeze blowing in through a giant portcullis overlooking the sea and out through the archways behind him, the courtyard sweltered in the heat of the furnace and the acrid smell of molten iron.

"Out of the way," a voice called out. Jaks jumped aside as the carter's horses snorted at his back and passed him on their way to coal bins by the furnace.

Recalling a mental image of the Academy map, he

weaved his way across the courtyard through stacks of sheet metal, cages of metal bars, piles of chiseled stone, spools of wire, and curious machines with moving cogs, levers, and rollers—some so peculiar that they looked like torture devices.

He skirted the furnace workshops, through an area with several wooden tables laden with books and documents. At one desk, a group of crafters appeared to be in a heated argument with raised voices and gesturing forcefully at various papers in front of them.

Grandmaster Mulgrave did not look pleased when Jaks found him in the Metals Laboratory.

The mage's lab was a maze of desks and benches that staggered the mind. Every flat space was covered with a plethora of partially constructed machines, machine parts, and tools. In addition, over-stacked bookcases and shelves partitioned the room into uneven sections.

Jaks had never seen a room like this before, and it took several moments to realize that at least half a dozen people were busy around the giant room, tapping, wrenching, and examining their contraptions or reading tomes and scribbling notes.

"What do you mean, 'new clerk'?" The bald mage glared at Jaks. Grandmaster Mulgrave had come from the back of the laboratory, after Jaks's inquiry had passed through several of the lab workers. The man now stood in front of him and studied him from head to toe.

Below his shiny head, the grandmaster's face continued as sharp as a knife down to a wild beard that covered his jaw and chin but left his neck bare. Threadbare eyebrows hovered above penetrating green eyes. A head shorter than Jaks, his chest and arms bulged with muscles. Dressed in an armless tunic and leather leggings, the old mage resembled a blacksmith of horseshoes and pots.

Jaks shifted from foot to foot. "Master Cranbrook said to come here today. I have just been released from conscription," he said.

"I don't need a clerk; I have a new apprentice already."

Jaks was lost for words for a moment. "He said . . . Master Cranbrook said that you would be able to help me with my magic, and that you needed help with your writing."

"I can write quite adequately, thank you very much —young whippersnapper." Mulgrave's face soured. "What's so special about you? Why would Master Cranbrook think I would help you with magic?"

A young man with ears that stuck out through sandy-colored hair ran up to the mage and handed him a plain leather-bound book embossed with silver lettering. "Here is the Navindi book, Grandmaster."

The mage took the book wordlessly but continued to ponder Jaks.

"I can't control my magic. Actually, I am not sure if I even possess magic," Jaks said.

"What? Preposterous! What is Master Cranbrook up to? Does he think I'm a nursemaid, taking care of any young pup who runs up to me? Why are you so special that he would have me teethe you?" Mulgrave demanded from Jaks.

Jaks felt the itch of many pairs of eyes on him from around the lab. His tunic was stained with sweat. Had he misunderstood Master Cranbrook last week? He searched for an explanation that might please the mighty mage, but all he could stammer was, "Electromancy?"

Mulgrave stepped closer, his expression unreadable. A vein on his temple throbbed like a pulsating worm. "Electromancy . . . that is a remarkable claim you make. Master Cranbrook is one of the least stupid administrators around here, so he must have seen something in you. Show me what trickery you can do." Mulgrave placed the book atop a pile of others and leaned against a workbench.

"Sir . . . my lord . . . I have only ever been able to invoke it once. I was under attack and there was lightning. I think it was lightning. It struck Baden and knocked him to the ground. It burnt a scar into his face."

"What makes you think it was not a fire invocation? You may have burnt him and he staggered backward and fell over."

"Master, I don't know, but it was incredibly bright

and cracked like lightning in a storm. I'm sure it wasn't flames."

"There are many types of flame, not just what you see under your mother's cooking stove." The mage put a finger to his chin. "What I want to know is what can you do with your conscious will?"

"Sorry, Master. Since that time, I have not been able to invoke again." Jaks described his failed session with Master Cranbrook and the subsequent panic attack at the Conscripts' Keep.

Mulgrave creased his forehead and began pacing a path between two rows of benches.

Big Ears, whom Jaks guessed to be the grandmaster's apprentice, lost interest in the conversation and meandered off to tinker with some tools.

The grandmaster stopped mid-pace and turned to Jaks. "Are you afraid of lizards?"

Jaks blinked rapidly, not sure he had heard correctly.

"What about spiders?" the mage continued, smiling broadly. "I think we will set up an experiment. I love a good experiment. Tavis!" He clicked his fingers at the apprentice, who scrambled over to his master.

Jaks looked at Tavis properly for the first time and was surprised to see a handsome face, solid chin, and a hawk-like nose, only spoiled by his forward-pointing ears. A couple of years older than Jaks, he dressed tidily with his tunic buttoned to the top and tucked into his pressed cotton trousers. He narrowed his eyes at Jaks.

"Well, are you, lad?" Mulgrave repeated.

"Yes, I'm afraid of them," replied Jaks.

"Which ones, lizards or spiders?" Mulgrave opened a desk drawer and shuffled the contents around noisily.

"Both, Master. And caterpillars and worms and . . ." Any critter with the wrong number of legs sent shivers up his spine.

"Hells, we don't need a zoo. Tavis, go find a spider and meet us over by the portcullis." He handed the apprentice a glass container stoppered with a wide cork.

The portcullis was a frame of rusted bars blocking a short tunnel that opened out to a neglected wharf and the harbor beyond. A salty breeze blew through the grilled barrier. Jaks welcomed the cool air dampening the furious heat of the courtyard behind him.

Seaweed covered the slimy green surface of the wharf outside, giving it the appearance of having been unused for years. Jaks imagined that if he tried to walk along it, he would end up sliding its length instead.

At the tip of the boat jetty, a couple of blue dragons squabbled over a fish: hissing, lunging, and swiping at each other with their front talons. And past them, waves undulated with creamy white tips and floated several boats traversing the city's port.

"Boy, what is your name?" Grandmaster Mulgrave was at a wooden bench dwarfed by the portcullis. He pushed aside empty beer bottles, cups, and dishes to clear a space.

"Jaks Rauhalik, Master." He turned away from the dragons, who had ripped the fish in two and were now eating their uneven halves.

"Rauhalik . . . name sounds familiar." Mulgrave removed his leather apron and draped it over the bench. "Anyone I would know?"

Jaks told him of the illumancer powers running through the female side of his family and Vixhana's additional gravmancer abilities, but he faltered at mentioning his father, simply staring at Mulgrave with his mouth opening and closing soundlessly, his mind and emotions swirling in a confused maelstrom of indignation and fear as he tried to think of how to describe him.

"Ahh, your father . . . General Rauhalik, yes? One of the king's old favorites, a shrewd strategist. Castellan now, I understand?" the bald mage interrupted, filling in the words that Jaks could not say. "From what I recall, also a gravmancer. It would seem that you have a fine lineage of magic. But let's see about you—and my experiment."

Jaks disliked the idea of being experimented on but said nothing.

"When that nice juicy spider gets here, it is going to help you." Mulgrave slapped his palms to the bench and grinned. "Hairy, leggy one, I hope. Ever eaten a spider?"

Jaks's face twisted in fear at the mere thought of a

spider near his face. "No, Master, please don't make me eat it! This is too much. I'm not sure I want to do this . . ."

The grandmaster's face suddenly turned serious. "Fear like that sweeps from an arc of simple worry and concern through to horror and terror. It is the fuel to electromancy, much like anger is to firemancy." The mage's lips thinned, his nostrils flared, and in his upturned hand, a ball of flame ignited and rolled in his palm. The heat reddened Jaks's face but seemed to have no effect on the mage.

"Fear is your reaction to threat of harm." He pushed the sphere of fire closer to Jaks, causing the youth's eyes to blink rapidly against its heat. He stepped back.

As quickly as it had ignited, the fireball was gone, and the mage looked up at Jaks. "Anger, though, is your reaction to an injustice."

A pinch in the arm surprised Jaks, then several more followed as Mulgrave pinched his arm repeatedly; he moved away, but the mage followed him with his pincering fingers. His face flushed again, but this time in anger at the irritating mage.

The bald mage ceased his assault when Jaks backed up against iron bars. "What starts out as one emotion can lead to the other. It depends on how you choose to perceive danger . . . a threat, or an injustice."

Jaks nodded. The words made sense, but he was too annoyed to think on their meaning.

The mage continued, "Electricity is the most

elevated of the energies we know of, so complex that we do not understand it well—so when Grandmaster Vinton died, our knowledge of it going forward also died. So, you could be our next chance of expanding on that knowledge."

"I don't think I am a grandmaster," Jaks said. "In fact, I'm probably nothing." The desire for magical power was not as appealing to him, with such a legacy laid on his shoulders. Better to stay unnoticed and out of danger.

"Yes, most probably nothing," sighed Mulgrave.

Tavis jogged up and clunked his jar on the bench, looking pleased with himself. An almond-sized spider with a green line down its back reared up against its glass-walled prison. "Found a good one, Master. I think it might be poisonous!"

"Well done, apprentice! Have *you* ever eaten a spider?" Mulgrave said and then laughed at Tavis's shocked expression.

"Emotion the fuel, imagine the goal, willpower the trigger, and power will go," intoned Mulgrave like a children's rhyme. "What my dramatic friend Master Cranbrook failed to do was to guide you in generating an appropriate level of emotion that you could control. He thought to dump a cartload of coal on a match and expected a bonfire; of course, you wouldn't be able to trigger anything."

The stocky mage nudged the glass jar toward Jaks. "Go on, open the jar and stick your hand inside. That will likely cause you a good amount of fear but should not be overwhelming."

He pushed it closer when Jaks hesitated, and continued, "Once the fear is strong, create a picture in your mind of lightning from your hand striking the spider. Then, the hardest part . . . you will need to *will* the lightning into being, all the while continuing to hold the image and your fear. That is the trinity of power." He bounced on his toes eagerly and drummed his fingers together.

Jaks looked at the jar. The spider disgusted him. He wanted to throw the jar into the furnace rather than open it. Even putting his hand on the outside of the jar sent a chill down his back, and he shivered.

"Okay, here goes." He plucked the cork from the mouth of the jar and placed it on the bench.

The spider skittered about but could not climb the slippery wall. He stared at it for a minute, his heart pounding and his hand trembling.

His hand slowly moved into the mouth of the jar and started to shake more coarsely, bumping the sides of the receptacle.

He visualized a white lightning bolt crackling into existence from his hand and held the image for several seconds and then, recalling Mulgrave's instruction to turn his mind to commanding the image into reality, he focused on cajoling, pushing, and building his expectation that the deadly bolt would trigger.

He closed his eyes, hoping it would help him focus.

Nothing happened.

Jaks opened his eyes and saw that his hand had drifted away from the jar, well out of danger.

"Try again," Mulgrave said.

Five times, he tried again.

Each time, the mage's face drooped further and further in disappointment.

After the sixth attempt, Mulgrave sighed. "Put the jar down, let's see if you can make a fire." He beckoned his apprentice closer and ordered him, "Tavis, start pinching the lad."

When the apprentice looked confused, he added, "Like this," and pinched Jaks in the arm.

"Ow . . . I don't think that is necessary . . ." Jaks said, pulling his arm away in pain.

"Nonsense. This is the second part of the experiment. Pinch him, apprentice," Mulgrave commanded with renewed fervor.

Tavis approached Jaks with an outstretched hand and pinched him in the arm.

Jaks yelped and backed away from him.

The older youth began grinning and chased Jaks around the bench, taking to his task with evil delight. He had surprisingly strong fingers when he could land a pinch on his target—an arm, leg, or buttock.

Jaks's temper brewed, and he turned to face Tavis, preparing to slap his hand away the next time he lunged. "Get away from me!"

"Imagine a wall, a wall of fire, boy. Between you and Tavis. Burning hot flames as high and wide as you are tall."

Jaks followed Mulgrave's visualization. The anger lingered in the peripheries of his attention as he willed the flame wall into being.

Nothing happened.

Tavis lunged forward and pinched Jaks on the arm where he had scored twice already and roared with laughter. "Gotcha!"

Jaks jerked away, feeling bullied and desperate. He was tired of being toyed with.

Tavis came for him again.

Jaks scooted backward and smashed into the wooden bench. Bottles, cups, and plates flew through the air and crashed around him. He fell heavily against the upturned edge of the bench, and pain lanced through his back. He cried out and slid to the ground. Face scrunched in pain, he closed his eyes.

A creeping sensation on his shoulder drew his attention as the back pain subsided. *Was I cut?* He felt for blood, but instead his palm found a hard, round object.

He drew his hand away to find a green-backed spider clinging to his wrist.

He yelled in fear, willing the monstrosity gone from

his arm. Suddenly, a sharp, needle-like pain barbed his arm and his yell turned into a cry of agony. His arm flexed in response and brought the persistent spider close to his face.

An abrupt crack sounded like a tree branch bent beyond its limit, and a brief flash of white sparked at Jaks's wrist.

The spider's fried husk fell from his arm and landed on its back with its legs curled up, dead.

Grandmaster Mulgrave froze mid-breath and stared back and forth between Jaks's arm and the dead spider for several moments, then exhaled. "Well, that was something."

Jaks did not hear, gasping at two fang marks and his swelling wrist. *I'm going to die.*

The mage ordered Tavis to fetch some ice and an aid kit, then turned to Jaks and grabbed his hand to extend the spider-bitten arm above his head.

"Stop being dramatic. The greenbacks aren't poisonous. I just needed you to think it was."

Chapter 11

The Meeting in the Bay

Lord Sicaro—Province of Sanford, Southern Ascoria

"Take down those damn banners." Lord Sicaro gestured at the pennants of the Ascorian king draping the throne-room walls of Castle Sanford.

The massive hall accommodated gatherings of several hundred people and was crafted by gravmancer masons so that no columns or supports were needed for its immense arched ceiling. High up the walls, stained-glass windows cast a dazzling palette of colors and patterns over the marble floor. Intricate engravings of battle scenes covered the west wall and holy scenes depicting The Creation were etched into the east.

Sicaro had glared at the pennants all morning as petitioners poured out their problems to him, as the castellan and surrogate governor for the province. The queue was longer than normal, following a long absence. A month lost to travel to the other end of the country and back, delivering the king his taxes at the Summer Solstice. A month lost to find and then lose his daughter.

He ground his teeth at the sight of the wall hangings, a reminder that he was a mere caretaker of this province and not its owner. A mere titled lord, not a landed lord as he should be. King Silas owed him this. This very land that General Sicaro had conquered for Ascoria only fifteen years before.

Instead, he was a general with no army and a lord with no land. *An affront that must be corrected.*

Two guards scurried off to pull down the banners, using the blunt ends of their spears to lift them off their hooks and then kneeling to roll them up against the wall. Several minutes later, they returned to their posts by a clerk and his small desk at the foot of Sicaro's dais.

A small white dog sat at Sicaro's feet, staring up at its new master with droopy brown eyes. He'd named it Kat in a twisted memorial to his dead wife. His henchmen had found it whimpering under a kitchen bench in the Dunberrin estate, and Sicaro had brought it back with him. As a reminder of his favorite daughter, it was pampered. Any who maltreated the dog spent a day in the stockade, and any who so much as smirked at their master's uncharacteristic tenderness was whipped and salted. However, much like how he should have kept his daughter close, the dog was on a tight leash and locked in a metal cage when unattended.

A royal herald entered through a side door to the throne room and bowed to Sicaro. "My lord.

Commander Lytton insists on an audience with you this afternoon. He repeats his desire to speak to you about the disposition of his troops, in particular, allowing him to position some of his battalion inside the walls."

Sicaro regarded the herald with dispassionate eyes. He disliked the fop immensely. Although every soldier in his garrison had been hand selected by him, this herald had been appointed by the king.

The man, as his role required, was pristinely dressed: tailored trousers, silk shirt, a vest emblazoned with a two-headed falcon crest. However, it was how he wore his feathered herald cap—jauntily tipped to one side—that made Sicaro want to crush the man's skull. But, for all his finery and dandyism, he was yet another agent that the Ascorian king used to keep a rein on him. He mentally shifted the herald's order of termination up on his list of people who needed to be purged in the coming months and smiled at the thought of the man's head mushed in his hands.

"What say you, my lord?" asked the herald.

"I'll see him tomorrow at afternoon court." He saw some potential in meeting the commander, even though he resented the presence of the newly arrived battalion. When the king had offered to send more soldiers to Sanford, Sicaro had been adamant that his heavily fortified town was already fully defended and had no need of the king's troops in his region. The Vor raiders were only striking the regions on the west coast of Ascoria, he'd argued. The battalion was an additional five hundred bellies to feed. Their encampment trampled two good pasturing fields, and Commander Lytton was another of the king's lackeys to challenge Sicaro's rule of the region. An unnecessary aggravation. He had been stuck in this rut for too long, stagnated, stalled, and underappreciated—it was time for a shift in power.

"I shall inform him, my lord," the herald genuflected and retreated.

Sicaro beckoned to his clerk. The twitchy man shot up from his chair and scampered up the throne steps.

"How many more?" the castellan said.

"Just one citizen awaits, my lord. Publican Unraster from The River Thistle tavern. He requests a month's reprieve from taxes." The clerk scratched at his thin mustache.

"Last month, he was complaining about the alcohol levy. The idiot should be increasing his beer and food prices to raise his income."

The clerk nodded like a drowning man keeping his head above the waves.

"Send him away. Halve this month's tax, but he must make up the amount next month," Sicaro said, and waved the man away. He was merciful to the Publican. Taverns dulled the masses and kept them happy, but he would not allow his coffers to suffer. Especially now that the coins would fill his personal coffers and not the Ascorian king's.

"Feed the dog, then lock it up," he said to a servant

girl waiting on the side. She scooped up the animal in her arms and dashed off to the kitchens.

He looked to the back of the hall and gestured to a man with blue rings tattooed around his neck and curved shortswords swinging at his hips.

His constant shadow and chief enforcer was a bronze-skinned ex-gladiator named Craeg Vesenira. From the Isle of Ellipta, he had joined the army in Sicaro's regiment many years ago. Truly a mercenary at heart, he had not intended to contract long with the Ascorians, but the man had a quality too useful to lose to another banner. A shadowdancer and skilled swordsman, Vesenira was a formidable assassin.

"Prepare the horses," Sicaro instructed the man.

At midday, Sicaro rode out of Castle Sanford on horseback, accompanied by Vesenira and six others of his personal guard, all veterans from his days as their commander. He informed the garrison captain, as he trotted past, that he was visiting villages along the coast and would return late in the evening.

The royal castellan wore a black cloak over a carapace of black steel-plate armor embossed with gold. Across his lap rested a giant warhammer: six feet of titanium topped by a huge fist holding a steel stake—pointed at one end and flat at the other—so tremendous in weight that only he, or another battle-trained gravmancer, could wield it in battle. Claimed in war, as it had been several times in the centuries since its creation, the weapon, called "Sorrow," was an apt symbol of the result of Sicaro's fighting powers.

They rode over Sanford Bridge, shadowed by the high walls of the castle and under the curious eyes of his soldiers on guard duty. If an enemy were to traverse the bridge, or sail the river, they would come under a hail of arrow, catapult, and ballista fire.

He had ensured that Castle Sanford was the strongest bastion in the region, and perhaps the entire realm.

The castellan and his retinue passed through two villages that afternoon, each time stopping to test a call to arms. A bronze bell would ring at the center of each settlement and summon every conscript-trained, able-bodied adult within earshot. Simple pastoral folk, both villages rallied a paltry twenty fighters armed with either a rusty sword, blunt spear, or frayed-string crossbow.

Inadequate fighters but obedient workers. *They will make good slaves.*

"My lord, the grain stores are filled to the brim. May I have your permission to sell the excess to the produce markets in Irin?" asked the mayor of the second town. A lanky, tough woman who bore too many opinions for Sicaro's liking.

"Build another silo if they are overflowing, Mayor Worten. You have done well with the crops this summer. I have a new market . . . overseas that I am working on. The returns will be far greater than what we would get locally. In the meantime, keep stockpiling," Sicaro said and flicked her a coin. It landed at her feet. She scowled at it as he departed.

At the last village, they supped early at a local inn on lamb and potatoes. As the innkeeper brought ale to his lord's table, he voiced his concerns that Vor raiding ships might spread to their region.

"You need not worry, proprietor. The only ships that touch this coast are the ones I invite," replied Sicaro.

As the sun touched the horizon, Sicaro and his men departed.

"What if the Vors are full of betrayal and break their promise, my lord?" asked one of Sicaro's henchmen once they had ridden several miles clear of the last settlement. The man was Kyle Halwoth, often called "Sneer" because of a left-sided facial droop that stretched his mouth in a permanent veil of contempt. A sycophant, he often rode close behind his lord, leveraging favor with flattering words and comments. Today, however, his words were full of worry.

Sicaro replied, "Never. Even after they land and have a foothold, they still need me to open the way north over the Reynford River. And besides, Harek knows he only has a moderate advantage in numbers. They need me if they are to anticipate and outwit Silas." The goal to replace the latter king relied on a successful war campaign, but his importance and station with the Vor invaders depended on making sure that they were forced to rely on him to win.

Since Sicaro and King Harek, the Vor ruler, had first met over a year ago, their initial distrust had settled to a mutual wariness. Their plan for the Vor invasion of the Kingdom of Ascoria had matured as Sicaro leaked valuable information piecemeal to the wily Vor in exchange for the promise of a dukedom over lands of his own. With final touches, their plan would be well-oiled and faultless.

The invasion would launch in two months' time. It would be early autumn and the conditions ripe for war: mild weather, summer harvests stored, and autumn produce ready for the horde of Vor warriors, dragons, and the monstrous *gargantors*.

"Fields will be toiled and turned with the changing of the crop." Sicaro spoke a metaphor of the upcoming invasion. "Our place is as the plowmen, and only I know how the machinery works. Harek needs me and will deliver his promise. You will all be richly rewarded, I can assure you." He spoke confidently and loud enough for all of his henchmen to hear.

He turned to Sneer as they directed their horses down a junction into the forest. "I have tasked Craeg with a task for the night of the invasion, but the signaler's tower on Dustun Cliffs needs to be taken care of. What do you suggest?"

Sneer flicked his reins to bring his horse alongside the castellan. "My lord, with the full moon and a wide field around, Arlo and I could sneak up on the tower around midnight. Two of us is risky but easily done with a silencing runestone to muffle our approach. We climb to the first floor and kill the sleepers, and then go up the internal stairwell to take out the night guard on the roof."

"Agreed, but not with Arlo. You just need muscle . . . take the brothers instead," said Sicaro. Sneer assented and nodded to the two red-haired siblings at the rear guard.

"Arlo is too important to risk this close to the invasion. The Vor king has agreed to take him into his retinue as an advisor whilst I am gone." Sicaro turned to the man himself: a fellow Vor emigrant who had fled their homeland as an orphan and later joined the Ascorian army as a mercenary—well before the Vor ships had begun raiding. A square-faced man with a braided beard who was the most loyal of Sicaro's men, and so entrusted to the most important of tasks.

The path ended at an abandoned woodsman's hut, but they continued through the small clearing and back into the swaying boughs, their horses pushing toward their meeting point with the Vor king.

By the time they had left the forest and descended to the edge of a sheltered bay, the sun had disappeared, but they still had a few hours to wait.

The twin brothers built a fire on the stony beach, although the evening was warm and the moon was full.

Staring out over the calm, moonlit ocean, Sicaro said a private word to his blue-necked enforcer. "Craeg, how fares your kinwife? How many months until her confinement?"

"Four months. She wishes to return to her mother and my other daughters in Ellipta soon. Which, in these turbulent times, might be a good idea, do you think, my lord?" Craeg had four wives, three of which were his daughters, a large family by Ellipta standards.

"By all means, send her off. Better she labor and birth in peace amongst her sisters. I hope to visit your enlightened country someday." Sicaro admired the progressive nature of Elliptan culture. Though most other societies found the island nation's practices repulsive, he saw much to appreciate. There were no barriers to who could consort with whom: cousins married freely, aunts married nephews, brothers married sisters, and fathers married daughters. And further fueling the liberal practices, polygamous families were the norm. The Royal Family of Ellipta, themselves, were a result of generations of inbreeding— the current king and queens were three siblings. That their religion involved the ritual sacrifice of physically defective children, of which there were many, meant they could breed strong pedigrees.

"Any word from Bako, my lord?" Craeg asked, referring to the one of the men Sicaro had left back in Dunberrin to continue searching for Karisa.

"He's found neither hide nor hair of her since the manse," Sicaro said levelly. His anger at Vixhana, after she interfered with his reunion with Karisa, had been fierce, and a week of further scouring the city had him think that the she-bitch had stolen his beloved out of the city against her wishes.

He had had no choice but to leave Bako and another man behind to continue the search, for he was needed in Sanford for this very appointment.

"She will come running to me at the first chance she has of escaping that devil. Bako will help her return when she re-surfaces." Sicaro returned to scanning the ocean.

A lantern flared in the bay, revealing the prow of a Vor longship. Rhythmic slapping of water soon followed, as oars dipped and pulled the boat toward the beach.

Several more lanterns lit up, and when the boat crunched onto the shore, a score of fleet-footed warriors leapt from the ship to take positions around the fire.

Another two ships slid onto the pebbles and spat out

even more armed men and women. They disappeared into the surrounding forest in groups of ten. Armored in leather, chainmail, or steel plate, they wielded swords, shields, and shortbows—except for several who carried the enormous double-bladed axes of gravmancer warriors, and a few who bore nothing but the sun-symbolic facial scars of firemancers.

Sicaro was impressed by the Vors' military operations, even at this small level. Seeing them in action gave him a respect for Harek's capability as a military leader. He had known that King Harek Raukela had been unifying Voros at the same time that King Silas had been unifying Ascoria; however, he only now saw the prowess required to subdue and diplomatize the fragmented country into one nation.

"Come join me, brother," Harek called from the deck of the longship.

Sicaro made an effortless jump onto the ship with his gravmancer powers, making him feather-light. Then, as he cleared the edge of the vessel, he steadily returned his weight to normal and landed gently—a graceful maneuver that was impossible for a plate-armored man of his immense size without similar magic.

"Bravo." Harek slapped him on the back and laughed. He had a face made for it, a broad smile and bright green eyes that glinted whenever he was in good humor, as he seemed to be that evening.

Slightly shorter than Sicaro, the king of Voros was more sinew than muscle. He was dressed plainly in battle leathers, with steel plates around his chest and arms, and wrapped in a finely woven gray cloak. But despite his fine garb and features, Harek was a renowned warrior—as were all Vor kings—for ascension to leadership was only by duel and fight to the death.

I could kill him, thought Sicaro. But this was not the time nor place. He would be seen as an assassin, not a contender.

They exchanged pleasantries and went to stand on either side of a thwart covered with maps.

He looked at the clean-shaven monarch. "As expected, Silas has spread himself thin along the coast of the western provinces in response to the raids. Word is that he has about a quarter of his army along the coast of Finstaff and another quarter along Hera. But, unfortunately, I was not able to convince him to leave the south completely unreinforced. Five hundred Ascorian soldiers arrived in Sanford a week ago."

Harek stiffened. "That is not many, but we'll need to amend our plan."

"I am meeting the commander tomorrow. I will get him to spread his force along the coast in small groups, which can be dealt with more easily; although, I expect most will lose heart and surrender when the head is chopped off the night before the landings—my man will deal with the commander directly."

Harek appeared happy with the idea. A smile reappeared. "My warriors will be better off for it if they can get their teeth into a few good fights. They will want some blood to begin with. Give me the location of each post and I will assign *torgues* to visit each of them," he said, referring to the battle groups of fifty warriors that his army was based upon.

Sicaro nodded. "We'll signal you the locations before you land."

They spent the next three hours poring over maps, running through the invasion plan, and fine-tuning their ultimate strategy for the weeks and months that would follow. Their scheme was meticulous, with a contingency for every eventuality.

"Another thing, Lord Sicaro," said Harek, as they were about to conclude their meeting. "We found a man recently. A hermit living in the jungle."

Sicaro waited in silence for the Vor king to continue.

"He had an artifact. With it, he killed half a torgue, even though he was physically weak and diseased."

"He lives?"

"Captured," Harek replied.

"And you have this weapon now?"

"Yes, but we cannot make it work. I saw the results of what it could do—it put a hole the size of my fist right through a breastplate . . . from a distance an arrow flies. It is unlike anything I have seen." Harek refocused his gaze on Sicaro. "I need someone who can make it work for me."

"The hermit cannot?"

"He is of limited help . . ." said Harek.

"And you think I can?" he said, confused at Harek's train of thought.

"The man reminded me of the spy you asked me about last time. The one found in the mountains. You asked whether she was one of mine," said Harek. "Of which, she was not."

Sicaro nodded.

Harek continued, "You described a vessel that had been found with her." He took a breath and stared at Sicaro as though about to reveal a secret. "Well, the man we found was near a vessel the same as what you described to me—silver with orange sails."

"Fascinating," Sicaro said, his mind churning through the ramifications of the two events.

"Is she still alive?" asked Harek.

"The woman? I think Silas has her locked away somewhere. The last I heard, she was in the Royal Infirmary with a broken leg."

"You must bring her to me . . . I would be very appreciative." Harek raised his eyebrows again.

"You want her?" Sicaro asked, his mouth agape. Why would Harek waste his time on a prisoner when they had a sea-born invasion with over a thousand ships to worry about? Was a single weapon that important? There was more to this than the Vor king was revealing.

"Alive. She is no use to me dead," said Harek.

If she was so valuable to Harek, and Sicaro could secure her, he could use her for leverage. For what, he did not know yet, but definitely something he could use as future capital.

"I have a couple of men in Dunberrin. I'll have my man Arlo signal an order when I return to the castle."

While Harek changed the subject back to the invasion, Sicaro could not help but puzzle over why the foreign woman could be of such importance.

Chapter 12

There Can Be Only One

Jaks—The Academy of the Arcane, Ascoria

The day after the spider experiment, Grandmaster Mulgrave examined Jaks's wrist. "It's fine. It'll be no more than a lump in a week. Those greenbacks have a painful bite, but no venom," he repeated. "Can't go killing you off yet, can we?"

They were in a spare clerk's office that Mulgrave had given Jaks to use as a bedroom. One of a dozen such vacant rooms along a cob-webbed corridor, filled with dusty shelves of documents and lined from floor to ceiling with ancient, yellowed books. A set of folding wooden panels bisected the room. A desk and chair on one side of the room divider, and a small bed on the other.

Jaks sat on the bed while Mulgrave inspected his wrist.

"But without a writing hand, you are not much use to me as a clerk," said the mage, releasing Jaks's limb.

"I could dust and clean," offered Jaks. He had noticed that the mage's quarters were in dire need of a brush; some rooms, like this one, had been unused for several years, or decades even, and were cobwebbed and cluttered with junk.

"Or, I could help Tavis set up experiments?" He looked at the apprentice leaning against the doorframe and noticed the young man roll his eyes at Jaks's suggestion. Tavis had some issue with him.

He had to find a way to befriend the apprentice.

Mulgrave stroked his beard for a moment. "Actually, I was thinking you could do some research in the library for information about an object that the palace has passed on to us. Come with me."

A door at the furthest end of the corridor opened into Mulgrave's private library.

Bookshelves marched in darkened rows around the octagonal chamber. Several desks were scattered around the room. Chairs surrounding a large, round table formed the centerpiece of the room and lead-lined glass windows looked out over a blue-green expanse of ocean.

One particular desk stood out amongst the others. It was covered with piles of letters, stacks of books with bits of leather poking out, stray styluses, and a taxidermied ginger cat. It was a wonder anyone could find anything on it. This was Grandmaster Mulgrave's desk.

On the opposite side of the library, a doorway led to a short corridor that housed the private quarters for the grandmaster and a smaller one for his apprentice. And through another door out of the library lay the main hallway and the rest of the Academy.

The fortress-like Academy was a continuous square building with a central corridor on each of the upper levels, linked by staircases.

Down into Mulgrave's laboratory and through the empty Metals lab, Jaks followed the bald mage to the main courtyard of the institute.

The giant furnace was quiet today, and they encountered only a handful of people, all of which were on their way out to spend the day off with friends and family or were rushing off to visit the city markets.

"Foolish love," Mulgrave said in a judging tone when two young women, an apprentice and a journeywoman, sped past them, hand in hand and laughing. "If those two devoted as much time to the lab as to each other . . ." he said to Jaks, shaking his head and returning to his path.

As they came to the outer ring of the courtyard, it surprised Jaks to discover it was a museum.

Where the main central area was dominated by the runic furnace, workshops, and their associated paraphernalia, the outer part was laden with old artifacts and relics from distant lands and countries. The objects rested on wooden platforms, some encased in glass cabinets and others not. Signs notified anyone would want to read about each object and its history.

At one curious object shaped like a chariot with a

sail on it, Jaks read that it was a "Zuran Flyer" used by gravmancers over two hundred years ago to levitate and fly around in.

Further on, an intricate machine of mirrors stood on rotating rods controlled by an array of levers and dials. "Howe's Signal Device – prototype" for long-distance communication between illumancers.

There were so many odd and fascinating devices that Jaks could have spent the entire day examining them. But Mulgrave came to a stop and stood with both hands on his hips and stared at one peculiar object.

Jaks joined his new mentor and gasped in surprise.

It was the metal pod from the mountains.

The capsule looked in even better condition than when he had last seen it over two months ago in the valley. Someone had taken a cloth to it and brought out a silver sheen to the surface.

"I know this!" Jaks stepped forward and touched the pod.

"Ridiculous. How could you?" Tavis challenged him. "You've only been here a day."

"We found it after that meteor storm last month. I was in the mountains on training and saw it come down. Minto and I found it the next day. It had an orange sail with it."

Mulgrave stepped up onto the stone platform beside Jaks. "Quite right. The material has gone to Grandmaster Hazeldine to examine in her lab."

Tavis's expression curled into a scowl.

"But I am sure anyone could have found it, if they had been around," Jaks said, downplaying the discovery, feeling that he had offended Tavis in some way.

Mulgrave pulled a sunken handle and a small door swung open to reveal the capsule's interior with seat, wall inlays, and glass panel—nothing had changed from how Jaks remembered it.

"Do you know anything about how it operates?" Mulgrave asked.

"No, we didn't really look at it very hard. I know there is a water pipe up there." Jaks pointed above the seat.

"Yes, which is why we think it was built for a long journey." Mulgrave rested a hand on the pod. "A ship of some kind, advanced beyond anything I have ever seen. I have not yet tampered with it except to take a piece of the internal frame that was loose. The alloy was incredibly strong and composed of materials I know not. Even more than that, that panel there is astonishing, but again, none of us can fathom its design or purpose."

Back in the mountains when Jaks had touched the object for the first time, a queer vibration had assailed his fingers. He touched it again now, and the buzzing sensation returned to his fingers. He jerked his hand away.

Mulgrave continued, "What I need you to do, my boy, is to find information about the machine. I want to know the significance of those inlays causing images to appear on the panel. You might find some references in the Academy library—"

"There was a woman," Jaks said in a rush. His heart thumped as he recalled the woman in the mountains, his emotions a mixture of guilt and excitement. "Her name was Meila."

"Remarkable." Mulgrave focused his eyes on Jaks as though seeing him in a new light. "So, you know of the prisoner, then? You spoke with her? Learned her name?"

"She did not speak any Ascorian at first, but I taught her some words."

"Was she able to tell you anything about this ship?"

"No. We were only together for a brief time. Our ranger arrested her and handed her over to the city guard. He thought she was a spy." Jaks pressed his lips together for a moment. "But she's not. I know she's not."

"An expert on spies now?" The grandmaster raised an eyebrow.

Jaks continued, ignoring the mage's sarcasm. An opportunity was forming. "I've visited the city's prisons. But I can't find her. I need to find her. Perhaps . . ."

"Why do you care what happens to her?"

"I promised her I would help. She saved my life." Jaks described encountering her on the mountainside. Wide-eyed, the grandmaster and his apprentice listened. But after he described the fight against the bronze dragons, they both looked skeptical.

"If she had a weapon of such power, why did she

not escape capture by simply killing the ranger?" Tavis snorted and crossed his arms.

"Don't you see? If she *was* a spy, she *would* have. It proves she is not." Jaks waved his hands excitedly and gave Mulgrave an eager look. "Grandmaster, we could ask permission from the king to talk to her. I could teach her Ascorian. And she could tell us all about this ship . . . and far more, I bet."

"Spy or not, only the king decides." The mage pulled his beard to a point. "I have not met this prisoner, but apparently no one has made sense of her except for a few basic words. However, it was Silas himself who ordered the investigation into this ship." He tapped the shell of the unworldly pod. "It shan't hurt to ask him for permission. Good idea, young man."

Again, Tavis's face crumpled, the way one defeated would on seeing an opportunity slip from his grasp. "Master, if the king gives us permission, perhaps *I* would be better to liaise with the prisoner. I have some skill with languages. I learned how to speak Pihaatian," said the apprentice.

Mulgrave nodded and turned to Jaks. "Oh, and how is the new lad with tongues?"

"My grandparents were from Voros. My sisters and I speak Vorosian, and I know some Fauconian," replied Jaks.

Tavis glared at him.

"And, you also already have some connection with her," Mulgrave said to Jaks and stepped down from the narrow platform around the ship. "Let's go back to the lab and we'll write a request to the palace."

Tavis scribed the letter that Jaks should have written but for his injured arm. The apprentice threw another dark look at him as he passed the completed letter to Mulgrave.

"I have some business with Master Cranbrook now. I'll have his office deliver the request to the palace in the morning." The mage pulled on a plain brown cap over his bald head. "You two can have the rest of the day off. We will start busy tomorrow."

The two young men watched the Grandmaster close the library door behind him.

Jaks was about to retreat to his corridor when the apprentice grabbed him by the elbow. His arm dropped, and he staggered as the weight of his forearm suddenly felt as heavy as stone. Tavis was using gravmancer powers on him.

"I can see what you are trying to do, and I'm not having any of it." Tavis glared at Jaks, whom he had magically dragged down to his knees. Flecks of spittle flew from his mouth as he spoke. "It took me four years to get this apprenticeship, four years of petitioning the Academy and breaking my back as a coal-hauler. If you think you're going to walk in and take my apprenticeship, you better think again, because I will fight you with everything I have."

Jaks had no intention of stealing the apprentice's job

away from him. He hadn't even known that he was a threat.

"I can see you're trying to prove you are better than me. All you city boys think you're better than us from the farm. You're just some stupid clerk straight out of conscription. You can't even control your pathetic magic. So, just do your scribbling and keep away from my apprenticeship or else I'll hurt you, do you hear?" Tavis's hand tightened around Jaks's arm.

Jaks winced in pain. Hand cold and numb from lack of blood, his arm was on the verge of breaking.

A small blast of light—brief, sharp, and white—erupted, along with a cracking sound, where Tavis held Jaks's arm.

The apprentice jerked his hand away and cried out in pain. He tottered backward and careened into a shelf of books, knocking down several. Righting himself, he then emitted a chain of expletives and curses. "You'll regret that," he said, rubbing his hand.

"I'm sorry. I didn't mean to, it just happened." Jaks reached forward to help the apprentice regain his feet. The invocation had been unbidden: he had not attempted to visualize or will the magic into being. Why was it so erratic?

Tavis shoved his way past Jaks. The apprentice augmented the push with magic and hurtled Jaks across the floor. The younger man slid into a chair and under a desk. "Get away from me. Stay away from my apprenticeship!" Tavis yelled and then stormed out the door to the main hallway.

Hyperventilating, Jaks crawled out from beneath the desk and slumped against a bookcase to calm his nerves.

He'd already made an enemy within a day of arriving at the Academy, and the job he had been promised was on tenterhooks.

It was apparent that rather than simply coming to work as a clerk and being trained in the arcane arts, he had been thrust into a bizarre contest for an apprenticeship.

To win, he had to remove the existing one and impress the grandmaster.

Could he displace Tavis by simply attaining control of his magic—electromancy was certainly rarer and more precious than Tavis's powers—or would he have to defeat Tavis through some form of duel? This place was turning out worse than conscription.

Chapter 13

The Wall

The next morning, the grandmaster and the two young men met in the private library. The stocky magesmith and Tavis, both dressed in little more than a leather apron and leggings, would be at the runic forge all day.

"Two tasks for you today, lad. First, go through that section"—Mulgrave pointed a stubby finger at several bookcases—"and record anything that might relate to your friend's vessel in the museum. Second, I have some exercises for you to practice."

Mulgrave instructed him on several exercises to invoke magic. Each targeted one of the three steps, and if Jaks could isolate and identify each separately, the mage told him, he might be able to bring his electromancy under control. However, the mage had his doubts.

"Unfortunately, some candidates with great

potential are incapable of learning how to control all three aspects. Whether it be labile emotions, a weak mind's eye, or poor focus, no matter how hard they try, their fledgling magic remains nothing more than a gimmick," said the grandmaster.

"I can do this. Don't worry, grandmaster, I won't fail you," replied Jaks.

"Focus on the three aspects. Don't attempt a full invocation yet—I wish my library intact." Mulgrave then slapped his bare arms as though warming up and departed into the main hallway.

Tavis followed, but not before throwing a glare at Jaks. If the apprentice's stare had been a knife, Jaks was sure his neck would have been severed.

He gulped. He would need a breakthrough today to keep up his chances of staying.

He drained hours into the invocation exercises that day, dragging up fearsome memories until despair blocked him, painted mind images until they grayed with boredom, and concentrated willpower until he was drained of any.

But disallowed from attempting any actual electromancy until he was supervised by the grandmaster, Jaks exhausted his progress and stared at the books.

At least a hundred books padded the "Vessels and

Vehicles" section that Jaks thumbed through. Although full of intriguing machines and designs—gigantic sailing ships, wheeled monstrosities, and more gravmantic flyers—nothing resembled the silver pod from the mountain.

So, it was with great relief when Grandmaster Mulgrave and Tavis returned that evening and the aging mage waved a torn envelope at Jaks. "Good news, boy! The king has signed a permit to interview the prisoner."

"Thank you!" Jaks leapt to his feet and reached for the letter—his hand pausing only a moment until his eyes gained permission from the mage—and read. Indeed, the document granted access to the prisoner for research. *I've finally found you.*

Additionally, it stated that any spy-like activity that the prisoner performed should be reported to the warden immediately.

"Let's hope she can illuminate us on the object," said Mulgrave as he rearranged the stuffed cat on his desk to weigh down some other papers.

"I'm sure she will, Master. She is very smart."

"If we can get her to talk and if she is willing to learn more of our language, I'll draw up a list of questions that you must ask her. If she can show us how to create machines such as this, the potential is staggering—perhaps even a revolution in technology."

"She knows me. She'll want to talk," said Jaks, hiding the uncertainty building in his mind. What would be her response at their reunion? *Will she believe*

I didn't intend to have her arrested? Might she still be bitter and see me as an enemy?

"We'll visit this prisoner of yours tomorrow," said the mage. "This evening, though, after I get changed out of these leathers and get something to eat, let's go down to the 'burn room' and see what you have gained from your exercises today."

That evening, the lab was dark when they reached the bottom of the staircase.

The mage carried a staff topped by a bronze eagle claw grasping a bright lightstone and led the way between cluttered benches and shelves of tools to a large room at the far end of the lab.

Mulgrave propped the staff up in a stand to cast a steady light throughout the cavernous room. A low stone wall stood close to the door and salty ocean air breezed through a barred opening in the far wall. The walls and ceilings were black with soot, and the acridness of smoke lingered in the air.

Jaks needed no explanation for why it was called the "burn room."

"Tell me about the exercises today. Which did you find easiest?" the mage asked.

Jaks explained that the easiest exercises had been conjuring the images: visualizing electricity discharges ranging in size from little sparks on a fingertip through to mighty forks of lightning arcing from his hands. He had never had trouble daydreaming and imagining fantastical settings. He had spent much of his childhood with his mind reeling with images of the stories his mother told him of immense battles of great armies of warriors, warlions, mages, fireballs, siege machines, and dragons combating the skies. To visualize magic was not difficult.

Mulgrave held up a finger and disappeared from the room. A minute later, he dragged in a burlap-sack dummy that he leaned against the far wall. "And the other two aspects?" he then asked.

"The willpower exercises got boring . . ." Jaks said. They were an extension of the visualization exercises and meant long periods of holding and intensifying the images in his mind.

"As an exercise, it might seem easy, but it gets harder when you meld all three aspects together in an invocation." The grandmaster rested his hands on the chest-high wall. "How about the exercises to control your emotion?"

Jaks shifted uneasily on his feet. "Difficult, Master. My feelings just seem to come and go as they please. Sometimes I think of a frightening memory, like you taught me, and my head feels like it's going to burst, my heart is jumping out of my chest, and the fear is so strong that it feels like it is happening again."

He was referring to an experience that he often tried to block but had, twice now, willed himself to re-experience: witnessing his mother's crushed head in his father's hands.

Occasionally, the flashback was triggered by some insignificant sound or sight. Like the time he was stirring a pot in the conscript-barracks kitchen and Baden lifted up the brain of a lamb he'd butchered and then, grinning, squished it in his hand—the squelch and mushed tissue had sent his mind reeling back to that bloody night and the sight of his murdered mother. Sometimes, the fear so overwhelmed him, he would blank out and rouse minutes or hours later lying on the ground, soaked in sweat and stinking of his own urine.

However, he did not tell Mulgrave the details of the flashback, fearing that just speaking of it might trigger a spiral of panic.

"And other times, I think of a terrifying memory, but all I get is a wall. I don't feel anything. My mind goes numb," Jaks continued. That day, he had reached a block in practicing the mage's exercises. He'd battled his emotions, trying to hold a constant level of fear. But his feelings had abruptly shut off and he'd stared at the bookshelves for an hour. "I admit, Master, that I cannot control my fear well . . . but I will keep practicing, though." He looked at the grandmaster, hoping for some empathy, but was met with a blank expression.

Mulgrave stroked his jaw and gazed at Jaks. "You have had a troubled past, I think," he said in a quiet voice. "Some evil visited upon you." The mage sighed, and his face deepened. "You must confront the past;

otherwise, your fears will always control you. For a mage, it must be the other way around." He rubbed his thick neck for a moment, then spoke again. "When you're ready, you must talk to someone about them."

"Yes, Grandmaster Mulgrave, thank you," Jaks said. He was grateful that someone wanted to help him. Tears welled in his eyes and ran down his face. "I really am trying my best, but I've failed at almost everything I've ever tried in my life. I'm scared that I'm going to fail you . . . I sometimes feel like giving up because it's so hard." The words spilled out in a hurry.

The mage stiffened for a moment and then slowly reached out to pat Jaks on the back. "Don't worry, lad. You'll be fine." After Jaks had recouped and wiped his eyes, Mulgrave stepped back and said, "Failures are learning tools . . . let me tell you a story few know.

"I was about your age when I discovered my firemancy powers. I was excited and did tricks and showed off to everybody. One day, I was visiting my friend, Davik, and I showed him the 'burning man' invocation that I had just mastered. It creates a skin of fire. I had practiced it by the lake, but I didn't think what would happen if I did it inside, in a house. I proudly invoked the burning man, and then the flames ignited everything around me. Rugs, cushions, chairs, curtains—the entire house burnt down. We escaped, but we didn't realize his little brother had been upstairs . . . he died in the flames."

The old mage shook his head, reliving the past. "It

was a small village and his mother wanted blood justice. Wanted me dead—even though it was an accident. My father rode me out in the middle of the night and we came to Dunberrin, where he left me to find work on the dockyards. In my grief, I didn't use firemancy for two years after that, but when I did come back to it, it was with much greater awareness of and respect for my surroundings."

Mulgrave arrived at the point of his story and said, "We all make mistakes, we all fail, but it's learning from them that is the important thing. The worst thing you can do now is give up and go on thinking you're a failure."

Jaks stared at the ground for a while, then looked up at the mage. "I'm scared I might kill someone. Sometimes the urge to kill is so strong, it frightens me." He averted his eyes in guilt as an image of electrocuting Tavis flitted across his mind.

"We all do, we all do. But it is always our choice whether we act on those impulses or not. We're not animals controlled by bestial drives. Again, it is about control," Mulgrave said. "Keep at the exercises, but instead of starting big, start small. Focus on controlling little things like . . . worrying about talking to a pretty girl and being rejected, or teetering at the top of a staircase, or worrying that you are going to fail me . . ." The mage grinned.

After that, Jaks attempted a full invocation several

times, visualizing a spark on his fingertip. But the magic would not invoke.

A half hour later, Mulgrave sighed one last time. "That's enough for today. Keep trying, boy. You'll get there."

Jaks prayed that was true. Tavis had a lengthy head start on him and wasn't going without a fight.

Chapter 14

The Prisoner

Meila—City of Dunberrin, Ascoria

The rattle of keys at her prison-cell door roused Meila Tahn from her meditation. She opened her eyes but remained cross-legged on her cot, waiting to see which of her captors was interrupting her.

For a prison, the cell was more comfortable than she had hoped to expect from these primitives. Larger than the ship cabin that she and her husband shared on the *UWFS Mendhelsson*, and furnished with a bed, table and chair, and sink and toilet-hole, it possessed the basic necessities.

But it was still a prison and she desperately wanted out.

After she had been captured and dragged from the crash site seven weeks earlier, they incarcerated her in a prison infirmary. There, she was strapped down, broken leg immobilized and splinted in a contraption of metal bars and leather braces. A series of interrogators then visited her: some gentle, with soothing voices; others evil, who tortured her with thumb screws and thrust hard fingers at her injured leg. Of course, she could not understand their words, but she guessed their accusations—spying on their country.

If she replied in her own language, it angered them. And using the few words she'd learned from the young man in the mountains seemed to anger them further. But eventually, the interrogators had relinquished and transferred her to this cell.

The prison surgeon, a white-haired man with a stoop, had been surprised to find that after only a month, her leg was perfectly healed. He was not to know of the medigel that infiltrated the hematological system and bone matrix for rapid healing.

The only visitors that came nowadays were the prison guards to deliver a tin-tray meal and a pail of water each day. The rest of her time was spent on calisthenics, meditation, and staring out her window, which overlooked a grand cathedral and its manicured grounds.

She had no support, no advocate, no defender. She must find a way to escape.

They suspected she was a spy already. *If only they knew . . .*

Seven thousand years ago, the Virgo-Supercluster Wars had destroyed the dimensional portals that allowed the first seeding of planetary colonies—of which this was one. And only in the past three centuries had the United Worlds Federation (UWF), led by old Earth, finally developed stardrives that allowed them to revisit distant galaxies and begin offloading their overpopulated and resource-depleted home planets.

She and her eight-person crew had been orbiting this planet, designated "Maya-four," for over two years, and were in the last months of their mission. Their data collection, on this planetary oasis of natural resources and habitable land, was almost complete.

On arriving at Maya-four, Meila's crew were not surprised at the devolved human civilization, given that most other Old Colonies had also regressed or gone extinct after the schism from their motherworld all those millennia ago. Maya-four, having barely clawed its way back to a pre-industrial age, was ripe for a UWF battle fleet to sweep in and remove the existing inhabitants, making way for a colony fleet to follow.

If they knew my mission, they would torture and execute me, and be fully justified in doing so.

She inhaled and exhaled.

It was a scenario that Meila and her husband—the mission's physician and geneticist—had witnessed on three out of the four planets they'd analyzed together. Only Old Colonies that had achieved specific criteria of civilization were eligible to continue alongside the new.

With their starship soon to return to Earth, the final report would have been straightforward: the humans of planet Maya-four were substandard. Feudal governments, archaic technology, and unusual genetic heterogeneity led to one conclusion: "Cleanse and repopulate."

She was not only here to spy, but to make a summary judgement of life or death for the entire human population of this world.

The sound of the cell door opening interrupted her thoughts.

Two men dressed in civilian garb and a guard walked in.

Meila surged to her feet. This was not a simple water-and-rations delivery.

New interrogators were here. The older one looked harsh. She vowed she would put up a fight now that her leg was healed.

The old man was bald and had a neck and arms like tree trunks. Although muscular and solid all over, his eyes gleamed with intelligence and guile. He wore brown leggings, a blue overshirt, and an armless cloak with frayed edging. He stood in front of Meila. Although he was short for the men here, she was shorter still and was forced to tip her head to meet his eyes.

He said something to her, and she understood it as the Ascorian introduction, "Hello, I am . . ." The rest of the sentence she heard as garbled syllables of their foreign language. However, she picked up his sentence when he said, "And this is . . ."

The other man stepped forward. He was far younger and taller than the bald interrogator. He looked familiar, with tousled brown curls and an innocent, slender face.

"Meila . . ." the young man said.

". . . Jaks," the old man finished saying.

She stared at Jaks. On many occasions during her captivity, she had retrieved recordings from her memory implants to review her interactions with the handsome youth at the crash site and knew his face intimately. But what was he doing here? He wasn't dressed as a soldier like the last time she'd seen him, but in plain gray leggings and a tunic that made him look like some form of servant. Was he now a lackey to this bald, evil-looking brute?

The young man said a few more words. When her stony expression made it clear to him that his words made no sense to her, he started gesticulating and acting out a scene: he made flapping-wing motions with his arms, talons with his fingers, and mimicked the actions of drawing a bow and arrow.

Amused, she could see he was trying to communicate his memory of their time together fighting off the dragon attack. She restrained a smile.

He finished by mouthing words and making large, round sweeping motions with his arms. Yes, they were here to interrogate her again, but it seemed they wanted to use someone familiar to her. He was a nice boy. Gentle and kind in their first encounter. When he'd sung to her, trying to distract her pain, she had laughed at first. But when she'd recognized the compassion of his act, she had been touched by the tender gesture. Her recall of them singing together almost brought tears to her eyes. However, she reminded herself, hardening her resolve, he had ultimately been one of the team that had incarcerated her. *It's either me or them.*

Perhaps she could manipulate him into helping her escape.

She had some influence over him—she remembered his yearning eyes over the campfire. *I can use that to my advantage.*

She thought quickly. Yes, here was an opportunity to exploit his youthful desires and manufacture a situation where she could escape from this prison.

She gave him what she thought was an appealing look, based on how her cousin Lezal, back on Earth, used to act around young men when they were that age. Although, that was a long time ago.

"Jaks. Hello. We fight dragons," she said in a stilted attempt at the Ascorian language, using words she'd snatched from what he had just said and from what she had learned earlier.

He gaped at her for a moment and then gave her a charming smile, and in doing so reminded her of Anton, her husband, with the same ability to melt hearts. So reminded, a pang of worry about Anton and the other crew tore through her. She triggered the emotion-regulation implant in her amygdala and quickly stifled the worried thought.

The bald man appeared surprised at her response

but then nodded a few times, as though identifying something in her voice. He spoke to the younger man and then gave instructions to the guard. The latter left and returned with two wooden stools for the visitors.

The rest of the morning panned out similar to their campfire lesson many weeks ago: Jaks pointing at objects and associating them with Ascorian words for her to repeat. It appeared his orders were to teach her their language. Did they expect her to learn it, just so they could interrogate her and force her to declare herself a spy?

She shrugged imperceptibly. Whatever their motives were, she would play along and turn the situation to her advantage. She'd survived worse imprisonments before. She'd get out of this one, too.

The bald man left after two hours, leaving Jaks with her, while the bored guard took the vacated seat and nodded off.

Without the older man there, she went to work. Sitting at the table next to Jaks, she leaned forward and touched his arm, laughing, breathing deeply, and staring into his eyes. She was disgusted with herself, but the young man was her best chance of escape, and she would do anything for her freedom.

Chapter 15

Defending the Village

Karisa–Province of Finstaf, Ascoria

Damn you, Jaks. Damn you, Vixhana. I shouldn't have listened to either of you, thought Karisa as she watched her company of soldiers line up on the crest of the hill. They were about to charge down into the village of Triserly, swarming with warriors of a Vor raiding group. *I could be safe in Faucony or Pihaat now, hundreds of leagues away from this stupidity.*

Karisa peeked over the hill. The village was one of a dozen farming settlements along the coast of the Finstaf province and housed about two hundred families. Tile-roofed wooden buildings—homesteads, barns, storehouses, and workshops of simple peasants—clustered around a village square.

Vor warriors, with green and brown war paint streaking their faces, darted in and out of buildings carrying armfuls of loot or dragging out screaming villagers. Variously armed with axes, warhammers, or

175

swords, they were clad in steel breastplates, pauldrons, and greaves, with chain or leather in less exposed areas.

Elsewhere, dead bodies littered the streets. Smoke poured out of a storage silo at the far edge of the village and flames leapt from building to building—the fires needed to be put out soon or they would destroy the entire village.

It was the pillar of smoke that had alerted them to the raid. Arriving within a half hour by horseback, they had left their ponies with handlers at the back of the hill before grouping to advance. As mobile infantry, they only used their mounts for transport and fought on foot, where their tactics and training were at their most potent.

She looked to the captain for a signal.

Captain Vale was a battle-scarred veteran and as hairy and ugly as a boar. He lifted his arm and pointed forward. A roar of voices and the clamor of armor and weapons crashed past him as one hundred and ten soldiers charged forward as one.

The mass of steel and blades accelerated away from Karisa, and she walked to the crest, where she and the senior signaler were ordered to hold and await further commands from the captain with his retinue of ten reserves. The captain took a vantage point nearby, placed his hands on his hips, and watched the charge explode upon the disorganized Vor warriors. The raiders had been too preoccupied with ransacking the houses and toying with the surviving villagers to notice the Ascorian infantry until they poured down the hillside like a thunderstorm.

The enemy called out in panic and ran in all directions. The most confused were impaled and sliced where they stood in the streets. Others scrambled to the village square and were joined as their companions spilled out of the buildings and surrounding streets.

"The bastards are rallying. Send a signal to pincer the village square," Captain Vale said to the senior signaler, a small man named Osiru who had a weasel-like face and breath like carrion.

"Yes, sir," Osiru replied, before lifting a horn to his mouth and blowing a trill of notes. He then stood steadily at the hilltop crest with both hands held in front of him and concentrated for several seconds. It annoyed Karisa that the man was taking so much time to formulate the invocation pattern; she could have flashed the message out in half the time. Finally, strobes of light flashed from his palms, signaling the message downhill. Osiru repeated the illumancy pattern two more times and then said to the company leader, "It's done, sir."

Skirmishes had broken out around the settlement as the outnumbered Vor warriors stood their ground against squads of soldiers. Most were just shot down with crossbows, but a few put up valiant fights despite bolts piercing their armor and trickling the life-force out of them.

However, Karisa was slack-jawed at a melee that defied the odds.

On a side street, five Ascorian sword-and-shield soldiers had surrounded a Vor warrior. The man wore a skirt of scalps and braids and brandished a giant double-bladed axe. Karisa expected he would fall after a brief clash like many of his other countrymen, but it became apparent that he was of an entirely different class.

Surrounded, the axeman ran forward and leapt into the air—three times his own height—and landed behind the three Ascorians who had been facing him; he then clove his battleaxe in a two-handed sweep and sliced through the chainmail-covered thighs of two of the infantrymen. They screamed as they collapsed to the ground, surrounded by their severed, bloodied limbs.

The third soldier turned to face the axeman gravmancer and steadied her shield while staring aghast at her fallen colleagues, grabbing at the stumps of their legs as their lifeblood pumped away.

The axeman advanced on the soldier, lifted his axe overhead, and then swung it as though chopping a piece of firewood. Her shield rose to block the blow, but it was not enough. The battleaxe split the wooden shield and continued down to cleave her iron helm in two—blood and brain splattered and the body crumpled under the magically augmented attack.

Karisa bent over to retch as a wave of nausea struck. Morbid fascination compelled her to return her gaze to the Vor warrior and the remaining two soldiers.

One of the pair dropped her sword and shield and grabbed a crossbow from her back while her companion stepped in front of her with his sword and shield, trembling.

The Vor gravmancer yanked his axe out of the dead body, then sprinted a few steps and leapt into the air, hurtling out of sight over a weathered barn full of hay.

Karisa, from her hilltop vantage point, followed the axeman's trajectory to see him land on the other side of the building. The Vor gazed about for new opponents, but finding none, he jogged around the barn back to the blood-stained street.

The two soldiers were back-to-back, looking skyward, as though expecting the gravmancer to return over the building. The one with the crossbow pushed a bolt into the dorsal groove.

As if time had slowed, Karisa watched in horror as the Vor charged around the corner of the hay barn. He gained sight of his victims and leapt with his axe raised above his head, targeting the nearest.

The swordsman dodged, barely evading the executioner's strike, and stumbled to the side. The Vor followed up, sweeping his axe from the left, knocking aside the shield and chopping the soldier's head from his body. The decapitated corpse tipped to the ground as the head flew a short distance and splashed into a muddy puddle.

Karisa screamed and put her hands to her mouth, but her eyes remained glued to the melee below.

The last soldier, looking over her dead companion,

raised her crossbow and shot the gravmancer in the chest.

He staggered back, staring at the crossbow, then lurched a few steps toward its owner—but thankfully, his legs buckled and he collapsed to the ground on top of his dreadful axe.

Even though the Vor was surely dead, the woman dropped her missile weapon and took up her sword. She stabbed the facedown body again and again. Four of her unit dead. She was lucky she wasn't the fifth.

Still nauseated by the horrific fight but relieved the gravmancer was dead, Karisa turned her gaze to the rest of the battle—and found the remaining Vors surrounded in the village square.

The few that had shields protected the rest behind them. A volley of crossbow fire dropped a few more Vors as bolts flew through unprotected legs or gaps in the shield wall. The remaining twenty or so warriors wavered and looked ready to break.

A movement from the woodland edge to the west caught Karisa's attention. The captain saw it too and cursed as a mass of Vor warriors spilled out of the forest and ran toward the village, their war cries loud enough to carry across the fields to their hill.

"It's a setup. They were hiding!" shouted Captain Vale. He then spat out orders to Osiru for another signal message.

There were several shouts from behind Karisa. She turned and looked down the slope. It was the horse handlers pointing and shouting at a second band of ambushers who were ascending the hill toward the captain's retinue. The captain was such an obvious target on the hilltop. Arrows whistled as some of the Vor archers targeted them, but at this distance and uphill, the arrows flew wild.

The captain drew his sword and ordered his soldiers to form a shield wall against the approaching warriors.

The rat-faced signaler kept at his job and sounded his horn; this time, he signaled his message without hesitation to the troops below, warning them of the Vors racing toward them from the forest.

Karisa was terrified and looked around desperately. She had been with the infantry company only a few weeks and, prior to that, had had just six weeks of conscript basic training. Although she had easily passed the proficiencies for fitness, crossbow, and spear—and to the surprise of her instructors, displayed heightened prowess with the sword—her illumancy had been her ticket out of conscription. Fast-tracked to specialist training, she had expected this signaler's job to be easy: staying back from the fighting and perhaps lazing up in a signaler's tower for the rest of the year before resigning and returning to her acting troupe. Fighting off a Vor ambush was not what she'd had in mind.

A second flight of arrows whistled toward them. Most flew overhead but several thunked against the shield wall. The captain barked some orders, and the squad shuffled into crescent formation with the captain and the signalers behind them. Osiru drew a shortsword and a dagger. "Get behind me, lass. Get your sword out," he yelled at Karisa.

Moments later, there was a roar and a crash of metal as the Vor warriors threw themselves against the soldiers. The shields of the Vors smashed against the Ascorians' shield wall. Swords slashed and jabbed between gaps while warhammers and axes smashed at the wooden barricade.

The Ascorians were fresh, unlike the Vors, who had charged uphill. And with their added height advantage, they struck three of the attackers dead or incapacitated from wounds in the initial clash.

However, the shield wall parted in the center when two Ascorians fell to longsword thrusts and more Vors arrived to throw themselves into the fray.

Several of the war-painted warriors flanked the Ascorians, and the organized defense crumbled before the orgy of violence. The defenders were outnumbered and falling one by one.

Captain Vale entered the fray, striding toward a Vor who had struck down one of his sergeants with a warhammer and had raised it for a deathblow with its spiked end. He swung his longsword, striking the Vor with an upward sweep to the pit of his raised arm. The blade impacted chainmail. Although it did not slice through, the impact knocked the hammerman to the ground. Without hesitation, the captain dropped his shield and shifted to a two-handed grip on his sword.

The Vor rolled to his front and began to rise with his hammer in one hand. Vale struck the man again: a diagonal overhead cut to the neck. The runic-forged blade severed the chainmail, enough for the edge to slice into the artery beneath. Blood spurting, the man fell to his knees, and the hammer dropped from his hand. The captain reversed his blade and plunged the sword tip down through the gap and into his thorax. The man spasmed in his death.

Three Vor warriors moved toward the two signalers cowering at the rear.

"Girl, listen to me. Focus a light blast to the right. I'll focus on the left." Osiru lifted his left hand up and concentrated.

Karisa raised both palms toward the snarling warriors. Despite her pounding heart and shaking hands, she was so practiced with invoking magic that it took little effort to trigger an emotion for illumancy—the memory of her little dog, Ella, sitting on her lap and staring up at her with big brown eyes sparked joy and happiness—where it mingled with terror. Armed with hatchets and shields, a stocky woman and two men advanced toward her.

She visualized and willed her palms to explode with light. It was as though a sun had suddenly birthed on the hilltop. So bright was the radiance, all three warriors brought up their arms to cover their eyes in reflex; the shields slipped from their grips and they stumbled around blindly.

Altogether, a dozen war-painted warriors, and one Ascorian, had been facing the signalers and were blinded by the light blast. They staggered and lurched. Some slid or fell down the steep hillside. And others, defenseless, were stuck down by opponents nearby.

Osiru ran forward and stabbed a blinded swordsman in the back, then turned toward another stunned Vor further along the hill.

One of the blinded hatchetmen continued staggering toward Karisa, but then tripped a few yards before reaching her. She watched in horror as he struggled to push himself back up, swearing and cursing. Although she had not spoken Vor in several years, she clearly understood his angry words and savage intent.

She had to do something before his sight returned.

She jabbed her sword at his heart, but the desperate attack merely scraped his breastplate and tipped him off balance. She cursed herself for not targeting his exposed face instead.

"You little shit! I'm going to rip your fucking arms off!" the man shouted as he staggered a few steps downhill. He fixed his gaze on her.

His threats angered her. She was not scared by his rant; he was just a pathetic man stumbling around. She had never killed anyone before, but she knew that, even against the burliest of warriors, a sharp blade in the right place would kill anyone.

With her sword in both hands, she lunged on her right foot and swung the blade at his face.

His eyes opened wide, seeing her intent. Unable to lift his shield in time, he flicked his head away from the approaching blade.

The attack clanged against his helmet and knocked him senseless.

Her opponent splayed before her, Karisa grimaced, but she knew no mercy in that moment and sought her finishing blow.

She slipped the sword tip beneath his chainmail skirt and pushed the three-foot blade upward with all of her strength. The weapon pierced his groin, his abdomen, and then his heart.

The Vor screamed and thrashed as her sword plunged in up to the hilt. Blood poured from the groin wound, and he sputtered bloody foam.

Karisa extracted her blade in a swift movement and then stepped back to stare at the dying man. A sense of exhilaration filled her.

She considered stabbing the man again but was distracted when Osiru came hurtling down the slope and knocked her down.

The weasel-faced signaler was lying on top of her and she saw that he was dead. A cut from the corner of his neck down into his chest opened up his internal organs to the air. Revolted at the mangled corpse, she writhed and pushed to escape the dead weight.

A warrior with a crocodile-hide cloak stood several yards uphill from Karisa, holding a double-bladed axe in both hands and sneering at his handiwork. He saw

Karisa struggling under Osiru's corpse and walked over to her.

One leg was still stuck under Osiru when the killer grabbed her by the hair—although it was far shorter than when she was a civilian, it was an easy handful—and pulled her up; she screamed and grabbed at his wrist with both hands, having lost her sword somewhere during the tumble.

In a frantic motion, Karisa extended one hand toward the man's face and invoked another light blast—much less powerful this time due to her lack of focus—but he merely grunted at the bright flash and stunned her with a slap to the head.

In the Ascorian tongue but with a Vorosian accent, he said, "Where you going, darling?"

It was the term of endearment her father used.

That one simple word cut deep and rattled her, leaving her even more powerless than the strike to her skull had.

He dragged her up to her feet, let go of her hair, and then punched her in the stomach, and Karisa buckled to her knees. "That's for killing Ritter, even though he was a hell-born sack of crap."

The brute tipped her onto her back with his boot and stood on her forearm. The blood-stained edge of his axe pressed against her neck.

From the corner of her eye, she saw at least a dozen dead Vors. But also dead were the Ascorian command group, including Captain Vale and the senior signaler.

Only she and one other captive, a terrified-looking soldier, had survived.

On the rear of the crest of the hill, she could not see the village, but her intuition told her that the battle there was just as bad.

Blood dripped from Karisa' brow and she ached all over from the beating she'd been given.

The Vor lifted his boot off her arm. "Watch out, she's a witch. Make sure she doesn't get up to any trickery," he said to two other warriors as they bound Karisa's wrists together, pulled her up, and then threw a bag over her head.

She sent her angry thoughts into the ether. *Damn you, Jaks, look what you got me into.*

Chapter 16

A Songbird in a Cage

Jaks—City of Dunberrin, Ascoria

Jaks entered Meila's prison cell and thanked the guard who had unlocked the door.

Immediately, a missile flicked into his vision, coming toward his face. He flinched, but not in time. The object struck him in the nose and bounced to the ground.

The cell filled with laughter as Meila grabbed for another ball of rolled up paper from her table. "Right on the nozzle," she cried out, then bounced another missile off his chest.

Jaks frowned at her, admonishing her playful antics. She was supposed to be his student. When he had been at school, infractions like this were punished with a swish of the cane, often several.

"Lighten up. It's not as though it hurt or anything," she said in a melodious accent.

He grinned, threw a ball back at her, and joined

her at the table. How could he think harshly about anyone locked in a prison cell as small as his little room at the Academy? For her, this space was her entire existence: she slept, exercised, and idled away in this box of stone, surrounded by hundreds of similar cells throughout the prison building. A songbird in a cage.

Jaks vowed silently, he would do whatever he could to win her freedom. He would challenge her wrongful imprisonment, stop running from conflict, and right the injustice.

It was late morning, and her playground attitude promptly turned studious.

"Read this," she instructed him, pushing a children's picture book from a pile he'd brought a previous day.

He read her the story of a man chasing a mouse and destroying the house as the pursuit unfolded. As he spoke, she wrote quickly in a notebook; Jaks thought her writing looked strange, with too many curves and dots.

"I use this when you are not here. Practice," she said. Her accent was thick, with a lilt and rhythm that was both confusing and intriguing. "I like these pictures. Paper books are . . . What is the word? Not many? Not common? Rare? In my world."

He had visited her every day for the past three weeks and barely kept pace with her ability to learn. It turned out that she had already acquired many of the Ascorian language sounds from listening to the guards and possessed an astonishing, precocious talent for languages—she did not forget any word or grammatical construct that Jaks had explained.

She had quickly taken over the instruction process.

Instead of waiting for Jaks's lead, she used her blossoming Ascorian to direct the instruction how she wanted. He was glad for her decisiveness once he learnt that teaching a language was very different from just being able to speak it. She told him that she already spoke eight other languages—none of which he had heard of before.

And most bewilderingly, later that day, she told him she was from a different world.

"The stars. Some of them are planets like the one we are on—but very far away," she explained and pointed to her caged window. "I am from one of those planets."

He did not believe her. She was teasing him. The stars were light stones planted in the sky by God, or so he had been taught. He had never heard of planets.

Certainly, she looked exotic, different from any other person he had ever seen, and she once possessed items and a weapon of foreign manufacture, but it was madness to believe she had come from the stars.

They did not speak for a couple of minutes while Meila flicked through the picture book looking for material, the rustle of paper the only sound in the room.

They were alone in the cell. The prison guards had decided a week ago that their interactions were so dull that they would stop sitting in on the language sessions and let Jaks come and go as he pleased. Since then,

Meila had relaxed and would sometimes brush his hand or forearm with her fingers; he thought the touches were by accident but wasn't sure.

Jaks took the silence as an opportunity to confess to her. So far, Meila seemed pleased with his visits and had not expressed any resentment or anger toward him about her capture. In fact, they had spoken twice about their first encounter, and she had complimented him on his bravery facing the dragons.

"I am sorry you are here. I did not want you to be arrested and put in prison." His remorse spilled out. "They think you are a spy. I want to help prove you are innocent."

"A spy?" she asked, her eyebrows creasing together.

"A thief who steals secrets," he explained further.

"And what is 'innocent'?"

"Someone who is not a thief."

She shifted her chair and faced him directly. "Why do you think I am *not* a spy?"

"Because you would be a terrible spy . . ." he said, waiting to see if he caused offense. She did not react. "You had no disguise. Your face is unlike any in Ascoria, it is so . . . delicate and strange, and your hair is so dark, it would stand out like a pillar of obsidian. Your clothes were peculiar, and people would have stared at you. Also, what use is a spy who could not understand our language? And lastly, why would you be in the mountains, in the middle of nowhere?"

Meila swept back a lock of hair behind her ear and

quirked the corner of her mouth. "Maybe I am a terrible spy."

Jaks was distracted for a moment—seeing the exposed nape of her neck seemed peculiarly intimate to him—and then he coughed and gathered his thoughts.

"If you were a spy, you would have killed me and Minto when you saw us, in seconds. I saw what it did to the dragons." The memory of the monsters dismembered by the violent blasts appalled him.

She leaned toward him, suddenly concerned. "What happened to my weapon—my *handgun*?"

"I don't know. All of your items were thrown into a sack and brought back with us. I guess they're locked up around here somewhere." *So that was what it was called*, he thought, visualizing the deadly object she had shoved in his chest at one stage. He couldn't blame her in the circumstances.

Meila reclined and stared at the door, lost in thought for a few minutes. "What if we told the judge . . . magistrate, that I can prove my innocence based on the items I had at the campsite."

Jaks was shocked and thought that she meant to trick the magistrate into giving her access to her weapon. "You can't mean to fight your way out—"

"You believe I should be free, though?" she said.

"Well, yes, but not by committing a massacre. It would be wrong. There must be another way." Jaks tensed. He wanted to help her, but not by evil means. "Is there anything else you could do, or show them, that'd prove that you are not a spy? What *were* you doing in the mountains?"

She stared at Jaks for a long minute, her face wracked by unspoken thoughts. Finally, she looked like she had come to a decision and laid her hands on the table.

"I crashed in an escape pod, the metal ship—I came from a starship," she said levelly.

Jaks sat stunned as Meila then elaborated on her claim that she came from beyond the sky, from a civilization of so many people that they were forced to live in gigantic buildings.

At first, he thought she was insane, even looking to the door in case her insanity was dangerous, but her earnestness and confidence in her descriptions kept him listening.

Over the next hours, in her broken Ascorian, she told him of concepts and technology that were truly alien to him, including the planets she had spoken of earlier, and ships that traveled between them. Although he understood little of what she described, the idea of an enormous universe with the possibility of life on other planets excited him. Somehow, it seemed right. If the night stars were suns like the one he saw in the day, then there must be millions of planets like the one they stood on. His eyes drifted as his imagination exploded with the possibilities.

Meila continued, her forehead furrowing as she drew drawings on loose bits of paper to accompany her descriptions: bulbous ships that housed thousands, buildings that covered miles of land, magnificent monuments, and bizarre animals. There was great beauty to the clean lines and geometry of the objects created by her people. Her artistry could line galleries if patrons could look past the alienness of the content.

She stalled when she returned to where she started —describing her starship. "The *Mendhelsson*," she said as she put down her pencil and stared at the drawing she had made of it. "It was a small ship. I commanded eight crew. We were . . . traveling between planets. It was home to me and Anton for many years."

"What happened?" asked Jaks, his elbows leaning on the table. He did not know who Anton was, but the sadness in her eyes told him that he was significant to her.

"A terrible accident . . . I cannot explain. I do not have the words," said Meila, leaving him hanging as her voice tapered off after speaking for almost three hours.

Dozens of questions arose at her vagueness, but it dawned on Jaks that he had made the breakthrough with Meila. The exact connection that he had promised Grandmaster Mulgrave. This was just the beginning. He had to find the mage and tell him of the incredible things she'd just told him, perhaps use it to prove she wasn't a spy.

"I have to go now, but I'll come back tomorrow," said Jaks. "Can I take these drawings to show my master?"

Meila nodded and rose from her seat. "You know, if

I got my possessions back, or get back to the escape pod, I could show you real pictures from my world that I have stored."

"Yes, I'd like that." Jaks stood. He wanted to hug her but kept his arms to his sides on seeing the movement of a guard outside. This was still a prison.

The next day, Mulgrave came with Jaks to see Meila. The mage was so bemused by Jaks's report of Meila's claims and her drawings that he wanted to see her again. "She's been monkeying around with your head," he had said to Jaks.

She greeted them coolly as they entered her cell.

Mulgrave studied her.

"Hello, Grandmaster Mulgrave. How nice to see you again," she said, her diction perfect with a musical lilt.

She gestured to the chairs around the table.

The mage smiled and sat down. "Wherever you are from, you know your manners." He did not like to banter and got to the point. "What is all this mysticism you are telling the lad here?"

She sat down and opened her palms to him. "I do not know what mysticism is, but what I told Jaks is all . . ." She paused for a moment, searching for a word. "True."

Mulgrave studied her for a minute and then stroked his jaw. "Tell me about where you come from."

"It is a planet called Earth," she began.

Meila repeated what she told Jaks the previous day, but to a far more skeptical audience.

The mage regularly interrupted her and demanded more details for each of her claims and greater explanation of the concepts and places that she described. He stretched her nascent language skills. It was hard to gauge how much he believed, but after several hours, as the clattering of the meal cart sounded in the prison corridor, they both seemed to have exhausted their powers of speech and fell into a long silence.

The next morning, Jaks found the mage asleep at his desk, lying over copious notes that he had written overnight. "I don't know why I have a clerk when I do all the writing myself," Mulgrave said.

"Sorry, Master. If you'd told me, I would have stayed up—"

"Never mind." The mage's chair scraped as he pushed it back and stood. "She's not telling us everything. It may be the language barrier, but I think she is withholding something . . . maybe a lot," he said. "We're going back today. There is one more thing I need to know."

In the prison cell, Meila smiled brightly and thanked Jaks for the bunch of scented yellow flowers that he had plucked as he and the mage walked by the cathedral gardens on their way here. Guessing his intent, Mulgrave had scowled at him and scolded, "She's not your woman. She's a prisoner."

Jaks had blushed and sheepishly replied with a muted, "Yes, I know."

"Did you rest well?" Jaks asked her when they were seated at the round table. The flowers sat in her wooden mug in front of them.

Before she could reply, Mulgrave interrupted, "If you were freed, where would you go?"

They had not discussed her imprisonment the previous day, although Jaks had mentioned wanting to petition for her release sometime before. At that time, Mulgrave had dismissed the idea as ridiculous.

"Back to the mountains. To my escape pod. I need to be close to it if . . . when . . . the rescue crew arrives. It is the only way they can find me here."

Mulgrave looked at Jaks. "You didn't tell her the ship is at the Academy." It was more of a statement than a question.

Meila frowned and glanced at the younger man.

"How long until they come for you?" Mulgrave asked.

Meila sighed. "Many of your planet's years,

unfortunately. Thirteen or more. This planet is very far from Earth. It takes many jumps and time to travel between each point. When our ship fails to return in seven years' time, the Agency may take a year or so to decide whether to send another mission. Then, if they do, it'd take a new ship about six years to find its way here."

"What'll happen if you stay in this prison here?"

"I would grow old. What else could I do?" She pursed her lips and stared at Mulgrave.

Keeping to his line of questions, he ignored hers and continued, "What do you know about the manufacture and materials of the vessel you were with—what you called your 'escape pod'?"

She was puzzled by Mulgrave's words and looked to Jaks, who took a minute to clarify the question for her.

"Why?" she asked.

The mage sat back, and his eyes flitted back and forth. It looked to Jaks as though the mage was trying to decide whether to reveal a hand of cards.

"You are either completely mad and what you say is just the ravings of a lunatic, or you are telling us the truth," said the mage.

"You think I am insane?" asked Meila, her accent thick and musical.

"If I had not seen your ship and the technology inside, I would not have believed you. But I have. And what you say is very convincing and explains a lot about why I can't comprehend its design." Mulgrave rubbed his chin. "So, how much do you understand about the manufacture of this technology and what can you teach us?" He leaned across the table. "If it is worth it, in exchange, we would petition your release—and you would come to the Academy and teach us all you know."

Jaks leaned forward. "Meila, the grandmaster knows the king personally—he could get you out of here," he said, louder than he should have.

Meila's look turned cold. She crossed her arms and furrowed her brow. "You will only help me if I help you?" Her voice became monotone, unlike her normal lilting voice, as though she were practicing the words for the first time. "I see things work here the same way they do back home."

Jaks hated the tension. He didn't know why she did not just say yes immediately. Surely, she could not be hiding something. "We are helping you. Please say yes?"

Chapter 17

Blackmailed

Meila—City of Dunberrin, Ascoria

Meila stood and paced the room. Indecision was a rare companion. It was not often that she was blackmailed for her freedom.

She needed to escape from this prison and had been willing to do anything—including murder—to escape. But the deal offered by the grandmaster contravened her code of duty. As a United Worlds Federation commander, she had vowed to never intervene with the politics of any colony that she was sent to evaluate; protocols dictated that no mission should contact or assist an Old Colony.

Violate her duty to the UWF and she would be court-martialed and decommissioned. Refuse Mulgrave's offer and she would waste away or die in this cellblock.

She paused mid-pace and looked at the mage. "What information do you want from me?"

"Everything. What metals make up this ship? What does the ship's machine do? How does it work? That would be the beginning." The bald mage paused. "Then, I would want to know, if the stars are planets, how do they stay up there? What keeps our world around the Sun? There are a thousand and a million questions I would ask."

Not difficult questions. Any UWF engineer could answer them. Her mission role, in addition to mission commander, had been engineering scientist, and she was as expert in that area as her husband in genetics and her other shipmates in their respective fields. It was not *whether* she knew the answers, but how sparingly she dished them out.

She was being offered a path to freedom. It was the best she could make of a poor hand. The only choice to take.

To hell with it, I'll deal with a court-martial when it comes.

She inhaled and triggered a memory implant. Reviewing information through her lens prosthesis she said, "The escape pod hull is an alloy of forty percent titanium, thirty-three percent lithtarite, seventeen percent xarcontate, and ten percent dothenide. I can tell you the alloying process and parameters and a million other details. But it won't help you, because you cannot recreate them here. The process requires elements and chemicals that do not even exist on this planet."

The old man remained silent and seemed to be waiting for more.

"That information is unhelpful to you, but I can teach you things that are far more practical and useful." She stood before Mulgrave and then said, "You do not know how *little* you know."

Chapter 18

Slave of the Vor King

Karisa–Magmatin Castle, Kingdom of Voros

Karisa did what she did best: act and play her part. Do it well and she would be a slave to just one man; fail, and she would be raped by many. The hungry gazes following her movements left no doubt of that in her mind.

She walked in a haze through the audience gathered in the throne room—blobs of shifting shadows and whispering shades held back by a lane of armored sentinels leading up to a dais.

Today, her performance was *The Seductress*.

Although trussed up like a child's doll in a tatty yellow dress, an uneven pearl necklace, and ragged slippers, her bearing was regal. She raised her chin high, squared her shoulders, thrust out her chest, and glided her steps.

The brute urging her along was the warrior in crocodile skin who had murdered her signaler-master and bruised her into submission: Hau Carric, a leader of a band of fifty warriors and a sycophant who made it clear to Karisa that she was a prize-mare to be offered to the Vor King.

After the ambush, and the raiding band had raised their sails for the motherland, Carric had gone to reappraise his loot in the middle of the longboat.

He scrubbed her face with a rag soaked in saltwater and stripped her of her leather armor.

Standing naked and trembling on the deck, she had thought of running for the gunwale and throwing herself into the ocean but knew it would be suicide. She would get out of this alive. Nothing was more terrible than what her father had already done to her.

Carric cupped her face, fondled her breasts, and parted her buttocks and labia. He huffed a satisfied grunt, then pulled out a dagger and pointed it at his leering troops, men and women alike, and said, "This one is for the king. Not a hand on her."

He had then thrown her a thick robe to cover herself those several days ago.

And now, before the king of Voros, Karisa stopped at the foot of the dais.

Marble statues encircled her, a stone honor guard of chiseled animals: lion, bear, dragon, eagle, and some hideous tusked monster she'd never seen before.

Between each statue, living guards completed the circle: steel-clad warriors keeping the mob away from their monarch. The hall looked to hold a thousand comfortably, but that day swarmed with twice that number.

A dozen steps led up to a cushioned granite throne, on which reclined a long-limbed man adorned in silks and velvets and a plain circlet of platinum atop his head.

The crowd fell into a hush as she curtsied and bowed her head as she had been instructed by Carric.

"Sire. Along with killing over a hundred Ascorian soldiers and taunting the Ascorian on their coast, I present to you a gift from our raid," Carric said, an arm pointing at Karisa. "A beauty unlike any I have seen before." A sonomancy runestone in the mouth of the dragon statue magnified the volume of all sound around them, so although Carric only spoke to the king, his voice was projected throughout the hall.

Karisa was glorious, a nymphet slathered in sensuality. She had ripped the dress that Carric had given her to expose her long lithe limbs and elegant neck. Her face was perfectly symmetrical, eyes opal blue, lips bee-stung and ruby red, and her hair haloed in gold. She hoped she had not overdone her illumancer enhancements—too much and she could appear an over-painted whore.

But she need not have worried, because King Harek Raukela was clearly smitten.

"What is your name?" Harek leaned forward, his eyes wide and drunk on her.

"Karisa, sire," she replied. "My grandfather once

lived in this very province—before you invaded it," she said, raising her gaze to meet his green eyes.

Harek laughed at her impudence and was soon echoed around the hall. "Rightly so. Magmatin would not join our union, so it needed to be forcefully . . . welcomed. But it has been all for the better. Isn't that so, Lord Magmatin?"

Karisa followed the king's gaze to a rusted iron cage to the side of throne room at his left—several listless forms huddled inside it—from which a crumpled man croaked out incoherently.

The king stood and strode down to her. Few men were taller than her, but the king loomed as tall as her father; however, unlike the latter's bearishness, Harek was a python: sinuous, smooth, and powerful with a crushing intensity. She drove back an impulse of fear and forced a smile.

He traced a finger from below her ear, down her neck, and stared at her for several long seconds as he lingered in the hollow of her neck. "Well done, Torgue-commander."

Two women swept down the dais at the king's command and led Karisa out the back of the throne room.

Karisa imagined and visualized the welcome she would deliver to the king as she lay and waited for him in his private bedchamber under the watchful eye of a guard. She thought that the seduction scene from *Lord Porten's Lover*, a titillating play in which she had acted as an innocent housemaid, would be the perfect enactment to complete her seduction of the Vor king. After their introduction in the throne room, she felt supremely confident.

The bedchamber was high in a tower, she deduced from the view out of a window overlooking battlements below and then a city beyond.

She could see a crescent-shaped port with hundreds of ships bobbing under a sky dark with rain clouds, neighborhoods of gray buildings tangled with streets and alleyways, and in the distance, a peaked mountain with a craggy top.

Seduction was a tool demanded of her at the most desperate times of her life. The first time had been to stop her father abusing her mother—a trade: herself for her mother, one for one. The second was when she had run away and sought refuge with her mother's old acting troupe. The playhouse owner had been more than pleased to give her a roof over her head—as long as it was in his bed. And now, she was forced to seduce yet another man to prevent being sold as chattel.

Or have I been bought already? For a moment, her confidence wavered and a wave of sadness swamped Karisa as the bedchamber walls closed in on her. It was her prison. She was trapped, bound, and paraded like an animal.

Surely, there must be more to life than running, hiding, and being a plaything of men.

Footsteps approached the bedchamber door, and Karisa composed herself. She clambered onto the four-poster bed, arranged her yellow dress, and then leaned gracefully on one arm.

A guard pushed the door open and stood aside.

Harek entered the room and fixed his eyes on her.

Karisa looked up in simulated surprise and formed an O with her lips.

The king gestured at the guard to leave and went to a table of stoppered bottles to pour and then quaff a glass of amber liquid.

"Stand up," he commanded her, motioning her off the bed.

She stood before him and chewed on her lower lip, staring at his chest.

He reached for her face as though to caress her. Then his fingers were around her neck. He stared at her with cold, soulless eyes and squeezed.

She pulled urgently at his wrists, but his grip tightened, lifting her off the ground.

The strangle-hold suddenly loosened, and he threw her onto the bed, where she lay gasping for breath.

She felt the front of her dress rip from the neck down and then a sharp pain shear across her face.

He slapped her several more times, grunting with each blow.

It was then that her act plummeted into a nightmare

of violence as the beast brutalized and violated her into the night.

———

In the morning, a guard dragged Karisa out naked into an adjacent chamber. Her mind was in a daze of fear and humiliation.

A silk-wrapped woman with red hair ushered Karisa to one of several velvet divans and snuggled a cushion beneath her head.

A moment later, a second woman appeared with a cloth and a steaming bowl in her hands. She tsked and tutted as she patted Karisa's face tenderly with the dampened cloth.

"You are strong, girl. You did not scream or cry," said the redhead. She grimaced at the black eye and red marks around Karisa's neck. "He is not a gentle man. Although he could have any of us, at any time, he is always as cruel as a lion toying with its prey. I don't know how you put up with it without making a sound. When he comes at me, I can't help but cry the whole time—I think he likes it the more I weep." She bent close to her ear and whispered, "He is a monster."

A third woman, also cocooned in silk, swept over and brought a mug to Karisa's lips. "Drink this. It is required after he gives his seed."

After a while, Karisa stirred from her daze.

The women fussed over her. They draped lengths of

red and blue silk over her battered body and asked her which she preferred. They puzzled over her accent and asked her how an Ascorian girl knew the Vor tongue. They showed her the harem and asked which divan she liked.

But despite the courtesans' warm welcome, Karisa shivered in despair. *Damn you, Vixhana. Damn you, Jaks. What of your damn oath now?*

Chapter 19

The Ward

Jaks—City of Dunberrin, Ascoria

Seated at the table in her prison cell, as usual for their lessons, Jaks contained an annoyed expression as his student soundly demolished his opinion on what was turning out to be one of her favorite subjects: frogs.

His disgust for the slimy animals was as severe as that for any belly-crawling, bug-eyed creature—and he had said so. However, Meila's defense decried the reptiles as beautiful guardians of the swamps with glorious traits that put human beings to shame.

She was launching into the fourth minute of the wonders of frogs when there was a rattle at the cell door that caused her to pause.

Jaks sighed with relief.

A female prison guard walked in. Typically, she would enter yawning with a bored expression, but today she was twitchy and nervous.

"Er, well . . . King Silas wants to see you," said the broad-jawed woman, her face sharing the same surprise as Jaks's and Meila's.

It had been a week since Jaks had delivered their petition for Meila's release to the Royal Palace, and they had been losing all hope of getting a reply.

Jaks tagged along with Meila and her escort of three Royal Guards, unsure whether or not he had been invited.

They led her from the prison to the Royal Palace through an enclosed bridge he realized was the famous "Wailing Bridge." Fortunately, today they did not cross paths with anyone weeping and crying after being condemned to death by the king.

He got as far as the waiting room of the king's private offices before a Master Herald barred his way and pointed for Jaks to sit at the end of a row of citizen petitioners.

He lost sight of Meila as purple-robed sentries guided her into an antechamber of white marble and flowing banners, but not before glimpsing Grandmaster Mulgrave inside.

An hour later, the stocky mage exited the king's court room and pulled on Jaks's arm as he swept by. "Come. The king is following soon. We are to go ahead of him and reconvene at the Academy."

An impromptu visit to the Academy by the king was an event to be excited about, but Jaks was doubly excited to see that Minto was part of the Royal Entourage. The apprentice herald waved enthusiastically to Jaks from the back of the group of soldiers and officials gathered along the land bridge in front of the Academy.

The king and twelve gleaming knights dismounted their horses while a throng of soldiers, advisors, and heralds, who had accompanied the entourage, waited on their king.

Meila was transported on a horse-drawn prison carriage by the same trio of guards who had escorted her from her cell. Her hands were cuffed in iron and her legs were in iron chains, heavy enough to cause her feet to drag.

Jaks frowned at the sight of the excessive bindings.

Along with Mulgrave and Tavis, he waited under the main gates of the Academy. Grandmaster Hazeldine, the Head of the Academy, and dozens of other mages had also stopped their work and had joined the welcoming party as word spread of the royal visit.

According to Mulgrave, the King had come to the Academy to see Meila reveal information in the escape pod to prove the existence of other worlds.

The entourage filed through the gate behind Mulgrave and the king; however, there was a pause when a raised word came from the king leading to

Meila's leg bindings being hastily removed by an embarrassed guard.

Jaks moved to the side to let everyone pass. He'd catch up later; he was eager to speak to Minto.

Slightly plumper than when Jaks had last seen him two months ago, the apprentice herald was finely dressed in a blue-bordered uniform and short cloak.

They clasped hands and clapped each other on the shoulder.

"They must be fattening you up for the king's table. They've even trussed you up like a roasted goose," said Jaks, grinning at a triangular hat sitting atop his friend's head.

Minto grinned, plucked at his sleeves theatrically, and bowed. "I thank you for your gracious compliment, m' lord." He then laughed. "I didn't think you could get any taller . . . you'll be bashing your brains out on doorframes if you don't stop growing!"

"It's a family curse," Jaks joked and pulled Minto aside. "I've got so much to tell you. No, I haven't got the apprenticeship yet . . . but that woman in the mountains we found. This is all about her! I've been seeing her in the prison for the last month."

"I know, beanpole, I hear a lot of the goings-on around the place. But, listen . . ." Minto glanced around and grabbed Jaks's arms. "The Vorosian Empire is going to invade Ascoria."

"They've been saying that for years," said Jaks.

Minto shook his head. "This time, it's for real.

Merchants and traders have been blockaded from Voros, and I heard a message read to the king with enemy troop and ship numbers. The king is sending even more reinforcements to the west coast as we speak." He paused, a look of concern crossing his face. "My master says there will be a call to arms. There's going to be a muster soon. You have to get a proper apprenticeship; otherwise, you'll get re-conscripted."

Jaks frowned as he considered Minto's warning. It was the king's prerogative to issue a call to arms where all fighting-age adults were summoned for active military duty. The only exceptions were people in essential jobs and their apprentices. At the moment, Jaks was a non-essential clerk and, likely in the eyes of the army, more useful holding a poleaxe or crossbow.

"No way. I can't go back to the army. To fight as a conscript against the Vors is a death sentence." Jaks faltered for a second. "Thanks for telling me, Minto. I have to work on it." *I have to get Tavis's apprenticeship. I have to get rid of him somehow.* His thoughts then turned to Karisa. *She was right. We should have run away to Faucony.*

"Look, we have to catch up with the group. We should try to meet again soon," Minto said.

In the covered courtyard of the Academy, the clang of anvils and thump of machinery continued at the hands of those who had been unable to stop midway through their creations to ogle at the king.

When the entourage arrived at Meila's metal ship,

King Silas said a word and the rest of Meila's restraints came off.

She clambered in without hesitation.

A guard went to grab her, but the king waved him away, then leaned over the lip of the metal ship to watch her. The grandmaster joined him.

Saying to the guards that he was "with the grandmaster," Jaks pushed up on the opposite side of the ship's opening—and found himself face to face with the king of Ascoria.

King Silas Montras had a long face, firm jaw, steely eyes, and silver hair. There was no indication of his status other than a gold collar made of small interlinking shields embossed with major insignias of his realm.

"Oh, hello there," the king said in a reedy voice that Jaks did not expect from such a distinguished-looking man.

Jaks turned red as soon as he realized his gaffe. "Sorry, my king. I didn't mean to, to—"

"This is the boy I told you about—the tutor," Mulgrave said. "He is a bit excitable."

"Understandable," Silas replied and winked at Jaks. "Shall we get on with it, then?" He redirected his gaze into the pod.

Meila was absorbed with the panel suspended on the metal arm. Symbols and images lit up and flickered across the surface as her hands slid and tapped at inlays on the pod's walls. "This is the taskwall. I enter requests through the keys, and they go to the onboard AI under my seat and send images to the panel." The images changed too fast for any of the Ascorians to comprehend.

"Here," she said a few seconds later.

The panel displayed a picture of her with eight men and women, all dressed in navy-blue uniforms, standing in front of a large window. On the other side was a sleek silver squid-like object with contours similar to the escape pod. It was completely enclosed and seemed to float in the night. "That's my starship, the *Mendhelsson*," she said. Behind the ship were huge extrusions and dark arms that Jaks couldn't make sense of. And, in the background, a glowing circle of large blue, brown, and white patches.

"This is a pre-launch picture. Those are my crew. Those are parts of the space station you can see there. And that is Earth."

She then showed hundreds of pictures including immense buildings, land and air vehicles, sophisticated objects, and sweeping views of cities that extended beyond the horizon.

Last, she played recordings that revealed minutes of life itself: people talking, laughing, eating, hugging, and living life on her planet and in her starship.

Once he saw the wondrous images, Jaks lost any doubt of the reality of Meila's claims. The amazed expressions on the faces of both the king and Mulgrave revealed they must have felt the same.

As Meila's eyes misted over as she watched the

recordings, Jaks wondered what she felt, severed from her past life, stranded here in their world.

The next day, Mulgrave received a Royal Decree declaring Meila his personal ward. She was to be transferred to his guardianship at the Academy, where technically, she was to remain a prisoner. The letter stated that if she complied with the demands of the king and Grandmaster Mulgrave's to supply knowledge, and did not attempt to escape custody for two years, she would be freed and released.

Jaks read the document several times, then whooped and danced around.

Mulgrave chuckled, seemingly infected by his clerk's joy. "We did it boy."

Only Tavis was not pleased with the news and went back to his room with a soured expression.

Chapter 20

Confrontation in the Library

"You're no hero," said Tavis, sneering at Jaks from a dark corner of the library. "Just because you got her to talk, doesn't make you any better than me. I could have taught her Ascorian—faster than you did—if I hadn't been helping the grandmaster with real work."

Mulgrave and Jaks had returned that afternoon from the prison, bringing Meila back with them.

When they had told her that Grandmaster Mulgrave was now her guardian, and that she would move to the Academy, Jaks had expected a more exuberant response. But she had just blinked at them a few times and then picked up her notebooks and said, "Let's go."

Mulgrave had converted another office on Jaks's corridor for her use. "Guard her close," he had said, creating an awkward moment between Meila and Jaks, who wondered at his seriousness.

So when Tavis ambushed him in the library, Jaks was distracted by thoughts of his new neighbor.

"Never said I was a hero," Jaks said. Tavis's presence brought Jaks back to the present and reminded him of his bigger problem: how to wrest Tavis's apprenticeship away from him.

Although Jaks felt like a hypocrite for going back on his word—he had told Tavis that he would not steal his position—the circumstances had changed with the threat of re-conscription.

"You are wasting your time here. You'll never get my apprenticeship, you slimy bootlicker." Tavis sheathed his hands in flames, showing off his pyromancy. "I've seen kids like you before, with your little tricks. It's not real magic, it's a vagary of childhood. And when your pimples clear, you'll find that you are just as vacant of magic as your mother is vacant of life." The apprentice snuffed out his fire-hands and snorted derisively.

Jaks's face colored, his ears burned, and the hairs on his neck stood up. The reference to his mother was tasteless but hit a sore point with him. Tavis was trivializing his mother's death.

They faced off between two towering bookshelves.

The veins in Jaks's neck throbbed as he clenched his fists and glared at Tavis.

The apprentice wrinkled his nose and scowled. "I'm just telling you the truth. You should leave the Academy today and save yourself the embarrassment," Tavis said. "The grandmaster doesn't need both of us; it's obvious he'll keep me and get rid of you eventually. We don't need you here."

They were interrupted by a female voice from the center of the library, Meila's lilting accent. "Jaks, there you are. I have been looking for you. Oh, pardon me . . ." she said, as though only just realizing the apprentice mage was also present. "I did not see you there, Tavis. Anyway, come here and help me now, Jaks." She turned from apologetic to commanding in an instant and gestured at Jaks to follow her back to their corridor.

Jaks glowered one last time at Tavis, then went to follow Meila.

The apprentice made a parting shot at his opponent. "Run to your mistress, slave boy."

Jaks slammed the library door behind him.

Meila stood in the corridor, waiting with folded arms. "What was that about?" she asked.

Jaks slapped the back of his hand into the palm of the other. "Tavis hates me and wants to get rid of me. He thinks I want to steal his apprenticeship."

"Is it true?" she asked.

Jaks pushed back from the wall as his anger waned. "It wasn't at first, but it is now—an apprenticeship is the only way I can avoid being re-conscripted."

Jaks told her of the incidents with Baden and Tavis, describing the dormant magic that had lashed out to defend him. "It's the rarest of magics, but I need proper training to use it."

He sighed and then told her about the history

between Tavis and himself and his fears of a war. "Raiders from the Vor empire have been hitting the coast for years, but my friend Minto says the king expects they are about to invade."

"So, if the kingdom is about to be invaded, why are you so desperate to become an apprentice?" asked Meila.

"It's the only way I can escape a Conscript Legion; they'll be the first to be thrown to the dogs. Imagine a bunch of old men and bumbling draftees like me fighting together. We'd be slaughtered."

"And you think the grandmaster must choose between the two of you?"

"A mage only has one apprentice," he said. "That's how it is with masters and apprentices in every occupation."

She paced for a minute, then turned to Jaks with a frown. "I think your problem is not Tavis—it is you." She pointed a finger at his chest.

"Huh? Tavis has had it out for me right from the day I got here. Just this morning, he threatened me and told me to leave the Academy," Jaks said in a defensive tone.

"Your problem is that you can't even do magic properly. It is not you against Tavis. It is you against *you*. If you can show that you can use this magic . . . this electromancy . . . properly, the other master, Cranbrook, you say, has already said it would be the first time in eighty years that anyone has had it. You don't think they would throw away a once-in-a-lifetime opportunity to have a fully-fledged electromancer, do you?"

"Well, I suppose not—"

"If you can show that you have this rare power, they'll find you an apprenticeship. You don't have to steal Tavis's apprenticeship. You only think that because he thinks that. You don't have to worry about whose apprentice you might be. The fact that Mulgrave spent so much effort to get me . . ." Her voice drifted as she struggled for a word. "To *acquire* me, for a chance at my knowledge, tells me he would do even more to help you—if you can show him electromancy." Meila pointed a finger at Jaks. "You should stop worrying about Tavis and worry about finding out how to do magic."

Meila made a convincing argument. This antagonism between him and Tavis was a waste of time. He nodded reluctantly. "You are right. I need to focus on the magic."

But the realization did little to lift the dark shroud over him as he recalled the failures he had experienced with invoking.

Jaks then helped Meila finish rearranging her room. "We can move the junk you don't want into one of the other rooms next door," he said.

She paused and puffed away a layer of dust from a wicker basket. "This room is smaller than my prison cell."

"Well, at least you can go out and walk around

whenever you like," said Jaks. "The grandmaster said that I can escort you if you want to leave the building and see more of the city. In fact, he said I *had* to accompany you if you wanted to go anywhere outside."

"Don't worry, I will not run away. I have nowhere else to go," she said to assure him. "But yes, show me around. It's nice having such freedom after months in prison." She smiled at him.

He led her on a tour of the hallways, libraries, and labs, sharing as much as he could about their common home; eventually, they ended up in the museum courtyard, standing at her escape pod.

"This is the only link I have left to my people," Meila said and clambered into the pod.

He peered in to see what she was doing and was curious to hear her speaking to herself in a foreign language.

"What are you doing?" Jaks asked, trying to make sense of the images flickering on the display panel in front of her.

She swept a wisp of hair out of her face but did not respond as she continued her tasks.

Jaks wondered if the pod itself could be used to escape. Was she about to fly away?

The pod did not move, and eventually, she sighed. "The emergency beacon is working perfectly—there is enough power to last three hundred years. If they don't come by then, I'll probably have forgotten about Earth anyway—or have been murdered by one of you barbarians."

"Three hundred years? You'd be dead of old age." Jaks wondered whether she had translated her words correctly.

She looked at him and smiled. "You pup! I'm already one hundred and twenty of your planet's years old." She laughed at his astonished gape. "I hope to live a few hundred more yet."

"No. I don't believe you," he said. "You're jesting me."

But she was focused again inside the pod and busied herself with the panel screen. An image settled on the screen; it looked similar to the background of the very first picture she had shown the king and Mulgrave earlier. A beautiful round disc, blue and green, with white patches.

"That is your planet. We call it Maya," she said.

It was a stunning picture that undulated as he watched an overhead map of their world. After a minute, Jaks was distracted from the panel by a pained look creasing Meila's face—a tear rolled down her cheek and she wiped it with the back of her hand.

"What's wrong?" he asked her.

She stared at the panel for a while and replied in a deadpan voice, "Four escape pods from my ship made planetfall." She stopped to wipe her eyes. "But over the past few months, they've all disappeared . . . I can't find any life signs of my crew. Even Anton, I can't find his implant signal anywhere."

She climbed out of the pod and shuffled off in a daze.

Jaks glanced at the panel.

The display blinked a single lonely dot.

Chapter 21

Guns

Meila–The Academy of the Arcane

Meila awoke to screeches outside her window. Two blue dragons lashed about as a furious ball of teeth and claws on the rocks below. An injured fish flopped nearby, inching toward the waves. The size of hawks, the two creatures were far smaller than the bronzes that she and Jaks had encountered in the mountains, but seemingly just as loud.

She pushed the window open, leaned out, and yelled at them.

Ignoring her, they continued their struggle for several more seconds. One then snatched the fish and flew away toward the wharves as the other winged after it in pursuit.

There was a quiet knock at her door.

She pulled the window shut and waited.

Bony knuckles tapped louder.

So used to the prison guards entering without

notice, she had forgotten the courtesy. "Oh, yes . . . come in," she said.

Jaks creaked the hallway door open and peered in. His eyes widened and he pulled back. "Sorry, I didn't realize you weren't dressed."

In nothing but a clerk's shirt, she grabbed her leggings draped over a chair and pulled them on.

"What's going on?" she said as she pulled the door wide open and threw on a green cotton jacket similar to Jaks's own.

"Grandmaster Mulgrave wants us downstairs . . . he's going to give you a tour of the Academy," Jaks said, seemingly embarrassed at seeing her naked legs. She was amused. *So naïve . . . surely, he has experience with women?*

A half hour later, down in the Metals lab, Grandmaster Mulgrave greeted her and Jaks. Tavis stared at the floor glumly.

"I'll show you around some of what we do, and then you must tell me what you can contribute," said Mulgrave. "I expect great things."

The old man did not waste any time. Deliver or go back to the prison. What could she give them that would prove her useful?

They began with the grandmaster's own team of magesmiths: Master Samis, the bug-eyed forgemaster, and his apprentice, the pretty Olire; Master Ivaleen, the wizened firemancer, with her journeyman, Benny, who never made eye contact; and Master Randell, obsessed with creating the perfect signaling machine.

Last were Doeg and Shazair.

A honey-skinned man turned from his bench as they approached. The bench was so covered in hammers, chisels, files, rulers, pliers, clamps, stones, screws, nuts and bolts, and metal panels that Meila was sure everything would slide off if anything else were added.

A woman with tight curls and a round face sat opposite him and looked up from her task of polishing a runestone.

"Master Doeg and Journeyman Shazair have a special interest. Why don't you show us your project?" said Mulgrave.

The man nodded and picked up a small square of metal. "A multi-cell sourcestone storage unit . . ." He slid open a cover on the container. Runestones packed the interior. "It's part of a battle flamer that we're designing."

"Flamer?" she said.

Doeg grinned. "Blasts whatever you point it at."

Meila stared at the mountain of parts on the workbench but could not see a weapon in the making.

Doeg plucked two stones out of the container. Shaped and polished, they were perfect cubes. "There are only twenty master firemancers in Ascoria, and only four battle-trained. So, we research ways to allow pyromancy to be used more widely. We use sourcestone devices, but most stones are so small that they need frequent recharging and generate weak magic."

Sourcestones, or as they were more often called, "runestones"—Jaks had told her during one of their lessons—were commonly used as light sources. Streetlamps, ceiling lights, chandeliers, and hand torches held the magical stones that could be purchased in any market or luminary shop. Any of thousands of people who were gifted with illumancer powers could rejuvenate the stones—for a price, of course. It made sense for families to store dozens of the stones in drawers and cupboards, ready to replace dimming lights.

Although other forms of magic were sometimes used—firestones to start cooking hearths, gravstones to lift granite blocks on construction sites, and sonostones for the hard of hearing—those types were rarer because of fewer mages of the corresponding power.

Doeg flicked one sourcestone to Jaks, who clapped his hands around it. The cold, gray stone was exceptionally well cut, highly polished, and barren of any lettering or marks.

The Fauconian offered another of the stones to the foreign woman.

"*Mayatite,*" Meila said unexpectedly, as the runestone tumbled into her hand like a dice cube. "Unique to this planet alone. Either formed or deposited in a single event millions of years ago. Its properties are unlike any other known mineral . . .

conducts like a metal but with an internal structure that changes dynamically like a living creature."

Master Doeg, Jaks, and Tavis stared at her as though she talked gibberish. Only the grandmaster followed her.

"You say it's alive?" Mulgrave asked.

Meila shook her head. She pincered the stone between two fingers and narrowed her eyes. "My geologist . . ." She stopped and sucked in her breath, eyes darting around the group.

"Geologist?" Jaks repeated the unfamiliar word.

"Never mind. Um," Meila said. Say too much and it would become clear that the *UWFS Mendhelsson* was doing more than just traveling past their planet. *They'll suspect we were observing them. They'll demand to know why.*

"How do you know so much about them?" Doeg looked at a runestone as though seeing it for the first time.

"Just general knowledge . . ." Meila said. Her eyes shifted quickly. "It's everywhere. The mayatite, that is. Dust particles. Pebbles. Boulders. Mountains of the stuff."

"Mountains!" Shazair interrupted, pausing her polishing to gape at her. "Where? No one has ever found a source that size."

"Beneath the sea," said Meila. Then turning away from the astonished woman, she said, "My hypothesis is that mayatite allows the creation and manipulation of energy out of nothing . . . what you call magic."

"The sea. I told you so," said Shazair, pointing a finger at Doeg.

Doeg continued as though hearing none of the last comments. "So, if you shape and polish the stones and then line them up in a row, they'll store far more magic. And here's the topper, if you stack them tightly together, they'll channel as much power as a master mage."

"If you don't blow us up first," said Shazair.

"Don't mind my wife—she's a killjoy," said Doeg, rolling his eyes.

"*Do* mind my husband—he's a daredevil," the woman replied, squinting at her partner.

"Come see our prototype," said Doeg, as he winked at Shazair fondly.

In the soot-covered chamber, a long metal contraption resembling a ballista with a steel tube but stripped of its limbs stood within an iron frame. Doeg inserted the sourcestone container that he had brought from the workbench into a cradle atop the device. "The full versions will be attached to frigates and shoot fire at attacking ships," he explained.

"Stand back," the master firemage warned. Meila joined the grandmaster and the two younger men behind a chest-high wall at the back of the room.

The Fauconian pointed the tubular end of the weapon at a sooty wall on the opposite side of the chamber and touched the sourcestone pack with his fingers. *Whoosh.* A fierce red flame shot out the front of the weapon.

A back-wave of heat smothered Meila. The fiery tongue scorched the far wall for several seconds.

"That's about half-power. A charged sourcestone pack will reach thirty yards and give about thirty seconds of flame," explained the pyromancer. "More than enough to set an enemy ship afire or burn down a dozen warriors."

Meila screwed up her face. "A flamethrower. Dirty weapon. So imprecise and short-ranged."

Master Doeg crossed his arms and raised his chin, clearly not pleased at her comment.

Don't be so critical, she thought to herself. *I need to prove my worth to them.* "However, I can see how useful it could be . . . at your level of technology," she added pathetically, doing little to repair her initial snub.

"Well, I think it's impressive," said Jaks. "I wouldn't want to be toasted by that."

"The design of the sourcestone pack is your limiting factor." Meila saw an opportunity to improve Doeg's weapon and pointed at the container. "If it follows the same principles as electrical battery cells, as it sounds like it does, I can help you calculate a setup that could double . . . triple the fire power? We'd have to develop a method to accurately measure mayatite power and start with some base calculations."

Doeg nodded his head and agreed enthusiastically. She could see none of them understood much of what she'd said, but they were open-minded. *Not too proud to take advice*, thought Meila.

"Good, good." Mulgrave took charge again. "But before you get ahead of yourself, come see what else we do here." Like an ambassador, he appeared keen to show off their feats, but the calculating look in his eyes betrayed his expectation for a trade that favored his needs.

The runic furnace glowered and roared like a caged beast at the heart of the Academy. Coal-shovelers fed the hungry beast and magesmiths worshipped with a chorus of hammers and anvils at its unholy maw. Blistering heat smothered anyone who dared go near.

Meila stopped as her eyes dried in the heat and sweat beaded her brow.

"Are there always so many workers here?" she asked Mulgrave as they neared the forges around the furnace. Dozens of men and women in leather aprons and leggings glistened with sweat and pounded away at lengths of glowing metal.

"A busy time. The Order of Nightblades put in an order for a dozen more whisperblade swords last week and requisitions from other divisions are coming in fast. There will be war soon. Damn Vors aren't happy with their own country, now they want ours," replied Mulgrave.

Five workshops encircled the runic furnace with a sixth space dedicated to the shovelers feeding the roaring inferno. The grandmaster stopped at the entrance of the closest workshop and nodded to the forgemaster.

The man looked up briefly between strikes of his hammer against a length of glowing metal. Another magesmith held the blade fast with a pair of tongs and was invoking a continuous wave of fire that spread over his bare hands and the steel.

Meila stared open-mouthed. "Why aren't his hands blistering?"

"Mages are not harmed by the magic they invoke, and if the tongs get too hot, he can dampen the heat in the metal. A mage can both produce and negate energy of their type." Mulgrave peered at the blade. "That particular blade has sourcestone dust crushed into the steel and will have a stone in the pommel. The stones can be invoked by anybody with training, even without mage abilities," he said.

"What about other types of magic?" Meila leaned into the workshop but retreated when the forgemaster snapped at her for getting too close. Moisture dampened her forehead, and she loosened her tunic.

"Any magic can be forged into an object. Flaming weapons, grav-balanced greatswords and hammers, blinding shields, and even armor that casts the wearer into shadows. Grandmaster Graywish once made a broadsword that invoked images of a dozen swaying cobras. When you held it, it looked like a handful of giant snakes poised to strike!"

At the next workshop, a handsome, muscular woman, near Mulgrave's age, came out to speak with them. She glistened with sweat, and ash smeared her face. "Mulgrave. What have you here?" She looked curiously at Meila.

"Grandmaster Arolee, meet my ward," Mulgrave said as he introduced the two women. To Meila, he said, "Arolee is the only triple mage in Ascoria."

The woman's gaze remained locked on Meila, and she reached out a hand to touch her face, as though she were a fragile object, but stopped and snatched it back mid-gesture. "You are exquisite. I wish I could cast you."

Meila frowned at the curious comment and responded instead to Mulgrave's statement. "Triple mage?"

Arolee gasped and stared at Meila's mouth with an incredulous look on her face. "Your tones are perfect. I bet you sing like an angel."

Mulgrave replied, "She commands fire, gravity, and sound. The only magics that she doesn't control are light and electricity."

Finally, Arolee snapped out of her reverie and stared into Meila's eyes. "Are you gifted?"

"We don't have magic where I come from."

"No magic. Ridiculous. There's magic everywhere."

"Not where I'm from," repeated Meila.

"I suspect you are gifted, though," persisted the female mage.

Mulgrave coughed and interrupted, "What is this you're working on?" He gazed at a suit of steel plate armor large enough for a horse.

Two of Arolee's assistants were working on the rear part of the armor, but it was the helm that demanded attention: a head cover molded to the face of a snarling demon complete with sharpened teeth, blazing eyes, and pointed horns.

"It's hideous." Mulgrave shook his head.

"Thank you," said Arolee. "It's also rune-forged to be as light and flexible as leather." She shifted her attention to Mulgrave and went to stand beside him.

"Is it horse armor?" Jaks asked as he and Meila moved around to appreciate the other side.

"Warlion armor. The beasts usually only tolerate leather armor, but this suit was commissioned for Pride Queen Kassindle by her rider. It even has a sonomancy runestone in the helm that augments her roar tenfold. Can you imagine a steel-clad warlion bounding toward you, screaming like hellspawn?" Arolee stroked the armor as though the beast were already inside it.

The last stop on their circuit took them from the forges to a fenced-off area of the courtyard. A flat-bottomed boat levitated several yards in the air at the center of the clearing, tethered by ropes to four granite blocks. The boat wobbled midair as Jaks and the rest of their group approached.

"Hazel?" Grandmaster Mulgrave called from the fence line.

The boat dipped backward suddenly, and a chorus of swearing and curses poured out from within. A voice shouted the others to order, and the rest of the vessel tipped down until it leveled off at chest height.

A woman with a head of wild curls and a heart-shaped face peered over the boat's side at the visitors. Three younger mages sat inside, the one in the front admonishing the two at the back.

"Shut up, you three," snapped the older woman, not looking so generous at that moment. "Put her down."

The wooden hull crunched to the dirt, and the mages climbed out. The younger three paced about, stretching their legs. The eldest came to the fence and picked up a clipboard lying there.

"Work in progress." Mulgrave offered a hand to the woman. She waved it away.

"Four gravstones aren't enough. Too vulnerable to incongruences in power. I'm thinking I'll have to double the number."

"Grandmaster Hazeldine's latest project. A reinvented grav-flyer." Mulgrave nodded at the plain-looking boat sitting abandoned.

"Previous flyers were limited by a single gravmancer and a sail," said Hazeldine. "With sourcestones and multiple gravmancers, I can get bigger ships into the air. And with more grav sources, I can propel the vessel in any direction without the need of a sail . . . theoretically. Getting it to work properly is proving more difficult." She pulled a pencil out of her wild hair and marked something on the clipboard.

"How do you coordinate direction?" asked Meila, climbing over the wooden barrier and examining the boat.

Hazeldine frowned. "I shout at them."

Jaks stifled a laugh.

Meila shook her head. "You'll need a better system than that. I could help you with a communication system for your boat. I used to design ships."

Hazeldine nodded approvingly but was interrupted by Mulgrave before she could question Meila.

"Later, later. One thing at a time, lass," said the bald mage. "It's time we sat down and talked about what you can do for me first."

***

Back in the lab, Meila, Jaks, Tavis, and Mulgrave gathered around a workbench next to a tall window. Rain pattered against the glass, creating tiny rivulets of water that dissolved the salt-crust on the outer surface. The sky was dark with storm clouds and the harbor swayed with several fishing boats urgently returning from sea.

"So, where do we start?" Mulgrave opened his hands as though to receive something. "You've seen what we do here. What can you do beyond that?"

"For your era, it's commendable that you can manufacture sheet metal, signaling machines, weavers, and printing presses . . . but disgraceful that you have little knowledge of chemistry, physics, engines, or even steam power." Meila got up and stood behind her chair. "You compensate for some of that with magic." She shrugged. "Maybe that's why those areas are behind." The sourcestones came to mind.

"Chemistry, physics?" said Mulgrave.

"Sciences that I could teach you but that would take years to benefit from. The question really is, what do you want from me?"

"Practical things. Weapons, armor, machines," said Mulgrave, steepling his hands in front of his chin.

"War machines," she said, "a warmonger." She shook her head disapprovingly.

"War is inevitable. In the likelihood that the Vors invade, they'll field an army far larger than ours. If we lose against them . . ." Mulgrave said in a somber voice.

"I get it. I lose too. My fate is caught in yours," Meila said. She stared out the window as though searching for something. Eventually, she sighed, resigning to the most obvious technological advance she could think of, and said a single word.

"Guns."

Meila described and drew diagrams of muskets and

cannons, the most basic of propellant-based weapons she knew of.

"You have the metal-working capability to produce the weapons, but you know nothing about propellants to fire them with," she said.

"Was it a . . . what did you call it . . . a *gun* that you used against the dragons that attacked us in the mountains?" asked Jaks.

Meila continued, talking over the apprentice's question. "Yes, it was a gun, of sorts. Similar idea, except mine used technology that is impossible to even consider making here." She twirled the pencil that she had been drawing with and tapped it on her drawings. "Gunpowder, however, requires only three chemicals. You already have charcoal sitting out there in the courtyard. It shouldn't be hard to source the other two."

"What do these guns do?" asked Mulgrave.

"Simply put, the explosive power of black-powder guns can shoot lead balls at extreme speeds that can penetrate even steel plate armor."

A doubtful look crossed Tavis's face. "Penetrate plate . . . not grav-forged plate." He shook his head. "Explosive. This powder sounds dangerous. Is it safe?"

"There are strict rules that we would have to enforce during manufacture and storage to make it safe," Meila said.

Mulgrave rubbed his hands together and grinned. "Yes, this sounds like just the thing. If it could be reliably used by common soldiers, it could change—"

"It *would* change warfare as you know it," Meila finished. She looked down at her drawings of the muskets and cannons scattered over the table and grimaced as if in pain. "If I ever get back to Earth, I'll be court-martialed for this."

"Where is the gun that you spoke of? That you fought dragons with?" Mulgrave looked at Meila and Jaks.

The pair looked at each other. Jaks replied, "Last I saw, it was taken away with her other possessions when Ranger Cromer arrested her. I assume they were all handed over to the prison."

"I'll see if I can track it down. It may very well still be there." Mulgrave looked back to the drawings scattered over the bench. "In the meantime, how long would it take to start making this gunpowder?"

"If we can find reliable sources for saltpeter and sulfur, we might be able to start mass producing quantities in a year or so."

"A year? We don't have years. The Vors already hound the coast and could invade at any time. The threat is high enough that the king is enacting a province cordon tomorrow," said Mulgrave.

"A province cordon?" asked Meila.

"No one will be able to travel out of a province except with a military permit. First step toward a call to arms. It prevents people from fleeing conscription. I know King Silas, and if he is calling a cordon, he will have strong convictions of an impending invasion."

"That might be so, but we won't be able to create workable guns overnight. It will take time," Meila said. "Time to find the chemicals and materials, time to develop a mass-manufacturing process, and time to perfect them. Ideally, we'd rifle the weapons but that would take even longer." She scribbled numbers on a new piece of paper as she spoke. "Solving the gunpowder recipe might only take a few months. But the whole process, mass gunpowder production *and* a safe weapon manufacture would take at least . . . twelve to twenty months."

She leaned over the table and stared at the bits of paper scrawled with diagrams and numbers.

"Are there other weapons like this that we could make faster?" Mulgrave asked, sounding deflated after his initial excitement at the gun concept.

"Gunpowder would be the easiest and fastest to get up and running. Unless . . ." Her face darkened, and she turned toward the window, tapping her chin. "I have another idea, but I need some time to think. I'll go back to my room for a while."

Mulgrave nodded and directed Tavis to gather up the papers.

Chapter 22

The Letter

Jaks–The Academy of the Arcane

After Meila wandered up the staircase, Mulgrave turned to Jaks. "Before I forget again, a letter came for you late last evening. It's on my desk; go get it if you like."

Jaks hurried after Meila, but by the time he caught up with her, the door to her room was swinging closed.

The letter had his name scrawled on the envelope and lay on the grandmaster's desk under the stuffed cat. He had hoped it was from Karisa, updating him of her experiences and to assure him that she was well; however, the handwriting looked more like Vixhana's messy scribble.

Back in his room, he tore the envelope's seal and unfolded the parchment inside. It read:

Jaks,

> *Karisa is missing. Her company ambushed during a Vor raid on Finstaf coast.*
>
> *One hundred and three of her company are dead. Eight missing.*
>
> *I am back in Dunberrin City on royal protection duty.*
>
> *Will let you know if I hear anything more.*
>
> *Vixhana*

Meila appeared at his door. "What's wrong?"

Jaks had not realized he had called out, and only now heard himself saying, "No," over and over.

"My sister, Karisa . . . the Vors," said Jaks. Then, composing himself, he described the contents of the letter.

Meila replied in a placating tone, "At least she wasn't among the dead. There's a chance she might have run off or hidden somewhere."

"Oh, God, I hope so. It was me who convinced her to join the regular army. If she had stayed as a conscript instead, she would have been doing light duties or training away from the coast. I told her she would be better off as a signaler and then she could resign after just one year . . . what an idiot I am." Jaks leaned against a wall of empty shelves and placed his forehead against an edge.

Meila stepped closer. "It's not your fault—"

"She has been through so much already. She trusted

me. I've already failed her so often, and I pushed her into danger again . . . and now she's gone. It *is* my fault." Jaks thumped a fist against the wall, shaking the shelves.

"I've got to help her. I've got to find her," he continued. "I made an oath to our mother that I would keep her from harm."

"Do you even know where she is?"

"I'll go to where she went missing and start from there."

"Sounds awfully dangerous. You might get captured too, or killed, and then you would be no use to anyone." Meila placed a hand on his shoulder. "Your older sister. Vixhana? It sounds like she is much closer to useful sources of information. There's no point throwing yourself into such an unsafe area with Vors everywhere."

"Yes, I suppose so," said Jaks.

"Until you know where she is, all you can do is prepare."

He turned to face her. "You're right. I need to prepare. I need power . . . magic . . . if I am to help her," Jaks said as he edged past her and then fled downstairs to the burn-room to coax his electromancy into control.

And when he failed yet again, his anger grew. Anger at his erratic magic, his failures to protect Karisa, his sister's captors, and his father's abuses. Unable to contain his frustration, he yelled and hurled himself against the uncaring stone walls of the chamber until his fists were raw, black and bloodied.

He sank to the ground in a crumpled heap and whispered a promise to Karisa, wherever she was: "Magic or no magic, I won't fail you again."

Chapter 23

Balance of Power

Meila–The Academy of the Arcane

How *much power is too much?* pondered Meila. After Jaks rushed out of the library, she welcomed the opportunity to stretch her legs. She kicked off the ill-fitting shoes the Academy had given her and ran barefoot through the hallways of the Academy.

She jogged and weaved through the hallways and stairs, leaving a trail of apprentices, clerks, and mages staring after her in surprise. Fortunately, she was fleet enough to escape anyone's lasting attention.

While she felt a burst of freedom from the running, her thoughts returned to the greater issue that hounded her. If she gave these people centuries of military advancement beyond any other civilization on this planet, would that be too much power? Would it create such an imbalance that the Ascorians would subdue or destroy every other nation? Was this King Silas a tyrant or a diplomat? An Attila or a Solomon? Her brief interactions with him told her little.

Meila's crew had not discovered the cause of this colony's fall of civilization after it had been severed from contact with Earth. If she accelerated their military capability tenfold with advanced weaponry, would it tip them toward another apocalypse of civilization?

Did she care?

What she did care about was providing her captors with enough capability to defend themselves against a superior enemy; if they succumbed, the probability was that she would be killed or made captive by even crueler masters.

A pang of self-pity struck her as she took inventory of her situation: ship destroyed, captured by primitives, impending invasion, her husband dead, and rescue at least a decade away. *Stop feeling sorry for yourself and think.*

After two circuits of the building, she was back in Mulgrave's library and breathing hard; it had been a reasonable effort, considering the month it had taken to recover from her leg injury and the limited exercise she had achieved in the prison cell.

She began a set of calisthenic stretches and considered the powerful weapons that already existed here: illumancers, firemancers, and gravmancers. Adding firearms was not that much of a step beyond.

But what if she could limit the numbers they could

make or use? Enough to defend themselves, but too few to contemplate world-wide dominance.

Even better would be if she could *loan* them a number of weapons.

To her, the answer was obvious now, but it could be a hard sell to get the old man to agree.

That afternoon, Meila found Jaks in his room, bandaging his hands.

He explained he had fallen down some stairs, then changed the topic. "Someone said they saw you running through the halls this morning. Was someone chasing you?" he asked.

"I just needed exercise. They locked me in a cell for a few months, if you remember." She helped him to tie up a bandage, but seeing his ragged knuckles, she looked up with concern. "You haven't been fighting, have you? Not Tavis?"

"No." He would not meet her eyes. "No. I just . . . fell."

She saw his evasion but did not challenge him; she would soon see for herself whether Tavis had injuries, too. "You want to come with me to find the old man? I've got an idea," she said.

Mulgrave and Tavis were in the ground-floor lab at a wide table mulling over blueprints and documents. The younger man had no obvious fight marks, Meila was pleased to note, and when the grandmaster asked Jaks about his bandaged hands, he received the same reply as she had. "Just a fall, Master." He then made a request to the mage. "The letter said my younger sister is missing. No one knows where she is. Could I go see my older sister in the evening?"

"I'm sorry to hear that. By all means—go now, if you want," Mulgrave said.

As Jaks left, Meila said to the grandmaster, "I have something to show you. Follow me." Without waiting for a response, she turned and walked through the lab to the Academy courtyard.

At the escape pod, she waited until Mulgrave and Tavis caught up with her. "What if we could get our hands on working weapons right now?" she said.

She put a hand on the hatch and pulled it open. "There are fractured sections of the *Mendhelsson* that crashed to the planet. It's possible that the wreckage will have weapons and ammunition still onboard." She climbed up onto the pod and slid inside.

"And you know where these sections are?" asked the old man, peering over the lip at her sitting in the one-person capsule.

She turned the panel screen to him.

A map of Ascoria flashed up in front of him, and his eyes grew wide as he absorbed the details.

"Amazing!" He traced a finger over the screen. "That's Ascoria . . . Ellipta . . . Faucony . . . Voros."

"Look at those three red dots. Those are some of the

larger sections of the *Mendhelsson* that broke off and scattered nearby." She pointed at one dot near the middle of Ascoria, one in Voros, and another in the ocean to the south. "There may be weapon lockers in those sections, and if we can get there, I can unlock them and we would have guns. Not just any guns, but darkcore weapons that could easily kill any man or beast walking this planet."

"Which ones have these guns?" Mulgrave asked, still staring at the brilliantly colored screen.

"That, I don't know. There were two weapons lockers on the ship. One fore and one aft." Her memory implant inventoried each locker with two handguns and two rifles, along with twenty magazines. "That section's the closest." She pointed at the red dot at the center of the Ascorian landmass.

"What are the chances of salvaging weapons?"

"Reasonable, I think. To show up on the scanner, the sections would have to be at least one-sixth of the entire hull in size. The hull fracture was mid-ship, so both ends are likely to have remained intact." The suicidal blast, whether or not intentional, had destroyed a central reinforcing beam. Although protected from exterior attack, the ship was not designed to withstand a darkcore event from within.

"And what about those?" Mulgrave asked, pointing at orange dots on the map.

"Escape pods."

"There are other survivors? You should have told us," the mage said sharply.

"No . . . I'm fairly sure I'm the only one alive." Meila repressed the stab of grief brought on by the words. "See. The green dot is me. Either the others have wandered beyond the ten-mile range of their escape pod —which is against Rescue Protocol—or they're dead."

Tavis leaned into the capsule to look at the map. "If we get to those weapons, what's stopping you killing us all and running off?"

"Nothing. Maybe I will." She glared at him, annoyed at the apprentice's distrustful tone, and enjoyed the shocked look he gave in return. After a few seconds, she sighed. "Of course, I wouldn't. I need to be near this pod; it's a beacon for my rescuers to find me— it's my ball and chain. Killing you would not help me."

She grabbed the edges of the hatch opening, forcing the mages back, and pulled herself out with a lithe jump. "I'm not familiar with your modes of transport. How long would it take us to travel to the nearest ship section?" she asked.

"Well, the closest one is in the middle of the roughest terrain in Ascoria: the Jurn Highlands. By horseback, we could get to the foot of the mountains in perhaps a week or two, but navigating the mountains . . . we would need a ranger to guide us. It is dangerous territory." Mulgrave rubbed his chin. "Reputed for impassable mountains, sheer cliffs, and ancient forests. It is largely unmapped. Do you know the area, Tavis?"

The apprentice shook his head. "All I know is, the woodsmen say it's a common place for bands of wildmen and packs of wulverions and dragons. No one goes there but the desperate."

The old man nodded and crossed his arms. "This is no small endeavor you're suggesting. Dangerous, in fact. I would want to know more about these weapons before we think about trying to salvage them, young lady."

Meila laughed at the reference to her age. "I'm twice your age in years. I should be calling you 'young man'." She winked at the bald mage.

Mulgrave and Tavis stared at her, unable to resolve the incongruence of her physical youth and stated age.

She continued, "If you want to know the value of the darkcore weapons, the best way is for you to see its power for yourself. If you track down my handgun, I'll show you what it can do."

Tavis looked up quickly but held back the alarm that shaped on his lips.

"Excellent idea. Let me find out what happened to your possessions. I'd like to witness these wondrous things," said Mulgrave.

She smiled in response. *I like how this man works; he does not waste time.*

That evening, Meila encountered Jaks in the hallway, returning from seeking his older sister. She asked if he had eaten anything that day. He replied he was not hungry, but she ordered him to follow anyway.

In the mess hall, they sat at an empty table, away

from the other diners, with bread and a bowl of fish stew each. Jaks picked at his food, holding his spoon awkwardly with a bandaged hand.

"How did it go? Did you get to see her?" Meila asked, dipping a bread roll into her bowl.

"It was pointless. Vixhana had nothing to add to what was in her letter. I asked her if Karisa might have escaped during the fight and gone into hiding, but it's been over two weeks now, so she thinks Karisa was undoubtedly taken by the raiders." Jaks stirred the stew around his bowl.

"I'm sorry, Jaks. You've done your best. I'm sure you will be the first person she tells if she hears anything new."

She then told Jaks about the crashed ship fragments and her idea for a salvage quest. She asked him if he knew anything about the mountains that harbored the wreckage, but he, too, drew a blank. "At school, it was just a blank area on the maps. Is it worth the trouble going all that way?"

"Remember the first day we met—the handgun I used on the dragons? That was the *least* powerful of the weapons onboard the *Mendhelsson*. It would be worth it."

What she did not tell him was she alone would have implant control over each and every weapon, including ammunition limits, power settings, and, most importantly of all, who could use them and for how long.

She would loan them weapons that could alter the course of battle, but only under the tightest of controls.

The next day, as Meila walked through the city, returning to the royal prison with Mulgrave and Jaks to seek the return of her possessions, she encountered a much-changed city to that of a few days before.

A somber mood hung over the crowds of people who all seemed on urgent business. In the market district, eyes followed her with whispers and pointed fingers—not curious this time, but suspicious. A group of urchins waved pretend swords and threw pebbles at her but gave flight when she boomed at them. Mobs jostled in the marketplace over food and supplies, with occasional scuffles breaking out in stalls and shops. Fresh posters depicting soldiers standing on duty were pasted to notice boards and walls of buildings; notices proclaiming the king's will for a province cordon. Dunberrin prepared for war.

At the prison, the Prison Magistrate admitted them immediately and greeted the mage with obsequious aplomb. "Welcome, Grandmaster. What an honor to see you again," he said as he bowed. "I see our lovely ward is doing well." His words acknowledged her, but his weasel eyes did not deviate from the mage.

After an exchange of pleasantries, Mulgrave requested Meila's possessions from the prison storage and the magistrate flicked his fingers at a guard to retrieve her items. While they waited a tedious quarter hour, the magistrate drew a reluctant Mulgrave into a conversation to whine about the prison's finances.

"Please accept this small donation to your facility," the mage said eventually and reached into his money pouch to place a gold coin on the man's polished desk.

The magistrate beamed and slid the coin into a drawer with a deft hand.

As they exited the prison, Meila remarked, "Greedy man. Is that the correct term?"

"You wouldn't believe how much that one slithers," Mulgrave replied. "Hopefully, he hasn't stolen and sold off what we are after." He looked at the prison sack that Jaks had accepted from the guard as they left.

An hour later, in Mulgrave's library, Jaks dumped the contents of the sack onto the central table.

Meila whooped in glee when she saw familiar objects in the pile. She pushed aside the bulkiest items: boxes of ration bars, silver insulation blanket, backpack with heat cells, medikit, and her old jumpsuit.

Picking up her handgun from the remaining small items, her implants confirmed that the black synthmetal weapon was still operational and had ninety-seven charges left in the energy cell. She checked both of the trigger locks, the first, a toggle above the grip, and the second, an internal lock activated by the implant in her forebrain through electrical impulses through her palm.

Satisfied, she looked up to see Jaks and Mulgrave

staring at the gun. She flipped it around to offer it to the grandmaster. "Take it. It's locked."

Mulgrave cautiously took the gun, weighed it, felt the texture of the grip and barrel, looked down the muzzle, and then examined the details of the trigger in the sunlight. "Not much to it. Is this all?"

"Let me show you what it can do. We'll need somewhere safe to use it," she said.

"The battlements. Barely anyone goes up there, and if we stay away from the dragon nest, they won't bother us," Jaks said, and then led them through the hallways to a spiral staircase leading up to the top of the Academy.

The roof was a wide stone walkway surrounding a huge bronze dome. The chimney of the runic furnace pierced the center and spat a column of smoke into the sky. Merlons and embrasures ran along the top of the outer walls, and thin towers crowned each of the four corners of the building.

Several blue dragons perched along the battlements while a pair of the hawk-sized creatures curled around the top of the furthest tower. Long necks sinuated as they tracked the appearance of humans in their territory.

"I could clear some of those pests out." Meila gestured at the blues, four of which took to the air as she watched, diving from the wall and then swooping long, tapered wings until they circled the furnace above.

"No, don't do that. Master Cranbrook treats them like pets. He throws them leftovers from the kitchens.

They're fairly harmless and keep the roof from being infested with filthy gulls," Mulgrave said.

"The ones in the mountains weren't harmless. But, it's your choice." Meila turned to gaze out beyond the battlements. To the north, the ocean stretched toward a thin line of clouds as a pair of warships carved the sea at full sail below. To the east and west, cliffs and stony beaches undulated along a craggy, gray coastline. To the south, a vista of rooftops was nobbled with chimneys and tall buildings, and in the center of the city, the triple peaks of the Royal Palace, the cathedral, and the army's main signaling tower—resembling a giant lighthouse— triumphed over the cityscape. She wished Anton were here to share the beautiful sight; it was a rare one to find on any planet of the United Worlds.

"Could you hit one of those gulls?" said Jaks, pointing at three gray and white gulls sitting sixty yards away at the end of the Academy's disused wharf.

The range would be an easy shot for her, but even so, she rested the butt on the battlement and magnified her right lens implant to train the gun sight onto the closest bird. As the small red dot hovered over the white of the bird's midsection, she paused her breathing and gently squeezed the trigger.

A capsule of darkcore matter energized and transformed a metal pellet into molten plasma.

The handgun emitted a barely audible hiss as the weapon spat the plasma out of its barrel.

The gull exploded into a cloud of feathers. Flesh

and bone splattered the wharf. The water behind the bird erupted into a plume of water and steam.

Jaks and Mulgrave gasped in synchrony and leaned over the embrasure to get a better look at the remains.

The younger man slapped the stone and laughed. "Not even enough left for the dragons to scavenge!"

"What form of magic is this?" Mulgrave asked, staring at the handgun greedily.

"Not magic . . . science," replied Meila.

"May I try it?" Mulgrave nodded like a little boy eager for a new toy.

She had known he would ask, and although her professionalism screamed at her not to allow an untrained civilian to handle the weapon, she briefly touched the grandmaster's arm to read his neuronal signature, then signaled her implant to unlock the weapon to him.

"Careful. Don't point it at anything you don't intend to kill." Her nerves settled once she had Mulgrave holding the pistol properly with both hands and pointed at the water below.

"Use your thumb to slide off the lock. Now, slowly squeeze the trigger to shoot."

The mage followed her instructions, and the weapon hissed again; the shot created another plume of water in the distance. She could see he was breathing rapidly and told him to slow his breathing before his next shot.

Wanting a live target this time, the mage aimed at a

seagull on the edge of the wharf below and squeezed off another shot. Miss. Too low. The tip of seaweed- and algae-covered wharf exploded in a ball of a fire. A loud boom startled nearby wildlife—birds and dragons leapt to the air and scattered. Fragments of rock flew through the air and splashed far out in the harbor. The end of the wharf fractured and sloughed into the sea, leaving a jagged ramp of freshly revealed stone.

"Ahh . . . Hazeldine will be mad," said Mulgrave. "But dog's balls, that is power!" he added, grinning. "Several blasts with this could bring down a castle gate in no time. How many of these are there? With enough of these, our armies could repel the Voros with ease."

"There are four per locker. But with limited ammunition, they would need to be used sparingly."

"They would be a stopgap until we could start mass producing the gunpowder weapons you spoke of earlier?" He toggled the trigger lock and hefted the weapon again.

"Yes. But only if we find all the chemicals we need for the gunpowder," Meila said, but kept her deeper thoughts to herself.

I'll make sure we don't find them . . . Just a few darkcore weapons should be enough to neutralize the invaders and keep the peace until I can get off this planet.

Chapter 24

The Salvage Mission

Jaks—Royal Palace of King Silas, Ascoria

Jaks was running out of time. The king's cordon on the province borders was a tightening noose, threatening to end his clerk job at the Academy and thrust him toward a pointless death in a conscript battalion. He couldn't go into the army, he had an oath to keep, he had to rescue Karisa.

Despite the flurry of activity over the past couple of days, following Grandmaster Mulgrave's decision to mount a salvage expedition to the wreckage of Meila's starship, he fretted over his personal dilemma: his magic was a dead end, so if he couldn't be the mage's apprentice, how else could he stay off the front lines?

A nudge in his ribs interrupted his thoughts.

"Here comes the herald. It's our turn. Get yourself together," Meila said as she smoothed the sleeves of her tunic and picked up her backpack.

The two of them, along with Mulgrave and Tavis,

were seated outside the Royal Court waiting to see the king. They needed a permit to cross the province cordon to pursue their quest.

Jaks hoped the herald would be Minto. It felt like a long time since he had seen his jovial friend.

Unfortunately, the red-capped official who called them out from the other petitioners was a middle-aged woman with a no-nonsense expression.

Expecting a majestic throne room, Jaks was surprised to enter an austere chamber plainly furnished with a row of chairs facing a long oak table. King Silas, adorned with a purple cloak and his gold monarch's collar, sat behind the table, talking with a clerk to his left. *Maybe I could get a clerk's job with the king? That would be important enough to keep me out of re-conscription.*

Armored sentries stood at each corner of the room, and Vixhana—fully armed and in nightwraiths' black armor—stood with crossed arms behind the king. She nodded at Jaks when they made eye contact, but her face stayed as hard and expressionless as a rock. Another nightwraith—older, male, and similarly battle-ready—stood to the side of the king's table and studied them as they approached.

A low growl sounded to Jaks's right—a sharp-snouted hound with bared teeth glared at him from the side of the chamber. The dog's handler pulled on a leash, and the animal sat back on its haunches but continued to menace Jaks with its eyes.

The silver-haired king looked up, over the maps and letters spread out in front of him, and smiled as the herald announced them.

"Mulgrave, my friend, please sit. All sit," Silas said. The clerk slid a document in front of him. "My apologies that I was not able to see you yesterday. As you can see, many call on the royal wax—and the situation with Voros becomes graver each day. I grieve for peace. Perhaps you have an invocation to summon it back?" The king grimaced, despite his joke.

"Sorry, my lord. If only I could. What news of the coast?" Mulgrave sat in the chair closest to the king.

"Five major raids on Finstaf over the past few weeks, each pushing further inland. The damned Vors appear to be searching for a beachhead." Silas looked down at a map for a moment and then continued, "Although I've reinforced the coast as much as I can, my generals predict a full-scale invasion within weeks. I will make a call to arms in the coming days."

Jaks tensed and his skin prickled at the king's mention of a call to arms.

"And ships?" Mulgrave asked.

"They outnumber our galleys and frigates, particularly after a heavy engagement some three weeks ago. Our navy still barricades the Gulf of Irin and the northwest tip of Ascoria, with the help of the Fauconians. But elsewhere, the Vors have free rein at sea."

"Can we count on the Pact Countries to send soldiers?"

"Strock promised troops, but they will not formally join an alliance. Faucony has promised more ships. But, Nera Boa has flatly refused." The king opened his palms to the air.

Mulgrave leaned forward on his chair. "My lord. It may please you that we might secure artifacts to greatly assist a war effort. May I show you something?"

He placed a cloth bundle onto the oak table and peeled back the layers to reveal the darkcore handgun.

They all stared at the alien object. King Silas and the clerk leaned forward with puzzled expressions. The two nightwraith soldiers looked on with the slightest of frowns.

"My ward brought this with her from her . . . planet," Mulgrave said, still grappling with the new concept. "Small as it may be, it is the most powerful weapon I have ever seen." He then went on to extol the destructive power of the gun with graphic descriptions of the dismembered seagull and the fractured wharf and then offered to demonstrate the weapon.

In the royal courtyard, a pole used for sword drills was mounted with a suit of steel plate armor. The better shot, Meila, received the gun from Mulgrave, but concerned over the confined area, she stood on the marble steps overlooking the courtyard to fire from.

Once the courtyard had been cleared of exercising

guards and palace staff, she took a two-handed grip on the handgun, aimed, counted down, and fired.

The back of the mannequin exploded with a spray of molten steel and incinerated splinters. Several paces behind it, the ground erupted, throwing up dust and stone. What little was left of the armor spun down the length of the courtyard.

The crack of exploding wood and stone, the scrape of metal, and the pitter-patter of falling fragments resounded in their ears for a moment until the area settled into silence.

In the aftermath, pieces of mangled armor lay strewn about the courtyard, with just a splintered stump of the wooden pole remaining.

None of the guards or administrators seemed alarmed that a foreigner had destroyed a suit of heavy armor only yards away from their king. The only thing that registered on their faces was shock.

"Bravo!" The king slapped a hand onto Mulgrave's back. "Spectacular. Can you forge more of these things?"

"No, unfortunately. They are forged back on her homeworld. But we know where we might salvage more of these weapons." The grandmaster looked at Meila approaching, the handgun sitting in the hoop of her belt. "As you saw at the Academy, her technology surpasses ours beyond imagination. I believe that with these weapons, we could repel any invasion force the Vors throw at us."

King Silas nodded. "Yes, yes, you must retrieve them. From where?"

"Damaged parts of her ship are scattered around the lands and may yield more of them. All we need, my lord, is free passage through the province borders," Mulgrave said.

"Of course. I'll have something drawn up. What are your plans?" Silas replied and directed them back to the audience chamber to continue their conversation.

Back at the oak table, the grandmaster and the king bent over a map as the mage traced a stubby finger over their planned route.

"Just the three of you?" Silas turned a critical eye over Tavis and Jaks in the row of seats. "You, my friend, can handle yourself—but these two lads are a bit green."

"I would take my ward too. I need her to access the weapons, as they may be locked away; also, she can identify any other salvage that might be of use."

"She is very . . . slight." The silver-headed king looked at Meila's svelte figure. "The Jurn Highlands are treacherous. You need more protection." He turned to Vixhana behind him and exchanged several words with her.

She nodded and returned to her position.

"The captain here will travel with you—she is a very capable warrior." The king gestured at Vixhana, who inclined her head to Mulgrave. "And you will need a ranger through those mountains . . ." He conferred with Vixhana again, then said, "We'll send a master to the

Academy to accompany you. And, if you need anything else, let my quartermaster know."

Jaks smiled at the thought of Vixhana joining them on the salvage quest. He caught her eye again and received a wink.

A letter was signed by the king naming Mulgrave a Royal Emissary and granting him and his party ease of passage through the kingdom and special powers to request aid from any Ascorian forces they should meet.

Taking advantage of his new privileges, they entered the Royal Stables and flashed the letter at the stable master to requisition four palfreys and a pack mule—the most placid beasts available, knowing that none of them were confident riders except for himself.

Meila had never even seen a live horse before, and although she was quick for the challenge, she rode out of the stables lying flat over the saddle, clutching at the horse's bridle with white knuckles and gritting her teeth.

In the Academy courtyard the following day, they packed food rations and supplies into saddlebags, readying them to be loaded for whenever their ranger and nightwraith companions arrived.

It was while Tavis crammed a rope into a pack that he expressed his displeasure at the mission. He spoke to Mulgrave, who was rearranging some hardtack in a saddlebag. "Master. Perhaps my skills could be better used staying here in the Academy and helping one of the others . . . maybe Master Doeg with his work?" said the apprentice. "Traveling and the outdoors are not my strong point . . ." He tucked back his hair behind large ears and looked up uncertainly at the grandmaster.

"Have no doubt, you will learn far more afield than crammed up here in this old keep. To be my apprentice requires more than forging and smithing—you didn't think your entire apprenticeship would have you stuffed up inside of here, did you?"

Tavis opened his mouth and closed it, then opened it again. "I just thought . . ."

"If I'm dragging my clerk along, you're coming too." Mulgrave laughed and returned to his task of packing hardtack into the saddlebag. A moment later, he said in a serious voice, "It will do you both some good. Maybe the two of you will learn to get along better."

Jaks looked up in alarm from the sack of dried apples he was holding and wondered how the mage knew of the conflict between Tavis and himself. He exchanged a look with Tavis; they both looked away awkwardly and hurried back to their tasks.

That afternoon, Mulgrave outfitted them from the Academy armory where weapons and bits of armor from the workshops were stored. Each piece was unique and often the result of magesmith experiments. Although the most valuable breastplates, helms, swords, and axes awaited distribution to the king's champions or generals,

Jaks, Tavis, and Meila were free to arm themselves with whatever else they wanted.

Hanging from the wall, Jaks found a set of riding leathers that were as flexible as cloth but as strong as steel, and he grinned when he pulled out, from under a jumbled pile, a round, steel shield with a lightning bolt emblazoned on the front. A barrel of swords gave up an intricately engraved shortsword, and Mulgrave handed him a light crossbow that could reload itself from a magazine of bolts with the single pull of a cocking-lever.

Feeling suitably warrior-like, Jaks helped Meila carry the arsenal of knives that she was acquiring. She had a wicked gleam to her face that he had never seen before as she examined dozens of knives and daggers spread across a bench from which she selected a couple more. There had been no armor small enough for her diminutive form, so she had settled for a short riding cloak that Mulgrave had stabbed with a dagger, demonstrating it to be as tough as chainmail. "Interwoven layers of steelinium alloy and wool," he'd explained. And, of course, she had her darkcore handgun.

Mulgrave pointed out his own midnight-blue plate armor with runestones encrusted in the greaves of both arms. He claimed to have forged the suit decades ago and then campaigned in it during the Unifying Wars as one of King Silas's battlemages. His weapon was a flanged mace with a red runestone pommel.

Tavis, however, was in a fit of indecision. Between

choices of armor ranging from a suit of full plate through to a mishmash of leggings, pauldrons, greaves, breastplates, and helms, whatever he tried always seemed better than the last.

After three hours, they abandoned him to his buffet of armor and descended to the mess hall for actual food.

The next morning, Jaks waited for Vixhana and the ranger to arrive. He sat on the wall of the land bridge, tapping his fingers on the sandstone blocks, excited about the salvage mission. In his mind, a quest to recover powerful artifacts was the stuff of dreams, or lived in legends and storybooks populated with mighty heroes. From his conscription experience, however, he knew the reality would be far less romantic and glorious: endless miles of boredom and trudging through wind and rain, over steep mountains and thick forests, and constant paranoia about snakes, wyverns, wolves, and other nasties. But, despite his worries, he took comfort that he was going in the company of a grandmaster battlemage, a nightwraith, and a ranger.

Jaks rose to his feet expectantly as two riders approached. The nearest sat atop a black courser and wore a traveling cape over black leather, while a bastard sword swung at the hip. Behind the rider, the haft of a massive axe rose like a flagpole, its double blades scabbarded in a riding holster attached to the horse. Jaks beamed at the sight of his sister.

Her companion rode a brown courser and held a recurve bow across his lap. Quivers of arrows were bundled into saddle bags, fletched ends sticking out like porcupine spines. The man was smaller than Vixhana but carried an air of immutable self-confidence, and together with his pointed beard, Jaks instantly recognized someone he had hoped never to see again— Ranger Cromer, his old survival instructor.

"Greetings, little brother," Vixhana said as she stopped and dismounted at the gates. In her nightwraith armor, she looked imposing; if it were not for the shape of her chest armor, she would be easily mistaken for a clean-shaven yet handsome man. "Set to go?" she said.

"Shouldn't be long. Let's go in," Jaks replied and glanced nervously at the ranger, who followed on his horse and stared blankly ahead. Perhaps he'd forgotten Jaks and his dismal failures during survival training?

In the courtyard, Mulgrave tugged the bridle straps on his horse and then popped an apple half into the eager animal's mouth and munched on the rest. As Jaks brought in Vixhana and Cromer, the mage welcomed them warmly and then pointed out the rest of their traveling party.

Vixhana nodded politely at Meila and then frowned at Tavis, who was wearing a mishmash of armor pieces and resembled a dress-up doll with push-on, pull-off parts.

"It's all excellent armor," Tavis said to her and showed off a pair of white leather gloves.

The ranger slid off his horse and nodded an acknowledgement to Mulgrave. "Grandmaster, what route do you favor?" he then asked, slipping off worn riding gloves.

Jaks tried to read the man's expression but couldn't tell the ranger's normal impassive state from resentment or even annoyance. *One thing for sure, he can't be happy that I'm coming along,* thought Jaks. He then straightened his shoulders, annoyed at himself. *I don't need to prove anything to him, he's not my instructor anymore.*

A bench was cleared, and the ranger laid out a map. Their route would be direct and simple. Across the riverplains of Dunberrin and then south through the province of Jurn to the Highlands. Paved roads until Jurn, from where they would skirt the fringes of a grassland sea, wandered by herds of antelope, wild horses, and longhorns, and prowled by lions and wolves. A dirt road would take them down this border between the two provinces. Although they might glimpse inhabited ranches of cattle herders in the northern region of Jurn, there would be naught but wildlands further south. It was from there on that Jaks expected they would be most thankful for the extra protection of Vixhana and the ranger.

To traverse the lowland expanse and reach the central Highlands, if undisturbed, could take a little over a week. But how long it would take them to find the ship wreckage in the uncharted area—rumored to be inhabited by exiled tribes of savages and dragons that curled around the tips of frozen mountains—depended on the ranger's skill to lead them through unknown perils to where Meila had marked the wreckage of her ship.

Jaks shivered, both excited and anxious. If they returned alive from this madcap quest, with darkcore weapons, they would return as heroes. But even with his new armor and weapons, he didn't feel the least bit heroic.

At least Vixhana was here. She could handle anything.

Chapter 25

Rivertown

They rode out of Dunberrin in the late morning, a party of three war veterans, two novices, and a foreigner.

The Grand Avenue led out of the city and became the southern road as it cut through a patchwork of farmlands and cottages. Gray mountains in the distant south painted the horizon. Clear autumn skies promised a decent day for riding.

Jaks sat atop his brown and black palfrey, a gentle mare who sometimes fretted in the city streets but in the open roads calmed easily as long as he used a light touch with his reins.

Ranger Cromer led the group, followed by Mulgrave, and then Jaks and Meila. Behind them, Tavis rode a brown palfrey and led a pack mule laden with tents and supplies. Vixhana brought up the rear of the party.

Jaks wanted to talk with his sister, but at the moment, he coached Meila in horse-riding and some finer points of controlling her gelding with the reins and her knees. After a few hours, she had relaxed enough to stop grabbing at the saddle horn whenever she felt unbalanced and shifted her weight on her feet instead.

"I could see myself enjoying horse-riding . . . ask me again in a couple of weeks," said Meila, "but my thighs are killing me right now." Despite her complaints, her riding had progressed within hours beyond what Jaks had taken weeks to develop as a youngster.

"You're lucky you're small. It's worse for tall people."

Around midafternoon, a wind blew in from the east and brought with it high clouds. Further south, a thick gray layer capped the mountain range to the south, heralding rain in those distant parts.

Meila rode confidently now—as long as she stayed in a straight line—and she gestured at a paddock of sheep. "This countryside is incredible. I've never traveled through anywhere with so much open land that animals can walk freely and eat grass out of the ground," she said to Jaks.

"Your land must be tiny." He laughed at her wide-eyed amazement at the unremarkable farmlands spanned out from both sides of the road.

"The opposite, actually. Earth Prime has greater land mass than this planet, but with so many people living there, there is no space for pastures and fields like this. They manufacture most of our food on other planets because agricultural land is so scarce."

"Sounds awful. I wouldn't want to live somewhere like that," said Jaks.

She went silent and returned to gazing at the fields. "Butterflies . . ." she said quietly.

With Meila losing interest in talking, Jaks slowed his horse with a tug on the reins—ignoring Tavis as he plodded by—and pulled alongside his sister at the rear of the group.

Vixhana leaned her massive arms on the pommel of her saddle with the reins held loose in her fingers. "Your friend is a natural rider. I'm surprised. She hasn't the legs for it," she said, thrusting her chin toward Meila. Directing her eyes at Jaks, she continued, "You spend a lot of time with her. She is nice to look at."

"That's not why I—"

"Sure, it is," she said and laughed as a flush crept across Jaks's cheeks.

"She's new here and doesn't know our ways. So, I'm helping her," said Jaks defensively. "She's the grandmaster's ward. He told me to guard her."

"Remember your loyalties, brother—country before heart. I could have killed you the other day for allowing her to handle that weapon so close to the king. What if she had been an assassin?" Her face frosted for a second.

"But she wasn't," said Jaks weakly, only now seeing the danger to the king had she been false with her motives. He consoled himself that the grandmaster had also trusted her enough to support the demonstration.

"Be careful with her. She may not be all that she seems. You must tell me if she makes any plans, okay?"

"Plans?"

Vix looked at him closely, as though talking to a child. "Escape, run away, that sort of thing."

He had not seriously considered that Meila would think of running away, but now that he thought on it, he realized he knew very little about what she wanted or desired. "I don't think she would. She said she has to stay near her pod for her people to find her." Could she be lying? His heart told him no, but his head warned him otherwise. "I'll tell you if she says anything strange."

They continued in silence, following the ranger at a turnfork, and then east for several more miles.

Jaks summoned the courage to ask his sister a question. The reason he had dropped back to see her in the first place. "Do you hate him?" he asked.

"Who?"

"Father." He rubbed at the stump of his missing finger. "I want to hate him . . . I need to hate him."

"What are you talking about?" Vixhana frowned at him.

"The grandmaster said I should talk to someone about the past. He thinks my unresolved issues are holding back my electromancy powers."

"I don't think I'm the best person to talk to about

that." Vix looked uncomfortable and shifted in her saddle, staring up the road. "I don't . . . do feelings."

A few minutes passed and then he asked again, "But, do you hate him?"

She looked at him squarely. "Do I hate him . . . Before you or Karisa were born, it was only mother and me. For ten years, I had her all to myself. Do I love her as much as you did? Do I miss her as much as you do?" Her eyes misted.

Jaks was shocked. It was the first time Jaks had ever seen his sister show any sadness, but then it flipped to anger.

"Of course, I hate him for hurting her. Of course, I hate him for molesting Karisa. I wish I could snap his filthy neck in my hands. I should have tried when I had the chance . . ."

Without warning, Vixhana stalled her horse to take up the rear and distanced herself from Jaks. Her face was granite and she sat upright, as stiff as a statue. He had picked at a scab covering his sister's emotions. She didn't approve.

She, too, had not dealt well with the past and obviously harbored bitter anger toward their father.

However, knowing that did not help Jaks with his torment about the same issues. He thought he wanted the anger that Vixhana had, but instead, he was mired in grief, guilt, and fear.

Later that afternoon, they rode into a picturesque riverside town nestled on the border of the river plains. White-washed cottages bordered with black beams were set back from the paved road by stone boundaries, apple trees, and gardens ablaze with summer yellows, blues, and reds. Bees hummed from flower to flower and several children, shouldering school satchels, returned home from school. An affluent township—inhabited by ancestors of the original gold-panners—was almost as cultured and wealthy as the Capital. However, unlike Dunberrin, the locals showed none of the anxiety and wariness that their big-city cousins had recently acquired.

The town center yielded several inns and shops, with most of the activity gathered around a few food and drinking establishments.

A group of local young men on the side of the road tumbled toward the closest inn, initially loud and jovial, but then quiet when they spotted the new arrivals. They stopped in their tracks and watched Ranger Cromer lead the others past them. A red-haired youth bowed his head toward Mulgrave, then stared at Meila—who, in response, pulled the hood of her cape over her head.

The ranger stopped at a traveler's stable and negotiated with the elderly stablemaster to attend and secure their horses and mule for the night.

The Drover's Inn, nearby, was a two-story stone building with a tiled roof and covered stairs running up the outside. The ground-floor tavern door stood open with a steady flow of locals going in and out. Wafts of ale, fresh bread, and roasting meat assaulted Jaks's nostrils as he followed the ranger inside. There was a brief lull in conversation amongst the bar patrons as the newcomers entered. A troubadour, however, playing in the corner kept up his strum and song.

A pudgy man in a beer-stained apron waddled up and bowed to the grandmaster. "Af'ernoon, m' lord. Will you be seeking lodgings and fare for the night?"

After agreeing to terms, the grandmaster and Tavis retreated upstairs to their rooms, with a serving boy running up some bread and stew soon after. Ranger Cromer joined a group of woodsmen who recognized him and called him over to a table on the other side of the tavern. Jaks and the two women huddled around a table by the wall and ordered a leg of roast beef, carrots, and mash.

As they waited, Meila quirked an eyebrow at Vixhana. "Jaks has told me a lot about you. You're some sort of elite warrior?"

Vixhana glanced at Jaks and then turned toward the dark-haired woman. "I've been in the nightwraiths since I finished conscription."

"King's personal guard?"

"No, not typically. But in wartime, we rotate royal protection duty with our regular duties."

"What do you usually do?" Meila leaned in.

"We observe the enemy and infiltrate behind lines

to ambush or take out important targets," Vix replied in a bland tone.

Jaks, eager to impress with his knowledge, added, "The Order of Nightwraiths started two centuries ago, after Kilka Entme used illumancy to take the guise of an enemy soldier, then slipped into the Elliptan camp and assassinated Warlord Ponti—ending the Battle of Bays. After she escaped, she gathered other illumancers and trained them as mercenaries to use stealth and camouflage in battle. Then decades later, the Order vowed to the king and have remained loyal ever since, mercenaries no longer."

"Quite so," Vixhana said, but keen to change the subject, directed her attention back to Meila. "And what is your purpose, where do you come from?"

Before Meila could reply, a serving girl with a hefty bosom glided up with plates and a platter of food and slid them onto their table wordlessly.

Vixhana grabbed a plate, spilling juices as she did.

As the young woman, he guessed of similar age to him, turned to leave, she laid an arm across Jaks's back and slid her hand along his shoulders. He looked up into her face and was captured by smoldering eyes full of invitation. She sauntered away across the tavern, leaving him hot under his leather armor and cape.

Jaks's attention snapped back to the table as Meila replied to Vixhana. Neither seemed to have noticed the serving girl's flirtation.

"I used to design and build engines for starships—

but I got bored and wanted to fly them as well. Joined the navy and made my way up to ship commander," said Meila.

"It must be amazing to fly," said Jaks, interrupting her as his imagination took flight.

"Exhilarating. Is that the word?" She stabbed a carrot on her plate and then continued, "You feel like you can go anywhere and do anything. The ground pulls away beneath you. People and buildings become tiny, but the land expands below you like a canvas. When you rise through the clouds, the world turns into a white blanket, leaving just you and the sun. And, when you reach space itself, you forget your worries and want to disappear into it forever . . ." Meila's eyes glazed over. A few seconds later, she stared at the carrot and bit into the vegetable.

Vixhana stared at her. "And anyone can fly on your world?"

"Not anyone can fly starships. But skimmers are everywhere. You can fly anywhere on a planet if you have one."

"Did you have one?"

She nodded and stabbed a chunk of steak.

"You must miss your home; it sounds incredible," Jaks said.

"The only thing I miss is my daughter." She looked away briefly before continuing. "But other than her, I don't miss Earth—I certainly don't miss the crowds or the pollution."

"Why are you so keen to be rescued, then?" Vixhana asked, pushing away her empty plate and wiping her mouth.

Meila raised her eyebrows and sat back, frowning, before she responded, "I have no place here. I have no one. But most of all, I have a duty to uphold." The words sounded forced, but once out, she looked satisfied with her claim.

"Duty is important." Vixhana nodded appreciatively.

"Despite how much I hate the issues back on Earth, I have a vow to assist my homeworld."

Disturbed by the idea of Meila leaving, Jaks spoke up. "But if you stayed with us, you could find work here —you're very clever—and could have another family."

Meila laughed. "Maybe." She looked at him with a glint in her eyes. "If I ever get released. Although I'm not locked in a prison cell, I'm not completely free either."

The serving girl returned and cleared away their plates, but this time, she gave Jaks no further attention. He was relieved, as he did not want to field awkward remarks or comments from his stern sister, or Meila, about romantic liaisons with a serving girl, or any other girl, for that matter. In truth, he was shy with girls and probably would have embarrassed himself with her, fumbling as she laughed at his inexpert hands.

Their meal finished and at an hour past dusk,

Vixhana announced she was having an early night and went upstairs to retire for the day.

Alone with Meila, Jaks noticed two men staring at them.

The first stood by a wooden column at the side of the room. Bald and clean-shaven, he dressed in riding leathers and had a scabbard at his side. The second, a short and stocky man, leaned against the wall.

Jaks glanced at them again. *Yes, they are definitely staring. Probably leering at Meila.* He glared at them as he'd seen Vixhana do.

The two men turned away.

Jaks felt a chill run down his spine and felt an undeniable desire to escape the room.

"Want to see the river? They pan gold from it," he said to Meila, keeping a sideways watch on the two men —but they seemed to have lost interest and spoke softly to one another.

Jaks and Meila stood and walked across the tavern toward the outside door.

A voice called out. "That one?"

A sharp-faced man with a crooked nose slid off a barstool from around a bench of several locals. He looked like a forester, one of the unkempt men who eked a living from hunting wild animals to sell as meat and furs.

Ranger Cromer sat with them, staring at Jaks, but made no motion other than to swig his tankard of ale.

"Wan' a dance, pretty boy?" slurred the man, his

breath reeking of alcohol and rot. Slack-faced, he opened his arms to Jaks. "Come on, come on." He wrapped the tall youth in a crude hug and started to sway, rubbing his crotch against Jaks's leg.

Rough hands pressing against his backside and the stench of the man's wiry hair pressed into his face. Laughter erupted around him and everyone in the entire tavern looked on as Jaks was pawed by the drunk man.

He pushed the man away in revulsion, but the hands of the slobbering man came back at him grasping like leeches.

Suddenly, the drunk was twisted sideways with his right arm wrenched behind his back. The man groaned, and his face distorted in pain. Meila stood behind him, contorting his arm, and with a tug, she threw him to the floor.

She stood over him and kicked him once in the belly, causing him to double up and retch.

The onlookers clapped and pounded their mugs against tabletops in applause. The evening's entertainment had started out well by their accounts. The troubadour continued strumming his lute and sang.

Jaks stormed out of the tavern into the dark with his head low and buttocks stinging from the pinches and gropes.

He followed the main street until he got to a bridge. Wanting to hide from everyone, he stumbled down to the riverbank and trod along the side of the river over rounded stones and patches of grass. Soon, the bridge and the lights of the town were distant. Stopping, he sat on an uprooted tree trunk and stared out over the river. Even with a full moon, the other side was barely visible, but with the mood he was in, he didn't care about anything but the solitude.

Minutes later, he heard rustling from the bushes above him, and Meila angled down the incline toward him. She sat down on the tree trunk with him.

Jaks picked up a stone and splashed it into the river. He felt humiliated and didn't feel like company—especially with someone who had observed his embarrassment and rescued him from it as though he couldn't do so himself.

They sat listening to the river burbling past and harmonizing with nightsongs of crickets nearby.

"I can't count the times I've been groped," said Meila. "The first few times, I was embarrassed and did nothing either . . . but now if anyone touches me like that, they end up regretting it." She bent down to flick a stone out into the water. "Don't beat yourself up about it."

Several more minutes passed by, then Jaks replied, "Thanks for helping me. But I can stand up for myself. I was about to knock him down." He found another stone and ran his fingers over its polished surface. "But perhaps you could teach me that arm-hold? They didn't teach us things like that in conscription training."

"Sure. In the daylight, though."

Jaks relaxed, and he started to enjoy being with a beautiful woman on a secluded riverbank. He sensed her warmth beside him. *What would she do if I took her hand or put an arm around her? Would she wring my arm like she did the forester?*

Meila, instead, changed the topic. "How are your mage exercises going?"

It took him a few moments to realize she inquired about his magic practice. He had all but abandoned his efforts since he last failed in his attempt to invoke magic. He had bashed his knuckles bloody in frustration.

"Haven't had much time to do them. Been busy the last few days." He rubbed his hands. Although they were not bandaged any longer, they were still scabbed and hurt when he clenched a fist.

"To be honest, I've about given up on it all . . . I can't get it to work." Jaks dropped the stone to his feet. "I'm running out of time and there's no point continuing the exercises—"

"Running out of time?"

"When the king makes a call to arms, I'll be drafted back into the army." He pulled his collar against the cold. "I need to find a job where I can support the war cause but without having to carry a spear . . . I'm not a good soldier. Vix got all that."

"What choices do you have? I thought you wanted to be an apprentice?"

He shrugged. "I don't know now. Perhaps instead, I could reapply to be a clerk at the magistrate's court, or maybe even the king's court." He thought back to the clerk organizing King Silas's documents. That was an important clerk.

"Don't be so stupid," said Meila. She leapt in front of Jaks onto a pebbled strip right at the river's edge. "You can't give up. You've got this . . . power. This magic that no one else has. You have a chance to learn how to do amazing things." Her voice became heavily accented, as it did when she spoke quickly. "Who cares about writing letters and contracts and whatever? If I had a chance to do magic, I would do everything possible to make it work." Her empathy for him had disappeared.

"I have been trying. It's so evasive."

With hands on her hips, she stood silhouetted against the moonlight and slowly shook her head.

Eventually, her face softened. "Tell me how it is *supposed* to work," she said.

He took a moment to collect his thoughts. "You summon up an emotion, which acts as fuel for the magic. Then you imagine a picture of what you want the magic to create, and then you concentrate on pulling the magic into reality . . . that's what I have been told how it works." He spread his hands and shrugged in futility. "The three times I *accidentally* invoked magic, I didn't do any of that—didn't do anything but panic."

"Well, that's something consistent. So, what happens when you practice?" She sat back astride the tree trunk.

"When I try to induce feelings of panic voluntarily,

I get to a point where something in my head slams shut and my mind goes numb. Thick and heavy like mud." Jaks bent over with his elbows on his knees. "Sometimes, I've practiced by putting myself in real danger. Once, I climbed up onto the battlements and hung my toes over the edge. But those times, I can't visualize or focus any willpower. I get overwhelmed and turn away. There is a point where I can't break past."

"What would happen past that?" asked Meila.

"A tornado. My mind would spiral and spiral without escape. There are things in the past that can't come out." He began rocking back and forth.

She paused for a minute, then said, "Being afraid of being afraid . . . is being afraid of paper tigers."

Jaks frowned. "Paper tigers?"

She placed a hand on his arm. "Every New Year's Day, my *gwama* would tie a paper tiger outside her window, to scare off evil spirits, she would say. It'd stay there, swinging around uselessly, banging against the glass, until the wind and rain blew it down." She dug her fingers into his flesh. "Although a *real* tiger can kill you and deserves to be feared, a *paper* tiger cannot and does not." She squeezed her fingers into his arm. "Fears of the past are just that."

"My fears are paper tigers?" said Jaks.

"Thoughts are just thoughts. And feelings are just feelings. They are not real. They cannot hurt you or kill you. When you stand back and see that fear itself cannot harm you, you can fold it anyway you wish."

Meila bent low, a hand on each of his shoulders, and caught his gaze. "Will you tell me what you're so afraid of?"

Jaks was quiet, considering, then said, "My father—" His voice broke and he coughed to clear his throat. "My father. I have nightmares of him coming from the darkness and crushing my head with enormous hands. Dark hands. The first few times that I tried to use that memory to invoke magic, I reached a point where I could almost feel my head bursting in his grip. But now when I try to use that image, a barrier smashes closed."

"Your mind is shielding itself," said Meila in a gentle voice. "Tell me more about your father." She sat back down on the tree trunk, half-turned toward him.

"My mother—" Jaks said.

"Your father."

"No, it starts with my mother." His eyes became unfocused. "We were happy when it was only her with my sisters and me. We were so proud of our mother. She was famous for her acting and singing, but she loved us fiercely." He paused for a breath. "Father rarely came home from the war when I was young, but when the realm was finally unified, he was back. He fired the house servants, drank all of the time, and he would beat her . . . accusing her of adultery. He kept her prisoner in the house for months at a time."

"Everything changed," she said sympathetically.

"Eventually, the beatings stopped. For a few years, at least. And we pretended to be a happy family. She even returned to acting for a while." Jaks could not bring himself to tell her the price of that peace—Karisa's sacrifice, her body for their mother's.

"Then, when I was about fifteen, he started beating her again and accusing her of sleeping with her patrons." He listened to the gurgling river for a minute. "One night, mother and I were in the upper kitchen when he stormed in. He started shouting the same accusations and waved around a play ticket as though it were some proof of her unfaithfulness. I cowered in the corner. I just wanted to get away. He is terrifying when he is in a rage. Then he started hitting her and hitting her. I can still hear her screams. She was telling me to run. He would start on me after he finished with her— but I couldn't. He crushed a table. He smashed the kitchen to pieces. She tried to run . . . the memories go blurry. I think he threw her down the stairs. The last thing I remember was his gloved fist. Her face destroyed . . . her beautiful hair . . ."

Jaks faltered as tears welled in his eyes. "Her neck was bent, and her head pulverized. There was blood everywhere."

"Oh, Jaks, I'm sorry. That's all awful." She touched his arm.

"He ordered me to clean up the blood. My mother's blood," Jaks said in a strangled voice and started shaking his head.

Meila slid over and wrapped her arms around him, holding his head to hers for a long while.

When his trembling stopped, she spoke quietly. "Fear and anger are lovers." She pushed him back gently. "They are entwined, and when danger rears its claws, they want to save their owner, but in different ways. Fear wants to run. But anger wants to fight. Fear says, 'We must escape the danger,' and anger argues, 'We must fight.' How can you *not* feel anger at your father? He has taken away your childhood, your peace, and your mother from you. You have a right to be furious at him—to want to shout at him, to hurt him, to want justice for her murder!" Spittle sprayed from her mouth onto Jaks's face; she wiped it away with a quick sweep of her palm and then grabbed his chin. "You are no longer a little boy. You have powerful magic, and you can stop him."

Jaks stared at her, wanting her words to be true.

"Embrace fear as it builds. Know you are strong, dwell on the injustice, and grasp your anger—there you will find courage." Meila pushed his chin away and sat back.

She was right. He had every right to be angry at his father, but for as long as he had known, fear was the only emotion he knew well. In the past, to have expressed anger at his father would have drawn attention to himself and thrust him into danger. He had been a coward. He should have been angry.

The monster had murdered his mother and abused his sister. Not only did he have the right to be angry, it was his duty.

Chapter 26

An Unexpected Journey

The evening chilled as Jaks and Meila watched the reflected moonlight on the river, preoccupied with their thoughts.

"It's getting late, we should—" Jaks was saying, when abruptly everything went silent around him. Even though he felt his mouth still moving in speech, his ears heard nothing.

Puzzled, he looked at Meila and saw a dark figure standing behind her. Its arm was raised above her head. He cried out in alarm to warn her, but, again, nothing came out of his mouth. Magicked silence. *Sonomancy!*

The arm descended and struck Meila in the head.

Her body slumped off the tree trunk onto the rounded stones of the riverbank, her face just inches from the water's edge.

Jaks jumped to his feet and turned to the attacker.

The watching man from the tavern.

Moonlight illuminated the bald man's face as he looked down at Meila. A blackjack was gripped in his hand, half-raised to club her again.

Jaks reached for the attacker's arm and shouted to ward him off—silence.

A dark figure moved in the corner of his vision.

Whack. A brick-like fist smashed into Jaks's jaw, spinning him around. He toppled to the ground.

The slobbering face of the second watcher from the tavern loomed over him, mouthing soundless words, and spittle dripped into Jaks's eye.

Thud. A shadowy blur cracked into the side of his head.

Darkness.

Jaks roused with a throbbing head, his thoughts thick and muddled.

In the pitch of night, he found himself lying facedown over a horse's back. Wisps of long grass brushed his rope-bound wrists as the beast walked steadily through a wild field. Unable to move his arms or legs, he was trussed to the horse like a deer hunter's prize.

Next to him, Meila's legs hung close to his face, bound facing the other direction. He called her name but received no response.

Three horses traveled together. The middle carried

the captives, while the other two—forward and behind—bore silhouettes of riders on both.

"The boy's a deadweight. Let me slit the shagger's throat. If we rid him here, the wolves and crows will clean his bones in a few days," the rear rider called out to his companion in a raspy voice.

"You know we can't kill him." The front rider turned around and replied in a cultured, city-born accent. "We'll dump him once we're far enough away that our trail will be cold by the time he makes his way back. We should get to the mountains by dawn. Then we can rest a few hours."

They continued all night through moon-lit paddocks, fields of corn and wheat, and at one stage along a shallow creek, as Jaks drifted in and out of consciousness.

At one point, he croaked a request for water to his captors, but they either did not hear him or ignored him.

He tried to rouse Meila again. She didn't stir.

Eventually, a rooster crowed in the distance, followed by another, and dawn sullenly reddened the sky.

The horses plodded single file through rows of ripening corn.

Jaks's hair was wet from brushing against broad, green leaves beaded with condensation. His back and head ached. Pain lanced through his jaw and temple whenever his head knocked against the thick, woody stalks of the corn plants.

Meila roused and began kicking at her rope restraints.

"Who the hell are you?" she called out to their captors. "Why are you doing this?"

"Shut up," said the rear rider.

"Untie me, now."

"Shut your mouth or I put a gag in it." He then yawned loudly.

She went quiet but struggled against her ropes for a while longer, and then eventually stilled.

The rear rider grumbled. "Damn it, we're nowhere near the mountains yet. I tell you, the boy's holding us up," he called out to his partner.

After a few minutes, the cultivated voice replied, "There's some sort of shack in the middle of the field up ahead. We'll stop there and rest."

The shack stood in the center of a small clearing. The doorless shelter covered a rusty horse-drawn plow, a farmer's hoe, shovel, and several buckets.

Jaks and Meila, hands and feet still tied, were man-handled from the horse to the ground. They wriggled upright and examined each other.

A bruise reddened the right side of Meila's face by her ear, and a bloodied graze marked her chin. Her knives and darkcore gun were nowhere to be seen. Her furrowed eyes and thinned lips were fired up with anger. She glared at their captors.

With a clearer look at them, Jaks was certain they were the two watchers from the tavern.

The man with the city-born accent was bald, pale-skinned, and moved with the confidence of a hardened warrior used to giving orders. Leather straps and molded armor were visible beneath his overcoat. A sword with a well-worn grip rode at his hip.

The other man was stockier than the leader and nurtured an impressive mustache under a wide, flat nose. He bore a flanged mace and a blade with a wide knobbed pommel: a rondel dagger used to finish off plate-armored opponents by pounding it through helmet openings or gaps in their armor.

"Jop, water the horses. I'll get them some feed," the leader ordered the other as he walked to the edge of the clearing and broke off heads of corn.

There was something familiar in the man's face. Jaks wracked his memory to place where he'd seen him before but could not.

"Who are you?" Meila demanded again as the bald man walked back with an armful of corn ears.

He paused and looked at her. "No one you would know, nor that you need to know."

"Then what do you want from us?" she asked.

"I want you to just do what I tell you to do," he said, stripping the corn to the yellow and dropping them to the ground. "If you behave, I won't have to hurt you or your boyfriend."

"Where are you taking us? Are you going to sell us?"

"You've already been bought." He laughed, standing over his two captives.

Jaks plucked up his courage and shuffled to face the man. "You'd best let us go now. We travel under the king's seal with Grandmaster Mulgrave of the Academy. My sister is a nightwraith who could kill you both before you even saw her. And our master ranger will bring them right to us. If you let us go, you could get a head start—"

The leader laughed. "They won't have noticed you missing until about now." He gauged the dawn-lit sky. "And I think your *master ranger* will be sporting such a raging hangover from his drinks last night that he won't know a piss-hole from a pothole until midday." He planted his hands on his hips and leaned over Jaks. "I know how to cover my tracks."

"You have to let us go," Jaks implored.

"Be quiet. That's enough talking," said the bald man. He then returned to tending the horses and ordered his underling, "Jop, tie them back-to-back against the wall of the shack. I'm going to rest inside. Keep them quiet and wake me in an hour. Then we switch."

He untied a bedroll from his horse and disappeared inside.

The man named Jop dragged Jaks and Meila to the shack wall and dutifully roped them together. He then sat cross-legged under the cornstalks, several yards away, and stared at them. He muttered to himself and pulled out a cloth to rub the ridges of his mace.

A breeze shushed through the corn field and

sparrows flew overhead as the sun arced higher into the morning.

After a while, Jop's hands slowed in their task and his head nodded and jerked up several times; after a few minutes, it slumped and he snored quietly—echoing louder snores came from inside the wooden shack.

By Jaks's estimations, hampered by night travel and an indirect path, they had only traveled fifteen or so miles from the rivertown. Their destination, the mountains that their captors had referred to, could only be the Northern Ranges Jaks knew well from his survival training. Their peaks were still twenty or more miles distant. But even so, he knew that Ranger Cromer would have a tough time even finding a lead from the tangential route of their kidnappers.

He found himself mired in defeat and hopelessness, in contrast to the defiance and anger he had seen smoldering in Meila's face. Although tied facing opposite directions, he could tell by the tugging movements and tension in her back that she hadn't let up—a wild dog who'd fight to the bitter end.

Defeatism wasn't going to help here; he needed to be more like her.

He needed to fight—and he knew the perfect weapon. *I can do it. I am not powerless. I can—I will—control magic.*

"Jaks, can you get at any knots?" Meila whispered, interrupting his thoughts. They leant back against each other, and her fingers brushed against his.

"No, how about you?" He bent his wrists and angled his fingers, but the rope was high around their wrists. "Are you hurt?"

"Just a pounding headache. I'm fine. We've got to escape. Do you have any ideas?"

Their guard emitted a loud snort and woke himself with a start. He looked up with groggy eyes.

Jaks and Meila desisted from testing their restraints.

He twisted his mustache and sat upright, blinking fatigue out of his eyes. "Did you say something?" he asked, smoothing out his mustache.

Jaks shook his head and stared at the ground.

A minute later, the man clambered to his feet, checked on the horses, and roamed around the clearing, looking for something of interest.

Thinking of her handgun and the half dozen knives and daggers she had armed herself with from the Academy armory, Jaks whispered to Meila, "Did they get all your weapons?"

"They got everything—even my boot knife."

"I can try to invoke magic. I might be able to electrocute them."

She paused before replying, "Not right now. Wait until either we're untied or you can get both of them at once. If you only get one, the other will end you . . . can you do it?"

"It's all we've got," he said, trying to sound confident, pushing away his self-doubt.

"You have to kill them, not just stun them." Her

voice hushed as Jop reappeared. "I know you can do it, Jaks. Be brave."

Bored with his exploration, the mustached man settled back down to watch them while chewing on a piece of jerky. When he finished the meat stick, he wandered over and crouched in front of Meila.

Jaks twisted his head and saw the short man lifting her chin to appraise her.

"You're a sweet pie. Where are you from?" Jop brought his face in close to hers, the caterpillar of hair below his lip quivering. "I wouldn't mind a taste of you."

"Get away from me," she snapped at him, "or I'll wake your master."

"Bako's not my master," the man replied, but then released her and stepped back. "You play along, you hear? We got a long journey ahead, and I can be nice . . . or not nice to you." He settled back under the cornstalks, took out his dagger, and skewered fallen leaves.

With the sun angling over the cornfield, the captors and hostages left the shack and continued their ride south.

Jaks sat upright, alone on the middle horse—wrists bound and tied to the saddle, but feet unrestrained—leashed to the lead horse.

The bald man, who Jop had named Bako, rode with his arms around Meila ahead of him. Ostensibly, they looked like a father and child riding leisurely through the countryside; on closer inspection, an observer would see her tied up like the hostage that she was.

Jop took up the rear again and shot envious eyes at his associate's closeness to Meila; however, the other man had no physical interest in her other than to keep her upright in the saddle.

They emerged from the cornfields into a prairie of green grass and sped up to a trot, aiming toward the craggy mountains. A flock of starlings startled out of the long grass and flew off with caws and a thrash of wings. A farm building was several miles to the west, with what might have been cows or horses clustered near a barn house.

Over several hours, the prairie changed from crop fields to pastures of roaming cattle several times over as the mountains loomed closer.

Bako veered away from buildings or human contact but could not avoid a chance encounter with a farmer erecting a scarecrow.

They were traversing another cornfield when the stalks parted and revealed the man digging a hole with a shovel and a strawman nearby. Reflexively, the man yelled out, "Hey, you're damaging my crop."

Without a word, Jop cantered forward, whipping out his iron mace, his horse crushing cornstalks.

The farmer, seeing trouble, turned to run but was struck down by a single blow with the head-crushing weapon.

Jaks lost sight of Jop and the farmer as his horse continued in tow of Bako, but a few minutes later, the mustached warrior returned to his rearguard and winked at Jaks. "Unlucky fellow. Lucky crows, though, feeding on meat instead of corn for the next few days."

Finally, with the sun at one finger above the horizon, they rode into a valley climbing up to a tree line at the start of the mountain range.

Their captors visibly relaxed as they entered the forest, slowing their pace and joking about the unfortunate farmer.

The giantwoods were immense guardians of the forest, their boughs wider than some houses and their canopies so far overhead that only the most determined, courageous climbers could reach their leafy tops. The scent of the forest was familiar: sharp and crisp over a mustiness of decaying leaves and wood.

Beneath the creaking boughs, Jaks recalled the little woodland creatures he had encountered on the hunting-and-gathering exercise—seeming an eternity ago—however, no matter how much he wished it, he knew he would have to rely on his own wits, not the gentle dryads, for escape. They were far too small and docile to combat two human warriors.

Bako and Jop dismounted at a clearing with a pair of

ten-foot-high ironwood trees at the center. Jaks and Meila were looped to one each.

After the horses were watered, fed, and secured at the clearing's edge, Jop held a waterskin to Meila's mouth and thrust a nob of bread into her hands, a task he then repeated with Jaks.

They ate hungrily—their restraints tied in a way that they could bring their hands to their mouths—and were surprised when Bako then dropped a thin strip of beef jerky and a carrot into their laps.

"Can you at least tell us where you're taking us?" Meila asked the bald man.

He looked at her with a wry smile. "Somewhere cold. You like cold?" he toyed with her.

Meila raised her eyebrows. "Look. You're a smart man. We'll cut you a deal. If you let us go right now, Jaks and I will head back down the valley and forget this ever happened. I can guarantee no one will even bother to look for you—we have better things to do. Deal?"

Bako smiled at her. "I'm not that stupid. You have no bargaining chits to offer; you'll do what I say, girly." He nodded to himself. "I think I'll keep ahold of you for the time being. Boy Rauhalik here, though, I will leave behind in the morning."

At the sound of his family name, Jaks spluttered, "How do you know who I am? Who are you?" Jaks asked.

The bald man frowned and flicked a hand at him.

"Never you mind. Now, shut up, the both of you. I think I'll gag you both tonight."

After a simple meal over a campfire, they then bickered until Jop, resignedly, sat the first watch as the leader lay down and rested his head on his scabbard and was soon snoring.

Again, Jop proved a sloppy guard and nodded off as well, slumped at the edge of the clearing against a giantwood. The campfire cooled to a glow, and darkness settled in. A warm night, the forest sighed and rustled high above where the leafy foliage met the abyss of night.

Jaks could see Meila's silhouetted form against her tree, two yards away, but couldn't speak through the cloth gag in his mouth.

Now wasn't the time to attack.

But it was time to prepare.

Closing his eyes, Jaks reached into the depths of his mind for the invocation and awoke to the nightmare of his father's horrific hands and his huge, bearded face emerging from the dark. He flinched, even though it was just a mental image, anticipating the hands on his throat. He clenched his jaw and bit on the cloth in his mouth.

Fear swirled around him and rose like flood waters, enveloping him and about to drown him when a numbness descended—a protective mist to beat away the flood—but instead of succumbing to it, as he normally did, he pushed it aside and summoned the image of his mother lying at the foot of the stairs.

Anger ignited and flared, recalling his father ordering him to mop up the congealing blood. Shoulders tensed and blood boiled.

Inner fire seared with the memory of being ordered to clean the carnage and the monster calling her "the whore."

With the Anger parting the mists of the Fear, he steadied the deadly emotions and held them ready. It was almost more than he could bear, but the anger spurred him to endure greater fear than he had ever felt before. *Courage.*

He cupped his hands and imagined a tiny ball of lightning nestled inside, pulsing blue-white like a miniature storm cloud firing out sparks every which way.

With the visualization vivid, and trembling with fear, he willed the lightning to be.

The hairs on his arm rose.

Acrid metal clouded his nostrils.

A white spark arced between his palms with a snap and then flicked out of sight.

Encouraged by the attempt, he renewed the visualization and channeled his fear again.

Blue and white flashed within Jaks's hand, but steady this time, gradually brightening. He tightened his fingers around a ball of scintillating sparks.

Through a gap between his hands, he stared at the magic he had invoked as if it were the most precious treasure he had ever found. Then his delight extinguished the fear and anger, and along with it, the electromancy.

Undeterred, he repeated the steps. And several times more, he channeled the ball of lightning.

Having forgotten to breathe while he magicked, he sucked in a deep breath and panted. Overjoyed at his accomplishment, he kicked his bound feet against the ground.

Meila grunted. She also kicked her heels, and the silhouette of her head nodded excitedly. She had seen his electromancy.

The mustached man, however, kept on snoring, having not seen a thing. Likewise, the bald man by the campfire lay unmoving, asleep.

Violent thoughts leached into Jaks's mind. *Come on, you bastards, untie me. Gather close. I have something for you.*

The giantwoods creaked and rustled their leaves as though to caution him. *Wait for daylight. Wait for dawn.*

Chapter 27

The Waterfall

The distant shrill cry of a wyvern woke Jaks, slumped against the ironwood. He shivered to throw off the chill of the night as a thin blanket of mist trickled down the wooded slope.

The bald man and Meila were already awake. Bako was crouched behind her and untying the rope that held her to the tree. With her wrists still bound, she groaned and struggled to her feet. Her eyes met Jaks's wearily— she hadn't rested well either.

"Give me some privacy," Meila said to Bako and disappeared behind some bracken.

The man followed, despite her request. The campfire was now just black ash and lumps, and Jaks could see Jop on the other side of it.

A few minutes later, Meila and Bako returned. "Sit back down," the man ordered. "I'm not having you wander around."

Jaks grunted and wheezed around his gag, drawing the attention of the senior man.

"I suppose you have to go now too?" said Bako, striding over to him. He removed the gag and released the knots behind Jaks's back.

After the rope fell slack, Jaks pushed against the tree to stand. It felt good to get to his feet. He ached all over from lying half-slouched all night, and his head still pounded from the whack it had taken a couple of nights before. He really did need to empty his bladder and stumbled behind the tree to tug at his breeches.

"When you're finished, get back there." Bako stood waiting with the rope in his hands.

Jaks hiked his breeches back up and turned to face his captor, arms tense and a bead of sweat forming on his brow. It was time. Even though his hands were still bound, he was on his feet and a lightning invocation would need only travel a few feet to strike Bako, then a second invocation against Jop. The second man had risen and stood yawning, arms outstretched. *I can take them out. Bako, then Jop—one, then the other.*

Jaks's and Meila's eyes met. She gave him a single nod.

"All right, sit down, boy. Haven't got all day. When we leave you here, I'll give you a blunt knife, so that you can cut yourself out of the ropes. It might take you a while, but you'll get free, and your daddy won't be angry with us. Well, I think so, anyway. Who knows with him?" Bako gestured with a finger for him to sit.

He gawped at the bald man and shook his head. "My father?" A memory flooded back. That was where Jaks recognized this man from. Back at his family's manse, months ago, one of his father's henchmen whom Vixhana had fought. Back then, the man still had some hair, albeit a mere crescent from ear to ear.

Bako placed a scarred hand on Jaks's shoulder and pressed him downward.

"Did my father send you?" asked Jaks. His knees buckled and he sank to the ground, mouth still agape. His plan to attack faltered. "Why would he send you? I don't understand any of this."

"You're not meant to." Bako tied him back to the ironwood. "Just don't try to come after us. You won't have any chance of catching up on foot." He ambled off to check on the horses and gave Jop an order to ready the saddlebags.

Jaks struggled against his restraints. Now, Bako was too far away to attempt a lightning attack, and being fully restrained again, he'd lost his opportunity.

Meila called out, "Don't just leave him here tied up. Cut him free before you leave him. A bear or wyvern might get him while he's still bound."

"He'll be fine. Few of those around these parts of the woods," Bako replied. Then to Jaks, he said, "Just head back the way we came and follow the valley to the plains. You'll find your way back easy enough."

"Cut me free," begged Jaks. "I promise I won't follow you," he lied. He couldn't just let them flit away with

Meila and leave him here trussed to the tree. He needed to take action now—but he needed to be on his feet, not tied up. *Could electromancy sever the rope?*

He curled his knees up in front of him and pressed his wrist binds against his legs. Bako and Jop were turned away. Meila's eyes jerked back and forth in fear.

He imagined a white blade of electricity against the loops of hessian, then summoned the fear as he had the previous night—his arms tensed, heart hammering to escape his chest. He *pushed* the mental image into reality.

A fine sliver of blue-white light appeared at his wrists, and the rope began to smoke. The pungent cloud filled his mouth and nose, startling Jaks into a spasm of coughing.

The blade disappeared, and he hastily blew the smoke away. The rope was blackened and singed, a few fibers parted by the brief invocation. He looked up at the two men, oblivious, busy with feedbags for the horses.

Meila's eyes were wide. She mouthed the words, *You did it.* She looked at their captors and back to Jaks, then shook her head.

It would create too much smoke. They would notice before he could sear through the ropes. *Unless I do it in short bursts while blowing the smoke away.*

He invoked the lightning blade two more times, burning a quarter of his wrist bind, until Bako and Jop finished fastening the saddlebags and walked back toward them.

"What's burning?" Bako peered around the clearing, and into the depths of the forest, but finding nothing, he shrugged.

A few minutes later, Jop had Meila untied and onto her feet.

It was all going too fast.

The bald man padded over to him and ran a thumb over a short knife. "It's even blunter than I thought, but you'll get there." The knife dropped to the ground by Jaks's feet.

He kept his knees curled up and wrists tucked low. Better not to say anything. *Just let them get out of sight, and I can sear through the ropes in a few minutes.*

Jop wrapped his meaty hands around Meila and pushed her up onto a saddled horse, then threw the tether to Bako on the lead horse. "Have a nice life, boy. If it'd been up to me—I would've slit your throat yesterday. Think of me having fun with your woman." He laughed as he clambered onto his brown gelding.

Meila and her captors rode into the forest. She cast back an agonized look as her horse was led away.

Jaks ignored the knife at his feet and looked down to his hands and once again invoked the lightning blade against the wrist bindings. He channeled a bright, thin edge. A swirling cloud of smoke and yellow flames rewarded his effort. Finally, the hessian fibers burnt through and he wrenched his wrists free. It had taken less than a minute.

Jop's back and his horse were still visible amongst the giantwood boughs and low-lying brush heading up the mountainside.

He didn't care if they saw the smoke now; he'd be out of the ropes before they could get back.

Hands free, he grabbed the knife and held it to the loop of rope binding him to the tree. He invoked lightning through the blade. Tiny arcs of electricity leapt and snapped over the steel, coming together where Jaks pressed it against the rope, and quickly burnt it through.

By the time the last strand fell away, Jop's horse had disappeared from view.

Each invocation of electromancy had fatigued him like a weight dragging on his head and shoulders. His emotions were frazzled, flagellating him like a whip. He needed a rest—but each minute was a minute that Meila and her captors got further away. *I've got to get them back in sight. I can't risk losing them.*

Jaks stumbled to his feet, stuck the knife under his belt, then began jogging through the forest in the direction he'd last seen the last horse.

A few minutes later, he paused to catch his breath.

No sighting of man or horse.

He looked to the ground for recent disturbance and breathed a sigh of relief when, not too far away, he found fresh horse prints.

Master Cromer would be impressed.

He laughed at the random thought and shook his head; now was not the time for self-congratulations.

Eventually, Jaks caught a glimpse of a brown horse a hundred yards ahead. He sighed with relief and hurried forward, keeping the giantwoods between them. Now that he was tracking them, he wracked his brain for a plan to rescue Meila.

If he called out to them while they rode, Bako and Jop would turn back, and he wouldn't know what direction they would approach—it would devolve into a melee and risk getting Meila or himself killed. No. Better to continue tracking them until they stopped for a break. Then he could sneak to within a few yards, ambush one and then the other before they could defend themselves. A simple plan, or so he thought.

As he scurried after Meila and the two men, he thought back to his lessons with Grandmaster Mulgrave for a clue about which aspect of invocation would increase the power of an invocation.

Willpower, visualization, or emotion?

The difficulty came when he focused on the mental control part of the invocation. The more attention he gave to willing the image into reality, the less fear he felt; not that it removed the fear, but that it became distant and detached.

Meila's wise guidance on the coupling of anger and fear had allowed Jaks to achieve enough fear for the electromancy, but his lessons with Mulgrave had never passed a beginner's level—he could play random notes of the instrument, but he couldn't play a melody.

Willpower, visualization, or emotion? He suspected it was all three—he would have to find out by himself.

Bako and Jop continued in the same southward direction as yesterday and skirted the inner edge of the mountain forest. Even so, the ground undulated across valleys and hills until Jaks's legs burned and his breath labored to keep up with them.

Thoughts of the grandmaster turned him to wonder whether the mage and the others were close by. His boast about Ranger Cromer's tracking skill had been fantastical, but it was possible that the eagle-eyed mountaineer might have picked up their trail by now. Despite his anxiety about his ex-instructor, Jaks respected the man's sharp mind and experience. However, with the situation as it was, it came down to just him.

If he failed to act, Meila could be lost to Bako's payman forever. He shook his head at the idea that his father was involved somehow. What interest could he have in her? How did he even know of her? Maybe Bako had a new employer, someone who wanted Meila for some inscrutable cause.

The riders stopped up ahead at a dark pool beneath an outcrop of rock. A waterfall fanned water from a crest several yards up and collected in the center of the pool with a churn of fine mist. Flat rocks lined the fine-looking pool. The horses dipped their heads to drink.

Jaks scrambled to within earshot of the group, colossal tree trunks hiding his approach.

One rider dismounted and crouched at the water's edge; the stocky figure of Jop cupped his hands, dipped them into the pool, and drank.

Bako looked down the wide stream feeding off the pool, as though searching for its end.

Meila flicked a look at Jaks, and their eyes met briefly. She knew he was there.

He slunk back behind the tree. Was she sending him a warning that he was too obvious?

"What a beautiful place." Meila's voice sounded in the distance. "Bring me some of the fresh water to drink."

Bako grunted. "You're a little princess, aren't you . . . yes, your majesty—would you like a slice of lemon with that?" he said.

Jaks dared another glimpse. Bako had dismounted from his horse with a flaccid goat bladder in hand, and now bent to plunge it into the rushing water.

"I need a few minutes," Jop said to Bako, then unbuckled his belt and walked behind a clump of ferns well away from the water. He dropped his trousers and crouched out of sight.

Bako lifted the full waterskin out of the stream and walked over to place it into Meila's bound hands.

She balanced on the saddle and drank deeply.

She passed the waterskin back to Bako and said, "Many thanks." It slipped from her fingers and bounced against Bako's chest and onto the ground with a thud.

Water drenched his front and poured over his boots.

"Oops. I'm so sorry," Meila said as he jumped away. At the same time, her horse scuttled sideways, obscuring Jaks's view of the man.

Had she fabricated the distraction on purpose? It didn't matter. Jaks scrambled up to and behind the giantwood closest to them—only ten yards from Meila.

Jaks's chest pounded. His mouth was dry as he pressed against the coarse bark and listened.

"Like I said, it just slipped out of my hands," Meila was saying. "That disgusting animal skin was slimy and slippery. Where I come from, we have bottles. Maybe you should look into it. Don't blame me." An imperious tone that Jaks had never heard her use before.

Bako replied in an exasperated voice, "You're acting like a child. This kidnapping business is ridiculous. The sooner I'm rid of you, the better."

Jaks took two breaths and stepped out from behind the tree.

"What . . . how in seven hells are you here?" Bako froze mid-dab with a cloth and gawped at Jaks.

"Let her go," Jaks said. He had hoped to sound commanding, but his voice quivered, and his throat tightened. "I don't want to hurt you, but I will if you don't let her go."

Bako laughed loudly, silencing the cicadas and insects nearby. "You won't . . . *hurt* me. That's a rare one.

What are you going to do? Fight me with that dulled knife I gave you?"

The warrior dropped the cloth, placed a hand on his scabbard, and tilted his head at Jaks.

"What's happening?" Jop's head poked up from behind the bushes.

"Wipe your arse and get a load of this," said Bako.

Jaks raised his right arm and pointed outstretched fingers toward the bald warrior. "Stand back, I'm telling you." His words were authoritative, but his soul was fearful. He retreated a step when Bako sauntered toward him with a grin on his face.

At that moment, Meila dug her heels into her horse's sides as Jaks had taught her a few days earlier and kicked her horse into motion. The animal whinnied, then leapt and trotted forward. She tilted dangerously in the saddle and gripped the saddle horn with her hands.

"Damn it. Get her!" Bako yelled and ran after the startled mare.

The horse hurtled past Jop, who stumbled to his feet and then lumbered after it. He struggled with his breeches and tripped after a few yards. Up on his feet, he buckled his leggings into place and returned to his pursuit—well behind the escaping equine and its rider.

"I'll get a horse." Bako stopped and turned to the two remaining horses.

Jaks stood in his way.

"Get out of the way. This has gone far enough, no

matter whose son you are." The warrior strode toward Jaks. His longsword rasped as he pulled it from the scabbard.

Jaks planted his feet and thrust a trembling hand toward Bako, but didn't have time to recall the practiced invocation involving his brutal father—the swordsman was almost upon him.

A hand reached forward to shove Jaks's arm aside; the other raised the longsword, preparing to strike.

Terrified, Jaks fought the instinct to flinch and instead straightened. Anger rallied his fear into courage. *How dare he attack and bind us like animals? How dare he dismiss me like a child? Die, you bastard.*

"Damn you to hell," yelled Jaks.

A fork of white electricity skimmed the air to Bako's hand.

Electricity channeled into his body. Excited tendrils of magic danced over the man.

A brilliance illuminated the area, and the crack of lightning shattered the tranquility of the forest.

The explosion lifted Bako off his feet. His limbs and torso arched, muscles contracted, and he was thrown back several yards.

The acrid smell that followed each invocation of electromancy filled Jaks's nostrils. Although its harshness made him wince, his lips curled and he welcomed it as a mark of a successful invocation. His arms fell to his sides, and he stared at the motionless body lying beside the stream. Smoke wafted from the man's blackened hands and boots. *Was he dead?*

The smell of burnt flesh hit him with a wave of nausea; he pursed his lips and clenched his throat to calm his stomach. He walked over to the body and picked up Bako's longsword. A well-balanced weapon, its grip was blackened but otherwise undamaged. He prodded Bako's body with the tip of the sword and dry retched at the sight of his burnt, peeled skin, and the man's melted eyeballs—congealed pulpy ooze in their sockets.

I killed him.

He staggered away from the corpse and squatted with his head low as he battled with the guilt of killing a man. *He deserved it. It was either me or him.*

He shook his head, remembering his purpose, then stood and gazed into the forest for signs of Meila.

Nothing but the giantwood sentinels and their shadows.

He would need to search for her; on horseback would be best. The warriors' two horses had bolted at the sound of the lightning bolt, but the trained animals wouldn't have gone far. He would find them and go after Meila.

However, as he followed the horse tracks—going back to their original trail—a voice called out behind him.

"Grafuk! What the hell happened here?" Jop was half-way down the hillside, gaping at Bako's lifeless body. He was astride Meila's brown mare, while she herself shuffled on foot behind him on the end of a long leather leash around her neck.

A cut and bruise marked the left side of Meila's forehead, complementing the purple bruise on the other side of her head.

"Boy. Who did that to Bako?" The stocky warrior's eyes narrowed and he surveyed the forest, not knowing that the killer stood before him.

"Me. I killed him," Jaks said, his voice so confident that he surprised himself. "I killed Bako. And I will kill you, too, unless you get off your horse and drop your weapons." He raised his arm and pointed at the stocky warrior.

Jop harrumphed and stared back and forth between Jaks and Bako's body several times. "*You* did that? You're a mage?"

"Get off the horse and lie on the ground," commanded Jaks.

In a swift movement belying his rounded shape, Jop dismounted and tugged on the leather leash, pulling Meila stumbling toward him. "I don't think so."

The same height as her, he spun behind her and flashed one of his rondel daggers to her throat.

Meila's face twisted in anger.

"Listen to me, boy. You may have got Bako by surprise, but I've got the upper hand now, don't I?"

"You can't harm her. You have to take her to your master." Jaks's outstretched right hand wavered while the left gripped the blackened sword at his side, parallel to the ground.

Jop shoved Meila forward until they stood alongside Bako's disfigured corpse. "Nasty work. Never liked the bastard, anyway. But you try that on me and you'll burn the girl too."

Despite her peril, Meila laughed. "I haven't been a girl for over a century, you filthy pig."

Without warning, she snapped her head back into Jop's broad face. The dagger fell from his stunned fingers. As he reeled back, she half-turned and kicked her heel into his right shin.

The man fell to the ground. But with the leash still wrapped in his fist, Meila was yanked down too. Both of them rolled to within a few feet of Bako's dead body.

Swiftly, Meila grabbed the leash with her hands to ease the tension. "Get him, Jaks."

With a roar, Jop surged up to his feet, one hand pulling on the leash and the other tugging on the mace at his belt. Crimson flowed freely from his nose and dripped from his chin.

Meila was too near.

The magic could kill her, even if the warrior was the target. He knew little of electromancy, but from his readings of Grandmaster Vinton's archives, he knew well enough that lightning could leap from victim to victim with indiscriminate lethality.

With magic out of the fight, Jaks grasped the longsword in both hands and raised the blade to a middle-guard position. During conscription, he had trained with the longsword but had never mastered the strikes and lunges, lacking the aggressiveness to react quickly or strike well. Now, he had no choice but to set sword against mace.

The mustached warrior sneered, released the leash, and shoved Meila away. "Yes, fight like a man."

She stumbled away from the warrior.

Nothing to protect him now, thought Jaks.

Jop hefted his mace over his right shoulder with both hands and lurched forward with a blood-curdling scream.

I won't fight like a man, I will fight like a battlemage.

Electricity hummed into being as Jaks visualized and bent his bristling fear. The blade sparked with crooked tendrils of the white energy as he intended—but a second later, stuttered and fled from the shining steel.

The mace smashed against the longsword, knocking it aside like a stick in a child's hands. The stocky warrior then charged bodily into Jaks and slammed him onto his back, knocking the wind out of him and causing the sword to spin out of his hands.

The warrior stood over him—face bloodied and contorted—and raised the mace two-handed over his head. The evil flanges of the mace would crush his skull easily.

Jaks threw a hand up to ward off the deadly blow

and frantically mustered the three aspects of invocation together.

Desperate, he willed up a bolt of lightning.

Snap. Light leapt out from his hand; however, instead of a powerful bolt, three thin forks of lightning crackled.

They struck Jop in the chest, but weren't strong enough to blast him off his feet as with the first warrior.

Regardless, the man careened backward in pain and alarm. His mace fell from his hand.

"You little prick," Jop yelled as he bent down to the mace lying next to the water's edge. The waterfall, just a few yards away, spilled its foamy discharge into the pool.

Suddenly, Meila appeared behind Jop with a dagger in her hands. She raised her rope-bound wrists and plunged the needle-sharp weapon into his upper back— ramming it through leather armor, skin, and lung.

Once. Twice.

The brute cried and twisted toward her. Pain etched his face and blood spluttered from his mouth.

Turning sideward to Jop, Meila balanced on her left leg and brought the other to her chest. Her boot lashed out in a side kick and smashed Jop in the face with a satisfying crunch.

He fell backward and toppled into the water. His face mangled with a broken nose and split lip, he splashed about on all fours at the edge of the pool, blood pumping from his mouth and nose. He managed to stand waist-deep for several moments until his footing slipped and his knees collapsed. Weakening fast, he thrashed about, stumbling further and further into the pool.

One more step—and the downpour of the waterfall pummeled him down and held him under a frothy, blood-tinged embrace.

Breathing heavily, Jaks rose to his feet and walked over to Meila. They stared for a long minute at where the body lay submerged.

"Should we fish him out?" Jaks asked. Even though they had killed these men who had been their captors, human bodies deserved some respect. "Bury him?"

"We have nothing to dig a grave with. Besides, that one already has a watery one. The other . . . the carrion eaters can just feast on. Such are the cycles of life," she replied in a dismissive tone.

The forest had now dimmed into late afternoon. A light breeze murmured through the wooded canopy and fantails flitted from branch to forest floor around the waterfall, oblivious to the violence that had scuffed up the ground to expose the bugs and worms they eagerly plucked.

Soon, a pair of small green dragons winged into the boughs high above and clung to the trees, necks sinuating as they eyed up the meat on Bako's corpse. Greens didn't worry him; the smallest of the dragons, they never attacked live humans, but dead ones, he was sure they would.

Jaks cut the rope binding Meila's wrists. "Are you hurt?" he asked, looking directly into her bruised face for the first time since the fight began.

"Nothing major. How about you?" Her eyes softened and her tense lips smoothed to a line.

He minimized his aches and pains with a head shake and asked, "Why did they want you?"

"I have no idea. Other than being a curiosity, I don't know why anyone would want to kidnap me. Unless they know about . . ."

"Perhaps they're after the weapons on your ship. Someone found out about them or was told about them."

Meila shrugged, looking deep in thought. She extended her neck as Jaks fumbled at the knot tying the leather leash around it.

"That man," Jaks nodded at Bako's body. "I think he used to work for my father. But I can't think why he would want to kidnap you. He's an evil man, but it's beyond me why he would do this."

"Your *father* organized this? What has he got to do with it? I can't get my head around any of this. We need more information . . ." Meila walked over to the body and rummaged through the clothes but found nothing of interest. She sighed. "We need to find those other horses. They may hold clues, and I need my darkie back."

Unwilling to let the man be ripped apart and eaten by the dragons, Jaks grabbed the dead man by the legs and pushed him into the pool. The waterfall greedily welcomed the second body into its depths.

"You know, they'll most likely bloat up and float ashore downstream," the woman commented.

Jaks frowned but said nothing and turned to leave. With the mare in tow, they regained the sunken tracks of the other two horses and left the waterfall to its gruesome new inhabitants.

A quarter hour later, they spotted Bako's stallion and Jop's gelding nuzzling through the undergrowth around a cluster of boulders. The horses looked up briefly and returned to their grazing.

They searched the saddlebags. Meila breathed a sigh of relief as she drew out her handgun from a jumble of hardware, including Jaks's shortsword, her assortment of knives, and a couple of runestone lights. She holstered the darkcore gun and secreted the sheathed blades about her body.

Their kidnappers had been well supplied with rations, blankets, and two tents, but nothing to reveal the identity of their employer.

"Is this a good place to camp tonight?" she asked Jaks, who was tethering the horses to a beech tree.

"Good as any. I'll get a fire ready. I've been in these parts of the woods before and there are wild animals we should watch out for." Green dragons were nothing, but a wyvern or frostbear sneaking up on them would be a disaster. He finished belting on his scabbard and then searched the area for sticks and branches.

"I suppose I'll go set up a shelter," Meila said.

As the last rays of daylight vanished, they sat beside Jaks's sputtering campfire in its circle of stones and ate hardtack biscuits from Bako's supplies.

A memory of him and Meila singing together the first time they met came back to him. He smiled. He would've loved to sing with her again, but now was not the time for noise and distraction.

She interrupted his thought, asking, "Where do we go from here?" She handed him a waterskin and he nodded thanks. "Back to the rivertown or Dunberrin?"

He wasn't thirsty but sipped a mouthful and gave it back. "I think we retrace our path back to the rivertown. If Vixhana and the others are on our trail, we'll hopefully cross tracks. If we don't find them along the way, we'll have no choice but to return to the Academy."

She nodded and after a few minutes placed a hand on his arm. "Thanks, Jaks. Thank you for coming to rescue me from those men. I know you didn't have to, and you put yourself in great danger to come for me." Her intense brown eyes bore into his.

"I had to." He looked aside as heat rushed up his neck. "There was no one else around."

Despite his earlier courage, he faltered from telling her that he couldn't bear a day without her, that she was his every waking moment, and that he would go to the ends of the world for her. It wasn't just her beauty—delicate features, lithe and graceful—it was her intensity and inner strength that drew him to her like a nail to a magnet. He revered and desired her. She was a goddess to him.

"I couldn't have done it without you. You stopped Jop when I faltered," he said and shuddered at the image of the man and his mace standing over him with murderous eyes.

"You killed the bald one—he was terribly disfigured. I'm guessing you used electromancy on him?"

He nodded. "What you told me the other night helped. It made sense what you said about fear and anger working together. Anger has always been an evil to me, I've avoided it. It was my father's domain, his rages, his beatings. But you made me realize that anger is neither evil nor good—it's just an emotion. I was able to draw on it when I was about to panic. And gathered the courage to complete the invocation against Bako."

"I'm glad you overcame the barrier. You did well." She picked up a stick and stabbed at the fire. After a long pause, she said, "That brute would have raped me eventually, even with the other one around. I know men; they're no different here than home. His eyes were always on me. He would have taken me when the other was asleep. I'm glad I killed the pig."

Her bluntness about murder, and that she had plunged the dagger so efficiently into Jop, sent a chill through him. She was callous sometimes. Regardless, he couldn't help but draw confidence from her self-assurance and grimaced at the memory of the violent thug receiving his comeuppance.

"You wouldn't understand . . . or maybe you would. When that man in the tavern grabbed you and forced you to dance. What did that feel like?" she asked with the tip of her stick flaming like a candle over the fire.

"Filthy. I was as disgusted at myself for not being able to get away from him as I was at his hands groping me—he had such a strong grip. I felt violated." He shuddered at the memory.

"Exactly. That's how you feel after you've been forced . . ." Her stick burnt out and she threw the rest into the fire.

He thought about what she had said for a few minutes, realization brewing, and then asked in quiet horror, "You've been raped before?"

She rubbed at her right wrist. "This isn't the first time I've been a prisoner. Last time, my captor was someone I thought I loved. I was only twenty, and I was so naïve that I didn't see the warning signs. He had eyes like fire and a voice like thunder. I joined his colony on a station orbiting Mars. Long story short, over a year, I went from being his wife to being a pleasure slave for all the men in the commune. I only escaped when a government raid came and arrested him for fraud . . . I've said enough." She jumped up and paced to the other side of the campfire.

"I'm sorry, I didn't mean to open old wounds." He rose and stood awkwardly, not knowing how to retrieve the moment.

After a minute, she came to him beside the

flickering flames and gripped his forearms. "It's okay, Jaks. It was a long time ago. Time heals. The scars are healed, and I've had much happiness and joy in my life since then. Even with Anton gone, I know that I'll find happiness again sometime. I'm pretty happy just to be alive right now." She smiled up at him.

He drank in oval eyes and wide lips, inviting in the firelight. Intoxicated with her nearness and the touch of her hands, he longed to embrace and devour her. Face filled with desire, he reached forward to wrap his arms around her and bent down to her lips.

"No, Jaks. Don't." She pushed him away and stood with a hand raised between them. "I'm sorry. I must be giving you the wrong signals. It's not right. You're still a boy."

He bristled at her words, wanting to reach for her. "I'm not a boy. I love. I love you."

"No, you don't," she said. "You're too young to know what love is. You're just infatuated with me. If I lay with you, it would be wrong. You should be with sweet things your own age—like that serving girl the other day." She crossed her arms, her face unreadable. "It's not going to happen." She retreated to the tent she'd pitched and huddled under a blanket.

The rest of the evening, Jaks toiled the fire and ruminated, rejection twisting like a knife. He shouldn't have just thrown himself at her. She deserved more respect than a rut in a forest. She was vastly more mature and experienced than he, and infinitely more knowledgeable. *What did I expect?* He would apologize in the morning and pray things returned to normal.

She woke around midnight, climbed out of the tent and over to the campfire—flames teased a dry branch that Jaks had thrown on just minutes before.

"I didn't expect you up so soon." He rose as she approached. "Meila, I'm sorry—"

"Don't worry about it, Jaks. It's not your fault. Sometimes these things happen when you're young. Let's just go back to how it was, okay?" She smiled at him, tugged her navy-blue cloak about her, and crouched by the fire. "Go get some rest. I'll keep the fire going. I'll wake you if I see anything."

He lay in the tent and closed his eyes, listening to her shuffle about the campsite for a few minutes; then, not realizing how tired he was, he fell asleep.

Chapter 28

Ascoria Invaded

Lord Sicaro—Province of Sanford, Ascoria

The sounds of battle were magnificent to Sicaro's ears. It had been too long since he had heard the clang of steel and the war cries of men and women hacking and stabbing each other to death. Grander than the ridiculous orchestras of the Ascorian king and sweeter than the screeching operas of his dead wife.

That morning, at an Ascorian encampment just five miles from Castle Sanford, he meandered amongst crushed tents, smoldering campfires, and dying Ascorian soldiers. He stopped at a man crawling through a pool of blood and kicked the man over to find he was, in fact, unwounded. Grimacing, he smashed down the steel tip of his six-foot hammer into the craven's skull against his shrill pleas for mercy.

Ahead of him, pockets of frantic Ascorian soldiers stood back-to-back as Vor warriors surrounded them and struck them down, one by one.

A young soldier broke out and ran across an open field, only for a broad-shouldered warrior woman to toss a spear at him that impaled him in the back. An impressive throw of sixty yards.

Elsewhere, other Ascorians had thrown down their weapons and were being trussed up into a slave chain—so many in number that Sicaro spat in disgust at the display of mass cowardice.

"Silas should be ashamed how low the army has fallen since I left command," he said to the Elliptan assassin shadowing his side, trailed by ten Sanford men-at-arms. "A clear reflection of the weakness of their leader."

"Aye, my lord. Quite so . . . Commander Lytton struggled pitiably when I strangled him. Couldn't command his bladder, let alone a battalion," Craeg Vesenira replied with his eyes fixed on the spear-thrower as she hefted an oversized battleaxe.

The woman clanked toward them, her plate mail pauldrons overlapping a chest plate emblazoned with the volcano crest of the Vor army. Taller than most Ascorian men, but average for women of the Burnt Lands, she threw her helm to the ground, planted her feet shoulder-width apart, and draped gauntleted hands over the end of her axe. Close-set eyes appraised him. "Lord Sicaro. I am *telsun* Cloete, leader of Zenith Torgue. We met briefly at one of your meetings with King Harek earlier this year . . . We are almost done with this camp."

"I see, telsun. How fared the initial assault?" asked Sicaro.

"They were forewarned. Probably by fires from the other assaults further up the coast. However, they didn't expect an ambush in their own camp. My torgue assaulted directly whilst Basalt and Granite Torgues attacked from the flanks. It was a massacre, my lord. A delicious bloodbath. We suffered one casualty to their hundred dead and captured." She delivered her report in a strong Vor accent—guttural and breathy—reminding him of his dead mother.

"Just make sure there are none feigning death to escape."

The woman nodded. "If the rest of the Ascorian army fights as poorly as these, we could be in Dunberrin by spring," she said, wiping her nose and sneering at the final prisoners being tethered to the slave chain.

"I admire your confidence, telsun. King Harek and I would be pleased if we could stretch so far, so quickly . . . but why rush? There is nothing more magnificent or beautiful than war. Would you not linger?"

Her gaze faltered and she pursed her lips. "Surely, my lord. I cannot say. That is up to the king to choose." She rotated her shoulders, moving easily despite her shell of steel.

"You are a griefmaster?" He used the Vor term for those gifted with gravmancy. He stepped forward and placed a gloved hand on her arm and *weighted* her elbow with his own gravmantic power. She staggered, her arm dragging her down under magicked weight, but within the blink of an eye, she recovered, standing tall as she countered his magic with her own.

"No match for you, my lord." She lowered her eyes, and Sicaro released her arm.

He stared at her and savored her deference, envisaging his defiant daughter Vixhana in a similar pose of submission. What he'd give to beat her down. Pummel her to a pulp for interfering with his reunion with Karisa.

"My lord, we should get moving if we are to receive King Harek at the castle at midday," Craeg said, interrupting his master's thoughts.

"Sergeant, have your men burn the bodies. Stockpile armor and weapons, but burn any Ascorian insignia—they have no place here anymore." Sicaro dismissed the woman and then returned to his destrier.

His armored retinue followed a cobbled road back toward his stronghold, a six-towered castle overlooking the town of Sanford. Pillars of smoke ranged up and down the surrounding coast, cleansing the Ascorian blight to make way for his Vor cousins and settlers to help bring this realm into a new era.

That his family, a generation ago, had been welcomed into Ascoria as refugees, was a great irony to him. For today, he had summoned war to its very shores.

His father had been a royal guard in one of the many fiefdoms of Voros—then known as the Burnt

Lands—back when borders rose and fell by the year. He'd impregnated the king's only daughter and, suffering her father's wrath, had fled with her to Ascoria.

As a son of royalty, Sicaro could have had claim to some nameless region; however, it was all meaningless now that Harek had annexed and conquered all the Burnt Lands, claiming them under one crown. Harek had done all the hard work for him.

His thoughts returned to the task at hand as he entered the outskirts of Sanford. His eyes trailed over the two hundred village folk corralled into the market square by his troops. Ironically, the same troops who had, until the previous day, been responsible for defending and protecting them. He caught sight of the town's mayor and ambled his horse over to tower above the man.

"Lord Sicaro, how dare you treat us like this." The mayor looked up, straightening as tall as he could. "You're a traitor to Ascoria. King Silas will have your head for this treachery."

Two men-at-arms stood between the town official and their lord, swords and shields shoved into the man's face.

Sicaro admired Mayor Trentholm's bravery, a rarity in this sedate country. However, such men with passion and a righteous cause incited rebellions amongst the peasants and could not be tolerated.

"Alas, it will be King Silas's head that shall be kicked through the streets." Sicaro, adorned in gold-embossed armor and a black cloak, slipped from his stallion and thudded to the ground, clutching the warhammer Sorrow in one hand. "Down on your knees, man."

The two soldiers prodded the mayor in the back of the legs.

The man stared up defiantly at Sicaro. "Do what you want, but God as my witness, you will burn in hell for all you have done."

Cries of fear and anguished sobbing rose from the gathered villagers. Parents shielded their children's eyes and averted their own.

Sorrow rose above Sicaro's head, six feet of metal topped by a giant fist bearing a sharp steel stake. It descended in a blur. The fist smashed down into Mayor Trentholm's head, pulverizing his skull and ripping through his torso in an explosion of blood and gore.

Screams from the village folk accompanied the crunch and squelch of the grav-augmented blow. What remained of the mayor's body slumped to the ground. Burst bowels stenched the square, and smashed bones and internal organs smeared the cobblestones.

Sicaro righted his bloodied hammer and gazed at the horrified villagers. Nodding to the captain of his men-at-arms, he said, "As you were, Captain. Continue your orders for the rest of them. You should be at the slave camp by nightfall. March well. Don't let any of them escape. I will need as many as we can get in the coming years." He returned to his destrier and climbed into the saddle. Yes, he would need tens of thousands for the ambitious works he had in mind.

***

At midday, a column of warriors traversed Sanford bridge. The array of siege weapons brimming the castle at Sicaro's sides could have made quick work of the warband if he had wanted; however, these warriors were his welcome guests—and perhaps one day, his loyal subjects.

He stood on the ramparts of Castle Sanford and had been watching King Harek's retinue approach for the last two miles. Below him, the gates and drawbridge gaped open with two lines of his garrison waiting as an honor guard.

The Vor king arrived with six hundred warriors: half on horseback, armed with axes and swords, and the rest on foot with crossbows and shields. At their lead, Harek rode a huge stallion who wore a horse-helm spiked with a vicious horn. The tall, slender man himself wore a robe of bear fur over bronze-colored plate armor; and, in place of a helm, wore a simple golden circlet. A longsword hung at his hip.

Curiously, in contrast to the mass of intimidating warriors, three riders wearing colored lace and silk trailed on ponies a few yards behind the king. Sicaro was surprised that, on this critical day, the regent would bring his own courtesans; the man was so confident of success that he had brought along his harem.

In the distance, yet to cross the bridge into town, the tail of the column snaked forward and brought with it scores of circling and swooping flyers that glinted with green, red, and gold.

Wardragons. Not small dragons as found in the wild, but wolfhound-sized beasts bred for war.

Even a mile away, he could hear their cacophony of screeches and yowls. The damned creatures had caught sight of a cattle herd and were diving at the defenseless animals stampeding in every direction around their grazing field. The dragonmasters whistled and blew their trumpets to rally their beasts of war but were only able to summon back the dragons after they had downed dozens of cows and bulls. But not to waste good meat, the handlers then sent the dragons back to feast on their kills. Sicaro frowned, hoping the dragons were better disciplined on the battlefield.

The main Vor column stopped in the now abandoned town square below, while King Harek, his harem, and a torgue of fifty warriors continued up to the castle. Back in the square, a gray-bearded warrior shouted commands at the remaining warband to encamp.

Sicaro descended the battlement steps to greet Harck within the castle courtyard. "Welcome, your majesty. The gods of the sea cradled you like babes last night," he boomed in a deep voice.

The Vor king dismounted and strode over to grasp arms with and then slap the shoulder of Sicaro. "That they did, Lord Sicaro. I could not have dreamed of a smoother invasion. Tell me, are the Ascorian forces all so poorly organized and craven? My commanders report that when they assaulted the camps, the sentries tried to flee and over half of the soldiers surrendered. Shameful."

Sicaro nodded and walked the king toward the main hall. "The Ascorians are rigid in hierarchy. They fare well in orderly battle but are slow to react tactically. Silas believes that when it comes to leaders: the fewer, the better. He thinks of his army in large chunks—easier for him to command—but it is a weakness, these lumbering masses of soldiers, easier to confuse and divide." At the entrance to the hall, he looked back to see that half of Harek's guard followed, along with the three women in silk.

The two leaders abandoned the guards in the main hall and retreated to Sicaro's war room with a few select commanders and Craeg Vesenira, his forever shadow. In the center of the chamber, a large table was shaped with molded plaster, painted and covered in sculpted landmarks showing a god's-eye view of Ascoria.

Messengers reported to the doorway, running back and forth with messages and reports from the continuing boat and ferry landings along the shoreline— all positive and according to plan.

"And how go the preparations for the gargantors?" Harek asked one of his generals, a barrel-chested man.

"Six will start the crossing tomorrow. Unfortunately, two of the males were injured fighting each other and won't be able to make the swim until their wounds heal. The pridemaster estimates three to four weeks," the man replied.

The gargantors were fearsome beasts with a thick leathery hide, saber-like claws, and snouted jaws with dagger-like teeth—and could tear an armored warrior apart in seconds. Giant tigers the size of elephants, they were almost as lithe and fast as the Ascorian warlions, but at five times their size, they were the most formidable of the beasts of war. Fortunately for the Vors, the gargantors' intelligence made them tamable and directable as long as they were caught young and rewarded with a steady flow of cattle and pigs.

"The monsters can't be coaxed onto a barge?" Sicaro asked.

The general shook his head. "Interestingly, they refuse to stand on a floating platform but will swim enthusiastically. In the ocean, we guide and speed them from island to island by pulling them with ships."

Sicaro nodded in appreciation. He had heard descriptions and stories of the monsters and was eager to see them tear into Silas's armies.

The king and his strategists spent the next several hours reviewing and revising their plans for the land campaign: troop movements, supply chain, harvest activities, and key engagements with the enemy.

At one point, two men-at-arms carried a large, padlocked chest into the room and placed it in a shadowy corner.

By late afternoon, light beams of green and red from a lead-light window slanted over the map table to illuminate motes of dust, lazy in the air. King Harek looked at the men in the war room. "Thank you, my friends. We are done for today. This evening, we banquet and celebrate our success. When you return to your warriors, assure them that there will be much bloodsong and victory to come. May the gods delight in our offerings," he said, clasping arms with each of his generals and commanders. "Lord Sicaro, stay a moment. We have one last issue to finalize."

The war room emptied, leaving just the two men.

The Vor king removed the circlet around his head and placed it on the map table. "My lord, I have been thinking on your mission," he said. "You have proved yourself invaluable so far. The landing could not have been easier." Harek picked up a pawn from the table and examined it. "Of course, as we agreed, Sanford is your fiefdom—settlers will arrive and it will grow into a city-state, I have no doubt—but I implore one thing more of you," he said as he replaced the pawn on the table.

The next phase of the conquest plan was for Sicaro to return "defeated" to the court of the Ascorian king and begin a mission of deceit. His man, Arlo, would remain as a strategic advisor to the Vor king, but the rest of his retinue would accompany him and a band of "survivors" to help sabotage the Ascorian defenses. That was the plan. What else could Harek want of him?

Harek walked to the steel chest that his men had brought in. He bent down to unlock the padlock and then lifted the lid. "Have a look," he said.

Inside were several sinister-looking objects, one hand-sized and the others as long as his arm. Individually, they looked highly crafted—sleek, black, and menacing. Sicaro's warrior instincts recognized them as weapons, but of a curious design. "What are they?"

Harek wrapped a hand around the shortest artifact and held it up to a ray of light. "Weapons. Such as the one we found on the foreigner who killed my men."

"You have many now," Sicaro plainly stated, staring at the beautiful weapon. He reached forward with his palm extended. "May I see it?"

The weapon was as light as oak and smooth except for diamond-shaped hatching where the hand went naturally to grip it. It was expertly designed to sit in a hand and point at a target. He had seen one-handed crossbows before—little more than toys—and this weapon looked as though it was missing the essential bow-limbs and projectile groove that would be necessary for it to be an effective missile weapon.

He guffawed and looked at Harek. "This little thing killed your men?"

The tall king nodded and then extracted another weapon from the steel chest and held it to display. Similar to the first weapon, but longer and heavier—made to be handled with two hands. "*These* artifacts came to me by way of a merchant from Volkre City in southern Voros. He said that he bought them from a group of desert gypsies, who said they found them in a ruined temple of the gods."

Harek laid down the sleek object on the map table and reached under his breastplate to extract an exact copy of the weapon that Sicaro held in his hand.

"However, this is the exact one that killed my warriors . . ." The king caressed the exotic object. "The prisoner called it a 'darkcore gun.' This one is usable by any holder. However, he said the ones in the chest are 'locked' and was adamant he could not unlock them. He told the truth; my interrogators made sure of that."

"What is it you want?" Sicaro suspected the answer but needed the man to say.

"You see, I need the foreign woman that Silas has captive. They are of the same ilk, wherever it is they are from. Although he could not unlock these artifacts, she might." Harek stared at the gun gripped in his hand for a moment longer and then slipped it back under his breastplate to a presumable pocket. "I want her. I want these weapons working."

Sicaro placed the gun back into the chest. "My lord,

the latest information I have on the woman is that they transferred her to the Academy of the Arcane. Still a captive, but I assume under interrogation by the grandmasters. Last I heard from my man Bako, a few weeks ago, he had not seen any opportunities to steal her away."

Harek pounded a fist onto the table. "I need greater action. When you go north, along with your primary task, you must personally take a hand at seizing the woman. I must have her. In the long-term, these artifacts could be even more important than the death of Silas."

"Certainly, my king. I may even be able to persuade Silas into giving her to me directly."

"Marvelous." Harek's demeanor switched in a heartbeat from commanding to affable. He grinned, locked the wooden chest, and walked over to the war room door, marking the conclusion of their discussion. "Let us go find some ale."

In the main hall of the castle, lines of banquet tables and benches had been prepared. Castle servants scurried about preparing for the banquet as the sun dipped into evening. Mouth-watering wafts of various roasting meats carried from the kitchens of the castle and the cooking pits in the courtyard. Sicaro's soldiers and Harek's warriors mingled like long-lost comrades, rollicking and jesting loudly about feats past and upcoming with the help of those who spoke both languages. The ale and beer had started to flow early, but Sicaro was not bothered in the least.

Four men-at-arms tagged along behind their king as he strode into the hall and met with a cluster of his captains.

At the arched entrance, Sicaro was accosted by his newly appointed chamberlain—an elderly, but efficient, man who was previously his head of coins.

Half-listening to the administrator, he was distracted by a woman sitting on the steps of the throne dais on the opposite side of the hall.

A courtesan from King Harek's retinue.

Draped in fine yellow silk, her long, willowy form and shapely legs were stretched out before her. But her face hid within the shadows.

He waved the man away and said, "That's fine, Master Feroz. Replace whoever you wish. I will be gone for a long while. Just make sure you keep my holdings well." He dismissed the chamberlain and gestured for Craeg Vesenira to follow him over to the throne dais, lured by his curiosity.

She leaned into a sun ray cutting across the steps. Sicaro's heart leapt as golden hair blazed in the light. He froze in his steps as he took in the features of the woman.

For a bewildered minute, he was looking at his resurrected wife: Katerin, the wife he married thirty years before. Aspiring actress, songstress, and dancer—liar, adulteress, and whore.

The woman's eyes grew wide and in the moment, he

realized it was not his wife, but his daughter, sitting before him.

Karisa, his princess, his queen.

She gasped as their eyes met, and then quickly retreated to the shadows, clapping her hands over her mouth.

"Beautiful, isn't she?" Harek drew up behind as Sicaro continued to stare at Karisa. "Exquisite bone structure. A prize from a raid a few months ago. My captain has a good eye for slaves."

Anger surged at the king's objectifying comments about his daughter.

"I never grow attached to them . . . even though this one is a true pleasure. If you like, you can have her when you return," offered the king in an affable tone. He gulped from a mug of ale in his hand and nodded to himself. "Yes, I'll give her to you as a reward."

Outrage rose in Sicaro's gullet at the liberties Harek spoke of with Karisa, but it quickly dampened at the thought of his daughter finally returned.

She was the only woman he had truly loved, born of his own loins, trustworthy and pure. As beautiful as his deceased wife, but as virtuous as a child. He had given her life; she was his.

Karisa flinched when he walked up the steps and bent down to her ear. "My darling, it won't be long before we will be together again. I will come for you soon."

Chapter 29

The Call to Arms

Meila—Northern Mountain Range, Ascoria

The golden rays of dawn illuminated a carpet of mist seeping down the mountain.

Meila grinned as she watched the vapor caress the forest floor around her legs. The bare ground higher up warmed to the rising sun and generated the mist that then swept down the slopes. She delighted in the natural phenomenon that she had only ever seen once before—yesterday.

Her eyes clouded with tears of sadness as she thought of the decades, the century, that it had taken for her to see this beauty. Despite studying recordings of geo-atmospheric physics as part of her pilot training, actually being present in the mist harmonized her to nature in a way she'd never known before.

A selfish thought teased her. She could live on this planet for the rest of her life. Find some secluded island where she could live simply: stand with nature and breathe fresh air every day. She needed at least a few decades alone. Away from people. Away from responsibility.

Marooned, imprisoned, kidnapped, and rescued—the last few months had been the most exciting she had experienced for a very long time. But also more than enough to last her for the next twenty or thirty years.

Her smile disappeared as she compared her memories of Earth with the spectacle of nature around her and felt a pang of sadness.

She ran a sensory recording of her birthworld; her intra-ocular and intra-aural implants overlaid her senses and took her back several decades to an outing with her daughter—only four years old at the time—and Anton. They played on the shore of a rectangular lake in a green field, several hundred meters wide, surrounded by sky-reaching towers and apartment blocks—looming like walls of an animal enclosure. Their daughter, Erin, in a toddler's bathing suit, looked at her and laughed, eyes full of mischief, then hurtled on tiny feet along a sandy beach into the artificial lake. It was a hot day, as was every day. Anton laughed as he stood ankle-deep in the clear water nearby and was caught by splashes from his errant daughter.

Hundreds of other children and families similarly frolicked and played in the water under a dying, red sun that was partially obscured by toxic clouds of brown and gray. Even at the center of highest society, purifiers were unable to cope with the fumes that enveloped the planet.

Sadly, it was the most cherished memory of nature that she had.

In the past, the memory recording had stimulated joy for Meila, but now it generated only sorrow. Sorrow at the thought of the cancer her homeworld had been and still was.

A noise within the campsite broke into her reverie. Jaks shuffled in the tent as he began to stir from sleep. He was a sweet boy, handsome with a noble face and a sweep of brown hair. If she were a hundred years younger, she would have bedded him without hesitation, but she was wiser now—and almost a species apart.

Although born human, her genes were spliced and augmented beyond semblance of anyone in the Old Colonies. Her implants and embedded technology systems made her a cyborg: part human, part machine. As such, she told herself that she shouldn't form an attachment to a sub-evolved human. For that, she was thankful for the implants that allowed her to turn her primal drives and libido on and off at will.

The youth clambered out of the tent and yawned. "Anything happen overnight? I didn't think I would sleep so deeply. Sorry, I should have woken to let you get some more rest," he said.

"That's all right. I'm rested enough," she replied,

thinking of the metabolic rejuvenation cycle she had run over the past hour.

A thought occurred to her. "Do you think there are more men out there hunting for us? That there could be a bounty in place?"

Jaks paused in his task of packing away the tent. "Maybe for you, but not me. They only took me because I was with you. They didn't want me." Again, he puzzled aloud about Bako and Jop's connection to his father. But he soon diverged from the idea, talking himself into thinking that the men must have switched to working for a slaver or harem collector. Far shores, he explained to her, such as Ellipta and Nera Boa still thrived on markets of flesh.

As she listened to Jaks debating with himself, a movement in the forest distracted Meila. Wary of predators—or possibly bounty hunters—she magnified her lens implants to examine the area closer.

Identifying the source of movement, she pointed at a giantwood. "Two or three animals over that away. Up in the trees. Can you see them? Monkeys?"

"Monkeys?" Jaks frowned. "What do you mean?"

"Little primates. Oh, of course, you don't have them here. Human-like animals that used to live in forests and jungles . . . before they went extinct." She palmed the grip of her darkcore pistol resting in its holster, reviewed its settings with her transdermal palm circuits, and adjusted the weapon to the lowest setting: one-fiftieth of full power—enough to kill any small animal.

"Little people." Jaks peered out into the forest. "Could be the dryads. Slender and about knee-high?"

She nodded. "Climbing around like squirrels. There's one there, halfway up. Whatever they are, their movements don't seem predatory." She took her hand away from her weapon and crossed her arms.

"It's probably them. They're peaceful creatures. I rescued one from a hunting trap once. They gave me apples in return." He smiled and stood beside her. "I hope they come out. I'd love you to see one up close." The youth looked at her, eyes flashing warmth for a moment, and then twisted back to stare at the trees.

Meila returned his smile, then brushed past him to the boulders where the saddle bags rested. Bako's stallion nudged at one of the bags. She opened it and extracted the feed bags, poured grain into each, and placed them on the ground.

Happy with her work, she dusted off her hands and foraged around in the saddlebags until she found some dried meat and fruit that she went to share with Jaks.

He was on the other side of the clearing, bending down. In front of him stood one of the small creatures with tiny clawed hands raised with an offering. A doll-like creature made from the forest, with skin the color of mottled bark, clothing of dried leaves, and hair of twigs and fiber. It turned to Meila with large green eyes, then skipped away to the trees on graceful limbs.

"Wait," Jaks cried out, staring after the dryad. A burst of mewling sounds followed in return, but the creature scampered up high into the overhead tree branches and away from view.

"Skittish," observed Meila. "Interesting little thing, though."

He held up a cluster of berries on a stalk. Crimson-colored, wrinkled, and the size of a grape, there were five of them, and they looked delicious.

"Are they safe to eat?" she asked.

"Only way to find out." Jaks plucked one fruit and tossed it into his mouth. "Mmm . . . tangy. Try one?"

She looked at it dubiously but popped the proffered berry into her mouth. Her tongue tingled and her lips puckered. "Sour. If you don't want them, hand them over. They're delicious." Mouth salivating, she crammed the last berries into her mouth and winced at the tartness bursting through her senses.

Jaks looked at her as though she had just grown a mustache and then laughed.

Meila grinned at him and wiped her lips. "All right, let's get going. Unless your little friend is bringing back some more berries."

They rode north, Meila keeping a steady direction as they retraced the exact same route from the previous day with the assistance of her memory implants.

"You have such good navigation sense," Jaks remarked to her after a few hours of riding through the wild woodlands. "I get lost unless I'm following a trail or something. Ranger Cromer said insects have a better sense of direction than me."

"He might be right. Some beetles, back on Earth at least, have excellent navigation sense. Some even use the stars to find their way around," she said.

Jaks frowned and looked wounded.

"I'm not teasing. It's true. Don't worry, everyone is unique in their own way. Scarab beetles navigate by stars—and you can literally do magic. You did well yesterday."

He raised his hands, studying them like they were foreign to his arms. "I felt sick afterward . . . Bako . . . it was gruesome. His body was so disfigured. Like a pig seared over a fire. His eyes—"

"You did what you had to do, Jaks. One of them would have killed you. Him or the fat one. They were professional killers. You saw the farmer they murdered. You couldn't have fought them on their terms. You used what you had," she said, directing her horse down a gully lined with skeletal trees almost bare from dropping their summer leaves.

A few minutes later, she asked in a small voice, "What does it feel like when you invoke magic?"

"It's hard work getting all the aspects to work together."

"But what does it *feel* like?"

He grimaced and narrowed his eyes. "Powerful. Like destruction bottled up and trying to force its way out. But uncontrollable. You don't know what will come. Whether it'll be a trickle or a flood. I want to invoke it again right now, but I'm afraid it would hurt you or the horses. I want to test it. Maybe blast that tree and see it explode." His voice took on a chilling tone.

"Okay, calm down. Let's just focus on riding," she said, surprised at Jaks's turn of mind. "Leave the experiments for some other time."

Late that afternoon, Jaks whooped in delight when they broke out of the forest at the top of the valley. Below, pastures and plains, green and brown, spread out like a patchwork quilt. Far to the north, through augmented eyes, Meila could see the city walls and smokestacks of Dunberrin; Jaks, however, despite his youthful eyes, reported he could see only clouds on the horizon.

Thankful that the rest of the forest had been uneventful, they set up camp within the tree line and rested for the night.

"What do you think's happening?" Meila asked the next morning as she and Jaks watched a great column of soldiers, horses, and wagons traversing a highway far off in the distance. They were just partway down the mountain slope and had caught sight of the organized mass. As far as she could tell, it began in the capital city and disappeared to the south. She magnified her intraocular implants with a thought and studied the constituents in detail.

"My guess is there's been more raids along the

coast," said Jaks. "The Vorosians scare me. I was only a kid when the last war finished, and we never really saw the effects of it at home, except my father coming back now and then. News of it all seemed very remote—like an entirely different country." He pulled his horse up next to Meila, who was at a standstill, holding her hand against the glare. "I suppose it was because Ascoria was conquering other kingdoms . . . but it's now us who might be invaded."

"About four thousand troops, by my estimate. Forced march, some of the heavily armored soldiers are struggling to stay in formation," she told Jaks.

"Maybe they've *already* invaded," he replied, chewing on his lip.

"If they have, our time's running out. Let's get moving." She pulled her cloak tight around her chest and flicked her mare to descend the green vale.

A few hours later, a cornfield ranged in front of them. The heads of the plants looked full and ready to harvest, but there were no signs of harvesting. The only movement, in fact, was the breeze shushing through swaying rows of cornstalks.

Jaks pulled his gelding up next to Meila. "Is this where they murdered that farmer? Don't know if we should trample through their field again . . . and if his body is still there, and someone saw us, they might think we did it."

"We'll go around. I'm sure I can pick up the trail from the other side. There is a risk that the grandmaster and the others could be going through the field at this very moment and pass us by, but I think that's a low probability." She nudged the mare left to follow the field's edge.

Soon, a farmhouse came into view, built at the corner of the cornfield. Tidy with not a loose board in sight, a tail of smoke trickled into the sky from its brick chimney stack.

"Let's give it a wide berth. Best if we don't interact with anyone." Meila applied gentle pressure to her horse's left side. Her thighs ached with the past few days of riding, but her muscles were firming up fast.

As they ranged away, four people walked out of the farmhouse. Despite being a few hundred yards away, Meila could feel their eyes upon her. A woman waved an arm at them as though to beckon them and began jogging toward them, hollering as she came.

"Just keep going. Pretend we didn't see them," Meila said, staring straight ahead at the horizon.

A few minutes later, the shouts were too close to ignore. She sighed and turned in her saddle to see a woman and three youths puffing after them. "Excuse me, excuse me," the woman called in a screechy voice.

"We should stop. Sounds like they're desperate," Jaks said in a too-sensible tone.

They stopped and waited for the farmers to catch up. "You talk to them. You're nicer," said Meila.

The woman had a weathered but kindly looking face with crows-feet wrinkles at the corners of her blood-shot eyes. Two of the lads puffing after her were plump and looked so similar they could only be twins. Trudging behind them came a stocky young man with wide nostrils opening out straight from his face. All the young men lugged sacks over their backs.

"Hello. Sorry to bother you, citizen. You're heading to the muster? Could you take my boys with you?" the woman said between breaths, leaning with one hand against her hip. "We only heard this morning when a herald came through."

"Muster?" Jaks asked.

"You didn't hear? The Voros army landed. The king has issued a call to arms . . . I thought you were heading to the muster point." The woman frowned. Her boys caught up with her, panting.

Meila and Jaks exchanged a glance.

"We're not going there," Jaks said—not knowing where "there" was—and looked to Meila for help. But she didn't meet his eyes. "We're going back to the capital."

The woman weighed his words and replied, "All right, my sons will just go with you to the main road, then. The muster is at Lohort village, a league from there. My husband would have taken them, but he . . . passed away recently."

Jaks looked at Meila again, who just nodded to him. "I'm sorry to hear about your husband," he said.

"Yes, well, he fell and hit his head last week. Dead and buried. Nothing I can do about that now." The woman's shoulders slumped, and she pursed her lips tightly. She then turned back to her young men and said, "Off you go, boys."

The woman—their mother, she guessed—grabbed the twins, one arm around each, and hugged them tightly. Her shoulders shuddered as she let out a loud sob and held them for a long minute until one of them pushed her away. "We'll be okay, Ma. We'll be back soon—don't you worry. Ma Kendall will help you with the harvest," the lad said to her.

She reached for the third son, but he brushed past her and patted her on the head, saying, "See yah, old bag."

The twin brothers, Meila learned, were actually twenty years old, a year or two older than Jaks—their rounded faces made them appear younger than they were. The oldest brother was five years older and lacked in wit but had a sly demeanor about him. They had been walking slightly behind Jaks's horse for just a few minutes when one of the twins asked, "How come you're not going to the muster? You must have done your conscription by now."

Jaks followed the burly youth's gaze to his upper arm covered by the sleeve of his leather armor. Self-consciously, he slapped a hand to where the conscript brand lay beneath and rubbed at it. "I'm . . . we're . . . on the king's business. We're on an errand."

The other twin looked back and forth between Jaks

and Meila, one eyebrow raised. "What is she? Someone important or something? She looks foreign."

Meila pivoted in her saddle to look back at Jaks and asked in amusement, "Yes, what *am* I?"

The twins stared at her, as though astonished she could speak, or perhaps surprised at her accent.

"She's a, she is a . . ." He fumbled for an explanation for a moment. "She's a master from the Academy. And I'm her guard. We're on a secret mission—"

"All right, that's enough," Meila said, glaring at Jaks as though scolding him, and then turned away.

"Ooh," the twins said simultaneously.

Jaks flicked his horse reins to distance himself from the brothers, but heard the eldest brother say to the twins, "She don't look like she'd be from the Academy. She looks like a dancer. I bet she's one of those dancers. You know." He sniggered.

"Shut up, Harold, you're an idiot," the first twin said, and they all fell silent.

Meila felt anxious to be rid of the farm boys, mixed with a little guilt that their father's death was related to her captors' actions.

Several minutes later, she swiveled around in her saddle—not confident to turn her horse at a sharp angle—and called back to the young men, "Our paths part here. We're heading over the field. The main road is not far; I'm sure you can get there on your own." She used her imperious tone.

The farm boys shrugged and dragged their feet

down the dirt path past Meila and Jaks. One twin muttered as he passed by, "Dunno why you just don't take the road."

Ignoring the comment, Jaks waved as they departed. "Bye, good luck ... You're very brave."

Meila laughed when the twins and their brother were out of earshot. "'You're very brave' ... what was that?"

"I felt bad that they have to join the conscript army. Technically, I should be going to the muster as well. I don't really have an excuse not to. If we run into a muster sergeant, they'll take me in." He nudged his horse to follow Meila, directing her horse again to follow the edge of the cornfield.

"All the more reason to avoid any further contact with people. Wouldn't want to be hauled off as cannon fodder," she said.

"Cannon fodder?"

"On ancient Earth, they shot enormous guns, cannons, at the front line of charging soldiers. So, the generals would send in the most poorly trained troops first as 'cannon fodder,'" she explained.

"Did your ship have a gun like that?" asked Jaks a minute later, probably having toiled over the idea since she'd mentioned it.

"No, nothing that large. It wasn't a warship. We only had weapons for protection if we were boarded or landed somewhere hostile."

"Could you design one? Something that

Grandmaster Mulgrave could build with the runic forge?"

She turned to him and saw a boyish grin. "Possibly. But if we retrieve darkcore rifles from the wreckage, they'll be almost as good and ready to use. Whereas a cannon of whatever design would take months or years to build. And, we would need to obtain an energy source—gunpowder, most likely. All hypothetical. Best just to focus on getting to the wreckage in good time."

They picked up their trail on the other side of the cornfield and continued their journey in silence.

Finally, they crested a hill and Meila spotted the rivertown, where they'd been kidnapped, several miles in the distance. With their goal clearly located, they took a direct route, rather than trying to follow the tangential one their captors had taken them that night.

Several peasants tended the wheat fields as they approached. Meila's augmented vision distinguished them as two women and three men with shovels—all wizened and old—no young helpers visible, perhaps sent off to the muster as well. One put a hand to his brow and squinted at them but soon returned to his digging.

"Well, it appears that Ranger Cromer didn't pick up our trail," Meila said. "Hopefully, we can find out where they've gone." Meila's horse broke out of the field and stepped over a ditch to surer footing on the road leading into the town.

Drear and gloom hung over the buildings, vastly

different from the lively cheer of a few days ago. The few people on the streets were twitchy-eyed at the storm clouds overhead and similarly at Meila and Jaks riding into their village. An elderly woman, pushing a cartful of wood beams, yelled at them as they passed, "The muster is the other way." She stopped and scowled when they ignored her.

They dismounted at the traveler's stable beside the Drover's Inn, and Jaks greeted the stablemaster.

"They been looking for you. The Ranger and all. Disappeared a few days ago—didn't yous? Caused them quite a kerfuffle. They thought you'd run off together . . ." His face then cracked into a knowing grin and he tapped his nose. "Yous done banging your bits together and back now, eh?" He winked at Jaks.

She didn't understand half of what he was saying but understood his lewd insinuation and ignored it. "Where has the grandmaster gone?" she asked, handing the weathered man the reins to the mare.

"Out looking for yous. I expect he'll be back soon." The stablemaster gathered the reins of all three horses in his hand.

Jaks pointed at a horse already settled into the stable. "That's Vixhana's horse. She must be here."

"Yep. They go out during the day looking for yous and come back in the afternoon. The captain and the ranger been back an hour already." The man nodded at the inn and led the horses to the stalls inside.

Jaks rushed up the outside stairs of the building to

the sleeping rooms and rapped knuckles hard against his sister's door, already grabbing at the door handle. It didn't budge, but he heard a loud thump inside the room. "Vixhana. Are you there?" he called through the door.

The door opened to a dark room, and his sister's powerful frame filled the doorway. Naked but for a bedsheet clutched to her front, sweat glistened on her skin, and her dark hair was tousled and loose. She stepped forward, pushing Jaks into the hallway, and closed the door.

"What the hell, Jaks. Where have you been? We've been looking everywhere for you two," she said, barely controlling her anger. She turned her glare on Meila and then down to her holstered pistol. "Did *she* put you up to this?"

Meila stared back wide-eyed at the muscular, strong-boned woman who, in her nakedness, radiated with primal energy. Together with the scent of passion, she suspected they'd interrupted Vixhana and a companion in the throes of lust.

"Ah, oh, I'm sorry, Vix. I'll go wait for you to get changed," Jaks stuttered and bumped into Meila, trying to retreat past her.

Vixhana grabbed her brother by his arm. "Stay here. Tell me, where have you been?" she said. "If you two just wanted to go and grind, you didn't need to run away to do it."

Jaks's face colored in a second, ears red as beets. "It's

not anything like that. We were kidnapped." He stared at the wall, unable to meet her nakedness or her glare, and then explained the events of the past four days as quickly as he could.

Vixhana released him and her face softened as she listened; by the end, she was studying the purple bruises on their faces and nodding in approval at their fight to escape.

The door to the bedroom then opened and the lean figure of Ranger Cromer walked out.

Jaks's mouth fell open, and he stared at the man.

The ranger leaned casually against the doorframe, exposing a mess inside the room with Vixhana's discarded nightwraith armor and weapons around a barren mattress.

"Now, let me get dressed and we'll go discuss this some more while we wait for the grandmaster to return. He should be back soon," Vixhana said.

Jaks looked uneasily back and forth between Vixhana and the ranger, clearly not liking what he saw. Meila nudged him in the back, rousing him from his bewilderment, and turned to go downstairs to the communal washroom.

Vixhana called out to her, "Wait. Wait here until I'm clothed. I'm not letting you out of my sight for the time being." The nightwraith retreated to her room and began hopping around in the shadows, donning clothes and armor.

An hour later, Mulgrave and Tavis burst into the

tavern, surprising the few diners sitting around eating and drinking, and stormed up to the round table where Meila sat with Jaks, Vixhana, and Cromer. "What's this all about?" the mage asked in an irritated voice.

This time, Meila explained the kidnapping, describing the events of the past several days in greater detail than Jaks had earlier, and attributing their escape to the electromancy invocations that Jaks had conjured.

Everybody stared at Jaks, and his face reddened again until he murmured dismissively, "It was nothing."

Tavis folded his arms and scowled, staring at the center of the table.

Mulgrave rubbed his chin, then looked over at Ranger Cromer. "Do you remember seeing the men?" he asked the arrow-bearded man stabbing a chunk of meat on his plate.

The ranger paused the fork halfway to his mouth. "Don't know who they were, but I remember the bald one and the fat one." He nodded his head at the back wall of the tavern where the men had been that evening. "I asked around for them, but no one knew who they were or saw them leave the village."

Mulgrave clasped his hands in front of him and said to Jaks, "Sinister, but I doubt your father would have any hand in this. I'm sure he has better things to do than organize a kidnapping. As you say, the pair were most probably slavers on the prowl for fresh meat." He nodded to himself. "I think our captain should keep a closer eye on our ward from now on."

Vixhana nodded briskly in response and settled her gaze on Meila.

The mage pulled a chair to join the table and then waved his hand at the innkeeper for more food.

From there, their discussions turned to the Vor invasion and speculations about the numbers and location of the enemy horde—and what King Silas would do to defend the country.

All the while, Meila listened and ruminated, aware that she was becoming dangerously entwined in the lives of these people—far more than she wanted. If she weren't so reliant on the escape pod back at the Academy for planetary rescue, if she had another transponder to signal her location off-planet, she could escape all of this to some isolated haven and wait for evacuation. *Damn these people and their problems.*

She contemplated toggling off her emotions, but then realized she was feeling something she hadn't for many decades—she was starting to care.

Chapter 30

Apprentice

Jaks–Jurn Lowlands, Ascoria

For one of them, it was going to end badly.

Jaks and Tavis stared at each other, rain beating a staccato on the tin roof of the open-walled shelter and dripping through rusted holes to the packed dirt floor beneath their feet.

That morning, they had gifted Bako's captured horses to the stable master as payment for stall hire, and resumed the journey interrupted several days before by the kidnapping. They followed Ranger Cromer out of the rivertown, pausing at the next village for Grandmaster Mulgrave to display the king's emissary letter to the soldiers at the border cordon, and then broke out onto the roadless riverplains of Jurn.

The horses forded countless streams and rivers—the namesakes of the delta plains. Often flooded and impassable by foot during the spring, in summer and autumn they were lush, fertile pastures for shepherds with their herds of cattle and sheep.

Midafternoon brought storm clouds rolling over the plains with raindrops falling fat and heavy. When visibility began to diminish under the downpour, the drenched ranger directed them off to a cluster of buildings in the foothills of the mountains nearby. A complex of old mining buildings crowded around an abandoned iron mine that, according to Cromer, had been exhausted and caved-in several years before. Only the tin-roofed shelters and warehouses in ramshackle condition remained.

With six humans, six horses, and one pack mule to shelter, the ranger commandeered the largest building in the abandoned site. The tall structure was simple but sturdy with steel beams propping up a rusted roof; it looked built to shelter heavy machinery and had no need for walls of any sort. Indeed, a rail track led from the mine entrance out to this very building and ended at a rotten wooden barrier with several wrecked ore carts marooned nearby.

It was here that Grandmaster Mulgrave had clapped his hands to summon Jaks and Tavis beneath the leaky tin-roof. They came together and stared at each other as the others settled at the other end of the warehouse.

Jaks knew this test was due.

Mulgrave had learnt that Jaks had successfully invoked electromancy when he had cut ropes and then fought Bako and Jop. Now, the grandmaster wanted to see it for himself.

If he failed to show it now, it would disappoint the mage, and Jaks's powers could be justifiably dismissed as chaotic manifestations that were as uncontrollable as the rain outside—unreliable, untrainable, and a waste of his time.

Then, Jaks reckoned, once they returned from their quest, the Academy would release him to be conscripted to the battlefront and likely suffer a meaningless death at the hands of a horde of axe warriors.

But even if he did successfully manifest electromancy, would it be enough to dislodge Tavis from his apprentice position?

Despite Meila's reassurance that the Academy would find Jaks a master if he showed electromancy potential, he wasn't so sure. Tavis, a dual-mage commanding gravmancy and pyromancy just like Grandmaster Mulgrave, could pursue a legacy to create powerful runic-forge weapons and artifacts, whereas Jaks, with only electromancy, had no creative potential, only destructive power.

"Show me what you can do, lad. I really hope your powers have matured," Mulgrave said, resting a hand on an upturned ore cart. Tavis moved to stand behind the mage and kept a wary eye on Jaks. "Something small. One of the first exercises I use with an apprentice is palming an energy ball—in your case, a lightning ball. Do you need a trigger . . . another spider, perhaps?"

"Um, that won't be necessary," Jaks replied, wishing to go and dry off by the fire that Vixhana was trying to start with a flint and tinderbox.

He raised a cupped hand in front of him and visualized a ball of brilliant white sparking to life. Nothing happened. Tense under the close observation of the grandmaster and the smirking Tavis, he had forgotten the other two aspects of invocation; without them, he wasn't invoking magic, he was simply imagining things. Under such scrutiny, away from the urgency of life-and-death, why was it so much harder to invoke magic?

Frustrated with himself, Jaks took a deep breath and began the invocation as he had been taught. He closed his eyes and recalled the memory of his father. Bestial and sneering, looming over his bed with a giant hand descending to crush his face—had it been a dream, as he had always thought it, or was it a genuine memory?—his body trembled, and his mouth curled unconsciously in fear. Forgetting the reason for summoning the memory, a haze descended and his mind fell numb and empty. *Dammit. Not this again.*

He cursed inwardly, kept his eyes closed and tried again, this time holding the fear. *Paper tigers. Thoughts are just thoughts, they are not real.* He then concentrated on willing the lightning into life.

His closed eyelids flashed red, and an odd humming sound grew in front of him. He flicked open his eyes and discovered a sphere of blue-white light in his outstretched hand. Feelings of delight surged through him—and the lightning ball extinguished. Out of the corner of his eye, he glimpsed Mulgrave's disappointed look at the fleeting demonstration.

Without hesitation, Jaks invoked the lightning ball again and resolved to sustain it for far longer. This time, the lightning ball sprang to his palm, and he carefully balanced the fear and his consciousness, teetering like a seesaw.

After a few seconds, the ball grew larger, stretching outward. Suddenly, it flashed up a column and struck the rusted roof. A loud explosion blew a man-sized hole through the corrugated tin, blasting chips and slugs into the sky, adding metal castings to the rain.

Surprised by the explosion, Jaks lost the invocation, and the warehouse went silent and dim. Rain poured through the hole and soaked him to the skin.

Laughter boomed from the other end of the warehouse, where the normally straight-faced Vixhana pointed at the hole in the roof and slapped her leather-encased leg. "You'll be the death of one of us one day," she called out.

Only Meila joined in the laughter, while the men stared with a mixture of fear and dismay on their faces. Tavis cowered behind an ore cart covering his ears, while Grandmaster Mulgrave swore loudly and started musing aloud about the magical properties he'd seen. Ranger Cromer's initial look of surprise quickly faded, and he turned to calm the horses still startled by the explosion.

"By gods, what a spectacle," Mulgrave said with a grin peeled to his face. "You've got potential, but you're going to have to work on reducing that volatility. At this stage, you will need to focus on sustaining a small invocation for as long as possible. That will get you used to channeling magic until it becomes as natural as breathing."

The mage looked at Tavis, who had recovered from his fright and had a pinched expression on his face. "How long can you sustain a fireball now, Tavis?"

"Two hours, Master," the apprentice proudly replied and invoked an oblong flame in his hand, recovering his display of cowardice.

"Well, go be useful and help light that campfire." Mulgrave gestured at Vixhana, who had returned to working a tinder at a smoldering pile of wood.

For the next hour, Mulgrave coached Jaks to maintain a pearl of buzzing energy in his hand. He could sustain it for a minute at the most. Maintaining the invocation drained his concentration quickly, until his head felt heavy and thick.

"That's good for now . . ." The grandmaster nodded and stroked his chin. "There's enough here to convince me to take you on as an apprentice—your gift is rare and needs much training. I'll keep you both on for now, but once we get back to the Academy, I'll need to decide which of you to continue with." He looked at Tavis, at the other end of the warehouse, drying himself by a crackling campfire, and back to Jaks.

Jaks grinned. "Thank you, grandmaster. I won't let you down."

———

The rain eased overnight, and by the morning, the clouds were mere puffs of white. Only puddles and mud remained as evidence of the rainstorm of the previous day.

Ranger Cromer rode out to scout the surroundings while the rest of them broke up camp.

Jaks felt a lighter mood while the ranger was gone. His anxiety about his survival instructor had taken on an additional layer of confusion since seeing the man walking out of his naked sister's room at the rivertown inn. He felt betrayed by Vixhana. How could she share a bed with the cruel man who had belittled him so often? Surely, it had been a one-off dalliance. He'd heard of soldiers having "pre-battle" relations with each other—the threat of death stirring febrile urges to seek company—but he couldn't stomach the idea of Vixhana and Cromer being together.

As they finished packing and began to wonder at the ranger's whereabouts, he returned. "The area from here is notorious for wulverions, but I didn't see any signs or tracks of them around. We'll need to remain alert for them, however," he said.

"Wolves, did you say?" Meila asked, vaulting onto her saddled mare.

"Wulverions," corrected Cromer. "They run together in packs of much greater numbers than wolves and can turn into shadows. Only the sound of their pounding feet will alert you before they attack. We should keep double-watch and a fire burning through the night."

"Fascinating beasts," Mulgrave remarked. "One of the few species that use illumancy in that way. A few other species, birds mainly, use it for attracting mates or to ward off predators, but wulverions use it to stalk prey. Truly, one of nature's assassins." Mulgrave looked at Vixhana in nightwraiths' armor as though comparing her to the wulverions.

"Well, if a pack of shadows starts tearing me apart—I'll know what they are." Meila laughed, trying to lighten the mood. "How long will we be riding amongst these land piranhas?"

"About four days to the Jurn Highlands. From there, there'll be different kinds of predators to watch out for," Cromer replied.

Now clear of the riverplains, a road led away from the mining camp and took them to the south—mountains to their right, and a grassy ocean of brown to their left.

The savannahs of Jurn were renowned for their savage wildlife and rugged nomads with their tent villages who once roamed the sweeping plains. However, exiled decades before, the plains folk had been forced by King Silas's armies, in his great land grab, into the wild mountains to the south and the great forests of Strock to the east.

Now, ranches of longhorns and fortified towns attempted to tame the wild expanse—their success thriving and failing on keeping out the lions, wulverions, and other predators that not only kept the humans corralled but also the immense stampeding herds of wild ponies and antelope under control. Of all Ascoria, the province of Jurn was the most lush but also the most wild.

As the group followed the dirt road skirting the edge of the savannah, they established a riding formation with Cromer leading, followed by Mulgrave and Tavis (with the pack mule), then Jaks and Meila, tailed by Vixhana, always at the rear. Mostly, they rode single file, but when he got bored, Jaks would ride up beside Meila and make small talk.

He enjoyed her company, even though she talked down to him like a child at times. He again pondered her rebuff of his declaration of love for her. Could she not see that he was a grown man of eighteen years, that they had a real connection? He kept his muddled feelings to himself and stared at her lovely, slender neck, confusing himself even more.

Midmorning, Ranger Cromer pointed at a large group of figures approaching through the plains from the west. Jaks saw several were on horseback, but the other hundred or more were on foot and carrying rucksacks. By their snail's pace, he guessed they would cross paths when their road met up at an intersection ahead.

When the group joined the main road, they headed straight toward Jaks and his party. As they neared, he recognized the king's pike and shield crest on the lead rider's chest plate and saw the people on foot dressed in conscript armor similar to what he himself had worn only weeks before. They all had spears, while a few had crossbows across their backs.

"Ho!" The lead horseman rode forward, the markings of an army captain visible on his shoulder. "Greetings, citizens. You going to the muster?" The gray-haired man—probably a garrison captain from one of the remote towns—eyed Cromer and Vixhana appraisingly, then fixated on the crest, like his own, imprinted on their saddlebags.

The column of male and female conscripts stopped and dropped their rucksacks to the ground, eager for a rest from their march. Most of them appeared fit and healthy, but some looked long past their peak fighting days. One elderly man wheezed, leaning heavily against a stick, and then dropped to the ground with his rucksack still attached to his back, resembling an upturned beetle.

Ranger Cromer sat forward on his horse and pulled at his beard. "No. We're on private business. You can be on your way."

"But we're at war." The guardsman licked his lips

and straightened in his saddle. *"Everyone* is called to arms. You're not deserters, are you?"

Jaks admired the man's courage to challenge the dangerous-looking ranger with the even more lethal-looking Vixhana behind him.

Even though any of the three—Cromer, Vixhana, or Mulgrave—could have intimidated the guardsman into submission, the grandmaster saved the man his pride and rode forward. "We're on the king's business," he said, pulling out the letter stamped with the king's seal.

The guardsman's eyes bulged as he read the letter. "Right you are, my lord. Sorry to bother you." He quickly handed the royal decree back to Mulgrave and saluted awkwardly. "I had to check—we've had some trouble with muster dodgers along the way." He glanced at a group of young men casting resentful looks around at the others. "Let me clear the road for you to pass."

"That won't be necessary. We'll go alongside. Your people are weary. It must have been a hard night under the rain."

As they rode past the conscripts, Tavis drew alongside Mulgrave and spoke in a loud voice that Jaks heard, even from several yards back. "Grandmaster, perhaps we *should* return to Dunberrin with the muster? With the Vors invading, surely our efforts would be better directed to producing weapons and such to aid the defense. We're maybe wasting our time chasing after artifacts that may not even be there," the apprentice said. "Even if we can find this wreckage, bandits or wildmen may very well have pilfered everything." Tavis's face creased with concern. "What if there's nothing there . . . and we've wasted all this time?"

Meila interrupted before the mage could reply, trotting up beside the apprentice and mage. "No one can get into a weapons locker without the ability to unlock it. Only one of my crew or I could do that. If there's a locker in the wreckage, the weapons will be there."

Tavis grunted. "Truly, what difference would they make against tens of thousands of Vors, anyway? We should be building proper siege machines back at the Academy."

"You moron. One of these"—Meila held up her darkcore pistol—"stores over a million megajoules of dark energy. On automatic fire, I could kill a couple hundred of your Vors in a minute. What could your stupid catapult do?" She waved the pistol around in the air. "And any one of the rifles on my ship could sight and kill your Vors from over ten miles away. If you think some piddly siege weapon would do better—go ahead and build your wooden toys."

Tavis scowled and mumbled, "They'd be iron and steel . . ."

Jaks grinned as the woman verbally cut down the apprentice. Mulgrave simply laughed.

Meila sighed, and shaking her head, holstered the pistol.

Tavis conceded defeat with a flap of a hand and grumbled quietly to himself. After a few minutes, seeking some other target for his agitation, he leaned back over his saddle to look at Jaks and whispered, "You should be with those conscripts. You'll never be a mage," then turned away.

Jaks's ears colored, and he glared at the back of the apprentice's head, wishing him dead. Then, in a surge of anger, he drew up behind Tavis and whispered forcefully, "The grandmaster took me on as an apprentice yesterday—so there. I bet he's going to get rid of you when we get back."

Tavis glared at him. "I don't believe you," he said, then flicked his reins to veer toward the grandmaster.

Jaks watched the apprentice confer with his master and then smirked when the older apprentice's shoulders slumped and his back sagged. Not long until he would be rid of his opponent.

Chapter 31

The Wulverions

It was two nights later that death stalked them from the dark.

Jaks huddled under a blanket with his back to the bulbous lower trunk of a dardan tree and flicked his eyes open for the fourth time in as many minutes. *Wake up, I can't fall asleep on watch with Ranger Cromer.* He looked at the tents and sleeping forms of his companions and found Cromer standing in the shadows near the tethered horses. The glow from the campfire flickered against the veteran's cloaked back as he stared out into the darkness surrounding their glade of trees.

His back tingled as though something was watching him. However, flashing his lightstone torch beyond the edge of the trees revealed nothing but the emptiness of night—nothing but lack of sleep playing tricks on his mind.

He shook his head, shed the wool square from his

shoulders, and lurched over to the crackling campfire. He scrunched his eyes several times, then threw more branches onto the fire and rubbed his hands over the flames. He yawned. Not long until the change of guard shift and he could get some more sleep.

The last couple of days of traveling had been tiring—sitting in a saddle for ten hours a day—but not dull, since Jaks had taken up a new hobby: zapping flies and insects, a fun, distracting exercise that required fast reactions and grew his invocation skill.

Grandmaster Mulgrave highly approved. Even more so since it reduced the swarms of biting gnats around them.

However, Vixhana hated Jaks's newfound skill; the sharp cracking sound and trail of fried bugs irritated her. She would snap at him, ordering him to stop. Jaks would, but then renewed with vigor each time a fresh plague assaulted him.

Jaks grinned, feeling he'd mastered the small, basic invocations. It must be time for more potent ones.

A tingling sensation suddenly ran up his back again. He looked around the camp and noticed the horses shuffling and grunting. *There is someone watching us.*

Vixhana's stallion let out a whinny and thumped at the ground. A loud whistle followed, and Ranger Cromer turned to him with his fingers dropping from his lips. "Get everyone up, we're surrounded." He held his bow in his hand with an arrow on the string and jerked his head back to the dark fields.

Jaks took up the call. "Wake up, wake up, wake up!" he shouted as he ran back to the tree where he had left his repeating crossbow, snatched it up, and ratcheted the first bolt into its groove with cold and trembling hands.

"What is it? What's going on?" Vixhana rose from her sleep mat, having refused the comforts of a tent, and pushed her way to her feet. Fully armored, she was ready in an instant, sword bared and into her hand before the others had even appeared.

Mulgrave and Tavis scrambled out of their tents. Tavis was in a cotton gambeson, his mélange of armor parts still piled up in his shelter. He looked about wildly and rummaged around for his sword somewhere back in his tent.

"Wulverions. They've surrounded the campsite," the ranger called to them without turning from the outward danger, an arrow nocked to his bow and ready to draw.

The horses snorted and shuffled, their dark eyes wide and searching. Jaks's palfrey, a brown gelding, pulled at its tether and came loose from the tree it had been bound to—finding freedom, it twisted about as though unsure where to run to.

Her longsword in her right hand, Vixhana stretched out her left and invoked illumancy. A bright beam of light shone from the end of her fist.

She took charge and shouted out commands to defend. "Secure those horses," she ordered Jaks. Then, directing her illumancy beam at Meila—standing by a tent with her darkcore pistol in one hand and a lightstone torch in the other—she said, "You, watch the road." She instructed Mulgrave and Tavis to watch a section each. They all faced outward with their backs to the campfire.

Jaks crouched as he approached the loose palfrey. He caught its attention, and then, whispering to it, stroked its mane. He placed his crossbow on the ground, keeping one eye on the trees as he retied the horse's tether to the trunk. Despite his presence, the animals continued agitating, and Vixhana's stallion snorted and pawed at the ground.

Jaks caught glimpses of eyes reflecting his torch beam.

"Looks like hundreds of them," Tavis said, having finally pulled on a steel breastplate and found a sword and shield.

Meila corrected him. "More like about fifty of them . . . I can see their heat signatures. Most of them are circling—makes it hard to count," she said, brandishing her pistol two-handedly in the direction of the road.

"Are they going to attack?" Jaks asked, having returned to the defensive circle. He gripped his crossbow tightly and considered whether he should use the weapon or attempt his electromancy if the wild animals pounced at them.

"Huh, the eyes just disappeared . . ." Tavis said, his voice rising higher. The apprentice unconsciously stepped backward, only stopping when the campfire flicked at his backside.

"They're circling closer," Meila said.

The sound of dozens of pounding feet surrounded the trees, but Jaks couldn't see anything beyond the tree line, despite the probing beams of the rune torches and Vixhana's invocation.

He tensed himself for an attack. He would use the crossbow, he decided, admitting to himself that his control of lightning was still largely untamed and might harm his companions or the horses close by.

With a roar, an enormous ring of fire sprang to life and encircled the entire glade. Raging, neck-high flames resembling a burning fence filled the darkness. Grandmaster Mulgrave held his arms widespread with an expression of intense focus on his face as he channeled the magical barrier.

Several wolf-like forms burst into flame. Ablaze, they leapt out of the ring of fire, howling, and writhed about on the ground. The curved trunks of the dardan trees were silhouetted by the fire, and several of the lower branches caught on fire. Smoke and the smell of burning wood, flesh, and fur wafted through the glade.

Several more shadows dared the flames and leapt through, but then vanished amongst the tree trunks as soon as they penetrated the ring of flame.

"A few came through," Vixhana yelled. "Near you, Jaks." She ran toward him while he looked about wildly.

Meila's mare squealed, and the other horses thrashed at their tethers. Hooves flew about dangerously, and Jaks backed away from the muscular animals.

The back legs of the mare collapsed, dragged down to her rear haunches by some unseen attacker. Its whinnying turned into an agonized squeal.

The other horses broke away except for the pony, which heaved about still on the end of its restraint.

Vixhana swung her longsword at a dark shadow attached to the leg of the mare and was rewarded with a howl as an injured wulverion lost its camouflage and was revealed with its spine cleaved in half and blood spurting from its severed aorta—it collapsed to the ground, spasmed, and died.

An arrow hissed across the glade and pinned another wulverion, causing it to expose itself as it twisted to snap at the arrow in its back leg. Even before it fell, Ranger Cromer had another arrow flying toward another shadow bounding toward the struggling pony.

"Look away from me. Look away," Vixhana shouted. A few seconds later, light erupted throughout the woods from where she stood.

Jaks dared a glimpse at her and saw her magnificent, as he had never seen her before. His sister radiated brilliance, looking like a warrior angel descended from the heavens. Her face, skin, and armor emitted pure white light. In her left hand, she had a struggling wulverion by the throat, held up in the air like a ragdoll. In her right hand, she held her sword above her head, about to strike at a blinded wulverion stumbling at her feet.

Awed but almost completely blinded by his sister's illumancy, Jaks immediately regretted his glance. Howls and brays of animals surrounded him. Snarling jaws attacked and pounding hooves sought escape.

He pointed his crossbow at something growling, a blurry shape moving toward him. He pulled the trigger, and the weapon shuddered. The bolt thudded into flesh.

Then a weight rammed into him, the blow spinning the crossbow out of his hands.

Within a second, something clamped his left elbow and crushed it painfully. *Jaws of a wulverion.* Even wounded, it wanted to kill him. The fangs, unable to penetrate the rune-forged armor, bit down several times more until they eventually found the unprotected flesh of Jaks's hand and sank in.

He screamed and tugged away desperately, but it held fast. Although his vision was clearing, he could only see a black shadow tearing at his arm. He fumbled for his dagger.

"Get down, Jaks!" Meila yelled from behind. He fell to the ground, kicking at the shadows with his feet.

The hiss of her darkcore gun sounded, followed by a sickening squelch.

Wet, warm globs of flesh pasted his face. The clamping force fell away around his arm. He scrambled backward and collapsed onto his side, holding his left hand up with his right.

A few seconds later, Jaks's burnt-out vision cleared. Pain agonized his hand, but he dared not look down, fearful of the damage he would see.

Vixhana was still glowing but not the blinding radiance of before; three furred beasts lay broken around her, while a fourth hung impaled on her longsword.

A dardan tree was ablaze, its lower trunk burning and flames creeping up, and scorched brown leaves tumbled through the air. Tavis was pointing his sword at a wulverion at the base of the burning tree and channeling a torrent of fire at the squirming beast.

Mulgrave shouted, "Apprentice, stop. That's enough. You'll burn the whole area down," while still holding out his arms, steadily maintaining the protective ring of fire.

Horses still lunged about the glade, running up to the fiery barrier and then turning back when the grandmaster flared the flames in front of them to keep them inside.

Meila's mare lay several yards from Jaks, with several chunks of flesh torn from its rear and its throat ripped open. Somehow, it held onto life as blood frothed at its neck wound.

The pack mule had suffered similar wounds but was already dead, lying near the western side of the glade by the magical barrier. Two dead wulverions lay near it, one punctured by arrows and the other with its head blasted off—presumably by Meila's darkcore gun.

Quiet settled over the glade except for the roaring flames of the protective barrier and the crackling flames consuming the burning dardan tree. And nothing moved.

A dozen wulverions lay dead around the campsite. Without their arcane camouflage, the beasts looked like common wolves.

"It's safe now. They're gone," said the grandmaster. He dropped his arms, and the flaming barrier vanished with a rush. Then, striding to the burning oak tree, he thrust his hands into the flames, and again, there was that rushing sound—like a door thrust open into a sealed room—and the blazing tree extinguished from the bottom up. The only light remaining in the glade was from the dying campfire and from Vixhana's illumanced sword and armor.

Meila holstered her darkcore pistol and surveyed the darkness beyond the tree glade. "They headed out west to the hills," she said.

Finally, Jaks summoned the courage to look at his ravaged left hand.

In addition to the finger chopped off by his father as a child, the rest of his hand was a mangled mess—torn skin and exposed muscle with a couple of fractured white bones jutting out of the bloodied meat. Blood streamed from the end of his arm.

"Grafuk, Jaks. Get something on that," said Vixhana, sheathing her sword and stomping over to grab his injured arm.

Meila ran to her tent and returned with a waterskin and a small bag of exotic packages and bottles.

"This'll numb the pain," she told Jaks, giving him a small white pill that dissolved in his mouth; within a minute, he felt nothing but a numbness in this injured hand and a tingling sensation all over his body.

After Meila splashed water over the wound, she patted it dry with a torn cloth and instructed Vixhana to hold his wrist firm. She grabbed his fingers and pulled on them, using her other hand to push the extruding fragments of bones in Jaks's hand back into place.

Vixhana swore aloud, her face creased in anticipation of Jaks screaming in pain.

Jaks sucked in a breath, also expecting excruciating pain—but when he felt only a slight twinge at her manipulations, he began to giggle.

Light-headed and slightly euphoric, he said, "That pill. I feel invincible."

Meila nodded. She studied his hand, and satisfied with her intervention, slapped a gel pad on either side and wrapped a bandage to hold them in place. "The medigel applies particulates that'll accelerate the healing," she explained.

Vixhana shook her head. "Nasty wound, Jaks. I've seen similar bites from warlions, and most go on to lose their hand—sometimes even the entire arm. It's mauled pretty bad," she said with a note of sympathy in her voice.

Meila frowned. "It'll heal fairly well with the gel

there. Although, it'll probably be deformed and impaired in function. Sorry, Jaks." A shadow of doubt then swept over her face. "Hmm, that is, as long as the gel is compatible with your physiology . . ." She gnawed on her lip and furrowed her brow. "Damn, I didn't think of that," she said, suddenly looking conflicted and torn. "Your genetics could have diverged from ours over the past few thousands of years. The healing gel might confuse your body's cells and see them as foreign."

"What does that mean?" Vixhana's eyes narrowed.

"The particulates could attack his body. Instead of assisting his cells in the healing, they might kill them . . . maybe we should take this off now, just in case."

Jaks hadn't seen Meila so void of confidence before. "If it was attacking me, what would it feel like?" he asked.

"Pain, swelling, hot. They will also distribute throughout your system. If it attacks your organs, the reaction could kill you." Meila gave him a fretful look. She then tugged at the bandage and unraveled it, undoing her handiwork to fling the material aside. "I'm sorry, I don't know enough about the differences in our immunology to know if it will help you or harm you. Here, I'll get some more water to wash the gel off." She strode off to the saddlebags lying by where the horses had been tethered.

The euphoria of the pill lingered, blurring Jaks's attention until it was drawn to the other side of the clearing by a horse's scream. There, Ranger Cromer had stabbed Meila's dying mare with his sword and watched as the horse shuddered its last breath.

He wrenched his sword from the animal's chest and said, "They were after horse flesh. But I doubt they'll be back tonight; I think Vixhana killed the alpha." He pointed his blade at a large beheaded wulverion at the nightwraith's feet.

Mulgrave appeared, having made a circuit of the fields outside, and wandered over to Jaks, who leaned against a tree. "How's the hand?" The mage placed a hand on Jaks's shoulder.

Meila returned with a water bladder and poured it over Jaks's outstretched hand until the blood and gel washed away. "It's about as raw as you can get." She wrapped Jaks's hand again, but this time without the sticky gel.

Under a quarter-moon, the dead wulverions and equines were dragged into the field and heaped into a pile. Once the mass of bodies reached chest-height, Mulgrave held his arms wide as though to embrace the corpses and spoke a single word: "Burn."

A dome of flames roared to life and smothered the bodies with incinerating heat. Tongues of fire leapt into the night sky and roared a crackling descant.

Jaks cradled his bandaged hand and wrinkled his nose at the odor of burning flesh. He stared, fixated on the cremation.

The next day's travel saw the road end at a village built around a ruined tower, surrounded by a palisade of sharpened logs.

Several farms, mere plots of pumpkins and cabbages bounded by rocks, and a piggery—that they smelled before they saw it—huddled close to the primitive settlement. A few peasants toiled at the soil but dropped their tools and ran for the settlement on seeing their group approach.

"I wonder how those pigs survive with wulverions around?" Jaks asked to distract himself from his throbbing hand. Although Vixhana had slung his left arm up around his neck that morning to keep it from knocking about, it pained him with every sway of his horse. He had accepted another of Meila's pain-dulling pills that morning, but he didn't want to ask for another, not wanting to seem weak.

"You just smelled their natural defense. Wulverions detest the stench and squealing. I expect the villagers can barely put up with the pig sty themselves," Vixhana said as she screwed up her face in disgust. She was marching alongside her stallion, holding the reins, with Meila sitting astride her warhorse; the two of them had been taking turns to walk, following the loss of a horse and the pack mule to the wulverions.

At first, Vixhana had ridden with Meila behind, but the warrior woman had grown uncharacteristically flustered with the smaller woman's arms wrapped around her; within a few minutes, she'd stopped abruptly and dismounted the horse to allow the other to ride alone.

Whatever the villagers' feelings were about the pigs, their feelings toward strangers were very clear.

"There's a body hanging from the wall," Meila said, her eyesight even sharper than the ranger's.

As they approached the gates, a horn blasted from within the settlement.

A thin woman peered over the palisade and trained a crossbow on them. A few minutes later, three more men and women appeared behind the wall with crossbows and spears.

"What do you want?" the first woman shouted, almost shrieking, at them. "If you're wanting conscripts, you'll be getting none here. This here is *our* land. We don't bow to no king."

Jaks gasped as he distinguished features on the hanging body. "That's the tabard and uniform of a royal herald," he said, hoping that it wasn't Minto's body hanging there.

"Pigfuckers," Vixhana spat, glaring fury at the fortified settlement and the mounting number of armed peasants bristling the wall. "How dare they kill a king's representative. I'll massacre the whole lot of them." She loosened the sword at her hip and then looked at the great axe strapped to her horse.

His sister's zealous patriotism was inflamed. She looked as though the assault on the herald was an assault on her personal being. He had not seen her so riled up since Karisa told them of their father's abuse on her.

Her form dimmed and her features lost definition.

"Vixhana, stand down." Ranger Cromer trotted his horse toward her.

She ignored him and completed her transition into a magical shade: a black blotch that bewildered the eye. Was it a shadow cast, a stain on the ground, or a trick of the light? The shade swept the axe from its holster and absorbed it into its magic. "Darkness, night. I will murder every one of the traitors," it said.

"Captain. Stop. We have no business here." Mulgrave backtracked toward them and stared at the shadow. "You will not attack." His face was stern and voice commanding. "The king will be notified, and he will deal with these rebels in due time—now is not the time. We have a task to complete."

The shade raced toward the village anyway, but then halted. Moments later, Vixhana snapped out of the blackness and back to her true form; the massive double-bladed axe was in her right hand and the bastard sword in the other.

She glared at the villagers, as though daring them to attack her.

The villagers cried out in alarm at her sudden manifestation. Their crossbows trained on her, and a single bolt hissed through the air and struck her in the chest. On anyone else, it would have pierced the leather armor and critically injured the wearer, but on Vixhana, it bounced off like a twig striking a stone column, then tumbled to the ground. An invisible shield of gravmancy protected her.

After what seemed minutes but was only several seconds, she turned and stomped back to her horse and slammed the axe back into the holster—the stallion sagged slightly with the weight. She slapped her palm against the leather scabbard and turned to Mulgrave.

"Apologies, Grandmaster. I forgot myself in the moment. As you say, the king will deal with these traitors," she said in a measured voice, but with eyes still fired with menace.

With the villagers watching from the fortifications, the ranger took the lead again and rode a wide arc around the settlement and crops.

Several miles to the south, the plains became rugged with brown and gray hills, and bare but for only tufts of limp grass and brush. And beyond that, the land rose into a wide mountain range that eventually joined the crags far off to their right.

"The Jurn Highlands," Mulgrave said. "Last time I was here, decades ago, we only reached as far as these hills. We'd broken the nomads and chased the remnants this far before they melted into those mountains. Silas decided it wasn't worth chasing them any further, and the army turned around right there," the grandmaster explained to Meila like a child. "Who knows what's going on in those mountains now."

They had lost their riding formation by now, with

no road to follow and their only landmark the mountains in front of them.

"I mapped the wreckage to the northeast, still some miles that way," Meila said, pointing up into the rough peaks. "A few days from here, perhaps?"

"Could be weeks, depending on the terrain and weather. Since we abandoned those saddlebags"—a further consequence of losing a horse and the pack mule to the wulverion attack—"we have fewer options for routes with no ropes and less cold-weather clothing."

"Needn't worry, the grandmaster and I can keep us warm." Tavis rubbed his hands, and pyromantic warmth radiated around them.

After a few hours into the barren midlands, they made the surprising find of a tiny, still lake—mirrorlike at the bottom of a wide basin of rounded, basalt hills.

A trio of goats startled when Ranger Cromer crested the hill overlooking the body of water. The wild animals bolted for the other side of the basin and clattered over the edge into the stony terrain.

"As good a place as any to stop for the day," the ranger said to Mulgrave. "The horses can water at the lake, but we camp up here."

Jaks walked his palfrey to the edge of the lake. The water was fresh from the recent rain, and he was amazed to see tiny, silver fishes flitting in shallows of the crystal-clear lake. His horse then dropped its mouth to the water and slurped, disturbing the surface and causing the fish to flit into the depths. It was a beautiful place: secluded, raw, untouched, with the wind pinching with every gust. Although tired from the day's ride, he daydreamed of living in a little house overlooking a lake.

With a couple of hours of daylight left, Grandmaster Mulgrave took his apprentices to the far end of the basin. "Even injured, every mage needs to be able to invoke magic to defend himself," he said, and then standing back from them invoked a suit of fire that enveloped his body from head to toe.

Tavis mimicked the grandmaster's invocation without hesitation and smirked a superior grin at Jaks through the flames.

Jaks concentrated on an invocation, but the best he could do was summon a halo of electromancy around his uninjured hand—far from a full shield of magic. The only point of redemption was, he kept it channeled for a minute longer than his previous record.

"Keep trying, lad. It'll come," Mulgrave said. "The second defense that you'll have to master, of course, is the wall. It will be beyond your capabilities at the moment, but you should at least start practicing."

"Like this," Tavis said to Jaks as though talking to a child. He stood back and invoked a chest-high barrier of flame two arm spans around himself. "I could push it out further, but I wouldn't want to burn you."

Mulgrave nodded. "Well done, Tavis. I'll spend some time with Jaks now. Run along and go keep watch with the master ranger." The mage perched on a flat ledge and ran a hand over his bald head. When the first apprentice had disappeared over the ridge, he said, "Try again. His presence probably wasn't helping."

"Yes, he's a distraction."

"Tavis is the most promising apprentice I've had for many years. His mastery of pyromancy is well beyond what I had at his age, and his gravmancy boons well in the smithery." The grandmaster spoke, but all the while scrutinizing Jaks closely. "I don't know what it is between you two, but you obviously antagonize each other to no end."

"He started it—" Jaks began.

"Never mind. You'll need to sort it out." The mage hopped onto a stone ledge overlooking the lake and sat cross-legged. "Now, let me see how you perform without distractions in the way. Go over there and try again."

Jaks retreated to the lake's edge. Reflected rays from the sun cast his shadow against the side of the stone basin.

Without Tavis sneering at him, Jaks settled easily into the three aspects of invocation with a level mind. In fact, the lightning armor came so swiftly that he laughed aloud, and it echoed around the bowl of the lake as he stood encased in a yard-thick suit of sizzling electricity. He stared at his body with white and blue arcing between his torso and limbs and leaping outward to threaten anything that came near him.

Grandmaster Mulgrave stood up on the stone ledge —a distance of twenty yards—and pointed a hand toward Jaks. "Hold steady. I'm going to test it," he shouted above the sound of crackling sprites.

A bolt of fire shot from the mage's hand toward Jaks's crackling armor.

An explosion met the firebolt on striking the outer limits of the invocation.

Several more bolts of increasing size battered the armor of lightning, each fusing and exploding before they could strike Jaks.

With each attack, Jaks felt the invocation losing power and his concentration wavering. With the sixth fire bolt, the armor shrunk and then abruptly dissipated. In fear that the mage would attack again, Jaks shouted, "Stop!" and held out his hand.

Mulgrave appeared in front of him, smiling, and slapped him on the shoulder. "That's it, lad. You have great potential," the mage said. "I think it's when your thoughts are contaminated by petty anxieties that your control is the poorest. Trivial threats make you indecisive and cloud your will."

Jaks nodded, finding truth in the grandmaster's words.

"Yes, that's enough for today. You can stay and practice if you like, but I need to talk to your sister again —I thought she was going to go off like a fireball at those villagers. I don't want her going back there in the middle of the night." Mulgrave shook his head, then wandered up to the camp.

Alone by the lake, Jaks invoked the electromancy

armor again. A familiar acrid odor filled his nostrils, and the hum of electricity filled his ears.

Nothing could touch him inside his shield. Cocooned, he was invincible.

Tavis might have both pyromancy and gravmancy, better magic control, and greater endurance, but Jaks was catching up fast. With the rarest of magic, he had no doubt the grandmaster would choose him over that other self-conceited smartass of an apprentice.

His smugness, however, was shattered a few seconds later when his armor of electromancy snapped out of existence and left him with only the lingering bitterness of metal in his mouth.

Chapter 32

The Jurns

That night, the group were forced down into the lake basin to shelter from the chill of howling winds.

Jaks swore they were the calls of wulverions and fought sleep throughout the night. But weakened from weeks of travel, invoking magic, and the pain of his mangled hand, he nodded off and cried out in his sleep as nightmare beasts chased him through a forest, caught him, and ate his hands and feet. And leading them was a hideous monster with the head of a wulverion on the body of his father.

In the morning, the winds stilled and left gray clouds to hide the mountain peaks of the Jurn Highlands before them.

Up to yesterday, the distant rocky titans had held Jaks's attention as they rode closer to their wreckage of Meila's ship. But today, riding one-handed, the midlands enraptured him with its great plateau of stone stretching in every direction.

Curious swaths of green trees peeked out of gorges, flowing like rivers of forest through this vast bed of flat, gray rock.

With no way to cross the ravines—some so long, one couldn't see where they started or finished—Jaks concluded they would need to descend into one and hoped that it would take them to the base of the mountains.

He gritted his teeth against the pain of his freshly re-bandaged hand and regretted refusing Meila's offer of her pain-dulling pills.

Earlier that morning, he'd barely stifled a scream of agony when she removed his bandage and examined his crippled hand. "Looks like the healing gel might have helped, although I washed most of it off the other day. This part here"—she pointed at puncture marks on his wrist—"probably didn't get the gel and is worse off than the rest of your hand."

A chunk of meat from the palm below the stump of his little finger was missing, and the wound was sloughed and red, looking like the side of his hand had been sliced off. Thankfully, the two bones that Meila had pushed back into place remained where they should, and the overlying flesh was a reassuring but messy red.

"Good. You didn't suffer any ill effects from the medigel," she said, peeling open a new pad of the stuff.

"Let's put some more on. The skin and muscle should heal up, but without a surgeon to fix the bones, those fingers will probably be next to useless." She pointed at the two closest to the stump of his little finger. "Sure you don't want a pill?"

Jaks shook his head, resolving to be strong.

That had been an hour earlier, and he decided he would continue to suck up the pain. He was getting used to it. Besides, it was a fitting punishment for his failures. He had spiraled into moodiness that morning.

He thought of Karisa and how their lives could have been so much happier if they had sailed away to Faucony as she had wanted to. He ruminated on how he had failed her and his mother, lived in a state of denial at the evil his father had perpetrated on them, and had done nothing about it. Yes, he deserved this pain for what he had failed to do for the two people he had loved the most—now both dead because of his weakness. He needed to toughen up, be stronger, or forever be a weakling.

"There's someone over there," Meila said. "Ranger—someone there is watching us," she repeated louder to the wiry hunter several horse-lengths ahead.

They all turned to her and saw her raise her finger and point to their far right. "Female human with some animal-skin headdress and facial markings."

Jaks squinted against the sun, but only saw the rocky expanse dotted with boulders and sheer ledges.

"Can't see anything, except those bronzes over the mountains," Tavis said, pointing at a pack of dragons flying into the distance. "Probably nothing."

"No, she's still there. About eight hundred yards out. Peering over that outcrop." Meila pointed again.

"Are you sure? How can you see that far?" Cromer asked, as he pulled out a metal-tubed spyglass that telescoped out as he pulled it up to his eye. The telescope ranged over the landscape and then froze as he focused. "I think you're right—there is someone there."

"Bandits?" Mulgrave asked, loosening the mace he carried at his side but never used, even when the wulverions had attacked.

The ranger shrugged and collapsed the spy glass, thrusting it into a saddle pocket. He fingered an arrow to his bow.

Over the next few hours, many more watchers appeared, surreptitious stalkers, none coming closer than the first. On this open plateau, Jaks wildly imagined he and his companions stood out like savories on a platter.

"Best you all prepare for a fight. This doesn't look good," Vixhana said, securing her shield and placing a hand on the pommel of her sword. "Unless we descend into one of those great ravines, we have no cover. What say you, mage?"

"We could put a ravine between them and us, if we

grav-jump across. We'd need to leave the horses and provisions behind," Mulgrave replied, speaking through the raised visor of his battlemage helmet adorned with a firebird with red wings. "Last resort, though. Let's find out how many there are."

Tavis was the only one of them that looked unconcerned, seemingly ignorant of how outnumbered they were. He grinned as he arranged his shield and hotchpotch of armor and flexed his hand as though ready to invoke a maelstrom of fire magic.

Jaks also craved a chance to test his newfound magic, but his experience with bullies and kidnappers had taught him to fear the unexpected, which in this case could come from a dozen fronts. With his crippled hand, he couldn't handle a crossbow, so he had only his rune-forged sword and his magic.

Ranger Cromer pulled his horse to a halt. "Here's a greeting party."

A figure emerged on a ledge overlooking them and leaned casually against a carved bone spear as several more figures with shortbows arrayed themselves behind. The man wore a horned goat skull over his head and a goat-skin cloak on his back. Bronzed and leathery with age, Jaks thought he looked like some wild medicine man.

"What are you doing here?" the goat man asked in a heavily accented voice.

The ranger, with his ironwood bow and an un-nocked arrow at his lap, narrowed his eyes at the man and then addressed him in a guttural flow of words in a language that Jaks had never heard before.

The goat man's face changed from wariness to puzzlement, and then he replied in the same heavy-syllabled tongue. His attendants stared at the ranger and lowered their weapons.

Again, Cromer replied to the leader and gestured at Mulgrave. The goat man examined the mage intently.

Mulgrave then spoke out several of the foreign words. Jaks was amazed. The grandmaster knew some of their language too, whoever they were. Partway through his sentence, he looked lost for a word and reverted to Ascorian. "Forgive me, my Jurn is very basic. I am Grandmaster Mulgrave from the Academy of the Arcane."

"You travel dangerously. Lucky we find you first. You will come. The Uwama will instruct you," he said in an inarguable manner, then pointed his bone spear to the east. "You must follow."

"Is *he* the Uwama, or is taking us to him?" Meila asked.

"Uwamas were the Jurn nomad chiefs before we drove them out of the plains . . ." Vixhana kept her shield raised but removed the hand on her sword. "They were all women, so I would guess this man is not one."

Thirty archers and spear-carrying men and women inched out of crevices, nooks, and from behind boulders to accompany them at a distance.

An hour later, a wide ravine yawned before them. A

cliff wall dropped twenty yards from where Jaks overlooked the edge, and its far side was shrouded from view by conical tips of a forest rising from the bottom.

For the horses to descend would have been impossible had it not been for a narrow path carved into the cliff side. Jaks and the other riders dismounted for the walk down, each leading their horses with caution.

The goat man, who had introduced himself as Witabu, waited for them at the ravine floor beside one of the tall pines. Along with the small forest, a pebbly stream meandered along the ravine and babbled quietly with the whispers of the pine needles releasing their sharp, refreshing scents. The overhead sun revealed the lush valley for a rich paradise hidden within the barren midlands.

"The waters from the mountains run through the ravines all year long," Witabu, the plainsman, said to Mulgrave, as Jaks made the final few yards of the descent in front of them.

"The ravines are gouged by water—surely, there are floods?" asked the grandmaster.

"At times. But, as you will see, our village is built to withstand the greatest of storms."

Witabu spoke an order to the youngest of his entourage. The boy dashed down the ravine ahead of them. As the last of their horses, led by Tavis, caught up with the group, the plainsman lifted his spear and continued along the wooded ravine.

They came upon a clearing with a corral of

pregnant goats, bleating as they gorged on a pile of food scraps; a goat herder nodded at Witabu and stared at Jaks and his companions as they passed by. A hundred yards more, and the forest opened up to a field of carrot, pumpkin, and potato plants, on both sides of the stream. The fields were joined by a flat wooden bridge and tended by tribe folk with hoes and wooden wheelbarrows. Fearful, despite the old plainsman's assurances, they stopped their work and watched on in silence.

As woods again filled the ravine, Jaks noticed rope bridges spanning the trees above.

A little girl gazed at them from ten yards overhead and giggled as she dropped winged seed pods that spiraled toward the ground in a blur and whirled amongst the riders. Witabu barked a reprimand at the child. Nonplussed, she made a face at him, sped off on bare feet along the swing bridge, and with laughter trailing behind her, vanished amongst the treetops.

The rope bridges became more numerous further on. Eventually, they were shadowed by a giant wooden platform the width and length of the Academy's main dining hall.

A raised open-sided structure, it stretched between at least twenty trees and was secured to each with braces and frames to support expertly placed joists and planks. Ropes hung from the underside for a variety of purposes—dangling lanterns, hanging deer carcasses, and benches bearing pots, pans, and cooking utensils.

Below the raised platform, a deck at ground-level mirrored the one above. A hole at its center accessed the running water. And around it, a group of women loaded kindling into several stone ovens and firepits. One dome-shaped oven, however, already spouted a trail of smoke while a sweaty man thrust a flat-bladed shovel into its small opening and retrieved flatbreads to cool on a nearby platform.

Witabu beckoned to a pair of spear-wielding sentries, who watched uneasily as they neared.

"Leave your beasts here. They will be guarded. We go up." He gestured to a set of wooden stairs on the side of the structure and ascended. The guards appeared delighted with the horses and began inspecting each one as though they were at a market: stroking manes, lifting tails, checking teeth and ears.

Vixhana looked down at the tallest guard, a half-foot shorter than her. "Watch out, he bites," she said, and then released her battleaxe from her stallion and gripped it in her hand as she stomped up the stairs.

Jaks followed his sister and paused when he reached the last step.

Several children ran and skipped about the immense wooden platform playing a game of chase, whilst a few even younger ones sat playing make-believe with toys of exquisitely carved wood, stone, and bone laid out on a brown animal hide. On the other side of the platform, a dozen women crafted as they knelt or sat cross-legged amongst rows of low tables near a woman seated on the only chair in sight. Four armed guards stood at attention beside her and cast wary eyes on the strangers.

Jaks jolted out of his wonder to see Witabu, Mulgrave, and Cromer bend and bow to the seated woman. He scurried over to Vixhana, Meila, and Tavis behind the tables and was followed by several of Witabu's hunters, who ranged themselves about the deck and shooed away the children. They scampered away over rope bridges to other platforms suspended throughout the forest.

"Welcome, Grandmaster," said the woman, who then looked at one of her attendants and spoke a few words.

The young woman rose and glided on slender legs to another set of stairs. Jaks swallowed and drank in her sharp features and long, auburn hair elaborately coiled around her head. She was beautiful.

"Uwama, I did not know your people flourished here," Mulgrave addressed the seated woman, taking his helmet from his head and holding it under his arm.

She placed her hands in her lap and rested green eyes on the mage. "We do not flourish, Grandmaster, our people survive by the grace of Hodrin and this oasis that He created for us." She cast her eyes upward momentarily as she spoke the name of her god.

It was the second time Jaks had caught himself staring, but he couldn't help but be enchanted by the Uwama. The chieftess was a gray-haired counterpart to the young woman who had fled down the stairs. Beautiful, the two shared grace of movement, slender long limbs, and intense, deep-set eyes that commanded attention. And she spoke in fluent Ascorian with a silky alto. Her voice reached into his heartstrings and plucked a desire to be near her and just listen to her speak. Unconsciously, he walked closer to her and stood behind the grandmaster to stare over his head.

"Can you tell me of the Highlands?" Mulgrave said. "We are just passing through these parts to reach them."

The Uwama frowned. "Truly, only a fool or a braveheart ventures into the mountains. There is little to be found other than wild beasts and monsters. Is that not why your king chased us here a decade ago, hoping we would expire against those cruel spires?" She rested a finger on her flawless jaw. "Tell me, what do you seek there? You are treasure hunters?"

The mage locked eyes with her for a moment and then removed his gauntlet and reached under his breastplate to extract a folded piece of paper.

Meila suddenly strode up to the grandmaster and grasped his wrist, preventing him from unfolding the map that she had marked with the location of the wreckage. "You can't show them. How do you know we can trust them?"

Mulgrave looked from Meila to the Uwama and back, then addressed the seated woman. "Uwama Xandu, Chieftess of Jurns, are your motives pure? Can I trust you to do us no harm?"

The Uwama laughed. "Of course, you cannot trust us." Although her words were antagonistic, Jaks yearned for her to keep speaking, that he could continue listening to her rich tones. "But even though your armies drove us from our pastures and plains, we know that we were only there because of the grace of Hodrin, and we bear you no ill will."

At that point, the young plainswoman reappeared bearing a tray of chiseled stone mugs and walked around offering one to each of their group. As Jaks took a mug, she studied his face and then his injured arm. "Are you sick?" she asked in accented Ascorian.

Jaks's face flushed as he searched for words, not wanting to embarrass himself while talking to this attractive woman. "I fought a wulverion."

"Oh," she said, scrutinizing him up and down, and then stared at his teeth.

He closed his mouth, wondering if this was how his horse had felt while being examined by the guards earlier.

She walked to Tavis and offered him a drink. "How about you? Are you healthy?" She leaned forward to examine him closer as the apprentice took a mug. He nodded and returned her brazen stare before coursing his eyes over her figure.

"Yes, you are better," said the beautiful plainswoman.

Tavis looked at Jaks and smirked.

Jaks sensed a burning in his stomach and clenched

his teeth. There had just been an unspoken competition —and Tavis had won.

Meila had removed her hold on Mulgrave's wrist by then but continued standing between him and the Uwama.

"The Jurns have welcomed us into their village, my cautious *ward*," Mulgrave said, stressing Meila's subordinate status. "That alone is a great trust." He waved a hand, gesturing for her to move aside.

Meila frowned but allowed the mage to unfold the map and hand it to the chieftess, who merely gave Meila a curious look as she received the paper.

"We seek a wreckage fallen from the sky. It has landed at this location." Mulgrave pointed a finger at a point on the map. "We seek to examine the debris."

"From the heavens? Is it an omen?" the Uwama asked, holding the map into the light.

"A magical skyship," said Mulgrave, glancing sideways at Meila and coughing, "that could unravel important wisdom and knowledge to us."

The Uwama interrogated the grandmaster for several minutes, probing his knowledge of the ship's origins and nature. Jaks was impressed with his master's disingenuous replies that avoided any revelation of the unworldly origin of the starship. Eventually, she exhausted her questions and sat for a minute, tapping elegant fingers on the chair arm.

"You seek this relic for knowledge? Through such peril?" she asked.

Mulgrave pulled a second paper from his pocket and passed it to the Uwama. "For the king. I am but his emissary."

The gray-haired woman leaned forward and examined the grandmaster closer. "An emissary. You are of status within your country. The king listens to you?"

Vixhana stepped forward. "The grandmaster is held with great esteem in Ascoria. His actions and words are of legend," she said.

The old mage laughed. "She exaggerates. I am but an old magesmith doing the king's work."

"But the king would bend his ear to you, if you asked?"

"Yes, of course."

The chieftess was quiet for a minute and then looked back at the map. "Dragons and other wild beasts roam the area that you search. Also, the terrain changes often because of landslides and rockfalls. Wandering there without knowledge of the Highlands, even with your mighty armor—especially with your mighty armor —could be a death sentence."

She then lowered her voice, as though telling a secret. "We know of this 'wreckage' you seek—"

"You have seen it?" The grandmaster's voice rose a half-octave. "You know where it is?"

"My hunters have seen it but most of it was buried beneath much rubble." She turned to one of her guards, whispered a command, and watched him run off over one of the rope bridges. "It is one of the areas they hunt rarely. As they described it, they saw a star fall from the sky and found their way to it the next day. It had struck a mountainside and slipped down, causing a great slide."

"Could these hunters take us there?" Mulgrave asked, excitement showing on his face.

The Uwama leaned back and accepted a mug from her attendant, sipped, and returned the vessel to her tray. She looked fondly at the young woman and said, "What is that phrase you always say . . . how does it go, my flower? 'I do something for you, and you do something for me'?"

"So wordy, Mother. It's just 'I help you, you help me.' Everything must be fair," the young woman replied, and walked back down the stairs with the serving tray.

The Uwama stood up from her chair. Diminutive, she was the same height as Meila, but where the gray-haired woman was wide-hipped and elegant, the outworlder was slender and graceful.

"Yes. If you help me, I will grant you my hunters to take you to your relic."

"What is it you want?" Mulgrave asked, stepping back as she came toward him.

The Uwama motioned for him and the others to sit with her cross-legged around a knee-high table.

"You must ask your king to allow us to live back on our lands. We were once a tribe of over a thousand, but now fewer than six hundred survive and lessen with every year." She sighed. "When the tribes fled the plains, most continued deep into the Highlands. Some survived, but most perished in the cold, starving, and savaged by beasts or bands of evil men. Hodrin led us to this abandoned village. But even here, we too slowly perish." The Uwama squeezed her eyes shut for a moment before she continued. "Hodrin created our people for the plains. The mountain gods are merciless toward us, their mountains and plateaus yield barely enough for the few of us living to survive, and they curse us with weak infants that die before they take their first breath."

Mulgrave's face took on a look of concern and he rubbed his scalp briskly. "Your tribes were offered peace, but they refused to submit to the king. That is why you were—"

"Were chased out," said the Uwama. "Yes, we fought to remain on our plains. Would you not have done the same? But, clearly, we had no chance against such an army. We chose to flee rather than submit." Her eyes flared for a moment, then dulled with sorrow. "But now we are a different people. Languishing, dying, barely surviving for over two decades, I would rather have my people back on the plains with our herds and ponies than slowly expire in these ravines. Even if it means bowing to your king."

"You would come under King Silas's rule? You would give up your chieftess rights?"

"Our people would still need a leader, but yes, we would submit to his rule in exchange for the right to roam the plains once again."

Mulgrave nodded his head. "It saddens me to hear of your tribe's struggles, and I bear some of the guilt of harming your people. In apology, I would be pleased to bring your plea to King Silas."

The Uwama and the grandmaster settled into a long discussion, with a plan for the mage's party to escort a representative back to Dunberrin once they had completed their salvage quest.

Bread and dried meats were brought to the table by the chieftess's attendants. But as the shadows lengthened over the ravine, Jaks ignored his pangs of hunger, wallowed in the pain of his hand, and suffered the gloating grin of Tavis while Xanra, the chieftess's daughter, doted on him.

Eventually, Jaks made an excuse to check on the horses. He found the palfreys and Vixhana's stallion resting by the rivulet, downstream from the lower platform, with the same two guards fussing about them.

As he approached, the tallest one lifted a small child to sit on Jaks's gelding. The brown-haired boy squealed in delight and thrust his face into the horse's mane and hugged the animal. Three other children bounced on their toes, waiting for a turn. Jaks shrugged and left the children to their entertainment and went to explore the surrounding woods.

A minute of wandering and Jaks came to the bottom of the ravine's cliff face. He gaped at a web of rope bridges and smaller platforms above him that spanned from the chieftess's deck to the walls of the ravine, where scores of open cave mouths dotted the cliff.

He flinched when a whirling disc whizzed past his face. A giggle erupted. On a bridge stood the rapscallion, the little loner girl, staring cheekily down at him. She threw another winged seed pod and dashed into one of the cave mouths, laughing.

He grinned at the girl's impish behavior and examined the cliff for a path up to the caves—which he guessed were where the villagers lived and slept—but the rope bridges appeared to be the only entrances.

A male voice startled Jaks from his study of the cliff face.

"You come see?" said a youth about Jaks's age standing behind him in the tree line. Wild-looking, he was attired in leggings and jerkin made of animal skin and wore a wolf-hide over his shoulders.

Pointing to the cliff caves, the youth repeated, "You see? You come?" He turned and beckoned over his shoulder.

Jaks was curious to see where the caves led. Were they just shallow alcoves or a deep network? Were they furnished? These people seemed to live like primitives, but could they have comforts within?

The young man seemed friendly enough. A knife dangled at his hip but his movements, gesturing and hopping like an excited child, lent him the role of an enthusiastic host keen to show a stranger his home.

Jaks hurried after him and caught up at the bottom of the stairs.

"I'm Jaks." He tapped his chest and examined the short tribesman, appreciating a grubby yet rugged, handsome face.

The youth pulled himself as tall as he could and grinned back. "Rakiyura . . . Raki. I show you village." His eyes fell on Jaks's bandaged hand and he frowned. "You are . . . a cripple?"

Jaks explained his injury but found no judgement in the youth's response, unlike the young woman's dismissive tone before.

"Hodrin bless you," Raki replied and then leapt up the steps in threes.

The two young men slipped across the Uwama's wooden platform, evading the chieftess's tables on the other side of the platform. Meila and Vixhana threw him quizzical looks, but he ignored them and dashed after his new friend onto the wooden planks of a bridge.

The two of them could have run side by side, but Jaks's head spun when the bridge started to sway, and he stopped to grab the waist-high guide rope with his good hand as the rocking continued.

Raki paused and returned to place a small hand on Jaks's elbow and muttered soothing sounds to encourage him across the planks; at one stage, the tribesman tipped Jaks's gaze up with a chin lift to jar him out of his contemplation of the fall to the ground below. In that moment, the youth reminded Jaks of his friend Minto, when they were young, coaxing him along a high wall to a hiding spot where they spied on pretty girls next door.

At the end of the bridge, Jaks found the little whirler girl standing there in the cave mouth, watching him and rolling her head from side to side while batting her temples.

The tribesman barked a few guttural syllables at her, "*Suli, oto bargen.*"

The girl slapped her forehead one last time and high-tailed into the cave mouth.

Jaks followed the tribesman and ducked into the cave. As the sunlight faded behind him, his eyes adjusted to a glow at the other end of the tunnel.

An excavated room with a wooden floor and a couple of knee-high tables greeted him. Light radiated from lightstone lanterns, revealing furs and skins blanketing the wall. Three similar rooms connected through short tunnels.

Raki ducked into the next room and beckoned Jaks along. Inside, two gray-haired men bent over a table taking turns to shuffle colored stones over a checkerboard; they greeted the young tribesman and stared astonished at Jaks. Raki spoke an explanation to the elders, at one stage miming someone swaying, at which the two men cracked toothless grins at Jaks.

Knowing he was the brunt of a joke, he mimicked wobbling on his feet, and then joined their laughter as he felt some gate of acceptance opening to him.

They left the old men to their game, and Raki led a

path through the cave complex, passing scores of tunnel offshoots blocked by hanging hides and skins. Jaks restrained an impulse to peer into the rooms, guessing them to be the private chambers for families and individuals.

Dozens more tribe folk greeted and gaped at the pair as they dashed by, with Raki proudly introducing his guest to each.

Jaks sighed in relief when, finally, he could stand straight in a tall, rounded cavern. A slit of sunlight cut through motes of dust from a long, narrow crack in the ceiling, and beneath it, a craggy hole fenced off with ropes occupied the center of the cave. In the closest corner, boxes of spears stood with iron tips upright. In another corner, unstrung shortbows were similarly stored with bowstrings draped over wooden spikes in the wall. Quivers of arrows lay stored nearby. Along with piles of animal hides, coils of rope, boxes of nails, and hundreds of other miscellanea, the cavern was a massive storeroom.

A staircase hewn into the wall climbed up to an open hatch filled with sunlight. Jaks blinked against the brightness at the top of the steps and found himself in a wooden shack with an open door.

"High village," Raki said as he stepped out of the hut.

Once Jaks's eyes adjusted to the midafternoon sun, he discovered himself in a settlement atop the plateau.

Dozens of stone buildings with black slate roofs

covered the tableland. Tribe folk toiled outside the buildings, darting in occasionally to access a tool or material, and settling back outside to complete their handiwork. Animal hides stretched over drying racks next to a woman scraping a fresh skin with a sharp blade. A circle of men chipped at stone blocks fitting together a new hut. Cooking pots boiled delicious odors as cooks stirred and commanded attendants busy at preparing vegetables and meats.

They strolled through the village and soon amassed a small following of gawky children who chattered and stared at the tall Ascorian invader. Soon, Jaks found himself holding a tiny hand and looked down to see the whirler-throwing girl parading alongside him, looking down her nose at any who dared to try and steal her prize. He smiled at her and squeezed her hand, eliciting a sparkle of eyes and a flash of teeth.

Raki was a popular youth. Adults greeted him warmly from their chores as they walked by, and he replied to each with a word or two and a nod. Jaks nodded his head congenially at each villager and repeated their greeting, *"Hodrin uhsaga,"* which Raki assured him meant "God's blessing on you."

At the edge of the village, Jaks looked out over another ravine full of pine trees, and then turning about realized the plateau was a tower of rock in the center of a single enormous cleft in the midlands with rivers of trees surrounding the village on all sides.

"It's like a castle," Jaks said. "No wonder they settled here."

Raki picked up his words and replied, "Caves here . . . before us. We find caves and build here." The tribesman led Jaks back to a pair of stone buildings where several women were sewing animal hides together as clothes and mats.

"Jaks, there you are," called out a voice from behind. Vixhana was staring at him and the circle of women and children. Grandmaster Mulgrave trailed several yards behind her and was gazing around the village in a group with Tavis, Cromer, and Meila led by the older tribesman Witabu. "I was wondering where you had got to. New friends?" his sister said.

The grandmaster called out, heading toward a small tower presiding over the village, and summoned Vixhana and Jaks to follow.

Jaks grasped Raki's hand and thanked him for the tour.

That evening, the Uwama dined with their party under the moonlight and lightstone lanterns on the platform in the ravine. As they ate, a tribeswoman danced before them to a flautist's melody. A gifted illumancer, the dancer weaved spirals of color through the air with her hands and entranced them with magical images of two forbidden lovers and their tragic story.

After the dancer finished, a dozen older tribe folk joined the Uwama's table and spoke politely with Mulgrave, Cromer, and Vixhana in stilted Ascorian that they'd learned to a greater or lesser extent. In the past, the Jurns had extensive trade with merchants and even welcomed the occasional outsider to settle with them— often having fallen for a beautiful tribeswoman. The Uwama's perfect fluency, she explained, came from having lived in Dunberrin learning the healing arts decades before, when King Irin, "the Roadmaker"— father of the current king—had ruled. Now, the only contact the Jurns had with outsiders was with fur merchants from Ellipta and the nearby villages in the plains.

From the plateau above, the sound of more revelry drifted down to Jaks's ears. Wilder, with chanting and beating of drums, he imagined villagers bouncing and swaying to the music.

After Witabu directed them each to a sleeping chamber at the conclusion of the evening, Jaks crouched inside the small room hewn into the rock, bare except for a hanging lantern with a thick, burning candle and a raised alcove with furs and goat hides laid out as a bed.

Several minutes later, Meila brushed through the animal-hide door-cover and smoothed out her sleeves. She was all business. "Let's change your bandage. Change your dressings now and we'll have one less to make later when the surroundings will be far less hospitable. Go on, sit down," she said, patting the ground next to a bowl of water and a cloth she had prepared.

A sweet odor permeated the room as Meila peeled

off the wound dressing and gently cleaned the wound. "Pretty good. The granulation tissue is excellent." She pricked the tip of his fingers with a wood splinter. "Feel that, sharp?"

"Blunt." His thoughts were elsewhere, though. He stared at her shoulder.

"We should get the chieftess, or one of her healers, to splint your hand properly, though. Get those bones healing straight." She spun a dry cloth dressing around Jaks's hand and tied the end off at his wrist. "The particulates in your system will continue to assist your muscle and skin regeneration until they're all used up. In two or three weeks, the soft tissue should be done. A month, and the bones should be fully knitted." She forced a smile, then picked up the bowl with the used bandages and stood to leave.

Perhaps it was her proximity, or the enclosed space, or the dangers of the Highlands that would invade their life the next day, but a heady desire took hold of Jaks's senses.

"Don't go." Words spilled from his mouth before he knew what he was saying. "Stay. Share my bed tonight?" The words were so brazen, he almost regretted them.

She froze, her face turned away from him.

He had said his desire. He couldn't take it back, didn't want to.

Her hand jerked away from his grip, and she

remained facing the door-hide. "No. You need rest. To heal . . ." Then she fled the room.

The rejection stung like a crown of nettles. He could not have been any clearer in his feelings for her, yet she had dismissed them again. Without even looking him in the face.

So, it was not disappointment that festered this time, but anger and indignation that left a sourness in his mouth. His heart turned cold.

Meila stood a little way down from Jaks's room, back to the wall, panting. An uneasy feeling cut through her with a saw-toothed blade. An emotion stirred that she had not felt for years, if not decades. Lust.

The last time she and Anton had been passionate, some anniversary or other, the act had been robotic and unsatisfying, and not attempted again since. But at this moment, propositioned by a tall, attractive man, her desires were ablaze.

But she couldn't succumb; she was loyal to her vows of betrothal.

She hurried through the tunnel, out onto the swing-bridge. The bowl dropped into the ravine below as she grabbed the sides and welcomed the night air nipping at her face and arms.

She shook her head clear and lowered her heart rate,

then stared at the silhouettes of swaying treetops and considered the irony.

She laughed aloud, not caring who heard. So ridiculous that she should be so confused by a young man, a fraction of her age, with annoying curly hair that demanded to be straightened, and a painfully handsome face that she wanted to slap or caress or both.

How had she become so cold and neutered that she had forgotten what it was like to have feelings unmodulated by cerebral implants—to be human?

Desire and affection enlivened her. The entire planet made her feel alive with the wonder of its unmarred landscapes, magical forces, mythical creatures, and the fight for life and liberty.

Alive again, after decades of deadening herself to the genocides that she and the *UWFS Mendhelsson* crew had brought to other Old Colonies. Guilt, yes. Regret, yes. She couldn't save those worlds, but hopefully, maybe, she could save this one.

Meila heaved the rope-bridge left and right, swinging and laughing. Caught up in the struggles of this world, she had been delivered from her own, unknowing that she had broken a heart in doing so.

Chapter 33

The Wreckage

They departed the village the following morning beneath a gray and foreboding sky. Witabu and three tribesmen led the way into the forest ravine and toward the Highlands of Jurn.

The tribesmen hunters were sinewy, hard men born to scramble over peaks and mountains. Outfitted with satchels over their backs, they were armed with stabbing spears and horn bows and dark-fletched arrows. The grandmaster was pleased to have the mountaineers with them, but Jaks merely felt indifferent.

Earlier that morning, the Uwama had expertly set the fractures in his hand properly in place and splinted them with wood. However, the effects of the pain-dulling pill he'd coldly accepted from Meila had worn off, and now both his hand and face were throbbing in pain—and the artificial sense of invincibility had wilted to a sense of annoyance.

Carrying on regardless, he rolled his shoulders beneath his backpack laden with provisions and essentials and picked up the pace to catch up with his sister at the back of the group.

Vixhana cast him a sidelong look. "What's with you? You look as glum as a pickle."

"Nothing," he muttered and stared at the path.

"Hells above, Jaks. You're a mess to be sad for."

He shrugged, unsure whether she referred to his appearance or his mental state. Whichever it was, he agreed with her on both counts.

Vixhana's concern, however, was brief, and she scolded him. "No excuse to dawdle. Don't fall behind." She had been snappy since giving up her great axe. Witabu had laughed at the oversized weapon. "You won't need that; there are no elephants for you to butcher here." Reluctantly, she'd left it at the Jurn village, along with their horses, and hitched her sword and shield.

Mulgrave and Tavis, sacrificing armor for agility, had abandoned their plate armor—gauntlets, boots, pauldrons, helms, everything except their breast plates. In their place, they wore borrowed leather boots, leggings, and furs from the Jurns.

Around midday, Jaks was tiring, and Vixhana prodded him repeatedly to keep up with the others. He hadn't realized how much stamina he had lost since conscription. Thankfully, the group stopped a half hour later, when the ravine floor rose and the cliffs fell away on either side to deliver them to the base of the Highland mountains.

Behind and below them, the plateau spread out, a cracked table of stone, and ahead of them, the Highlands were close enough for Jaks to see a thunder of dragons, or perhaps just a flock of large birds, circling one of the peaks. Pine trees hugged the mountains and a cap of white topped many of the higher peaks.

The terrain steepened from there on and enveloped them in mountains all around. Witabu and his men blazed the trail and assisted the less experienced adventurers over sliding shale slopes, narrow canyons, and at one time, over a makeshift rope bridge that traversed a short crevice that yawned between cliffs. Fortunately, the wind was mild and one less hazard to worry about, certainly a boon as Jaks tight-rope walked across the rope with only one good hand to stabilize himself over the two-yard length.

The tortuous landscape afforded no lack of concentration. A misstep here or there meant slipping to his death or sliding into injury. So, for the rest of the day, the trek forced Jaks to clear his mind and forget his aches and pains. There was nothing better than danger to focus his head.

That evening, they stopped beneath a rocky outcrop to camp. Although lengths of slimy algae dripped from the overhang, underneath it was dry and sheltered from the wind. A fire crackled, and the food was passed around the hard shelf, barely capable of fitting all nine of them.

Meila approached him and made idle chatter about the day. Still hurting from her rejection the night before, he moved away as though he hadn't heard her and warmed himself with the tribesmen around the campfire.

The next morning, a crashing boulder on the other side of the valley startled awake most of those who slept. The startled screech of several dragons echoed high above, and a subsequent rockfall of stones and pebbles followed for a couple of minutes and then settled into a pile of debris.

Jaks clambered to his feet, heart pounding at the sound of the avalanche and the dragons.

In the dim dawn light, the hunters yawned and stretched without a care. Reading their calm as a signal of safety, he settled back to his sleeping mat and stilled his pulse with a breathing exercise.

Once the sun had risen enough to march safely out of the valley, the group trekked until they came to a rapid, white river—heard well before they saw it. Jaks sighed in relief when Witabu declared they would only need to follow its length and not attempt a crossing.

The river remained their deafening companion for the rest of the morning, a leviathan desperate to slither through the mountains and carve a channel to the sea. If it had been calmer, they could probably have sailed right back to the lowlands, but even Jaks—with his lack of boating experience—could see that a boat would soon be smashed to pieces by the chaotic, watery maze of boulders.

"The site is over the ridge in the next valley," Witabu translated from one of the hunters to Mulgrave as they veered away from the river and began ascending a steep hill.

The sun hid behind rolling clouds, and a brisk wind howled past them as they crested the ridge. The next valley lay between three mountains and had yet another river coursing through it; however, this one was a calm cousin to the monster that had humbled them earlier that day.

The valley floor was flat and the easiest terrain they had walked for the past day. Lone skeletal trees and small bushes struggled to grow even near the river.

"Around the side of that mountain," Witabu again translated for a hunter pointing at the largest of the three mountaintops. Nothing grew on its sheer slopes, and vast tracts of loose and broken stone marked the surface. Even the top was cracked, resembling the shape of a horn.

Daylight faded as they reached a point where the hunters told them they would see the wreckage.

Witabu was the first to reach the rock—a giant extrusion from the side of the mountain. He suddenly crouched and waved his hand downward.

"There are people there!" said the head tribesman, pulling back behind the rock.

Ranger Cromer, Mulgrave, and Vixhana pushed their way to the front, pressed against the stone, and carefully peered into the valley beyond.

After a few minutes, they withdrew, and Mulgrave swore. "Hell and damnation—they're excavating."

In his place, Jaks poked his head out to spy on the interlopers.

A mile away, at the bottom of the horned mountain, humanoid figures toiled at the base of an avalanche; this rockslide, however, at its base, had a large alien structure. Ragged walls and twisted pylons stood out of the stones, looking like part of a ruined house made of metal. The figures appeared to be carrying stones away one by one to deposit them in a distant pile that, by its size, Jaks guessed they had been working on for at least a couple of days. One of them appeared to be giving orders to the laborers, while a couple of others—near several lean-tos and tents—tended a spitted animal over a cooking fire. Three sentries stood listlessly around the perimeter of the excavation.

"Who are they?" Jaks asked when he turned back to the whispering group behind him.

"Vixhana will scout them once night falls," Mulgrave said. "Could be wildmen curious for loot, but we need a closer look."

"It's definitely the *Mendhelsson* . . . a sizable fragment," Meila said quietly as she crouched at the rock, watching the excavation. "No instruments operating. Only the emergency beacon is functioning."

She looked away, and Jaks saw her face downcast and eyes moist. "She was a beautiful ship."

Vixhana peered around the rock again. "They're finishing up for the day and look to be settling into the camp. I'll wait until a couple hours past dusk and then move in. The rest of you should find cover—"

"No cover. It is very open." Witabu waved a hand at the darkening valley.

Mulgrave made a decision to withdraw back to the ridge overlooking the valley, an hour's trek under the moonlight. No fires were lit, and a fearfulness kept everyone in hushed voices and whispers as evening fell. Thankfully, the grandmaster channeled pyromancy to warm the air and remove the chill as they waited.

"Is there going to be a fight?" Tavis said to Cromer, within earshot of Jaks.

The ranger ignored Tavis's question but could be seen running wax over his bowstring and counting his arrows.

"Damn, I wish I hadn't ditched my armor," Tavis said to no one in particular, his voice sounding high-pitched and thin.

Vixhana had stayed behind at the observation rock, dropping her backpack and securing her black leather armor against stray straps that could create any noise. That had been two hours ago, and Jaks imagined her nightwraith form now slipping through the darkness toward the excavation camp.

The wind piped an eerie harmonic as it coursed

over their heads; fortunately, on the leeward side of the ridge, they were spared a direct battering. Waiting seemed an eternity.

A whistle and then a voice called out a few hours later—the tall warrior woman returned from her clandestine task. She materialized suddenly in their midst, breathing heavily. The hunters scrambled away in fright and brandished their spears at her in the dark until Witabu rasped a command.

"Well, what did you find, Captain?" Mulgrave stepped closer to Vixhana, who seemed to have forgotten her backpack on returning. He invoked a yellow flame that hovered in the air to illuminate the night.

"Warriors of Voros. I counted twenty-four, armed with swords and at least a dozen crossbows. Probably a half-torgue." She hunched down and looked around until her eyes fell on her brother. "Pass me something to eat, Jaks."

"What are Vors doing here?" Tavis asked from somewhere in the dimness.

"I'd say they've been here two or three days excavating that wreckage. I was going in for a closer examination, but somehow, I was spotted." Vixhana then swore uncharacteristically. "I've never been uncovered before like that. They sent out search parties, but I outdistanced them and misdirected them to the other valley."

"Maybe they had a dog that caught your scent or a

trained dragon that heard you while you were 'manced?" Mulgrave suggested.

"No. I had a clear view of their camp, and they didn't have any guard animals."

"How do you know they're Vors? Could they just be bandits?" Jaks asked as he handed his sister a handful of goat jerky and a waterskin.

"I know my Vors, Jaks," she said in a cold voice. "I see one every time I look in a mirror. Besides, the ritual tattoos on the face and neck give them away."

"Mages?" Mulgrave asked.

"A firemancer and at least two grav warriors with them."

"Do they know what they're digging out from the avalanche?" Jaks asked.

"Ten leagues from the closest coastline, in the middle of a mountain range . . . of course they know, stupid. Right, Master?" Tavis replied.

Anger inflamed Jaks's face, and he resisted an impulse to punch the other apprentice.

"Someone must have told them about the wreckage . . . and the weapons," Meila said in a hushed voice.

Mulgrave turned and the magical flame followed to illuminate Meila, deep in thought. "I thought we were the only ones who knew about this?"

"Apparently not," Vixhana said, looking at the smaller woman suspiciously. "What else is she not telling us . . . what are you not telling us?"

"No one else knows. I'm telling the truth. I have told no one else of this location. There must be someone else with an implant and access to a scanner—"

"Like who?" Vixhana challenged her.

"I don't know. Maybe someone else did survive . . ." Meila grabbed the warrior by the arm and spoke quickly. "If someone else is alive, we have to rescue them. I have to know if one of my crew is there."

Ranger Cromer spoke for the first time since Vixhana had returned. "If they are there, he or she is on *their* side—not ours. That makes them the enemy."

"No. My crew wouldn't side with the Vors. We saw the atrocities they committed against their own people. Their culture is vile and evil—"

Vixhana placed a hand on Meila's wrist. "How do you know that?" She tightened her grip. "You are a spy. What lies are you hiding? You are no traveler—you have been watching us." She pulled Meila until their noses almost touched.

Meila struggled against Vixhana's grip but stopped when her other hand was equally pinned by her side.

"What is this all about? What is your mission here? Did you lie to us about the weapons?" Vixhana asked in an acidic tone.

The outworlder slumped against the warrior's grip and her gaze fell as her energy fled. After several seconds, she looked up to meet Vixhana's interrogating eyes. Despair painted her face. "The old worlds are dying. Trillions of people have ravaged dozens of planets over the millennia." Meila sighed heavily. "My ship has been searching for lost colonies, like this one, for recolonizing."

"Recolonizing?" Mulgrave said, frowning.

"Hundreds of millions of new colonists." Meila turned to face Mulgrave, while Vixhana maintained her vice-like grip on her wrists. "The truth is, your people arrived here as a fringe-world colony over seven thousand years ago. But soon after it was established, the supercluster colonies and the origin worlds descended into a century-long intergalactic war that destroyed the wormholes that allowed us to travel between galaxies. The fringe worlds were isolated and forced to sustain themselves. A few thrived. Most collapsed and disappeared. And some, like yours, regressed to primitive remnants of humanity."

"You didn't answer the mage. What do you mean by *recolonizing?*" Vixhana said through gritted teeth.

Meila wilted under the anger of those around her, but drew in a breath and continued, "The first wave of ships come to cleanse the planet. If the old colonists have been classified as 'peaceful' and unwarlike, they are corralled to a less desirable part of the planet. But if they are not . . . the world is 'depopulated.' Battle fleets remove the old colonists, clearing the way for the second wave of ships and their burden of new colonists."

"That is outrageous, monstrous." The grandmaster's eyes protruded, and his teeth were bared.

"That is recolonizing," Meila replied weakly.

"Much like how your own country was subdued under one rule."

"That's completely different. Every territory had the opportunity to submit and continue under Ascorian rule. None were eradicated for mere convenience." Mulgrave wrung his hands in agitation.

"And what is your part in this?" Vixhana jerked Meila's wrists. The smaller woman flinched in pain.

"My ship was scouting your planet, collecting information about the condition of the surface—how survivable and sustainable it is—and the well-being of the original colony. We would have then returned to Earth and submitted a report to the Ministry of Colonies."

She then looked to Mulgrave, who was rubbing his head in agitation. "Look, I'm sorry I didn't tell you the full truth—I didn't think it would help for you to know. If they do decide to repopulate this planet, it wouldn't be for decades or possibly centuries. But it changes nothing about why we're here, right now. If anything, it makes it even more important that we get those weapons before the Vors do."

Surprisingly, Jaks heard his own voice pierce the night. "She's right." He coughed and then continued, "We still have to defend our country from the Vors, regardless of what is coming later."

"So, there are weapons here?" Vixhana's voice leveled, and she loosened her grip.

"Yes . . . I'm almost certain there are. If I'm correct,

that section of the ship is rear-portside and housed part of the engine and shielding. There was a weapons locker in the engine room. It's partially covered in rocks, though—so I can't be a hundred percent sure."

No one spoke for several minutes. Thoughts churned and glances were exchanged; Mulgrave and Vixhana stared at Meila as though attempting to read her mind. The hunters and Witabu watched on, uncomprehendingly, sitting on the rocks near the crest of the ridge.

Eventually, the grandmaster folded his arms, anger abated. "Jaks is right. We can only deal with one invasion at a time. We need those weapons to repel the Vors, and then we can worry about the greater foe from there."

"I can help. I might be able to persuade the Ministry to preserve Maya—your world—or at least ring-fence the continents that you are living on. I want to help you," Meila said. Her eyes flicked around them all and settled on Jaks.

"You can let her go, Captain," Mulgrave said after a long minute and placed a hand on Vixhana's wrist. "She withheld information from us, but she did not lie. Disingenuous, but not malicious. Just doing her job, so to speak."

"Yes, in the beginning, but not anymore. I've seen your world for what it is—beautiful and pristine. It deserves to be protected." Meila rubbed her wrists and stepped back from Vixhana. "Your civilization is backward but verges on an industrial age, and it has something that needs to be preserved that no other colony has."

"What's that?" Jaks asked.

"Magic." Meila smiled wryly, then raised her hand and opened her palm; in an instant, a tiny green dragon danced lightly in the air, and she smiled, holding out her illumancer invocation for everyone to see. "I'm one of you."

Chapter 34

Ambush

Meila–Jurn Highlands, Ascoria

Meila did not sleep that night but instead directed her cortical implant to run a thirty-minute rejuvenation protocol that replaced her need for sleep. Alert, she sat guard—with one or another of the others who took turns sleeping—and gazed down into the valley, wondering which of her crew could be alive.

Now more than ever, she regretted the absence of a long-distance communicator in her cybertronics. On the *Mendhelsson*, her home for the past three decades, it had been unnecessary; the starship comms had been built into the ship, surrounding her, always close enough to allow her to talk with shipmates and the AI in any part of the vessel. Outside of the starship, she had no way of sending out a signal to find out who might be out there.

Because she was sure someone was there.

And that someone must have used a UWF scanner

445

to locate the starship debris, just as she had. There was no other way a large, organized group could have found their way here, so determined to spend days excavating an avalanche.

Her heart lifted with hope that it was Anton, her eccentric biologist husband. But it could also be any of the seven other scientists who had been aboard the starship.

Except Stefan.

Stefan Knight, in hindsight, had been poorly equipped for life aboard a starship. Although highly qualified as a Planetary Actuary—one of the geniuses who analyzed and calculated the overall worth of each Old Colony world—his claustrophobia and anxiety had grown with each year they spent in space. In the last months of their orbital mission around planet Maya, it had seemed that he was improving—keeping to himself more but complaining less about the suffocating, confining starship.

With their return to Earth soon coming, Meila had missed the man's deteriorating state. He had become suicidal.

With a darkcore pistol, he had blown his head off; in doing so, he'd triggered a critical fracture in the hull of their ship. Whether the Actuary had been trying to kill all of them along with himself, Meila had never found out. They had only had a few minutes to reach their escape pods and evacuate the ship.

But one of her crew was alive.

She had to find out who.

She scanned the desolate valley again, her visual implants adapted to the darkness with night-vision augmentation. A nocturnal bird—an owl?—circled in the distance, outstretched wings buffeted by air currents. It swooped toward the ground, several hundred meters away, near the river cutting through the valley. She magnified and focused her vision on a movement dashing below the flying predator. A small animal bounded in a zigzag toward some unseen escape. Left, right. It didn't reach its bolt-hole fast enough—the predator snatched it from the ground with great talons and plunged a saber-like beak into the helpless creature and then flew off with its prey.

On the *Mendhelsson*, she'd had an overvalued sense of invulnerability, protected by millions of tons of synthmetal and shielding. But now, with death as common as a pair of talons from above or a spear through the back, she felt scared but also exuberantly more alive than ever before. Decades of leading lost-colony missions had turned her hard and remorseless. It had taken danger and threat to her life for her to rediscover her humanity.

She patted her legs and the reassuring lumps of her knives and darkcore pistol.

A quick glance at the sleeping forms, and she snuck over the ridge and down into the valley on a scouting mission of her own.

Alone with her superior vision and nimble feet,

Meila made it back to the massive rock within half an hour. There, she found Vixhana's backpack and left it hidden in a crack.

Peering around the rock to the Vors campsite, a mile away at the base of the horned mountain, it was too far to discriminate faces. She crouched and crept behind boulders and scrawny bushes, stalking toward the campfire where three guards kept watch over the campsite. Hopefully, whoever or whatever had alerted the guards to Vixhana earlier on wouldn't see her skulking now.

She stopped behind the skeleton of a lone springfell tree, a half mile from the Vors camp. Here, she could see several sleeping faces beneath the lean-tos. Although partially obscured, she easily recognized them as localized humans—not one of her crew.

One figure, though, caught her attention: a long, thin individual curled by the fire with a coarse blanket pulled up to his neck, asleep. Not a typical Vor male, too delicate of bone and muscle. Although full-bearded, like the guards, the man was unkempt and had what appeared to be a collar around his neck and a chain trailing away from him.

A prisoner.

She stared for a long time. Magnified her implants to their maximum resolution. Her mouth went dry, her breathing quickened, and the hairs on her neck stiffened.

It was Anton.

She emitted a sob at the condition of her husband. He was even gaunter than his usual leanness, and his face looked as though he had aged a dozen years since she had last seen him several months ago. Scars crisscrossed his face and over his eye. Patches of hair were missing. *An ear missing?* His decrepit condition caused her heart to lurch. Although their passion had gone, she still loved him at his core. He was a pitiful sight.

An impulse to rush into the camp took ahold of her. She had boasted to Tavis that she could kill a hundred Vors in a minute, but that was if they were lined up waiting to be shot—not under battle conditions. There were twenty-five of them. Could she guarantee the high degree of accuracy she would need with the pistol to kill enough of them, forcing them to abandon their hostage? Some of them were mages too, and she'd seen what a firemage and gravmancer warriors could do in a fight. No, she couldn't take the risk of a rescue attempt by herself.

She'd need to go back for help.

A while later, just as the valley took on the amber hue of dawn, Meila scrambled over the ridgeline back to their resting point.

"See, she didn't run away," Jaks said, a relieved look on his face.

Ranger Cromer grunted as he stared at the dark-haired foreigner.

Meila walked to Vixhana, who was sharpening her

dagger, and dropped the nightwraith's backpack at the warrior's feet. "Here," she said, breathing hard.

"Where did you go?" Jaks asked, offering her a waterskin, which she waved off. "I knew you wouldn't leave us."

His icy demeanor toward her since they left the Jurn village was gone, and he seemed genuinely eager to see her return. A stab of guilt reminded her she would need to make amends with him—her rejection of his invitation to his bed had affected him harder than she'd thought it would. But now that she knew Anton was still alive, she did not regret that denial.

She flashed a small smile at him and then leaned against her knees to catch her breath. When she looked up, it was to focus on the grandmaster, who had just woken on her return and was rubbing his eyes.

"They've got my husband. They have Anton prisoner. I saw him shackled and injured. We have to rescue him," she said, stepping over to the mage as he stood.

"Were you seen?" Vixhana asked.

"I didn't go as close as you probably did . . . and I think the person who saw you was Anton, but he was asleep the whole time I observed them. Listen, we need to rescue him, we need to change the plan."

The previous night, Vixhana, Cromer, and Mulgrave had decided on a strategy for the following evening. A daring ambush that required them to creep into position and then have Meila snipe the firemage—

who they assumed was the leader—and the two gravmancers, while Ranger Cromer shot the regular guards. Subsequently, the grandmaster and Tavis would enfence and blast the Vors with fire magic as Vixhana leapt into the killing zone to finish off any survivors.

Jaks had looked aggrieved at being told his only task was to stay with Meila and protect her if things went wrong; he had glowered when the grandmaster told him that his electromancy powers were too unreliable and unrefined to be involved in the coordinated attack.

The four Jurn tribesmen initially refused to be involved with the assault, worried about the aggression involved. "We only bring you here," Witabu said. "This is not our fight." However, after Vixhana pointed out that their efforts in fighting the Vors would greatly assist the Jurns' plea to King Silas, Witabu and the hunters agreed to join Meila and Jaks as reserve fighters.

"Impossible. Too dangerous," Cromer said. "The plan relies on complete surprise. If we make a rescue attempt first, we lose the initiative."

"What if we begin the attack as first planned, taking out the three mages and guards, but then in the confusion, you"—Meila nodded at Vixhana—"go in and snatch Anton and carry him away? I take it your magic would allow you to get in and out quickly. Then we carry on with the rest of the plan?"

Jaks wrung his hands together. "That would be dangerous for Vix."

"This prisoner, is he worth it?" the nightwraith asked flatly.

Meila looked appalled, her small nose wrinkling and her eyebrows creasing to a point. "He's my husband. Of course, he is *worth* it." After a minute, her scowl dissolved, and she continued, "He is an expert in biology and medicine . . . healing, what you would call it. He could advance your planet's healing arts by centuries, millennia. If you're wanting something tangible out of it."

A clatter of rocks and several animal-like snorts interrupted them. A crowned stag and three does skittered out of thick brush below them at the bottom of the hill. Before anyone could say anything, a bowstring twanged and an arrow from one of the tribesmen streaked over the top of the deer. Meila heard the hunter swear as the animals leapt back into the bushes and trees. Witabu and the other hunters laughed at the embarrassed man.

"What do you think?" Vixhana turned to Mulgrave, her face revealing a conflict of emotions.

"Certainly, we should try to keep him out of danger. If we don't extract him first, it will be difficult to avoid harming him with fire area-magic in the main assault. Tavis or I could attempt to grav-jump in and then out with him . . . but you have greater experience in that sort of thing."

Vixhana nodded. "All right. Let's go with that plan. As soon as the first targets go down, I'll retrieve him and we carry on with the plan as before. Is there a way to stop him ratting us out if he sees us with this super-sight you have? Tell him that we're attempting to rescue him?"

"Sadly, no. The most I could do is try to get his attention in the dark at a distance that no un-augmented human could see—and hope he recognizes me. But if that failed, he would probably alert the guards. I doubt he has any hope of rescue out here in this wildland." Meila sat down to rest her legs. "It'd be best if we just wait until late enough that Anton will be asleep like the rest of them."

The day passed with the group waiting and watching the Highlands unfold around them. The roar of a mountain lion echoed later that morning, perhaps announcing a successful kill, perhaps one of the deer they had seen earlier. That afternoon, clouds roiled overhead, threatening rain, but passed by with just a brief shower and then cleared to a peaceful, blue sky.

Meila marveled at a thunder of dragons that soared over the valley episodically; she invoked miniature illusions of them in her palm and crafted the tiny figures to amuse and calm herself against the excitement of being reunited with Anton—and the anticipation of the necessary violence to free him. She thought she should feel guilty about plotting murder, but she couldn't help but think the Vors deserved what they had coming to them for torturing her husband and attempting to steal her starship.

Two hours after a stinging, chilly night fell over the Highlands, a wedge of moon slunk over the clouded peaks.

Meila and the group of nine men and one other woman took only killing implements and snuck down to the junction of the three valleys. There, a bend of the river meandered from the Vors' vale and into the other valley. A journey that would have taken one hour in the daylight took three in the dark.

The riverbed had the advantage of being the lowest part of the narrow valley and allowed the ambushers to inch their way beside the tinkling waters to within a half mile of the Vor camp.

"Tell me what you see from here," Mulgrave whispered to Meila as they lay against the stones of the riverbank, finger-streaked mud across their faces and exposed skin.

Meila peeped over the riverbank and spotted the closest Vor guard exactly 641 yards from her position—indicated by the rangefinder built into her visio-cortical implant. Only he and two other guards appeared to be awake.

A score of almost motionless bodies were sprawled under lean-tos and tents protecting them from the cutting wind. She tensed when she saw Anton curled, as he was last night, in the open near the fire, but relaxed upon seeing him asleep.

The previous night, she had observed a heavily tattooed firemage using the largest tent; the fierce-looking woman had pushed open the tent flap and invoked a bright flame as she wended her way to a makeshift latrine on the outskirts of the campsite.

Meila's other two primary targets, she guessed, were the two men lying next to huge double-bladed battleaxes. No one but gravmancers like Vixhana could wield such mammoth weapons in combat. No one had told *them* there would be no elephants to butcher.

Reminded of the nightwraith and the others waiting for her reconnaissance report, she shuffled backward on her belly and then informed the others of what she had seen.

Mulgrave gave the order, and they dispersed to take up their ambush posts.

"*Hodrin uhsaga*," Witabu said, invoking the Jurn blessing as Mulgrave slipped away with Tavis, cautiously treading up the riverbed with just moonlight guiding their steps.

Ranger Cromer cast a quick look at Vixhana and then, with quiver in hand and recurved ironwood bow in the other, hunched low and started his stealthy advance to the north side of the camp—opposite where the grandmaster and his apprentice would be positioned.

"Let's go. Keep quiet. Secure your weapons. Watch where you step," Vixhana warned and then crested the riverbank, followed in single file by Meila, Jaks, and the four tribesmen. The nightwraith invoked an illumancer shield in front of herself, an eerie impenetrable black wall hiding them from the guards, two arm-breadths to either side and as tall as she. Meila switched to an infrared visual filter and confirmed the heat signatures of the Vors still blissfully unaware of the ambushers closing in to set their trap.

At a hundred yards from the closest guard, Vixhana signaled a stop and carefully lay down amongst the scattered stones and boulders that peppered the valley floor.

Meila mimicked her action and listened to Jaks and the Jurn hunters shuffle for several seconds until they all lay in nervous wait. Thankfully, the whistling wind covered the sound of any stones that clattered with their movements.

Cromer was to her distant left. Her respect for him leapt a level at seeing him hidden a mere sixty yards from the Vor guards who sat around the sputtering campfire. Anton's pitiful form lay a few yards behind the guards.

On the far side of the Vors' fabricated shelters, Mulgrave and Tavis hugged the ground, unmoving.

Minutes seemed to stretch for hours as she waited for the ranger to trigger the attack. Sweat moistened her grip on the darkcore pistol, but fortunately, the diamond-hatching kept it firmly in her hand. Jaks was muttering nearby but quietened at Vixhana's low shush. What was going on with the young man? He seemed troubled since leaving the Jurn village—friendly one minute and then glowering and moody the next.

Her thoughts returned to the present as her attention was drawn to the slowly rising figure of Cromer lifting his bow and drawing back a strung arrow.

"Get ready," Meila said in a low voice, then rolled into a kneeling firing posture and pointed her weapon with both hands at the firemage's tent. The handgun's low-temperature aiming beam pierced the fabric and rested on the enemy leader's chest. The wonders of her visual implants would make it an easy shot.

Vixhana dropped the illumancer shield and pulled herself into a crouch, fists to the ground, looking like a giant panther ready to pounce.

As soon as the ranger's first arrow hissed through the air, Meila pulled the trigger, and the buzz of the pistol firing was immediately followed by the firemage's torso exploding inside the tent. The canvas billowed outward with splatters of flesh and bone, collapsing the shelter on top of her mangled corpse.

Meila looked back to the campfire and saw a guard slump to the ground with an arrow through the back of his head.

The other two guards stared in astonishment at the dead man and rose to their feet.

The tribesmen's bows twanged around Meila, and four more arrows hissed through air to pierce and stagger the remaining guards.

The closest gravmancer stirred and rolled to his side under the lean-to he shared with three other warriors. Meila blinked and then traced the targeting beam to his chest and squeezed the curved trigger again.

Pzzt . . . the blast blew the man's chest apart and exploded into the ground behind. Dirt, rock, and viscera pelted his sleeping neighbors.

There was a pounding of feet as Vixhana ran forward eight paces, leapt into the air, and hurtled toward the middle of the camp.

Meila needed to find her third target quickly.

Confused voices called out around the Vor camp, and several figures sat up and looked around.

The second gravmancer sat up, looking around, confused. His hand rested on a giant battleaxe beside him.

Vixhana landed gracefully on the far side of the campfire, a few yards from Anton.

The aiming beam flicked to the single remaining enemy mage, and Meila squeezed the trigger as she kept the beam focused on the gravmancer's chest.

He stood at that moment and the darkcore bolt struck him in the belly. The effect was the same as with the previous shots—flesh and organs burst out of his back, removing a quarter of his body mass and folding him in half. The wooden lean-to collapsed as the follow-through blast splintered and smashed the crooked branches that supported the structure.

Shouts and alarmed voices cried out all over the camp. Men and women staggered and lurched to their feet, throwing aside the furs and blankets that just a few minutes before had been warm havens of peace.

Meila stood for a clearer view as Vixhana lifted Anton in her beefy arms. His neck lolled back abruptly as a chain attached to his iron collar yanked against a heavy boulder rolled onto the distal end of the restraint. Meila gasped, fearing his neck broken by the sudden tug; however, relief came when Anton's hands grabbed at the chain, indicating him alive.

Vixhana deposited Anton and stepped toward the boulder.

Suddenly, there was a thud and the ground near the campfire erupted into a cloud of earth and rock.

A second later, another explosion blew Vixhana off her feet.

Darkcore blasts.

Meila had the only such weapon in sight—but something else, powerfully explosive, had just detonated a half-ton of earth and rock in front of her eyes. Her eyes darted around for the source.

Vor warriors stumbled out of their lean-tos toting swords, axes, or crossbows; a few more clambered out of the largest canvas tent at the far side of the camp, calling out orders, or perhaps demanding explanations, from the confused mass of men and women.

Vixhana lifted and threw aside the boulder that only a gravmancer—or three men—could move, freeing the end of the chain restraining Anton.

At the flap of a small tent, thirty yards from the

nightwraith, partly hidden by lean-tos, a warrior with a face tattooed in geometric symbols aimed a sleek-looking weapon at Vixhana.

Meila targeted the tattooed warrior with the hand weapon, but the man began to dart toward Vixhana, firing off shots as he moved. They landed randomly, creating bursts of dirt and rubble.

The explosions caused the nightwraith to stumble, and she fell to a knee.

Meila's heart pounded and her hand jerked as she attempted to track the gunner's loping movements.

She fired the darkcore pistol, despite the fleeting, intervening blurs of other Vors obscuring an accurate shot.

She missed.

Instead, a Vor warrior moving in front of her target took the shot in the hip. He spun forward and smashed his head against the stony ground.

The Vor gunman—unknowing that he was now a target himself—fired another couple of shots in Vixhana's direction, steadily approaching her. If he knew how to use the weapon properly, he would have stopped for a more accurate shot; instead, he used the foreign weapon bluntly, pelting his target with blasts. One shot hit the campfire and slammed the stack of burning wood into a spray of embers and flaming branches. Other shots further disrupted the earth and scattered debris everywhere.

Further chaotic shouts sounded as the campfire faded and left only the moonlight for the Vors to see by.

Vixhana scooped Anton into her arms a second time. He sagged into her like a child, and she flipped his loosened chain over her shoulder.

The gunman drew up directly behind the two. Meila couldn't target him; Vixhana stood in the way.

The next blast from the gunman ruptured the earth underneath Vixhana's feet and heaved the two of them forward to smash against a heaped pile of rocks.

Time slowed leadenly while Meila could do nothing but stand paralyzed in shock and watch the horror unfold.

Jaks cried out a moment later, only grasping Vixhana and Anton's dire position as the two crumpled together in a heap. This could not be happening. His invincible sister.

"Get up, get up," Jaks yelled at Vixhana and started loping toward her before he knew what he was doing.

An arrow sprouted out of the Vor gunman, who was lining up another shot. The missile penetrated his leg up to the fletching, with the arrow-shaft emerging from the other side. The man twisted in agony and fell.

"Get up," Jaks called out to his sister again as he ran.

"Stop, boy," Witabu shouted after him. And, just as

the words left the tribesman's mouth, a wall of fire roared to life just a few yards in front of Jaks.

Jaks skidded to a halt, the heat of the flames drying and stinging his eyeballs as he stared through the fire wall for glimpses of his downed sister. *I need to help her.*

Despair and fear swamped him as he looked for an opening around the burning, neck-high barrier, but it encircled the camp.

He gulped. His only way was *through* the flames.

Jaks hesitated for only a moment, before running forward and leaping into the fire. But blinded and deafened by the roar of the surrounding inferno, he faltered and fell within the flames, his momentum too weak to reach the other side.

Flames lashed at his face and hands as he lurched, not knowing what direction he faced. He screamed in pain, fearing he would burn to death.

Jaks's panicked thoughts leapt to the lightning cocoon—his one protection. He rammed his emotions into the image and willed it into reality.

Lightning crackled to life and enveloped him in a ball of white and blue pulsating energy. Where the electricity sparked, the flames withdrew, as though intimidated by the greater power. The familiar metallic smell filled his nostrils, and the pain of his exposed skin retreated.

With the flames driven back, his vision returned, and he focused on Vixhana.

Like a rolling storm cloud, Jaks erupted out of the

fire wall just in time to see Vixhana staggering back to her feet with Anton still in her arms. He breathed a sigh of relief and dropped the magical armor.

However, the gunman, too, rose from the ground, having broken off the arrow penetrating his leg and then pulled out the shaft. He knelt on his uninjured knee and pointed his darkcore weapon once again at Vixhana, grimacing as his aim wavered back and forth.

"Get down, Vix," Jaks shouted and raised his arm for an invocation. But his sister continued to stumble and lurch as blood streamed from her scalp and over her face.

Her movements blocked a clear attack on the gunman; however, he couldn't wait a moment longer, he had to kill the man before he fired another shot.

An attacking pulse of bright white and blue arched from Jaks's hand toward the gunman with an ear-splitting crack—but instead of striking the Vor, the lightning pulse forked toward Vixhana and Anton.

In the split second that he realized the deviant path of electricity, he snapped out of the invocation, but it was too late.

The energy pulsed through Vixhana and Anton in an instant. Limbs stiffened, bones snapped with the powerful involuntary contraction of muscles, neck muscles corded, and eyes bulged.

Anton's body flew out of the nightwraith's grasp, his weedy figure tumbling amongst the rocks.

Vixhana's muscular mass dropped heavily on top of him and crushed him.

Facedown in the rocks, neither of the two moved again.

Meila's horrified scream registered in Jaks's periphery, but he was too shocked to do anything but stare at the bodies splayed before him.

If he had had greater awareness, he would have seen Mulgrave and Tavis at that same moment—attacking the Vors with fire and flame—and Tavis felled by a blow to the head by a maniacal hammer-wielder who in the next instant received an incinerating blast to the face from the grandmaster.

But, for Jaks, nothing existed other than the aftermath of his lightning strike on Anton and Vixhana. She couldn't be dead. Not his invincible sister. Frozen in place, not knowing what to do, he yelled at her to get up. *Don't be dead. Don't be dead.*

The Vor gunman, seeing his targets taken down, grinned and sought a fresh target; Jaks found himself staring back at the black metal of the hellish darkcore gun.

In that second, an arrow sang through the dark and thunked into the gunman's chest. He stared at the foreign object incredulously. Moments later, another of the ranger's arrows joined the first and slammed the Vor into the dying embers of the campfire. He flopped about for several seconds more and went still.

Stung with grief, Jaks ran to his sister's side, fell to his knees, and rolled her off Anton's body.

His hands came away sticky with blood. Her skin was hot and her leather armor smoked where it touched metal. The smell of cooked flesh assaulted his nostrils.

Despite vigorously shaking her by the shoulders, her mouth lolled open, and her eyelids remained shuttered and unmoving.

"Vix, I'm sorry, I'm so sorry." He collapsed beside her and sobbed.

Time passed in a haze with Jaks lost in grief, oblivious to the panicking Vors running around him and the torrents of flame and waves of arrows that ended their lives.

A while later, Grandmaster Mulgrave placed a hand on Jaks's shoulder. The wall of fire had smoked out, cries of the injured had silenced, prisoners were secured, and the dead were being counted and laid to rest.

The fight was over, and Meila staggered forward with her darkcore pistol held limply in her hand.

She stared at her husband. His skull was crushed against the rocks. And similar to Vixhana, the skin of his hands and face was blistered and dark. Where the iron collar had touched his neck was burnt and raw. As Meila rolled him over, his eyes stared back dull and lifeless. She murmured quietly over the body and closed his eyes.

"Did you see that?" Jaks said suddenly.

Vixhana's chest rose and fell almost imperceptibly.

"She must be alive." He grabbed her by the shoulders again and shook her.

"Stop, lad, you'll just injure her more." Mulgrave knelt beside her and pressed two fingers against her blackened neck, then peeled her eyelids open. A magical flame hovered over his shoulder to illuminate a face marred not only by charred skin but by many cuts and grazes. "Yes, she breathes, but her mind is not there," he said.

Relief flooded Jaks, and he cleared her hair from her bloodied face. "I'm sorry, Vix," he said. "I'll stay with you."

Although she was not dead, she was not truly alive. No one knew if she would eventually recover or be cursed to remain in a coma and slowly die.

Tavis, too, having suffered a blow to the head, was incapacitated. In a mumbling stupor, however, his breathing was steadier and stronger than Vixhana's, so he seemed more likely to live. A day earlier, Jaks might have felt happy at seeing his adversary for the apprenticeship crippled, but today, all he could feel was overwhelming guilt.

Jaks and Meila stayed with Vixhana and Tavis that night; unfortunately, there was nothing in her healing bag to bring either of them out of the darkness. But they did what they could for them. And fortunately, his sister's burns were less significant than they had originally looked. Bandaged with medigel, Jaks hoped

Vixhana would pounce back up and scold him, but that she did not.

The next day, they cremated the dead bodies. The Vors went in a single heap, but Meila created a separate pyre of sticks and branches for her husband. When the grandmaster channeled flames to consume his body, she stared expressionless as the wind scattered smoke and ash across the valley.

Then, with the ashes cooling, the group—except for Jaks, who stayed to monitor Vixhana and Tavis—turned to the avalanche and began clearing the shale and rock from the wreckage of the *Mendhelsson*.

After several hours, Meila scrambled over the blackened and twisted starship debris, eager at first, but then sagging when no weapons were found. But as the day progressed, she brightened again at the discovery of other relics, and ordered their removal, sometimes requiring the elder mage's smithing magic to cut away objects and parts.

The reality, though, was that after all this effort, at the cost of Vixhana and Tavis incapacitated from injuries, the only weapon they gained was pried from the fingers of the Vor gunman.

Two darkcore pistols were not enough to repulse an invasion force.

Ranger Cromer fumed over the wasted time and risk.

Mulgrave said nothing.

Chapter 35

Consequences

Jaks–Jurn Midlands, Ascoria

The Uwama of the tribe folk frowned at the wounded man and woman being carried toward her.

Jaks and the able-bodied members of the salvage party had arrived at the canyon village of the Jurns. Mulgrave and the ranger carried Vixhana on a makeshift stretcher, and a couple of tribesmen carried Tavis on a second.

"Put them down over there." The Uwama pointed to the platform below the wooden deck spanning the canyon trees. "Xanra, fetch my tools," she directed her elfin-faced daughter, whose bare feet skimmed her up the steps in response. The chieftess then nodded to the grandmaster, but her greeting turned to a frown as she saw Witabu and Meila leading a group of Vor prisoners.

Tavis moaned, and the Uwama turned her focus to

the injured apprentice. "What happened to him?" she asked.

"A hammer to the head and a blow to the back on falling." The bald mage pointed at Tavis and then, having noticed her expression at the Vors, said, "We ambushed a group of Vors. Needn't worry, they'll leave with us in the morning." He gestured at the three miserable-looking men and one woman who had been hauling a long metal object and now thudded it to the ground.

"And her?" She looked at Vixhana, immobile on the canvas between two long branches.

"I electrocuted her," Jaks said in a toneless voice. Head hung low, he then stood mute.

Meila stepped up and continued Jaks's explanation. "She's been unresponsive since then. Four days now. I got a naso-gastric tube into her." Although they had not found the weapons they wanted from the wreckage, they had uncovered medical supplies that Meila had used to help treat Tavis and Vixhana. "So, we've been able to keep them hydrated, at least," she said, and picked up the refillable bag of water to allow the fluid to drain into Vixhana's stomach. "Keep her lying on her right so the water doesn't backflow into her throat."

The Uwama nodded, then bunched her long, silver hair into a bun and stabbed it into place with two carved sticks whittled for the purpose. She knelt to examine Tavis and then Vixhana with expert hands.

Jaks stepped away from the platform, offloaded his

backpack, and slumped against a tree. Footsteps padded up to him, and Meila knelt in front of him.

He glanced at her warily, readying himself for the outlash he expected from her. They hadn't spoken since the night of the ambush. She hadn't yet taken an opportunity to wail upon him for his dangerous use of electromancy. It would probably be now.

"I killed your husband. I tried to save him, but I killed him. And maybe Vixhana, too," he said in a rush and then hung his head between his knees. He had to confess to her and endure her anger. It was what he deserved, for her to shout and rage at him, or worse—to show her disappointment in him.

Meila grabbed his arm and pulled him up. "Let's get away from here. I need to say something to you." She shoved him toward the pine forest darkened under the overhead bridges and platforms that were the Jurns' connection to their plateau village.

"Stop," she ordered once they were out of sight, the trees their only witness.

He hung his head low and gritted his teeth.

"Stop it," she said in a harsh tone. Her hand gripped his arm again. "Yes, you fucked up. Fucked up badly. You made a huge mistake, and if it wasn't for you, they might both be alive and walking." She scowled at him and shook his arm. "Isn't that what you want to hear?"

"It's what's true. It was my fault—" Flashbacks of Vixhana and Anton as lightning pulsed through them, faces contorted and eyes bulging, tormented him.

"Be quiet and listen to me." She released his arm. "Wallowing in your self-recrimination and self-pity isn't going to bring them back. Harboring this blame will only fester and rot you inside like an abscess."

"It's what I deserve."

"Deserve? What about the blame I deserve? I'm the one who asked Vixhana to rescue Anton. I pleaded to have her risk her life. If she had refused, if she just said it was a bad idea, maybe Anton would have just laid low the entire time and survived. I don't know. All I know is that other people had a hand in his death too, not just you. The Vor gunman, for one." She chewed on her lip and leaned against the rough bark of a pine. "Maybe they would have died anyway? Maybe his death and her sacrifice saved others of us from dying?"

"I'm going to give it up," Jaks blurted, interrupting her. It had been in the back of his mind ever since the incident, and now that he had said it, it made perfect sense. "I'll never use the electromancy again. It's just destructive and evil. All it does is kill. If I keep using it, all I will be is a cold murderer like my father . . . I can't live like that."

"You're not listening to me, are you? Nothing you do is going to make amends. Giving up your power—"

"If I didn't have this power, I wouldn't have electrocuted them." He felt a weight lift from his shoulders. It was the right thing to do. He needed to tell the mage. Then it would be done. "I need to find Grandmaster Mulgrave."

"Jaks, wait," Meila called after him, but he loped off unheeding.

He found the stocky mage and Cromer with Witabu and the Uwama, seated around the low table on the elevated wooden platform. When Jaks appeared from the stairs, the wiry tribesman beckoned to Jaks and pointed at the bread, fruit, slices of meat, and cups on the table.

The Uwama gestured to a cushion at the end of the table and addressed Jaks. "*Hodrin uhsaga*, apprentice. Come and eat. Your sister and the apprentice have been taken up to the village, where I will attend them again later. There is little more I can do for them. They need time to heal," she said.

"It is kind of you to help us, Chieftess," he replied stiffly.

"Sit, lad." Mulgrave patted the cushion. "Vixhana and Tavis will stay here with the Jurns to recuperate while we return to Dunberrin," he said. "She is a trained master of the healing arts."

"A long journey would hinder any recovery," the Uwama said. "Even worsen their injuries."

Jaks nodded. If Vixhana and Tavis were staying, it would make his next words easier to say.

"Grandmaster." Jaks had remained standing and now inclined his head to the mage. "Since I came to the Academy, my wish has been to become an apprentice, and I thank you that you gave me the opportunity." He licked his lips and screwed his hands together.

"However, I do not want the responsibility any longer. This power I have . . . I will never use it again. I must relinquish my apprenticeship to you." He heard footsteps behind him, and Meila came up beside him.

"Did you tell him to do this?" Mulgrave asked the outworlder.

"I had nothing to do with it."

"What arc you talking about, lad?"

Jaks repeated the explanation he gave to Meila earlier, and with each word, he felt more certain it was the right thing to do. "I can't live with this unpredictable energy; it's like a viper inside me that, if let out, strikes at anything around me. It killed Meila's husband. It put my sister into a coma."

The bald mage stared at Jaks for a long minute, after which his face softened and he pushed himself to his feet. "It was a dangerous mission with a bad outcome. But your country still needs you. Needs *us*. No one is going to force you to use your magic until you're ready again. Once we return to the Academy, we can restart your training."

Jaks shook his head. "No. That's not it. I'm not going back." He then turned to the Uwama, who was watching expressionless. "Uwama, would you allow me to stay and live with your tribe? Your people are peace-loving and gentle—how I wish to be. I would help in the village in whatever way I can. I can help look after my sister. And, maybe I could teach. Teach the children numbers and how to read, write, and speak Ascorian."

"Of course. The Jurns welcome all who desire our simple life. For, are not we all one under Hodrin? However, I would not wish to *steal* you from your master."

"He is no slave. He goes about as he wills." The grandmaster turned to Jaks. "Think on it, lad. You have a power that no one else has had in almost a century. Our understanding . . . your understanding of it is so little. If you can learn to control it, there are incredible things we might discover. You could be the master of great power one day." He toiled with his beard for a moment. "Do you remember the story I told you, when I burned down my friend's house and his brother died in the fire?"

Jaks nodded.

"It was not my friend's house. It was that of my family. And the boy who died was my brother." Mulgrave locked eyes with Jaks. "Our mother was distraught and drove me away into the woods, decrying me as a sorcerer. However, what I told you about my father was true. It was he who arranged a new start for me—although I couldn't stay with them any longer—he forgave me for my stupidity."

The mage's words gave Jaks some small comfort but did little to soothe his guilt.

"My father forgave me, but it took me years to forgive myself. No one blames you, lad. Don't waste your years like I did—especially in a time like this, when your country needs you." Mulgrave's voice fell to almost a whisper, and he looked reluctant to say his next words. "Choose wisely. If you stay, there may be no turning back."

"I know this is the right thing to do. I'll stay here with the Jurns. Help look after Vixhana and Tavis."

"Well, that's that, then," Ranger Cromer said, dusting off crumbs from his legs as he stood from the table. "There's a war to finish. If he's staying, he's staying. We've been away too long chasing . . . scrap." He waved a hand at the piled backpacks, sacks, and the metal tube they had salvaged from the starship wreckage. "We need to be on our way tomorrow." He then turned his attention to Jaks. "I should drag you in for desertion, but out of respect for your sister, I'll leave you to find your peace." Sadness marred his face, the first time Jaks had ever seen any sensitivity from the ranger, but it was gone as quickly as it came, replaced by a laugh. "However, if she does recover, I wouldn't be surprised if she, herself, charges you with the crime and drags you in by the ear."

That evening, Jaks stared around the carved-out cave that would be his new home with the Jurns. He hung up the lantern he had used to navigate the dark and slid down against a wall. Was it the right decision? Should he have just kept following the grandmaster blindly, growing his power so that he could kill more people faster? Kill legions at a time?

If he'd had any of the other energies, he could have used it for some good. Crafting, smithing, or art. But electromancy was so raw and ruinous, like the lightning that fueled it. He had to discard this power in the same way he would have tossed away a dagger, had it been that he'd injured her with.

Not only was the electromancy a reminder of his mistake, it dishonored her to keep using it. Abandoning it was a repentance.

He had a chance at a new life here with the tribe folk. A peaceful, simple life.

A voice startled him out of his thoughts.

"You're giving up so easily?" Meila stood in the entrance from the cavern hallway. "I thought you were better than this."

He lurched to his feet. "I'm not—"

"Do you think she would want you to give up? Run away? Was Vixhana one to quit anything?"

"I'm not her. It's not that simple. It's everyone I've loved . . . My mother, Karisa, and Vix, all dead, or almost dead, because of me. Whatever I do, or don't do, people die around me. I'm a curse. The best thing is for me to keep away from anything that matters. At least here, I can't do much harm."

"These people, they're not just things. They matter too." Meila paused, drawn into her thoughts. Tense lines in her face suddenly softened. "This world matters. It's worth fighting for."

"There are many thousands who can fight, all better than me." Jaks waggled his bandaged hand.

"And what about us?" she asked in a hushed voice, staring into his eyes.

"Us?"

Her face abruptly hardened. "You're supposed to be my guard, aren't you? I'm the ward. You're the guard."

"Anyone could be your guard . . . you don't even need guarding," he said, confused.

She huffed loudly. "You're impossible," she said, then turned and stormed out of the room.

It was done, his decision made.

The next day, she cornered him again as he watched from the Uwama's platform while the grandmaster and the ranger prepared the horses for their journey back.

Meila approached Jaks from the stairs. "You may have given up on yourself, but I haven't," she said. "Take this, it's a long-range comm." She pressed a gray disc with a floppy strap into his hand.

"What is it?" Jaks said, turning over the coin-sized object. Although it was hard and inanimate, he had the uneasy sense that it was alive in his palm.

"You wrap it around your wrist." She took it back from him and folded it over the wrist of his uninjured hand, where it tingled on his skin. "It lets us communicate over great distances. It'll reach across the entire realm. I've got one too from the salvage." She pulled up her sleeve to reveal a similar contraption on her arm.

"I don't need it. I'm not going to change my mind, if that's what you're thinking."

"Look, Jaks. I owe you. I would still be in prison if it weren't for you, and I can't imagine what would have happened if you hadn't rescued me from Bako and Jop." She looked up at him with tender eyes. "This village may be where you want to be now, but if you change your mind, you'll be able to find me and let me pay my dues." She slid her hand down to his and held it for a moment. Then, at the sound of Mulgrave calling up to her, she turned and strode over with a flick of her raven hair.

Jaks watched the travelers depart. The ranger, grandmaster, and Meila followed by Witabu and two other tribesmen—the Jurns' representatives to petition their union to the king of Ascoria.

A pang of guilt stabbed at him as they walked into the trees of the distant canyon. But once they had gone from sight, he shook away the unwelcome feeling.

With them gone, so was the burden of responsibility. With them gone, he could live peacefully.

"It will not be the last you see of them." The Uwama appeared beside Jaks at the wooden railing. "Although you are welcome to live among us, the *energies* will not be denied. You cannot refuse the call for long." She arched her brow. "This, I believe."

Jaks turned to refute her but stopped when she shook her head and walked back to her entourage.

He would stay with Vixhana and pray that she would live.

As Meila nudged her mare through the canyon, leaving the Jurn village, she cursed Jaks's stubbornness. Like a mule, he had refused to go on, but she wouldn't give up on him yet. The long-range communicator would keep them close. She nodded to herself. *He'll come out of it.*

But meanwhile, she could not lose time waiting for him, eager as she was to return to the Academy with the grandmaster. A horde of these damn Vors needed dealing to.

She grimaced as she looked at the innocuous synthmetal tube the prisoners carried in front of her. Yes, there was no time to waste. She would need all of it if she was to design and construct a super-weapon.

Chapter 36

A Viper in the Wheat

Lord Sicaro—City of Irin, Ascoria

The crippled man sagged in the saddle, teetering on an angle that threatened to tip him from the back of his black stallion. Rain soaked a blood-tinged bandage that covered his head and left eye. Fat droplets fell from an elbow slung to his chest, low enough to display the torn insignia of Sanford Province to the guards ahead.

Sicaro grimaced beneath the hood for using the mummer's trick. Although distasteful, it was necessary for his plan-within-a-plan to work: for two kings to die, and he to rise in their place.

A score of hobbled and drenched Ascorian soldiers trailed behind him, scattered along the road for a mile, bent and trudging in mud-caked boots, with the most depleted riding tandem on bedraggled horses. The stronger ones assisted their comrades, who limped on makeshift crutches and picked up those who fell. A group of battle-weary survivors, four days after the horde of Voros first bloodied Ascorian soil.

The horseman straightened as the road ended at a stone-walled city, hedge-hogged by a palisade of sharp wooden logs.

Ascorian sentries lined the wall, and a guard captain called down from the tower gate to confirm them as more of the same casualties that had been trickling in over the morning. Horrified at the pitiful state of his fellow soldiers, he called for the gates to be opened and hurried men down to assist the injured.

Despite his obvious wounds and weakened state, the leader, recognized by the guard captain as the Castellan of Castle Sanford, entreated to see the king, vowing vital news of the Vorosian horde that the monarch needed to hear.

The castellan's men slumped into the cover and warmth of the gate tower. The injured castellan, however, waved away offers of assistance and followed the captain and two escorts through the town, over a giant stone bridge, toward the palace on the northern banks of the Irin river.

Even through the pouring rain, it was clear that the city prepared for war. Lines of sodden soldiers with shovels marched the streets. Horse-drawn carts laden with bricks and planks splashed through puddles. Humans and beasts alike headed toward the south city wall where, no doubt, their burdens were delivered to strengthen the Ascorian defenses.

Pity their labors. They will cry in terror when they see the gargantors leap even the tallest of their walls, thought the castellan.

At the palace stables, he slid off his horse and threw the reins to a stable boy.

As Sicaro shuffled toward the basalt staircase that fronted the building, the guard captain followed and quietly said, halfway up the stairs, "My lord, are you sure you would not freshen before you present yourself to the king?"

The castellan shook his black-bearded head and continued the climb.

An entrance hall, a long corridor, and several pillared guards led to a pair of doors traced with iron leaves.

Two sentries encased in steel and embellished in platinum issued a last challenge. The castellan and his escorts then waited as one of the two whispered through a grilled windowlet.

Finally, a door clunked open to the inner sanctum of the Ascorian king.

"Lord Sicaro," said King Silas. In simple robes and the royal collar of shields around his neck, he left a wide table surrounded by military men to meet his loyal subject limping into the throne room. "My friend. I feared you lost to the invaders."

The guard captain bowed at the foot of the dais. "My king. The Lord Sicaro arrived just this hour through the storm with a score more of injured soldiers."

Silas thanked the soldier and dismissed him with a nod.

"My lord, come warm by the fire. News of Harek's damnable horde is surely welcome, but first tell me of your ordeal." The king gestured to a raised fire pit crackling at the side of the room with an inverted iron funnel suspended above.

At his signal, guards scraped over a pair of chairs from an audience area, empty but for two restless messengers. Sicaro slumped into one of the offered chairs and studied the king's retinue.

The Ascorian king was not without considerable protection; in addition to a dozen King's Guard on sentry duty, four nightwraith warriors, a pair of silver war dragons—tongues flicking the air—and two hounds with armed handlers were in attendance. Even the eight old generals at the war table could probably put up a fair fight.

Sicaro recognized them all. He had argued, strategized, and commanded with each of them during the Uniting Wars in his previous commanding post. However, they had all kept their military ranks while he had lost his for a peacetime role as a caretaker. He withheld a frown at the frustration that had long dogged him and brought him to this point. Although he officially outranked each of them, his true sphere of influence was small and his command over armed forces insignificant. He needed to rectify this inequality.

Sicaro slid to his knees in front of the king. "My

king, I am at your mercy. I failed to preserve Sanford. They swept over Commander Lytton's regiment and the castle by surprise—"

"No need. Sit, my lord." Silas assisted Sicaro back to the chair. The castellan's wet clothes squelched as he sat. The king sent for a blanket and then sat in the opposite chair.

It could all end here. A flash of a dagger through Silas's neck and the Ascorians would be leaderless, kingless. However, Sicaro estimated his chances of escape as low, and besides, there were other ways of subduing this enemy.

As though reading his mind, two nightwraiths took up positions behind their monarch, and he cast the thought from his head. A white-haired clerk then joined them from the shadows and waited on his monarch's needs.

The warmth of the firepit and the wool were a welcome comfort as Sicaro selected words to continue. "I should have followed my intuition . . . but I knew Lytton's men would have lost respect for him if I had countermanded his orders. Having been in his place, I humbled myself to allow him his poor choice rather than belittle him." He looked to the tiled floor and shook his head.

"What orders?" the king's clerk asked. Sicaro turned to study the man and took a moment to place the man as the king's senior civil magistrate, Lord Jor Hummerford. The ring of hair around his bald pate had turned white, but his eyes were still bright, mirroring his razor-sharp mind. A dangerous man, despite never having borne a blade to battle.

"Lord Hummerford." Sicaro inclined his head to the king's childhood tutor promoted to run his courts and treasury. "The commander spread his troops thinly along many miles of coast. When the Vors landed in the late of night, they cut through so swiftly that we only learnt of an attack as the first raiders leapt and scaled our walls at the break of dawn. It was then that I saw the extent of the invasion, my king." He shook his head slowly, with a tormented look to his face. "Thousands upon thousands of Vors . . . it was clear this was no simple raid. Spread far down the coast were plumes of smoke from Lytton's fractured encampments and our damaged signaling towers."

"Why Sanford, of all places? There are hundreds of miles of coastland closer to Voros than there," Hummerford asked.

"Strike where least expected?"

"How did you escape?" the king asked, leaning forward with wide eyes.

"Yes, my lord, how did you escape?" Lord Hummerford repeated, eyes narrowed and lips pursed.

Sicaro sensed the bald man's suspiciousness but ignored him and looked to Silas. "Your majesty and I have fought many battles together in the past—and I know an impossible fight when I see one. They had already taken the gate and were pouring through. The castle was lost. As soon as I saw the odds, I rallied my garrison and fought a retreat pursued by the Vors' for many leagues."

Lord Hummerford opened his mouth to speak, but Sicaro pushed ahead with his next deceit. "After our pursuers fell behind, we hid, and then I returned with two of my best men to gather more information on the invading force. It was an opportunity no good commander could waste." He adjusted the bandage around his head and winced.

"You went back?" the magistrate interrupted, only to be ignored again.

"It goes, my king, that I am born of Vor parents but am your loyal servant; however, I still bear the appearance of my ancestors, and when we came across a dead warrior near an encampment, I took on his armor and markings to slip into the enemy—"

"You dressed as one of them?" Hummerford asked, eyebrows rising.

"Keep up, old man. That's what I said."

"Let him finish, Jor."

Sicaro stared into the king's eyes in his best attempt at earnestness. "I slipped into their midst amongst their drunken, wretched rejoicing. It took all of my resolve not to reveal myself and stop their rapes and defiling. But in my subterfuge, I infiltrated far enough to glimpse this Vor who calls himself king. But in poor fortune, I never got close enough to make a chance on his life."

Silas shook his head. "A pitiable shame."

"His warriors speak of him in great fear and respect. Respect not for his personal prowess or politics, but for his cruelty and cunning. His person is plain, however. Tall, not of a warrior's build, but slender like his lordship." He nodded at the frowning Lord Hummerford. "Sharp jaw but clean-shaven like a boy, the little that I saw."

Silas looked enthralled, so Sicaro pressed on, "However, that night as the camp slept, I returned to Castle Sanford through tunnels made for escaping the keep but accessible if one knows the riverside exit. Halls heavy with sentries, I sought the Vor king a second time but was again thwarted by guards. Maybe a nightwraith could have gotten to him, but God did not design me for sneaking and creeping in shadows."

"That he did not. Go on."

He grinned and leaned in close. "Luck found me in another way, though. In the chamberlain's office, a guard slept at his post over a table of maps and papers. After I disposed of the man, I discovered a trove of the enemy's information. I studied their plans, examined their maps, and learnt of their strategies. However, before an hour was out, I was discovered and fought my way out of the castle while suffering these wounds." Sicaro lifted his injured arm and touched his bandaged forehead.

"Incredible, my lord. Your courage is heroic." The Ascorian king nodded and inclined his head.

"Yes, incredible . . . almost unbelievable," the magistrate said, his hands clasped in front of him with a forefinger tapping a knuckle. "I beg your forgiveness, but how can we know the truth of this? Perhaps, my lord, you were knocked unconscious, and a memory formed from a dream?"

Sicaro froze his expression before a scowl could form. He itched to strangle the man right there. "Your concern is touching, Lord Hummerford. But you do not think I would chance upon the enemy's map horde and leave without one?" He reached into the recess behind his chest plate and extracted a tattered, folded map.

Silas accepted the Vor map and held it to the light. "By God, I had thought they would immediately move on us here at Irin. But they are splitting their forces to Cerik and Hera. There may be an opportunity here."

"Exactly, my king. If we strike quickly, half of Harek's army will be to the east and half to the west—we could cut them right down the middle back to Sanford. We could retake the province and then pick their forces apart bit by bit."

"The war council must see this map." The king stood, glancing at the gathered generals where one of them was ramming a finger emphatically onto the table as he spoke over the others, and turned back to him. "Lord Sicaro, I would be grateful if you would join my war council and advise me as you have in the past, my friend. I have grown battle-weary, but dragging you—and that other lot—back into this makes it easier, and maybe then I can finally retire in peace."

Sicaro repressed a smile at the words he had been waiting to hear. "Aye, my king. I am but your servant."

A viper in the wheat.

Scion of Lightning closes here, but The Stormcrafter Chronicles continues in book 2.

In *Blade of Lightning* . . .

A month after Jaks abandons Meila and Mulgrave to stay in the Jurn village alongside Vixhana, the tribe's emissaries return from the king of Ascoria with a royal ultimatum. If the Jurns want to return to their nomadic life on the plains, they must send warriors to join Ascoria's fight against the Vors.

In addition, Jaks discovers that Karisa is a slave to the Vor king. Remembering his oath to their mother and seeing an opportunity to redeem his failures, he embarks on a mission deep into the heart of the Vor-captured city of Irin to rescue her.

Here is an excerpt from **Chapter 4** from *Blade of Lightning,* The Stormcrafter Chronicles, book 2.

The warband needed a leader in front—a champion—to stiffen the Jurns' morale and stir their ferocity. Not the Uwama. She was their heart. It had to be him: he was the only one with the power to do what was needed. "Stay back. Stay away from me," he yelled at her.

White and blue flickered around the edges of Jaks's sword and shield as he ran toward the charging Vors. Routing, Jurns scrambled out of his path, leaving him facing hundreds of screaming Vor warriors.

The electromancy, suppressed for months, rushed to his bidding. The triple steps of invocation merged as one and crackled around him in a sparking, magical aura. Half-panicked, half-enraged, he willed the magic into a dazzling ball of lightning as he sprinted forward. Grass burned behind him and left a trail of smoke in his wake.

Forks of electricity leaped and blasted arrows that targeted him. The projectiles burst into flashes of fire and banged with every strike.

All eyes on the flank drew to the glowing lightning god thundering across the meadow. The charging Vors faltered and hastily formed a shield wall to meet this new adversary.

A Vor griefmaster, teeth bared and eyes rounded, pushed through the wall carrying an enormous two-handed battleaxe. He took three steps, leaped again, and then soared through the air with the crescent of his weapon bearing down on Jaks.

Jaks pointed his sword at the gravmancer. Lightning lanced down the weapon to strike the enemy battlemage. A brilliant flash splintered the axe and hurtled the charred torso backward to thud at the foot of the shield wall.

"Regroup. Follow me," he yelled at the Jurns behind him.

Jaks frowned as the shield wall parted fifty yards away. A red-robed woman marched through the gap, weaving her arms through the air. Flames appeared in her hands and grew as her arms continued their intoxicating dance.

The visage of a burning dragon flew out of the fire and flapped flaming wings above the firemage.

Jaks shuddered, fearing the powers of this woman who so masterfully conjured this draconic invocation to life. His nerve almost broke when the dragon spat a column of fire into the air and flailed its neck from side to side, hovering above her.

The firemage stared at Jaks and then thrust her arms at him.

The dragon swooped and raced across the field as though to engulf him.

An electric wall crackled in front of Jaks; a bully's sneer, a biting spider, an armored fist, and his mother's crushed skull fueled the shield into existence.

The draconic missile smashed into the shimmering barrier with a conflagration of flames. The detonation deafened and blinded him momentarily, even though he had turned away from the blast. When his sight returned, the wall of lightning stood crackling, but nothing was left of the firemanced dragon except the smoking dirt around him. Jaks staggered, fatigue sapping his concentration and focus—his lightning wall disappeared.

A second fiery dragon swooped into the air above the mage. He couldn't absorb another massive assault like the last. He would have to destroy the source.

As the firemancer's arms snaked the air, the conjuration grew with every motion. The dance focused her attention, building up another magical assault.

Jaks sprinted toward his enemy, jumped over a ditch, and dared to close half the distance to her. His electromancy had not stretched out this far before, but he had to strike now.

The dragon visage continued to grow until it was the width of a ship's sail. The red-robed woman's gaze homed in on Jaks.

He plunged down on one knee and pointed his sword tip at the firemage. Although his mouth was open and his throat shook in exhalation, he heard no sound— and saw nothing other than her scornful eyes.

Her scream only lasted a couple of seconds, before all the air burst out of her chest, and her flesh sizzled and crisped from the lightning channeled into her from Jaks. A curtain of electricity cut the field to her and then forked outward to strike the hundreds of Vor warriors sheltered behind the battlemage.

Lightning vaulted from limb to limb through the enemy flank. Weapons and shields fell from stunned hands, and spasming bodies toppled to the ground. He savored the familiar taste of metal in his mouth and poured energy into the chained lightning until every Vor warrior within a hundred yards lay twitching or still. As he stared at the bodies, a sense of power surged within, and he laughed at the thrill it gave him.

A war cry sounded from behind and a fresh charge of Jurns, stirred on by the Uwama's rally and Jaks's devastation, pounded past him and into the Vor mainline. Drained and depleted, he leaned on his shield and watched the enemy defenses crumble under the warband's renewed assault. Satisfied that they no longer needed his help, he collapsed to the burned ground and closed his eyes as the sounds of battle faded.

Don't miss out on future books by J.T. Moy

Signup to J.T. Moy's mailing list to receive special offers and updates about upcoming releases.

Mailing list: https://linktr.ee/jtmoy

About the Author

J.T. Moy is from Auckland, New Zealand. A medical doctor and careers consultant, he retired in his mid-40s to write scifi/fantasy novels. He is married and has two children.

www.jtmoy.com

facebook.com/jtmoyauthor

instagram.com/thestormcrafter

www.ingramcontent.com/pod-product-compliance
Lightning Source LLC
Chambersburg PA
CBHW032036050726
47590CB00001B/11